Bitter & Twisted

Simon Temprell was born in Chesterfield, Derbyshire, and raised in nearby Clowne. He attended the Plymouth Art and Design College before moving to London in 1982. After working as a window dresser at Harrods, he started his own interior design business in 1986, moving to Brussels in 1990 and Washington DC in 1992. Continuing his design business, he lives in Virginia and began writing as a hobby in 1994. *The Rich Man's Table* was his first published novel, followed by *Previous Convictions*.

Praise for *The Rich Man's Table*:

'An astonishingly accomplished comic novel that out-fabs *Absolutely Fabulous*, outpaces *Tales of the City* for plot, and outcamps E. F. Benson's Mapp and Lucia novels for waspish social commentary . . . Temprell's nerve is breathtaking'

Robb Cassy, Bookseller

Also by Simon Temprell

Bitter & Twisted

SIMON TEMPRELL

MACMILLAN

First published 2002 by Macmillan
an imprint of Pan Macmillan Ltd
Pan Macmillan, 20 New Wharf Road, London N1 9RR
Basingstoke and Oxford
Associated companies throughout the world
www.panmacmillan.com

ISBN 0 333 90660 8

1 3 5 7 9 8 6 4 2

A CIP catalogue record for this book is available from
the British Library.

Typeset by SetSystems Ltd, Saffron Walden, Essex
Printed and bound in Great Britain by
Mackays of Chatham plc, Chatham, Kent

To Dan

Truly, madly, deeply

Thank you to Anne and Peter for preventing me from becoming too bitter and twisted in my writing and for making me believe in happy endings.

Bitter & Twisted

PART ONE

Bitter

One

When people describe Annie they skirt around her as though there is a band of yellow police tape that says DO NOT CROSS THIS LINE. They struggle with euphemisms, avoiding the one thing that sets her apart from most other people. They describe her chestnut-brown hair, so glossy and smooth. They wax lyrical about her translucent, blemish-free skin and her perfect little teeth. Her personality is akin to March sunshine, open windows and newly baked bread. Annie is everyone's friend.

And she is fat.

Bonny. Heavy. Ample. Stout. Plump. Buxom. Comely.

Anything but fat.

She has gone through her entire life being labelled in this way. Of course, things weren't quite so courteous when she was younger. School kids can be so heartlessly cruel towards anyone who deviates from the norm. They called her Bunter, after the famous comic-strip character, and they made snorting noises through the toilet partitions whenever she had to use the facilities.

Pig. Cow. Fatty. Hippo. Porker. Lard-arse.

Did they care that she hid Mr Kipling's frangipani slices under her mattress so that she could eat them at night without derision? Did any of them stop to wonder if she might be stigmatized by their heartless name-calling and insinuations? She was just an object of ridicule and therefore impervious to their cruel taunts. Thick-skinned and thick-ankled, watching for confrontation on the lacrosse field through her impossibly thick National Health glasses. 'Come on, Bunter, move your arse!' they would shout.

Girls in pleated gym skirts and white Aertex tops. Girls with blonde bunches and enviable waistlines. Girls who afterwards ran around naked in the shower room: perky-breasted and firm-buttocked, ample and ready to hand-pick the best of the boys for the Christmas social.

So now, at thirty-seven, Annie is having the last laugh. She is standing in front of her full-length mirror in a cream satin wedding gown and she is laughing. Laughing at all those spiteful girls who said she would never amount to anything. Laughing at the relatives who ridiculed her at the dinner table for taking second helpings. Laughing at all the women she knows who have settled for compromise and have lived to regret it.

Annie is getting married to the most popular boy at school. Athlete. Scholar. Most likely to succeed.

Spencer Noble.

She can barely believe it herself. Here she is in a custom-made wedding dress, while her father waits downstairs looking uncomfortable in a tuxedo. The car will be here any minute and her bridesmaids are fussing around with her veil, clipping it securely into her enviable chestnut-brown hair. They are probably thinking how beautiful she looks for a fat person. They are probably shocked that she is eating a Mars Bar while finishing off a McDonald's strawberry milkshake through a jumbo straw.

'Mind your lipstick, Annie,' chides Spencer's younger sister, Jasmine.

'Don't get chocolate on your dress,' admonishes Annie's cousin Diane.

Where is Betsy? Where is Annie's chief bridesmaid? 'She's in the lav,' says Diane, 'probably got her fingers down her throat bringing up her McNuggets.'

Trust Diane to be so vitriolic! Sometimes poor Annie despairs of her family and their lack of decorum. Whatever must Mr and Mrs Noble think of them all, as they gather on opposite sides of the church?

Mr and Mrs Noble with their Victorian conservatory and double garage.

Annie can see them now – glancing surreptitiously across the aisle at her mother all decked out in periwinkle-blue chiffon. At her grandmother clinging to her zimmer frame in a pre-war astrakhan jacket and support tights. At the motley collection of aunts and uncles, cousins and family friends, all of them gathered in mismatched lines along several pews, wearing unsuitable hats and tight collars.

It doesn't bear thinking about.

Spencer's father is on the county council. Spencer's mother is chairperson of the Women's Guild. They give cheese and wine parties and hobnob with the mayor at social functions. They have a real tree at Christmas and drink dry sherry.

Annie's father is a fishmonger in the market. Her mother works at the Trebor factory, operating the machinery that wraps the mints and then packages them into cartons of thirty-six. For many years the locals have been able to sniff the air around Chesterfield and thus recognize the day of the week: peppermint on Tuesdays, pear drops on Fridays.

'The car's here, Annie,' says Betsy Brown, popping her gaunt little face around the bedroom door. Annie takes a final gulp of her milkshake, and Diane gives her a quick squirt of Opium.

'Oh God, I'm so nervous,' admits Annie, looking to her best friend for reassurance.

'It's going to be brilliant, love. You'll be the envy of everyone there. You're such a lucky cow! Spencer Noble – who would have dreamed, eh?'

Spencer's sister Jasmine obviously finds it difficult to keep quiet on this subject, because she screws up her pretty face as though attempting to dislodge something painful from her throat.

'Shift yourself then, Annie. Your dad's looking constipated down there in his monkey suit!'

And so this is it.

Annie steps gingerly down the narrow staircase, with umpteen yards of cream satin trailing behind her. This is the same staircase, where she played as a child halfway up, on this same nylon carpet, dangling her dolls from the banister rail and pretending it was a ski lift. Her veil brushes the low ceiling and she fills the space like an enormous meringue that has expanded too fast in the oven.

'Don't get wedged in there, Annie, otherwise we'll need a couple of hefty blokes and a length of rope to get you out!' Cousin Diane has never been one for subtlety. She is thwarted and mean, with a pinched face that looks spiteful even when it's smiling.

Dad waits in the living room. He stands with his back to the empty hearth as though warming his bum at an imaginary fire. In his rented tuxedo he appears fenced in and itchy, shifting his neck uneasily in his collar and flexing his hands into fists. Father and daughter overwhelm the cramped space with incongruous glamour: he in his dicky bow and she in her twenty metres of cream satin. The room seems to have shrunk, like one of those optical illusions at the Fun House in Blackpool where the walls are all skewed in order to deceive the eye. Annie has to duck to avoid the ceiling light.

'Crikey, love, you look smashing.'

Annie beams with joy. She *feels* smashing. 'Ta, Dad.'

'I have to admit, your mum and me were beginning to wonder if we'd ever see this day. What with our Frank wed at eighteen and our Erma knocked up before she left school, we thought you were going to be living with us until we popped our clogs. Looks like we were wrong, eh?'

'It looks like it, Dad,' and Annie kisses her father on the cheek. Even now, with a liberal splash of Brut, she can still smell the wet haddock lurking beneath his aftershave. It is a smell she has grown to associate with her father, and there is something comforting about it.

'Come on, Mr Stamper,' urges nimble Betsy, pinning a pink carnation to his lapel. 'The car has been waiting out there for ages. They'll be wondering where we've got to.'

'Betsy, love, it'll be you next, standing right here where our Annie is.'

'Pigs might fly, Mr Stamper. The day I land myself a husband, the moon'll be as blue as your jokes.' You

7

see, Betsy is as thin as her best friend is fat. She has been battling anorexia since she was fourteen years old.

'Looking the way you do today, I'd reckon there's a grand chance of you finding Mr Right at the wedding reception!'

But Annie's dad is just being kind. Betsy, in her bottle-green Dupion two-piece, looks like a shrivelled spring onion. Someone has misguidedly suggested that she should put her hair up for the wedding, so now it sprouts at the top of her narrow little head like the waving roots of a chive – milk-bottle white and wispy as candyfloss.

When Betsy and Annie walk out together of a week-end, they elicit the kind of stares usually reserved for circus freaks.

'Oh, I wish you were *my* dad,' smiles Betsy, raising a skeletal hand to her lips and blowing him a kiss through the breakfast hatch, as she rinses out her coffee mug and leaves it to drain with the others.

The neighbours have come out to see the bride. They stand in clutches near the ends of their paths, awe-struck by the spectacle of Annie Stamper emerging from number 11 in what looks like a cream satin barrage balloon. She can barely get through the gate. What on earth does somebody like Spencer Noble see in her? They've talked of nothing else on Clitheroe Street for weeks. It was rumoured that she must be up the spout, but who would even *know*? At fourteen stone, Annie wouldn't even need maternity clothes.

'Good luck, love!' they shout over the privet hedges.

'Congratulations, Wilf. She looks a picture!' They don't say what *kind* of picture.

It's a bit of a squash in the back of the car. Annie's

dad has to hold down her dress in order for the driver to see through the rear-view mirror. It is warm in the car and Annie can feel beads of sweat along her hairline. She can only hope that her extra-strength deodorant holds up until after the ceremony.

It is unseasonably warm for September.

The car sweeps down Clitheroe Street, dominating the narrow road and even causing the Bleesdale twins to stop playing hopscotch for a moment or two, as the limousine glides past and turns into Lebanon Avenue.

This is familiar territory for Annie. These are streets she has known all her life. The chip shop, the pet shop, the newsagent's, and the cobbler's. The people out on the street are familiar too; maybe not all by name, but with faces that fit into their surroundings like bricks in a wall.

There is a hearse standing outside the funeral home, heaped incongruously with vibrant flowers and ominously solemn in the early afternoon sunshine. Annie wonders who has died. Not much happens around here without everybody knowing about it.

'That'll be Charlie Finch,' supplies her father, nodding in the direction of the floral tributes. 'Liver cancer – passed away on Wednesday.'

Annie has to suppress a shiver. Is it a bad omen to see a funeral on the way to one's wedding? She wonders if there is any wood to touch, but the inside of the car is all vinyl and upholstered panels, so she just has to keep her fingers crossed beneath her bouquet and hope for the best.

*

Spencer Noble is supposed to be at the church by now but he is still sitting on the arm of his old Habitat sofa willing the telephone to ring. His best man Timothy is fretting in the hallway, checking his watch for the thousandth time and wiping his brow with the back of his hand. 'Come on, Spence, we're really late as it is. I promised your mother that I'd have you at the church by half past, and it's already a quarter to. She'll go berserk.'

Timothy is Spencer's oldest friend – they were at school together – Spencer can wrap Timothy around his little finger, so he isn't unduly concerned by his friend's discomfort. Timothy idolizes Spencer, as did most of the boys at Frechville Grammar.

There is an unsettling silence in the flat: the silence of departed friends. It hums along with the motor of the fridge-freezer in the kitchen. This is the flat that used to belong to Spencer before he moved up in the world. This is the flat that his family keeps on for the sake of wise investment and unwanted houseguests. It is small and unassuming – rather like the life that Spencer left behind when he moved to London.

'Just another five minutes, Tim, and then we can go.'

Shit, shit, shit! She promised she would call. *She promised.*

Spencer can look down at the school playing fields at the rear of the building, as he is on the ninth floor. There is a game of football going on and he almost wishes he was out there kicking the ball around instead of sitting up here in a bloody cravat and cummerbund. He is absolutely certain now that he is making the biggest mistake of his life. That is why he needs her to call him, that is why she *must* call him before he goes through with this ridiculous fiasco.

The plane tickets are on the coffee table. The honeymoon suite at the Prescott Hotel is booked for tonight, along with the banquet hall for the sit-down reception, and the ballroom for the informal disco afterwards. The prospect of it all is dismal, and Spencer has never felt so trapped in his entire life. He can't tell this to anyone, because nobody knows. They all think he's gone mad, but they don't know why exactly. Everyone is too polite to ask him why he has chosen Annie Stamper to be his bride after such an extended bachelorhood. How come, at thirty-seven, Spencer Noble would decide to marry a lump like Annie Stamper, when six months ago he was reputed to have three beautiful women on the go down in London?

What must he be thinking?

Right now he is thinking that if the phone doesn't ring he is going to scream. There is a pressure inside his head that threatens to break free at any moment, and if Timothy sighs one more time he will chuck the fucking table lamp at him!

Irritable spoiled Spencer. He would call *her* but he knows that her husband is home and he just can't risk another street brawl like the last time. Spencer isn't the fighting type – he prefers to pop his grievances through the postbox on a monogrammed notecard. And there is always the risk of violence to others, and Spencer cannot subject anyone to physical danger just because he needs reassurances on his wedding day.

Even under this extreme pressure Spencer appears cool and collected. Transparently grey-blue like the uninviting colour of northern seas. Nobody ever really

11

knows what he is thinking, and that is why he does so well in business. He knows how to bluff his way through the most difficult situations. He knows how to oil the wheels. If he were less attractive, people might label him ruthless, but he charms everyone he meets and so he gets away with murder – just like he always did.

'*You should be a politician.*' People are always saying things like that. They think just because he looks good in a suit and pretends to like babies that he would be an asset to local government, but politics does not interest Spencer, too much hard work for too little reward. Forget the wankers who work alongside his father down at the town hall, Spencer is too embroiled in the machinations of the legal profession to entertain the idea of anything less demanding.

If Spencer were an animal he would be a panther.

He would rather not consider what kind of animal Annie might be. That would be cruel.

Poor Annie. They have been unlikely friends for over twenty years. Nobody ever understood why the most popular boy at school would knock around with such an unfortunate individual. They tolerated Annie whenever she was with Spencer, but the same people who pretended then to like her also called her the worst names behind her back. They failed to recognize her intrinsic qualities. Spencer is surprised that she isn't already married to some overweight welder with tattoos and a hairy navel, but even those overweight welders have passed her up for slimmer, more vivacious types. Spencer is quite sure that Annie is a virgin. Why is that thought so utterly distasteful to him? A virgin at thirty-seven? He wonders if she ever masturbates. Now that's a mental image he'd rather not dwell on.

Is it Christian to have such thoughts? Spencer doesn't know all the rules of godliness but he's pretty sure that it's a sin to judge someone for the way they look. Spencer, however, has never had to worry about that. People admire and love him because he is so utterly adorable.

He could have married many beautiful women. He is a great catch, and there have been a number of flirtations that could have been very lucrative for him in the long run. But they would have demanded too much of him, smothering him with their cloying sexuality and their overwhelming perfume. Women have a nasty habit of taking over, of suffocating him even when he makes it totally obvious that he's not interested in anything other than a casual relationship.

He needs a wife who will ask no questions. A wife who will be so overawed by the mere fact that he is her husband that she will overlook just about anything. He needs a wife because he just can't go on like this any longer – something has to change otherwise he will be lost for ever. Just last night he had been tempted to go down to London for one last bite of the apple but somehow she – the woman he needs so badly right now – persuaded him that it would not be a good idea. Oh Christ, why doesn't she call him now when he needs her the most? He can't get through this without her.

'OK, Spence, you've had your five minutes. It's time to go, otherwise we'll lose our slot at the church and you know how much trouble your mother went to in order to arrange the damned place.' Timothy is standing in the doorway, jangling the loose change in his pocket. Bespectacled, fair-haired Timothy, he looks at Spencer imploringly. He is the same age as Spencer but he looks so much older. That's what a wife, two kids and male pattern baldness can do to a man. Is that what is in store for himself, Spencer wonders?

'Fair enough then, let's go.' And right then the phone begins to ring. Spencer answers it before the second ring.

It is her.

He places the palm of his hand over the receiver and asks Timothy to go down to the car – he'll be there in a couple of ticks. Timothy makes a face and points to his watch, but he nevertheless leaves Spencer alone so that he can talk in private.

'I can't go through with it, Maggie. It is bound for disaster. I need more time – more time to get my head straight. Can't I just come down to your place and talk about it some more? I'm just not ready. I'm sure I could make some kind of excuse.'

'And what kind of excuse do you think Annie is going to swallow if you leave her standing at the altar? Be sensible about this, Spence. You've had plenty of time to back out and it seems just a trifle selfish, even for you, darling, to start thinking about this just as the church bells are ringing. I told you repeatedly that this was a bad idea, but you'd got the idea in your head, and once it was there I couldn't get through to you. Yes, it's a bloody bad idea and I think you're mad, but I honestly don't think you can back out now. I'm thinking about Annie more than anyone.'

This is not what Spencer wants to hear. He was hoping for Maggie to reinforce his belief that this marriage would be good for him. 'I should be marrying *you*,' he says.

Maggie laughs. 'Oh, now that's a really sensible

suggestion! What do you think Frank would say? Sometimes, Spence, you say some pretty stupid things for a bloke who is supposed to be so clever.'

'You know exactly what I mean.'

'Look, it really is too late to be having this conversation. You've dug your own grave, and if you want to chicken out now, then on your own head be it. You can call me later if you like, I'll be here – Frank's in Scotland so you don't have to worry about him answering. Billy's playing football and then going on to a friend's house for tea. I tell you what, why don't you set up a conference call from the honeymoon suite?'

'OK, OK, very droll! I suppose I'm just a bit worried that I'm doing this for the wrong reasons.'

'Darling, you *are* doing it for the wrong reasons! You are not going to find happiness in a marriage created from lies and deceit. You don't love this woman at all, so how are you going to sustain a relationship with her for longer than a few weeks? When I first met Frank, I did at least have *some* feelings towards him, and before you say it, yes, I caught him on the rebound from you, but that's not the point. Oh, we've gone through this a thousand times before – I'm tired of talking about it.'

'OK, I'm doing this for myself: pure, unadulterated selfishness.'

'That sounds about right! I love you, Spencer, despite the fact that you're an egocentric pig. I care about what you do with your life, even though you messed mine up so badly. I can't believe I'm saying this . . . to you of all people.'

'I'm sorry, Maggie. You know I love you, but you and I have always been at the wrong place at the wrong time. I'm just going to take a deep breath, and I'll see you when I get back to the surface.'

'As long as you are not found floating face down,' sighs Maggie.

'If I am, you'll just have to give me the kiss of life.'

'Oh, go and get married before I get really pissed off!' yells Maggie. 'And before you ask . . .'

'Yes?'

'I didn't bother with the bridal registry at Heal's. I wanted to save you the trouble of taking the breadmaker back next week.'

'Fuck you!'

'Ditto.'

And Spencer Noble puts down the receiver and prepares to take an enormous leap of faith.

Two

'I don't give a flying fuck if the embassy is closed, we need that waiver by Monday morning, so hustle that skinny ass of yours round to Juanita and rattle her cage!'

Marla Philips has a headset so that she doesn't have to pick up the telephone. She minimizes effort in any way that she can and employs a sycophantic entourage of personnel to do all the things that normal people would usually do themselves.

She is in the office on a Saturday. This is not unusual for Marla because she lives for her work. She is an immigration lawyer, and she can't afford to sit on her laurels and let some other hotshot come along and knock her off her self-made pedestal. She is one of the best lawyers in London. Her clients are mainly rich Arabs who can practically *buy* their way into the country, but she also has a Manhattan office which means she is the very best person to see in London if you want a green card.

She is a mess.

Her hair beneath the headset is daffodil blonde, and as dry and brittle as fibreglass. It may have been professionally styled a few days ago but she has slept on it for three nights without combing it out and now it has the wild, unmanageable texture of kapok.

She wears no make-up and her skin is sallow – the

unhealthy colour of cigarette smoke. She smokes sixty a day, and most of her lipstick is now stubbed out in an overflowing ashtray atop a mound of legal papers and documents. It is hard to believe that Marla Philips was at a black-tie gala reception on Wednesday evening sitting just three tables away from Camilla Parker-Bowles.

The phone rings constantly.

'Sue the redneck son-of-a-bitch!'

'Hey, Chuck! I hope you've got good news for me otherwise I'm hanging up on you right now.'

'Julie, get me a Diet Coke and see if you can get hold of Spencer. Yes! I know he's getting married today but I need to know where the Al Sabah files are.'

Spencer Noble and Marla Philips are partners. Marla brought Spencer in last year as an equal partner and it is working famously. Spencer is everything that Marla isn't: smart, efficient, methodical and meticulous. Marla is everything that Spencer isn't: arrogant, ruthless, unorthodox and infamous. They complement each other in a way that chalk and cheese never could.

She has a coffee stain on her Chanel suit. Her bony chest and the edge of her black bra create an untidy V between the ash-flecked lapels of the bouclé jacket. One of the brass buttons hangs by a thread. She looks older than her years. She could be pushing sixty but she's only forty-nine. Too many late nights, cigarettes and transatlantic crossings. Too little sleep, food and relaxation.

Marla's secretary comes through on the intercom. Her broad, cockney accent still grates on Marla's nerves even now, and Julie has been with the firm for almost two years.

'Miss Philips, that psycho sent another letter. Should I get in touch with the Old Bill or ignore the toerag?'

'What did he say this time?' asks Marla, lighting up a cigarette from the butt of her last one.

'Oh, the usual tripe! He reckons he's going to kill you. He says he'll be waiting for you when you get home, so you'd better watch out. I think I'd best contact the law just to be on the safe side, don't you?'

'Yeah, call the cops and talk to Inspector Blake. He's the one dealing with this creep.'

Marla inhales deeply. The nicotine no longer has any effect on her; it merely drifts around her lungs, unable to penetrate their tar-clogged membranes. She breathes the smoke out through her nostrils and closes her eyes for a moment. *Who is this crazy shit-head?*

It started out with pornographic messages on her email from an unknown source. Then she started getting letters and faxes describing the sexually humiliating situations that she might find herself in. Whoever it is, this wacko, he's obviously turned on by the idea of dominance in a big way. Last week she received a dead crow and a dog turd in a gift box from Fortnum & Mason.

If it wasn't for the overt sexual nature of these messages and threats she might be inclined to believe that somebody has found out about her past, but there is no mention of Jessica or the murder trial. She did her best to escape from the front-page headlines and the wicked, manipulative news reports of her tragedy, but even now there are times when it all comes back to her with a prickling at the back of her neck, like the fear of an unturned corner in a haunted house. Why else would

somebody scare her like this? And what can they possibly gain from dragging up the past, unless it's just one
of those asshole religious freaks who wants to see her
burned in hell?

She had wondered if it might be her ex-boyfriend
Pierre. She had stopped sending him money when he
got married recently, but he denies her accusation vehe-
mently and Marla believes him. He now has better
things to do with his life than bug her.

She can't think of anyone else, unless it is some
disgruntled client who failed to get a visa or a work
permit. She certainly knows plenty of people with the
power and connections to get her obliterated at a
moment's notice. But *why*?

Marla isn't the kind of woman who scares easily.
She goes skydiving, bungee jumping and white-water
rafting when she needs a break. When she is in the
States she carries a pearl-handled revolver in her handbag, and in London, because of the antiquated gun
laws, she carries a silver-plated knuckleduster and a flick
knife. Anyone foolish enough to mess with Marla Philips
will get more than they bargained for. She went through
years of psychotherapy to be the woman she is today.
It's hard to believe that just a few years ago she was
practically comatose with fear and vulnerability.

Damn the Brits and their lack of air conditioning! It
is like an oven in the office, even with the windows wide
open. The noise of the street below rises up on an
unseasonably humid cloud of afternoon heat. This is
very peculiar for late September, and Marla wishes she
hadn't worn this damned thick suit. The desk fan is
broken and somebody never bothered to get it fixed –
who would that be? Marla expects things to happen on

their own, like magic, and usually they do if she leaves them long enough. She had no hot water in her bathroom for three months before anyone bothered to get it fixed. Her maid, Hetty, complains that she cannot read Marla's mind, but isn't that what Marla pays her for?

Julie brings her a Diet Coke. 'Inspector Blake weren't there, Miss Philips, so I left a message with another copper who said he'll get him to call back on Monday, when he gets in from Southend.'

'*Ice*, Julie! How long have you been working here? I can't drink this stuff without ice.' Marla shakes the Coke can at her secretary as though it is a collection box.

'It's not good for you, Miss Philips, all this ice. No wonder you're always coming down with colds.'

'Julie, just get the ice and save the layman's diagnosis for somebody who gives a shit.'

Julie smiles. Nobody around here takes offence at Marla's abrupt turn of phrase. She's *American* – what more can they expect? 'Couldn't get hold of Spencer. I left a message at his flat and called his parents' house but I reckon they'll be at the reception by now.'

'So call the damned hotel then! I have to have those files before I leave today.'

'All right, but he's not going to be a happy camper.'

'Go! Go!' yells Marla, pointing the way out with an imperious, nicotine-yellow finger.

And Julie goes – clomp, clomp, clomp in those ridiculous platform soles of hers.

The phone keeps ringing and ringing but Marla's eyes are diverted to the flashing screen of her computer. 'YOU HAVE MAIL!' it announces cheerfully. She clicks on the envelope icon and a message appears in bold red letters: ARE YOU SCARED YET? 7899. SHE DIDN'T DIE IN VAIN!

Oh, Christ! He knows the security code to her apartment, and she only changed it this morning . . .

He's going to the Oscars. A letter arrived today from the Academy of Performing Arts in Hollywood, and they have invited him, all expenses paid, to attend the award ceremony in LA next March.

Lester Philips is so overwhelmed by this news that he practically brings up his Weetabix and instant coffee.

His wife Tina looks up from her bowl of Alpen and stares at him impassively across the breakfast table. She has those funny rubber-sausage things in her hair that make Lester think of Medusa.

'They want me to go to the Oscars.' He has to modulate his voice because he is in danger of screaming out this news at the top of his voice. He can barely remain seated and his voice is shaking.

'Give over, Less. You're having me on,' responds Tina, eyes still made up from last night, her nails the colour of bubblegum.

'No, darling, it's true! They want to do some kind of tribute to Oscar winners of the past, get us all up on stage. They want me there for a whole week, to rehearse and everything. You're invited too, darling. A free trip to LA next March – what do you think about that?'

Lester can no longer control himself. He leaps up from his IKEA blonde wood chair and grabs his wife by her arm. They stagger around the tiny kitchen together, bumping into the fridge and the cooker as they pantomime a waltz across the six-foot square of lino that is patterned to look like Mediterranean tile.

'I can't believe it, Tina. After all these bloody years I'm going to be back there with the big guys! You'll probably get to meet Jack Nicholson and Tom Cruise – all kinds of celebrities!'

'Yeah, sure, Less. More likely we'll get stuck at the back with a load of has-beens like yourself.'

'Charming! Is that how you see me, Tina? A has-been?' Lester stops spinning his wife around for a moment and looks into her ashen face.

'You know what I mean. All those big film stars and then *us*. We're hardly up there with the likes of Tom Hanks and Meryl Streep. There are people in their twenties who've never even heard of *Five Farthings*. It's not as though any of the cast are still famous these days. Even the soundtrack is in the bargain bin at HMV.'

'How can you say that, Tina?' Lester feels hurt. 'I'm not exactly in the dole queue, you know, and what about Shani? She's doing that thing for the BBC with Maureen Lipman.'

'She has about three lines in every episode, and it's not as though either of you have been in a film since the early '70s. *Five Farthings* was your one-hit wonder, Less. I'm sorry to sound harsh but try to get a grip on reality – going to LA isn't going to change any of that.'

This is the first time that Lester has heard such views from his wife. They have only been married for a few months and she previously always seemed so impressed by his minor celebrity status. He gets asked to sign autographs all the time – usually young kids with their parents who recognize him from his daily TV show. OK, so it's not Oscar-worthy stuff these days, but it pays the bills and it gets him on the cover of the *TV Times* occasionally. At least he's not doing adverts!

When Lester looks back to 1969 – and he looks back a lot – it all seems like it happened to a different person. Everyone says that, don't they? When something happened a long time ago it gets this kind of otherworldly feel about it, sometimes as though it never really happened at all. That's sad because it makes you realize that maybe your fifteen minutes of fame have already passed you by. What hope is there for Lester of ever recapturing the heady excitement of celebrating his fourteenth birthday on the sound stage at Elstree Studios, with all those people singing 'Happy Birthday' to him?

Karl Steinbrenner was probably the most sought-after director of the day. He had just finished making *Heads or Tails* with Glenda Jackson and Oliver Reed and everyone thought he was going to be a tyrant to work with. As it turned out he was a real gentleman and if it hadn't have been for Karl, Lester would never have won his Oscar for best supporting actor.

He wants to call Marla but he knows that Tina will be pissed off if he does. Tina reckons he's still in love with his ex-wife but Lester knows that he isn't. It's just that Marla, being American and having lived with him for so many years, will appreciate the magnitude of this news. She would break out the champagne and take him to dinner somewhere nice, boosting his ego and making him feel important. Tina, on the other hand, is more interested in reading her *Cosmopolitan* than in her husband's triumph. She flips the pages idly, stifling a yawn with the back of her hand.

Lester wishes that it wasn't a Saturday. He would have liked to go into the studio today, to nonchalantly mention that he has been invited to Hollywood, to act cool and unaffected, as though this is no big deal. Half the people there don't even know that he once won an Oscar. Half the people there don't even know that he can *act*.

Pigbeet and Little Pud is a children's programme that airs on weekdays at 11 a.m. It has been reasonably successful over the past five years or so, although it cannot rival the *Teletubbies*, or some of those American imports. It is aimed at the five to ten year age group and has an old-fashioned approach to entertainment, unlike so many of the vulgar, brash shows they make for kids these days. Lester plays Pigbeet – a kind of overstuffed purple pig with a forgetful, slightly stupid personality. He appears on T-shirts in Debenhams, alongside Rosie and Jim and Barney. Hey! It's better than nothing, and the salary is decent. This flat isn't particularly palatial but it's smack in the middle of Kensington, and they've got their own patio. They're hardly paupers.

Tina brings in a pittance with her massage therapy. It had been lack of finance that prevented them from getting married for so long, but Tina had then threatened to leave if Lester didn't make an honest woman out of her and so they'd thrown caution to the wind and dropped in at the registry office to pick up a licence.

They are eating breakfast at three in the afternoon. They were out late last night at a terrible dinner party given by some of Tina's friends in a council flat near King's Cross. They didn't get to eat until almost midnight, because the hostess was pissed out of her head on home-brewed beer that she siphoned from a plastic sack hanging from her kitchen door handle. They had to endure two hours of amateur porno movies which had been thoughtfully supplied by Tina's mate Brandi, a so-called actress whose most inspiring role so far has been the 'Girl With Dildo' in a brief sequence that takes place in the back of a Range Rover.

It isn't that Lester dislikes Tina's friends – they can be very amusing at times – but last night he wasn't particularly in the mood for cheap plonk and mindless conversation. They act like a bunch of students who have never grown up, sitting around on beanbags, smoking dope and discussing the merits of various recreational drugs. Lester has never really been into the whole drug culture, although he has nothing against people who like to drop the occasional E or smoke a joint. He just doesn't see the point of *analysing* it.

The afternoon is hot and sticky. It seems to smear the windows with its cloying stillness, and Lester feels enervated even though he's only been out of bed for fifty minutes. The ceilings are low because the flat is in the basement. Daylight struggles to reach them from beyond the pavement above the kitchen window. Tina turns the pages of her magazine and Lester feels bored with the day before it even starts. They have no plans, which means they will probably squander the weekend doing nothing. Lester wishes that there was something to look forward to, but March is a long time to wait and he isn't getting any younger. Instead of feeling revitalized by marrying Tina, he feels cheated – cheated of the rejuvenation he felt sure would come from marrying a younger woman. It seems so passé to have a mid-life crisis these days, but Lester has started waking up in the mornings with an unsettling sensation of urgency. Grab it while you can, says the little voice in the back of his head, it's now or never.

So Lester Philips, at forty-seven years old, rereads his letter from Hollywood and pours himself another mug of coffee from the cafetière with the broken filter.

Three

London swings like a pendulum do . . .

But there are no bobbies on bicycles, as far as Annie can see.

Annie Noble (née Stamper) stands on the pavement in her flat, black court shoes and looks up at the buildings that line Bond Street.

It is 9 a.m and there is barely room to breathe. The road is choked with taxis and cars, bumper to bumper, filling the grey morning air with a city smell that Annie cannot get used to. Her palms are damp and she's got butterflies in her tummy. First day at work and she has never felt so uncertain of herself. Clitheroe Street is a million miles away and Annie has to swallow a small lump of nostalgia for that familiar territory. The girls in her previous office will be drinking coffee and sharing weekend anecdotes over the Xerox machine. Are they wondering about Annie? Who is using her desk beside the filing cabinets? Who will fetch the sandwiches and buns at lunchtime?

Annie steps back to allow busy people to pass by. They seem annoyed with her for taking up so much pavement, and nobody smiles. Sharp, professional faces look straight ahead and not at Annie. The shops are not open yet but their windows are filled with expensive things with famous labels. Down in this crack between buildings it all feels so enormous, so impersonal that Annie has to bite her lip to stop herself from crying. She feels homesick.

Spencer has had to stay in Paris. Their honeymoon consisted of two short nights near the Pantheon, and then Annie had to come to London to start her new job at Spencer's office: without him.

'You'll be fine, darling,' he had assured her last night, as they drove through the tunnel where Princess Diana was killed. 'Marla will be there, and the other secretaries are very friendly. Anyway, they won't dare be anything but nice to you – after all, you are the boss's wife!'

Quite frankly, Annie is scared stiff of Spencer's business partner Marla. She has a voice that grates like unpolished metal and, like most Americans, she talks to everyone as though they are off in the next room. Marla is a powerful woman and power frightens Annie.

The law offices of Philips Noble are above a leather handbag shop. There is an unassuming doorway with a brass plaque and an intercom, and standing on the door-step there is a Federal Express man with a clipboard and a large envelope. He smiles at Annie with a whiff of Juicy Fruit, and his teeth are pointed like a dog's. 'You going in, love?' he enquires.

'Yes,' says Annie.

'You work here, do you?'

'Well, I . . . yes.'

'Well, sign this for us, love – save me the trip up-stairs.' He hands the clipboard to Annie and removes a plastic biro from behind his ear.

'Well, I'm not . . .' stutters Annie, accepting the pen.

'Right there,' says the courier, pointing to a line where she is supposed to sign.

Annie scribbles her name, taking the large envelope before she can get a chance to explain any further. The Federal Express man hops back into his van, and off he goes into the stream of Bond Street traffic.

Annie presses the buzzer. Women with expensive perfume breeze by on important business. Annie can't help but feel marooned in her drop-waisted dress from Evans, and realizes her jacket sleeves are too long.

'Come on up,' says a scratchy voice on the intercom, and the door buzzes open.

Inside the hallway they've tried to modernize with plate mirror and up-lights, but Annie can see that the building is fighting the attempt by messing up the stream-lining with bumpy, over-painted cornices and dado rails.

There is a lift that was obviously an afterthought, and it is too small for Annie to fit inside without compromising her box pleats. Even the stairs are narrower than usual, and Annie's hips brush the vinyl wallpaper as she pulls herself up to the first landing.

Terror pounds in her temples. She wants to turn around and go straight back out of the building, but what would Spencer say if she did such a foolish thing? He would smile and call her a 'chump' and then she'd have the added humiliation of having to come back here with everyone knowing that she chickened out on her first day. It makes her feel about ten years old and ancient fears crowd in on her. She thought she had forgotten how it felt to be a schoolgirl in a size 18 gymslip, hanging around the tuck shop with all the other freaks and misfits.

Marla's personal secretary, Julie, is the first person that Annie meets as she enters reception. She slides back a mirrored window and smiles redly at Annie through the hole in the wall. 'All right?' she enquires cheerfully. 'You must be Mrs Noble. We've been expecting you. Mr Noble called this morning to tell us to look out for you. Come on through – that door on the right.'

Annie feels enormous in these tiny rooms filled with artificial plants and framed certificates. In the mirrored panels she has a shiny face that catches the light from the recessed downlights.

Behind the door there are offices – and people. An atmosphere of business prevails; leaving Annie stranded on a patch of purple carpet like an uninvited guest at a party. Julie reappears from around the corner. She looks a bit tarty in that figure-hugging black dress but she's got lovely legs. Her hair is jet black and shoulder-length. It curls up at the ends and she's got it tucked behind her ears to show off her earrings.

'What's that you've got?' asks Julie, indicating the envelope that Annie is carrying.

'Oh, it was being delivered as I came upstairs.' Annie hands the envelope to Julie.

'Shit! He was supposed to wait while we sign the papers. Hang on a second love.' Julie dashes off, leaving Annie alone in the corridor with nothing to do but stand there fiddling with the clasp on her new handbag.

There is a globe on a metal stand.

If I didn't have my socks on, I'd show you the Northern Hemisphere.

Annie remembers Spencer saying that all those years ago when they were watching *Saturday Night Fever* at his parents' house. His legs were hanging over the arm of the sofa and he was attempting to spin the world with his feet but his socks were too slippery to move the globe of his parents' cocktail cabinet. Annie loved him even then. She probably always loved him but he never knew it. How could Spencer Noble possibly ever love a big lump like Annie? He had girls swooning at his feet and yet it was Annie he chose to be his friend.

Disorientated, uncomfortable Annie.

She doesn't know which foot to stand on and these shoes are killing her already. Her mouth is dry and she's gagging for a coffee. She steps to one side of the corridor, moving slowly, with her head thrust nervously forward as though somebody might leap out and startle her at any moment. On each side there are offices with open doors and the efficient rattle of people at work. What is she supposed to do? Where should she go?

Marla Philips appears at the far end of the corridor. Today she is wearing an acid-yellow skirt and jacket with a lime-green blouse that gapes open to reveal a black crew neck beneath. Her heels are high, her stockings black. The hairdresser has puffed up her hair into a yellow helmet of lacquered waves, and she looks every inch the international lawyer. When Marla spots Annie dithering at the far corner of the corridor, she squints through her cigarette smoke. 'Is that you, Annie?' she enquires, her voice as soothing as chalk on a blackboard.

Annie nods but no words come out of her mouth. She takes a few steps forward, wondering if she is now expected to approach Marla.

'What the hell are you doing hanging around in the hallway like that? Hasn't Julie showed you where your office is yet?' Marla takes a final long drag on her cigarette and stubs it out in a convenient flowerpot. Her rings flash in the halogen lighting.

'Well, Julie had to, erm . . .'

'Christ Almighty! *Julie!*' screams Marla at the top of her voice. '*Julie!*'

'Blimey, where's the fire?' asks Julie, popping her head out from an office doorway.

'Take Annie to her office and fetch me some pantyhose, I've got a run in these and I'm due in court at eleven. And where is my coffee? I thought you were bringing it an hour ago . . .' Marla vanishes, but her voice continues to drone as though it somehow operates independently of her body. Julie smiles at Annie and rolls her eyes.

'You'll get used to it, Mrs Noble, she's always cheesed off on Monday mornings but her bark's worse than her bite – *most* of the time, anyway! Come on, I'll show you where your office is.'

Annie could kill for a Twix. She's got two in her handbag but she daren't get one out in case people think she's a pig eating chocolate so early in the morning. In Paris it was different – she could dunk her pain au chocolat in her coffee without raising an eyebrow, but this isn't Paris, it's London and Annie wishes she was anywhere else rather than here right now.

'Here we are, then. This is where you'll be working. And this is Richard – you'll be sharing with him for the foreseeable future.'

'Richard Carruthers,' says the rumpled-looking gentleman who jumps up from his desk as they enter the small office space. Annie shakes his hand and smiles with a confidence she really doesn't feel.

Richard is not wearing a suit, just trousers and a

shirt with the sleeves rolled clumsily above his elbows. Annie wonders if that is allowed: she had imagined all law offices to be staffed with smart-suited professionals – sleek and immaculate like Spencer. Richard's watch is not silver or gold; it is yellow and red with Mickey Mouse on the face.

'This is your desk, Mrs Noble.'

'Please, call me Annie. I keep thinking my mother-in-law is here whenever anyone calls me Mrs Noble.'

'That's enough to put years on you!' laughs Julie. 'And you ain't seen *my* mother-in-law!' She shows Annie an empty desk by the window. 'Not much of a view but sometimes, if they have the lights on, you can see through the net curtains opposite.'

Marla shouts for Julie down the corridor.

'Her ladyship awaits, I've got to dash. Richard'll look after you, won't you, Richard?'

'Most certainly! How about we start with some coffee?'

'Lovely!'

'Follow me, then. I'll give you the grand tour.'

Annie is concerned to see that Richard walks with a pronounced limp. It isn't the kind of limp that comes with a broken toe or a bunion; it is the lilting, unwieldy kind of limp that comes with something more permanent, like polio or some congenital deformity. He drags his left foot behind him like a heavy weight, using his arms to balance himself as he tilts from left to right. Annie, being a sentimental person and terrified of appearing insensitive, walks beside him and makes inane observations about his aftershave being so pleasant.

How dreadful!

Annie can't wait to get out of this place, but it's only

half past nine and there's a whole day to get through before she can rush home and hide herself away in Spencer's little house on Fulham Road.

Their house.

But it has been Spencer's house for so long that it will never feel like their house and Annie still doesn't know where the cutlery goes or how to work the dishwasher.

'Unlimited Jaffa Cakes,' announces Richard as he shows Annie the small kitchen where the coffee machine is. 'Marla buys them in bulk from the cash and carry and we've got enough to last us well into the next decade. Help yourself.'

And when Richard's back is turned Annie stuffs an entire biscuit in her mouth before he can witness her gluttony.

So much for her promise to Spencer about starting a diet. He wants her to go to WeightWatchers, but she can't be faffed with all that measuring and weighing of calories and fat – she'd rather buy a few Lean Cuisine frozen dinners and have done with it. Of course no diet has ever worked for Annie, because she just doesn't have the necessary willpower to survive on celery and water for thirty days. It's depressing, and what's the point in being depressed if you can cheer yourself up so easily with a bar of Fruit and Nut and some crisps?

Annie takes another Jaffa Cake. To hell with it! She'll go to bed early tonight and skip supper.

Four

Spencer has no business to conduct in Paris.

He just cannot face being in London with Annie right now. A sickening dread has set into his bones, like rheumatism, making his joints ache, making his stomach churn. He found a little church this morning, a dark place where light came through the darkened stained-glass windows in murky red and green. He sat alone at the back pew and listened to the sound of a distant barrel organ while he bowed his head and prayed for guidance. He found no comfort in prayer, so he merely closed his eyes and spoke softly to the colours inside his head.

He sits now by the open window of his hotel room, listening to the sounds of the traffic in the street below. There is a soft, filtered sunlight that turns the Pantheon to the colour of honey, and beyond the surrounding buildings there is the deepening blue of a September sky. An idyllic spot for romance. The honeymoon suite, no less: a four-poster bed and a separate sitting room with CNN and watered silk curtains.

What has he done?

He has made a terrible mistake and he doesn't know what to do about it. For the first time in Spencer Noble's life he is unsure of what comes next. If he could, he would run away from it all, go into hiding somewhere quiet with sunshine and olive trees. Tuscany, maybe? Or Provence? He could hole up in one of those crumbling old farmhouses that they always show on cooking programmes, sustaining a simple life on bread and wine, with oil lamps, and a mosquito net above the bed.

Pipe dreams.

He is surprised at himself. Pragmatic and unromantic, Spencer is not one to be caught up in such fanciful daydreams. He is the type of man who never goes out in the rain without the right clothing. He has to *plan* everything, from a trip to the supermarket to an 'impromptu' supper with friends. Nobody knocks at Spencer's door without an invitation. His friends know what he's like in that respect.

Marrying Annie was a foolish and reckless action spurred on by a brief but enigmatic message that popped into his head one day without warning.

'You must change your life and marry,' said the voice in his head that day as he walked past a display of video recorders in Rumbelows. Spencer had stopped in his tracks, looking around to see who was speaking, but there was nobody there. The voice had come to him from within, but it was not his own.

Spencer feels in need of salvation. What is he going to do?

A distant clock strikes five. He doesn't want to call the office to see how Annie is coping on her first day. What the hell was he thinking, getting her a job in his own damned office? Now he is going to have to see her all day long unless he's out of town. He obviously didn't think things through. She will be there every morning and every night, looking at him with those trusting, adoring eyes. Love me, is what she will say. But Spencer cannot love Annie. Not in the way she wants him to.

Their honeymoon was a charade. Attempting to have sex with a woman you have known since childhood is not very easy, especially when she is a virgin and several stone overweight. Spencer doesn't have the largest of penises, but under normal circumstances it has proved adequate for the purpose. With Annie it had taken several awkward manoeuvres before he could enter her, and he had felt rather like a mouse mounting an elephant. She made no indication of pleasure or discomfort so Spencer had rummaged around for a while before rolling over and acting as though he was satisfied and tired.

She had a smell. Nothing offensive – just an off-putting smell of talcum powder that had settled in her creases, making Spencer think of his mother.

This will never work!

Annie had made clumsy attempts at oral sex on the second night. Having never done it before she was obviously nervous and her sharp little teeth scratched the shaft of his penis so that he had to grip the pillow in order to remain silent. Her mouth was dry, her mouth was impossibly small and not made for such vulgar acts. In the end she tried valiantly to jerk him off, but her fingers gripped too lightly and her stroke was far too slow. Spencer groaned as though he liked it, but his groans were not those of pleasure, they were the groans of a man who has to admit he has dug his own grave.

'I hope that was all right,' said Annie afterwards. 'You didn't . . . you know.'

'A bit exhausted I think, darling. But it felt great,' lied Spencer, turning off the light and staring into the blue wash from the window like a man afloat on a piece of wreckage.

The bed was too small with Annie in it. Her nightie was hideously feminine – pale blue with frills and bows, like something that Hattie Jacques would have worn when 'carrying on' with Kenneth Williams. Every time she moved, that talcum smell would puff up from beneath the sheets, keeping Spencer awake with its persistent taunt.

'Let's not cuddle,' he whispered into her soft chestnut hair, 'it's a bit too warm in here for that.'

And she had touched his cheek with the back of her podgy little hand, the hand that now glitters with the gold of his vows, and she had told him how much she loves him. 'Me too,' he replied. And the words had battered his tonsils and made him gag.

Oh my God! The full truth of the situation threatens to suffocate him, like a polythene bag tied under his chin. He breathes in, and the transparent plastic forms to his face, blocking his nostrils and stretching tight over a silent scream.

He can't stay in Paris a moment longer. He longs desperately to be back in London where things are familiar to him, but he can't go home, not with Annie there, sitting wedged uncomfortably into one of his Shaker-style armchairs. No, Spencer will go to Maggie in Holloway. She will let him sleep in their spare room, along with the spider plants and the sofa bed with the creaky springs. Frank might get pissed off, but Maggie will think of something clever to say – a feasible explanation that appeases her husband. Frank is not an intelligent man but he isn't as stupid as everyone thinks. He is the kind of man who watches old reruns of *Love*

Thy Neighbour and says they don't make sitcoms like they used to with a wistful melancholy in his voice. He went into mourning when Enoch Powell died. Not that racism has anything to do with the way he views Spencer: it's just that people like that are bound to get overexcited if they suspect that something is not as it might seem. When you work on a North Sea oil rig ten months out of the year, you tend to become just a little bit oversensitive.

And nothing *is* what it might seem.

Spencer takes the 7.20 flight to Heathrow.

It is almost nine by the time his taxi pulls up outside Maggie's house, and it is dark and slightly damp, as though Bonfire Night has arrived early. The narrow road she lives on is dimly illuminated with inadequate street lamps which hide between the trees that rustle slightly in a breeze that smells of damp leaves and woodsmoke.

The lights are on in the upstairs sitting room, but the curtains are drawn so that only the thinnest scraps of light show through to the outside. The gate is open. The porch light is off. Spencer is aware of – but can't see – the stained-glass panel in the front door that depicts a hummingbird about to feed from the open petals of a flower. He knows that this encounter is going to be awkward but he's here now and he has to go through with it. What else can he do?

Ding-dong, ding-dong goes the doorbell.

Spencer's feet scrape on the tiled area inside the porch, and he clears his throat, wondering what he is going to say.

A light comes on and the hummingbird appears in rich jewel tones.

It is Frank. Frank is wearing his white vest and a flannel shirt with the sleeves rolled up high enough to cut into his bulging tattoos. He stands in the doorway, blocking out the light with his antagonism. His face is rough with several days' growth, and Spencer knows what his breath smells like, even before he opens his mouth. Lager and pepperoni pizza.

'Hello, Frank, I'm sorry to impose at such an hour but I was wondering if Maggie is home.' Spencer smiles as he talks, keeping his tone light and hoping that Frank doesn't catch the whiff of airline gin.

'She's out at one of her women's meetings in Hampstead – doesn't usually get back until about eleven.' Frank announces this information as though delivering an ultimatum. He doesn't bother to hide his animosity, because they all know that any attempt at social grace would be ridiculous at this point.

Spencer weighs up his options and realizes that this was a stupid mistake. 'Oh, look, it doesn't matter. I can call her tomorrow . . .'

'I wouldn't bother if I was you, mate. We'll be out tomorrow, and I thought we'd decided that there is no point in you coming round here again? Maggie doesn't want anything to do with you, and I don't want you acting all pally with Billy either. I suggest you just piss off back to that new wife of yours and stop fucking around with mine.'

Once again Spencer wonders whether Maggie was so desperate to get married that she had to choose such an uncouth, brutish man as Frank. 'Just tell her I stopped by, will you?'

'You know, I might just like to forget that you were ever here. I'd invite you in for a drink, but I'm not sure

I could stomach the sight of you in my living room. Now, if you'll excuse me, I'm watching a documentary about cancer and it's a hell of a lot more interesting than standing here looking at you.'

'Point taken, Frank. Your subtlety is wasted on the rigs, you should have taken up politics.'

'You are such a wanker, Spencer!' As Frank says this, he takes hold of Spencer's lapels and pulls him close.

Spencer jerks himself away from Frank's grasp and straightens his jacket. He is halfway down the path before he turns back and shouts, 'You are a bully, Frank – a fucking headcase. You should see a doctor.'

'Up yours!' shouts back Frank, making obscene gestures from the open doorway of the house as Spencer hurries away to the safety of the main road.

So a taxi takes Spencer from Holloway to Fulham, and he wonders if Annie will still be awake when he gets in. She goes to bed early because she likes to read for an hour before lights-out. The books she reads are usually fat and glossy with gold-foiled one-word titles like *Shame* or *Destiny*. With any luck she'll be tucked up in bed and then Spencer can creep around downstairs before sleeping on the futon.

Spencer's house is by far the nicest on the street. He spent thousands renovating the exterior, bringing it up to scratch, and now it puts all the others to shame. The drainpipes alone cost more than most people would spend on a widescreen TV. He knows that Annie hates it, but she's too polite to say anything, and Spencer's too selfish to offer her the chance. The last thing he wants is a house filled with Annie's cute little orna-

ments, frilly cushions, and framed posters from Debenhams.

Good! There are no lights on at the front. Spencer
turns his key very carefully, so as not to make a noise,
but he anticipates the shrill warning signal from the
burglar alarm and jabs at the conveniently placed key-
pad before it has a chance to wake Annie up. He is
surprised that she even remembers how to set it cor-
rectly, but maybe he is being too harsh – it's not as
though she's stupid. All these years she has been his
good friend, and suddenly, because she is his wife, he
is projecting this image of incompetence on her. Why is
that?

The recessed, low-voltage, directional lighting has
been turned up to its most harsh, white glare at the top
of the stairs and Spencer dims it down to a more
acceptable level. He enjoys the subtle tones of shadow
and light that play against his soft white walls, and
bright light has always offended his sensibilities.

The perfectly sanded, perfectly stained, perfectly
waxed parquet floors still glow from a recent buffing by
Iris, the cleaning lady who comes in three mornings a
week. Not that she has much of a job, because Spencer
is hardly ever here, but he likes to keep everything dust-
free and smelling of polish. Iris lives in the next street,
with her three daughters and a couple of Rottweilers.
'I've never known a man keep a house so tidy!' she likes
to say, folding her satisfaction beneath her arms as she
surveys the gleaming surfaces of Spencer's house every
Monday, Wednesday and Friday. And Iris is right –
Spencer's house *is* incredibly tidy.

'A place for everything,' beams Iris as she hangs the

dustpan and brush on their special hooks behind the utility room door. Of course she doesn't understand the *concept*. Asian simplicity meets western aesthetic.

Iris just thinks the house is a bit 'sparse' and keeps leaving Dulux charts on the kitchen counter with ticks at the side of certain colours she thinks might look nice in the bedrooms – colours with names like Shrimp Bisque and Calypso. But how could she possibly understand? A woman of her class? She watches *Blind Date* on a Saturday night and doesn't even realize that it's 'fixed'.

Spencer doesn't like this feeling of being an interloper in his own house but he really doesn't want to face Annie right now. He will fix himself a glass of Scotch and sit in the conservatory with a quiet concerto and some figs that he knows are still in the fruit bowl from last week. He creeps down the passageway and the perfect parquet groans and creaks beneath his feet. The hob light is still on in the kitchen – he can see its glow reflected in the polished black granite and the stainless steel of his industrial-quality fittings.

The first thing that assaults his eyes as he enters the kitchen is an open box of coffee-flavoured Matchmakers and the remains of a Terry's Chocolate Orange resting on his butcher-block island. And then he sees the dark shape of Annie sitting deep in the shadows of the conservatory, clutching an oversized mug in both hands as she stares out of the windows on to the unlit garden beyond. She hasn't heard him come in. Bang goes any thoughts of avoiding her; he's going to have to say something. 'What are you doing, sitting here in the dark?'

Annie throws her mug halfway across the conservatory and gasps with startled surprise. Coffee, or tea, or maybe even hot chocolate splatters the sisal floorcovering, soaking into the deceptively expensive, absorbent fibres in a way that Spencer knows will never come out. He has to stop himself from voicing his alarm as he grips the edge of his Sub-Zero refrigerator with fingers turning white with anxiety.

'Spencer! Darling! What are you doing home?' Annie is obviously overjoyed.

'Couldn't stay away,' he replies, staring at the dense black stains on his natural fibres.

'Oh blimey, I'm sorry! Have you got a J-Cloth and a bucket?' Annie is standing there looking hopelessly large in the rectangular conservatory that was only finished in April.

'It's OK, Annie, I'll get the steam guy in tomorrow. I knew I should have got it Scotchguarded.'

'Good job it's just coconut matting – I would have felt awful if it had been new carpet.'

And Spencer just smiles. What is the point in explaining the intrinsic qualities of sisal floorcovering to somebody who judges the calibre of home design by the number of toilets a house possesses.

'*Five* toilets!' Annie had whispered to him the first time she went to his parents' house, and Spencer, at fourteen, had proudly taken her up to his own private bathroom that was decorated with red and white tiles.

'This is a bidet,' he had told her, pointing out the porcelain oddity to Annie as though it were something precious and rare. And Annie had been suitably impressed. That was one of the things that Spencer always liked about her – she was *always* suitably impressed.

'I was in a world of my own just then,' she says, already on her hands and knees with the sleeves of her blouse rolled up above her elbows. 'I set the alarm and I was all ready to go to bed. What brought you home early?'

Spencer removes his jacket and hangs it over the back of a chair. All he wanted was a few quiet moments in the peace of his own house, with a drink and some pleasantly soothing music. Instead he has to make polite chit-chat with his wife, who seems infinitely more at home with her hands plunged deep into Fairy bubbles than in contemplating Mozart over a glass of something expensive.

'How did your first day at the office go?' he enquires, popping open the top button of his shirt.

'It was fine,' answers Annie, wringing out her reply with reddened knuckles. 'Marla took me to lunch at an Italian place that served lovely spaghetti. It was supposed to have clams in it but I had it without. Got tomato sauce right up the front of my skirt. I'm sharing an office with Richard. He's very nice and he was dead helpful with the computer.'

'Yes, Richard is invaluable when it comes to computers. I hope he doesn't bore you to death, though. He is apt to ramble on a bit sometimes. Bit of an eccentric, I think. He spends too much time on his own.'

'Well, he's been very nice to me so far.'

Annie pours her soapy water down the sink and wipes the inside of the stainless steel bowl with a dry cloth to maintain its showroom sparkle. Spencer knows that she has watched him do this himself, and her thoughtfulness pricks his conscience.

'We should do something nice this weekend. Let's go out to dinner on Saturday night, eh?'

'That would be lovely,' smiles Annie, her face lighting up with gratitude.

Oh God, can she be so utterly dependent on Spencer to make her life worthwhile? Will he have to constantly offer her these morsels of affection to keep her sustained, or will she begin to expect more of him? Spencer is not sure he can find the necessary reserves to keep Annie smiling.

They both jerk to attention when the doorbell rings. Who could be calling at this time of night?

When Spencer opens the front door, he almost slams it shut again once he sees who is standing on the doorstep. 'Nolan! For God's sake, what are *you* doing here?' he hisses, allowing only a narrow crack of space for his question to pass between them. 'You'll have to go. This is not a good time.'

The man on the doorstep is wearing an airline uniform: navy-blue blazer, white shirt, with gold stripes on the cuffs. He appears distraught and runs his hand nervously through thick, blond hair. 'You've changed your phone number,' he whispers. 'You've returned my letters unopened. What was I supposed to do? I *had* to come here.'

'I thought you were over in Singapore?'

'Who is it?' calls Annie from the kitchen.

'It's business, darling, I'm going to have to see to it, so why don't you go up to bed and I'll be up as soon as I can, OK?'

'Who's that?' asks the man on the doorstep.

'My wife,' says Spencer.

47

'Your *what?*'

'You'd better come in, Nolan. It's been an eventful three months. Let's go into the living room.'

The living room is almost dark. Spencer closes the blinds and turns on a table lamp which casts a soft glow across the sparse furnishings. It is an uncomfortable room, with very few practical pieces of furniture. There is a large bench-like sofa made from the polished trunk of a tree and several tortuous-looking chairs, some of which cannot be used because they are too old and unstable to take a person's weight. On the stark white mantelpiece there are three small celadon vases – prize trophies from a recent business trip to Japan.

Spencer indicates a safe seat for Nolan to occupy and they stare at each other across the wide expanse of antique Gabbeh carpet (hand-dyed with beetle blood sometime in the seventeenth or eighteenth century).

'*A wife?*'

Spencer nods.

'Why the hell do you need a wife?'

'You wouldn't understand, Nolan. It's just something I needed to do. It was going to happen sooner or later – you knew that.' Spencer looks at Nolan, and it is as though two worlds are colliding right before his eyes.

'Spencer, you and I were friends for three years. You were pretty comfortable with the fact that I'm gay and I really hoped that you were coming to terms with your own sexuality. I know we never had sex but we did have a relationship – a very strong relationship. When you told me to get lost back in February with all that reformation claptrap, I thought it was just some kind of mid-life thing so I left you alone. But I can't believe that you've changed, Spencer – I just can't. And I can't believe that you're now totally straight just because you got married.'

'Well, believe it, Nolan. I'm married and I'm very happy, so just don't come around here any more. Our friendship was special but you were getting too close. You always seemed so sure that I was like you, but I think you were just projecting your own hopes on to me. I just can't live that kind of half-life any more. I'm a different person now.'

'You're fooling yourself, Spencer. I *know* you, remember? I know how passionate you are and I know how much I meant to you. You can't suddenly tell me that everything you said and did in the past was due to you being fucked up in the head.' Nolan stands up and approaches Spencer by the fireplace. He places his hand around the back of Spencer's neck as though to kiss him, but Spencer jerks away and glares at Nolan with open hostility.

'Don't! It's useless, Nolan. You've got to move on and forget about me. I am not interested.'

'You're a fool if you actually think that you mean that,' says Nolan. He straightens his jacket and pinches the bridge of his nose as though he has a headache.

'You'd better go now.'

'Yes, I think I've heard enough for one night.'

And Spencer shows his former friend to the front door.

'You know where I am if you need me,' says Nolan, raising one eyebrow with resigned acceptance.

'Goodbye, Nolan. Drive carefully.' And Spencer closes the door of his house.

Up in the master bedroom Annie is already propped up in bed with one of her historical novels. She is wearing her apricot chiffon number, the hideous one with the little ribbons threaded around the neckline. 'Who was that, love?' she asks, smiling up at him as he enters the bedroom.

'Oh, a worried client, that's all.'

'Is he an airline pilot?'

'Cabin attendant.'

'How come men who work for the airlines are always so dishy?'

'It must be the uniform, darling – they're just normal blokes underneath.' And Spencer goes through to the bathroom, where Annie has thoughtfully laid out his dressing gown and slippers.

Just a normal bloke. That's what he sees in the mirror as he pauses by the washbasin. A married man, a successful lawyer, a credit to his sex. Bisexual men all around the world would be proud of him. 'Well done, Spencer!' they would say, clapping their hands and smiling enviously. 'You did the right thing.'

But Spencer wonders just how many of them really believe that, deep down inside. Those self-deluding men who kiss their wives goodnight, then dream of the guy they saw pouring concrete on the building site. Men who renounce their homosexuality in deference to a wife and children and half an hour every night on the gay chat rooms, getting off over the computer keyboard.

Spencer wants so badly to be 'normal', but he is beginning to wonder just what normal really is.

Five

Marla Philips lives in a high-rise tower with a rather spectacular view across the Thames. It is a new building designed by American architects and decorated by a New York interior designer who succumbed to a falling chandelier and died shortly before the building was finished. At night the building glows richly from within, and the main lobby is so clean and white that the doormen wear sunglasses against the ferocious glare of the halogen lighting.

The concierge tonight is George. George has acute psoriasis and carries pictures of his wife's shaved vagina in his wallet. He likes to whip out the photographs and boast about their liberated sex life.

George scratches a raw patch of dry skin on the side of his forehead, and makes a move to help Marla with her bags as she staggers through the plate-glass doors in an unsuitable pair of Versace heels.

'Grab these files, will you?' she demands, leaning dangerously to one side to counterbalance the bulging briefcase, which hangs from a strap across her left shoulder. 'Jesus, I think I've broken my fucking elbow!'

George chuckles. He gets a kick out of Miss Philips and her dockyard vocabulary. He often tells her that she is always welcome to join him and his wife at one of their 'key parties', but Marla prefers to keep a wide berth and remains fairly aloof whenever she encounters him.

'There's a package for you, Miss Philips. I left it outside your door.'

'A package?'

'Yes, came by courier about half an hour ago. I signed for it and everything. Is something wrong, Miss Philips? You look as though you've seen a ghost.'

Marla offers George a watery smile and jiggles the books and papers under her arm. She doesn't want him to know of her recent fears, so she merely indicates the lift with her chin and George presses the button for her.

Inside the lift it is cool as chrome. It rises rapidly with barely a whisper, and the floor numbers pass by, illuminated in neon blue. PH for penthouse. That is where she gets off. That is as far as she can go.

Silent carpeted luxury. Walls painted pale greenish-grey and uplit with dim, state-of-the-art fixtures made of iron and cobalt-blue glass. Black-framed pictures are bolted to the walls and depict artful architectural scenes in black and white. The corridor stretches away in both directions and Marla approaches her door with apprehension. She can see the brown cardboard box from here, innocuous and threatening, like a sleeping tiger on her threshold.

The silence is broken before Marla reaches her door. Mrs Whatshername from number 6 is obviously on her way out for the night, tarted up in black stockings and fake-fur bomber jacket. 'Is it still nippy out?' she enquires of Marla as she secures the locks on her door with scarlet fingernails. 'I'm off to a party and this bloody skirt barely covers my snatch!'

Marla is not sure how she should respond to such a

candid statement, so she merely stands there, folders slowly slipping from beneath her elbow, briefcase strap sliding gradually from her shoulder.

'You're really loaded up tonight. Working at home, are you?' enquires Mrs Whatshername from number 6.

'Yeah, working at home,' states Marla. 'Do you think you could get the keys out of my pocket and open my door for me?'

'Sure.'

An overwhelming fog of musky perfume surrounds Marla as she allows her pocket to be assaulted by . . . 'I'm sorry, I don't know your name. Lived here for two years and I don't know anyone in this damned place. I'm Marla Philips.'

'Yes, I know. I've seen your name on all those Federal Express envelopes you get from the States every day. I've chatted to your cleaning lady a few times. My name's Therese but my friends call me Treez.' Treez jangles the door keys in Marla's face with a triumphant grin. One of her front teeth has an inset diamond and it catches the light as she turns to unlock Marla's door. 'There we go, love. You want me to help you with this parcel?'

'Thanks,' says Marla, eyeing the brown paper package with trepidation. 'Just put it on the hall table.'

Treez turns on the lights and Marla's marble foyer gleams in recently polished splendour. 'Fucking hell!' exclaims Treez, catching sight of herself in one of the several enormous gilded mirrors. 'I look like shit. I knew this colour wasn't good on me but the poxy French hairdresser said it would bring out my natural skintones. Natural! I look about as natural as Cilla fucking Black!'

Marla drops her briefcase and folders to the floor.

Several sheets of paper slide effortlessly across the sleek marble tiles, and Marla leans against the doorjamb in an attitude of complete exhaustion. She has a ladder the size of a cucumber up the front of her leg.

'You look done in, love. You should climb into a hot bath with a bottle of bubbly and get Tom Jones on the hi-fi – that's what I do when I've had a shitty day. I close my eyes, listen to the music and imagine a big hairy bloke with a nine-inch tongue going down on me. Does me the world of good I can tell you!' Treez jabs Marla in the ribs with her elbow and cracks another leering smile. 'Now, then, I'm off to the land of the living, and if I get lucky don't expect to see me again until sometime next weekend!'

'Thanks,' smiles Marla and she watches her neighbour teeter down the sleek corridor towards the lifts. For a moment she forgets the package on her hall table, but as she turns to close the door she sees it there, silent and deadly between the elephant tusk lamps that were sent to her by a grateful client in Zimbabwe.

The box is quite light and when she shakes it Marla feels a dull thump inside as though something soft is shifting around there. Her name and address are printed on a white label, but there is no return address or indication of the courier service that delivered it. She takes it with her to the kitchen.

Marla has a gourmet kitchen not unlike the one in Spencer's house on Fulham Road, but Marla's kitchen is twice the size and has been abused beyond belief. One might think that a family of rugby players lived here, or that Marla hadn't cleaned up in several years, but actually her cleaning lady, Hetty, came in only yesterday and this is merely the detritus left behind by Marla this morning.

An entire pound of ground coffee has been spilled across the granite counter and on to the marble floor, and the coffee machine has regurgitated itself over the butcherblock island because Marla removed the jug before the coffee had finished filtering. Boxes of American cereal and Entermann's fat-free pastries litter the breakfast table, each box torn asunder with a letter-opener, scattering their contents as though pounded by the fists of a gorilla. On the draining board there are cartons of milk and orange juice, and a pair of puce gold-tipped shoes. On the floor by the industrial-sized fridge there is a mound of spilled chop suey alongside a casually discarded jacket from Nicole Farhi.

Marla pulls open a drawer to find the kitchen scissors. The parcel opens easily and she lifts the lid very slowly, standing slightly away from the countertop as though expecting an explosion of some kind.

The box contains a blouse: a rather lovely silver-blue silk blouse from Emporio Armani. There is a note beneath the blouse and it is written professionally, like the calligraphy on a wedding invitation: *Try this next time. The one you wore today makes you look like a whore.*

Marla looks down at the sheer purple shirt she is wearing today. Her black bra is clearly visible through the wrinkled fabric, but that is the way it was displayed in the window of Harvey Nichols. It is a look that is fashionable right now. 'Freak!' she screams, throwing the box across the kitchen so that the blouse skids artlessly over the polished surfaces, catching itself over the back of a chair.

She has had enough of this charade. It has been going on for too long and those assholes at Scotland Yard are about as useful as shit. Marla calls Police Inspector Mark Blake and gets one of his frigging assistants. Apparently Inspector Blake is out of the office until tomorrow, and Marla cannot be placated meanwhile by some minion with a voice like Rowan Atkinson.

She slams down the phone and searches for cigarettes. There is usually a carton of duty-free Marlboro by the fridge, but Hetty must have moved them somewhere. In the spacious living room the white walls are washed by a pale orange glow from the lights across the river, and everything here looks serene and impeccable. Marla never uses the main rooms of her flat unless she is entertaining clients, and so they remain as Hetty leaves them week after week.

There are cigarettes on the coffee table. Marla lights up in the semi-darkness and closes her eyes as she inhales. The heating system ripples the surface of the light, transparent curtains, and it is very quiet here. There are very few moments of calm in Marla's life, but that is the way she usually orchestrates it.

'I sometimes wonder if anyone really knows who you are . . .' That is what her ex-husband Lester once said to her after a particularly acrimonious argument. Lester probably knows her better than anyone, yet Marla keeps her arms around her privacy as though it is a small child to be protected against all dangers. She has no friends, she has no family and the only people who think that they know her are people who mean nothing to her.

Since they lost the baby, Marla has shied away from all close personal relationships, and Lester is the

56

only person with whom she can share her lingering insecurities and fears. Lester and Marla had had a daughter, but she died when she was only one month old. It was Marla's fault that she died, and because of this fact Marla must live with the guilt for the rest of her life.

She smokes her cigarette with a contemplative air uncharacteristic to one so driven and unsentimental. This most recent personal attack is puzzling and frightening to her, mainly because she has no idea who could be targeting her in such a cruel, vindictive fashion. If she knew who her enemy was she could fight them, but these anonymous and intimate invasions of her privacy are terrifying to a woman prepared to reveal so little of herself to the outside world. She habitually stands on an island of her own manufacture, fists clutched at her breast and eyes clenched tight. Don't get any closer or I'll bite is the message that Marla Philips offers to the world.

The email message mentioning her new security code this morning was the first indication that her pursuer knows all about Jessica and the murder trial. Up until today the anonymous threats were mainly sexual in content – the work of a frustrated pervert who gets his rocks off scaring defenceless women. Well, he's picked the wrong woman this time!

We watch Marla as she stubs out her cigarette in the oversized crystal ashtray, and it might be interesting to follow her as she climbs the spiral staircase to her bedroom suite. After all, doesn't everyone like to sneak around in other people's houses?

Opulence prevails of course, but chaos litters the surface of Marla's bedroom. On days when Hetty hasn't been in to tidy and clean, there is a sense of destruction to every room that Marla makes use of. The king-sized bed has been left unmade with both duvet and sheets tossed angrily to one side, covering a mound of magazines, papers and food wrappers. A hand-held neck massager remains plugged in as testament to her nights of rigid sleeplessness, and on the bedside cabinet, instead of the usual bedroomy accoutrements, there is a fax machine and an oversized container of sleeping pills prescribed by a lax Manhattan doctor.

Pink is the predominant colour: salmon pink and ivory, like the bedroom of a faded Hollywood superstar. The curtains are lined with blackout fabric and they remain closed so that there is a perpetual sense of midnight. Some of the furniture is transparent Perspex that reeks of '60s glamour, and even the headboard of her bed lights up with pink neon against the mirrored wall. Clustered atop her TV cabinet there is an incongruous display of stuffed toys and Beanie Babies. Marla buys them at lonely airports when there are no business acquaintances for her to talk to.

She goes through to the adjoining office area where her computer screen illuminates the gloom with a greenish hue. The flashing envelope in the top right-hand corner of the screen announces that she has mail. Taking a seat at the built-in desk, Marla clicks on to her mailbox.

Seventy-three new messages!

Usually she is lucky to get *any* personal mail at all so she is surprised by this announcement. She does not recognize any of the sender addresses that wait patiently on her screen. The first message came in at nine-twenty this morning.

UnMeNow@starlight.com

Dear Marla,

I am replying to your intriguing advert as a man who enjoys the same erotic pleasures. I too live in London and would very much like to get together with you. I could come to your place or I have a company flat in Shoreditch that we could use most afternoons. I attach a photograph for your personal pleasure and look forward to meeting you soon.

Doug

Marla clicks on the little paperclip icon and reaches for a cigarette, conveniently located on her mouse pad. She watches the photograph unloading until, line by line, it fills her screen. Even before the image is fully complete Marla recognizes the substance with which Doug is smeared and surmises that he has a huge personal hygiene problem.

'Gross!' Marla deletes Doug from her monitor and lights up her cigarette, inhaling deeply and leaning back in her chair. How the hell did he get her email address?

The second message comes from a guy called Frank who is married but looking for weekday perversions with a like-minded woman. The third is from Chris, a dentist in Wapping who requires dominance and abuse in order to reach a fulfilling climax. Every message is in the same vein, some of them referring to personal details of Marla's life such as her address and phone number, her office location and even her physical appearance.

As she scrolls through the messages Marla becomes increasingly frightened. Nausea forces her to stub out her cigarette and she leans forward, with one hand over her mouth, as she stares at yet another disgusting display of human depravity. Tears blur her vision and she blinks them away, fiercely denying herself the luxury of emotion.

She has to know who is doing this to her. The police must do something about her security; this has gone too far.

And, by the subterranean light of her computer screen, Marla stares up at the ceiling and imagines an aerial shot of her face, camera panning away until all that remains of her features is a tiny speck on the screen. Anonymous and minuscule like a single grain of sand.

Six

Lester unzips his costume and places it on a hanger in his dressing room. He is about ready for a replacement outfit, but Zelda in Costume reckons this one has another month left in it yet, and it's not as though they have an extravagant budget. Pigbeet, the purple pig-like character that Lester personifies every weekday morning now hangs from the rail as though recently slaughtered. Without Lester the costume is inanimate.

Pigbeet and Little Pud is now into its fifth year, and the ratings are down. There has even been talk of cancellation and morale is low. They are bringing in a new producer, some young hotshot from one of the Saturday kids shows, who wants to inject new life into the programme. Today, in a valiant effort to pep up the content, they featured a pre-pubescent pop band that lip-synced to their latest hit, gesturing and prancing across the set in a precocious attempt to emulate sexual maturity. Hardly suitable for a children's show but poor Matilda, the show's current producer, is at her wits' end and she knows that her days are numbered.

Someone taps at his dressing room door. It is young Michael from the sound crew. 'Phonecall, Less!' He hands Lester a cordless phone that is greasy with something that looks like the sauce from a hamburger.

'Hello, Lester Philips.'

'Darling! It's me . . .' Shani, Lester's long-time friend and soulmate, is calling from her car and the line isn't very clear. 'Are you still there, darling? I can't hear a damned thing with these maniacs on the M25.'

'Yes, I'm here.'

'Karl has died. I just heard on Radio 4. Heart attack, darling. Dropped dead on the set of his new film in Sicily.'

Karl Steinbrenner was the director of *Five Farthings*, the musical that first brought Lester and Shani together, and won Lester his Oscar. Lester hasn't seen or heard from Karl in twenty years. 'Poor old Karl! At least he died doing what he loved best.'

'Hang on, darling, I'm going through the Blackwall Tunnel right now and some bitch in a Fiesta is trying to overtake me on the inside.' There is a lot of static, and sounds of Shani swearing, and then the signal fades and is lost. Lester is left with a dead telephone in his hand.

So, Karl is dead. Lester wonders how old he would be now. He had always seemed like an old man even when directing *Five Farthings* but he was probably only in his forties then. Everyone seemed old to Lester back then; even Shani and she was only twenty. Karl was instrumental in Lester's Oscar success, coaching the young boy with compassion and patience, bringing out the best in him at a time when Lester had no conception of 'character' acting. He remembers that summer as one might remember a loved one struck down before their time. It hurts him inside to think about it too much; the memories twist in the pit of his stomach and he can actually bring back the smell and atmosphere, as though they are trapped somewhere forever between the layers of his skin.

'You are going to be a great star, my boy.' Lester remembers Karl saying that to him at the wrap party, drinking champagne for the very first time and loving it. There was Shani in that amazing dress, dancing with Bill Danvers, and the make-up girls fussing around him as though they were favourite aunts.

'You're going to get a taste for the good life, Lester,' they mocked, ruffling his hair and hugging him to their maternal sides.

And there were stars in his eyes that night. Everything was suffused with a warm, golden light that melted his heart and romanced his soul. This was the world he ached for, at fourteen; this was the place he wanted to spend the rest of his life – cherished and loved, with these marvellous, colourful people around him. It felt like the beginning of something incredible, and the excitement was tangible. It had fizzed in the air that night like static electricity.

'My darling, I have a feeling we are all going to be famous!' Shani had yelled, over Bill's debonair shoulder, as they waltzed past with the lights shining in her magnificent red hair which was still pinned up in that Victorian style.

Lester places the dead phone on his dressing table and stares for a moment into the mirror. Postcards and yellow sticky notes surround the frame, and his face is florid by the light of the exposed bulbs. A vase of long-dead roses stands in a mess of spilled face powder and paperclips. This is how life is now. The bubbles rose to the surface of Lester's life many years ago, leaving it flat and sour and barely palatable. He enjoyed his fifteen minutes of fame that night when he went up to collect his Oscar from Julie Christie, with the orchestra playing his solo and the cameras flashing on all sides.

That night he had dinner with John Schlesinger and a very giggly Goldie Hawn. The Best Film had been *Midnight Cowboy*. John Voight shook Lester's hand and said that he would be watching out for him in the Best Actor category the following year. But Lester's second film was a major flop and his third never even made it to the cinemas. At sixteen Lester was already a has-been: undereducated, disillusioned and unprepared for real life. He was still living with his parents in those days, and fortunately his father had been shrewd enough to put all of Lester's earnings into a trust fund that he couldn't touch until he was twenty-one.

He worked for a while in a local hotel, serving roast beef and croquette potatoes to the dinner-dance crowd. His agent tossed him the occasional scrap of theatrical work but it was mainly seasonal stuff in pantos, Lester always being billed as an Oscar winner but never drawing much of a crowd. By the time Lester was nineteen his acting career appeared to be over, and he was living in digs with two girls and a cat over a pawnshop in Blackpool, selling ice cream sundaes in the summer and helping fix the rides at the Pleasure Beach during the winter.

It was in 1975, when Lester returned to London for a dubious audition, that he met up with Shani again. She was appearing in a West End revival of *Hayfever*, sharing a dressing room with Penelope Keith. Shani's career had proved slightly more successful than Lester's, due to the fact that she had slept with several influential directors and married a glam rock musician called David

Lane. David died of a drug overdose six months after
the wedding, leaving Shani with a seven-bedroomed
house in Epping and a three-year-old stepdaughter
called Aurora.

'They're looking for short-term contract actors on
Crossroads, darling. My friend had dinner with Noele
Gordon last week and apparently they need new blood.
I could get you an audition, no problem.'

And Shani kept her word. Not only did she put in a
good word for Lester but she also took him out to lunch
and introduced him to Marla, who had just moved to
London from New York. 'Marla is an immigration
lawyer,' enthused Shani over her beef stroganoff, 'fresh
from the States.'

'*Junior* immigration lawyer,' corrected Marla through
a cloud of cigarette smoke. And Lester remembers how
exotic she seemed to him then; silver platform boots,
leopard-skin jeans and a pink feather boa.

They had sex in Marla's Camden Town flat, with
the gas fire hissing and a flimsy curtain pulled across to
hide the kitchenette where the sink was piled high with
dirty dishes. Marla asked him to do it to her 'doggy
style', with her head jammed up against the hot-water
boiler, and afterwards, while Marla rolled a couple of
joints, Lester ate baked beans out of a tin and they
listened to Cockney Rebel on the portable record player.

He did get a part in *Crossroads*, and ended up staying
with the series for six years, during which time he
married Marla and opened twelve village fêtes, seven
supermarkets and a retirement home up near Wakefield.
His popularity on the show reached something of a peak
when he jilted Amy Turtle's niece at the altar and

instead became a priest. They wrote him out of the series shortly after that, burning him to death in a car accident.

1981 was a bad year. Marla gave birth to their daughter, Jessica, but one month later Jessica was dead and Marla was in a mental hospital. Lester's mother died that same month and he was passed up for a job on a new television programme called *Game for a Laugh*, usurped by a total nobody called Matthew Kelly. It was the beginning of a ten-year wasteland for Lester, and while he watched Marla make a slow and painful recovery, he languished in her shadow, drinking and partying with his show business friends. It was inevitable that they would finally divorce – two stars shooting in opposite directions. Jessica's death and the subsequent therapy made Marla ruthless in her professional ambitions. She no longer had time for a husband.

'Are you coming down to the pub, Less?' Charlie from editing pokes his head around Lester's dressing room door.

'Yeah, give me a minute, Charlie. I'll follow you down there.'

And Lester Philips, forty-seven years old and small-time celebrity, grabs his jacket from the back of the chair and turns out the lights. In less than six months he'll be back up there on the stage with the cameras flashing, the audience cheering, and the world at his feet. It's going to be fantastic.

He can feel it in his bones.

Seven

Drip, drip, drip . . .

When it rains there is an annoyingly regular beat
outside the bedroom window where the guttering
allows water to fall against the sill. It is almost seven
o'clock and the alarm will sound at any moment.
Annie has been awake for quite some time, waiting
for it to grow light, watching the sweep of car head-
lights on the ceiling. It is going to be a dull, rainy
morning.

Beside her, Spencer is dead to the world. He is
snoring lightly, arm thrown above his head, mouth
slightly open. The duvet is pushed down to his waist
and Annie marvels once more at this handsome man
who is her husband. Even in sleep he is beautiful.

Perfect.

How did she catch him when he could have had any
beautiful woman he wanted? Annie looks at the rise of
his chest in the shadows of the morning, and her eyes
fill with tears of love and admiration. She wants to reach
out and run her fingers across his skin, through the hair
that grows in all the right places, and down beneath the
duvet where he will be warm and soft and sleepy. But
Annie doesn't want to wake him; she wants to look at
him as one might look at a piece of jewellery that is too
precious to wear.

Should nice girls like Annie be even thinking about sex?

She has been unable to think about hardly anything else since they got married, and when she looks at Spencer with his perfect body exposed like this she can't help but yearn for something physical to happen between them. Last night had been another disaster, but she had smiled and kissed him and said that it didn't matter. He blamed it on the pressures of work and Annie had to hide her disappointment, as though tucking a love note into an apron pocket. She is beginning to have indecent thoughts, and her fantasies are becoming increasingly graphic.

She presses her thighs together and attempts to suppress the rising warmth that comes with these sexual thoughts. She has considered the idea of satisfying herself manually but she has always shied away from *that*, mainly because it seems so vulgar to fumble about with your own private parts. She once came very close to doing it while watching a Brad Pitt film on video but she overcame the urge with a bowl of ice cream and some Smarties. Annie has the suspicion that it is an itch that, once scratched, will only grow more insistent.

The alarm clock beeps and makes her jump. Spencer lashes out at it with one hand, then groans with his elbow across his eyes. Annie closes her eyes, then pretends to be just waking up herself. She yawns, but does not exhale in case of morning breath.

Now is the time for her to slip her hand across his warm, furry chest. Now is the time to press up against him under the duvet. Spencer groans again and shifts slightly to avoid contact with Annie's legs. She feels as though she could grind her hips relentlessly into the mattress; it is unbearable.

'Morning, love,' whispers Annie, kissing Spencer on the back of his neck.

'Morning,' he replies, throwing back the duvet and forcing himself out of bed.

Annie looks at his naked body as he crosses the room. His shoulders taper down to his perfect little bottom and the hairs on his muscular thighs stop right at the ideal point. He is better than Brad Pitt. Better than David Beckham. Better even than Robson Green, and she's had a crush on *him* for years.

She reaches for the remote control and turns on the little portable TV that sits at the foot of the bed. They are talking about the horrid weather and a five-car pile-up on the M1 that is causing massive tailbacks. The bedroom is filled with a comforting, flickering light, and Annie buries her sexual frustrations as a dog might bury a bone.

Annie's best friend Betsy is coming down to London for the weekend. She has never been to the capital before and Annie is looking forward to her visit. Annie has taken the day off work to prepare, and Betsy is arriving on the afternoon coach. Spencer is taking them to a posh restaurant for dinner tonight and tomorrow they are going shopping on Oxford Street.

Spencer is in the shower now. It is a big shower space, made for two people, but Annie has never been invited to join him. It is Spencer's bathroom and Annie has her own down the hall. Hers is smaller but Spencer said she could decorate it herself, so she has chosen a very pretty paper from Laura Ashley and a shower curtain that has daisies embroidered down the edges.

Spencer's bathroom is cold and sterile: bright chrome, white towels and speckled granite. On the wall there is a black and white photograph of him taken by a famous photographer. He is scowling and looking away as though somebody just attracted his attention. It doesn't look like Spencer at all, but he seems to like it.

Victoria coach station on a rainy Friday afternoon.

Annie hesitates just outside the glass enclosure, with the steel tip of her umbrella standing in a puddle of water by her unsuitable beige court shoes. Betsy's coach is late coming in, because of the weather. The smell of fuel turns the air purple, or so Annie imagines as she watches harassed commuters wander by aimlessly, laden with heavy luggage and straggling children. It is a depressing scene and Annie now wishes that she had offered to pay for her friend to come down to London by train instead. But Betsy would have refused such an offer; she always pays her own way.

London – and everything in it – still seems overwhelming to Annie, who arrived here almost forty minutes early due to her ignorance of the underground system. Spencer had urged her to take a cab, but Annie was determined to force herself out into the confusion of the city, despite her naive apprehensions. If she doesn't apply herself to life here, she will never grow to love it. And everyone has told her that she *will* grow to love this sprawling, noisy, confusing place.

'Do you know where I'll find the buses to Bristol?' A bedraggled woman in what looks like an oversized plastic sack stands before Annie, wiping rain from her face with a handful of toilet paper. Her hair has given up: it hangs flat around her blotchy face, clinging to her scalp with squid-like tenacity.

'I'm sorry, I don't know. I'm just waiting for a friend,' explains Annie, offering the woman a sympathetic smile and looking down at her own sodden shoes as though they might somehow transmit some kind of empathy.

'Well, at this rate my mother's bowels will have been stitched up and she'll be back on solids before I ever get down there. Never again! Next time I'm taking the Volvo, motorway or no bloody motorway.'

Annie watches the woman blend into the crowd. One of the National Express coaches coughs up an expansive cloud of exhaust fumes and people cover their faces and flap their hands in a futile attempt to clear the air. There is a snack bar inside but Annie is trying not to think about it. She's already eaten two Flakes and a Picnic bar and Spencer thinks she is on a fat-free diet.

'Annie! I thought it was you!'

Annie turns around when she hears someone call her name. It is Richard from the office, fumbling with an oversized umbrella, and his padded ski jacket is dripping on to his shoes. 'Oh, hello, Richard. What are you doing here?' Annie cranes her neck to see any sign of the Chesterfield coach coming in.

'I'm meeting a cousin who is coming to stay with me for the weekend. He lives in Wales and I only see him every couple of years. Boring as hell but he's family, so what can one do?'

Richard pulls an apologetic face and wipes his face with a large linen hankie – the kind that nobody uses any more, the kind with a dark red initial in the corner. He smiles at Annie and his eyes crease up at the corners.

She wonders how old he is. Forty maybe? Perhaps a few years older? It is hard to tell because he gives the impression of someone already way beyond middle-aged. His glasses have steamed up from the rain outside.

'My best friend is coming down to visit, but her coach is really late. I'm a bit worried that it might have broken down or had an accident in the rain.'

'Oh, I'm sure it'll be nothing so dramatic. Probably just the traffic on the M1 which is always bad when it rains – especially on a Friday. I'm just going to get myself a coffee. Can I get you one while I'm at it?' Richard indicates the snack bar inside.

'I've run out of change,' explains Annie, patting her coat pocket.

'Oh, I'm sure I can run to the price of a cup of instant. Milk and sugar?'

'Yes, please. Three sugars.'

Richard hurries inside the glass enclosure and Annie continues to look out for the Chesterfield coach.

'Here we are,' he says, returning with two styrofoam cups. 'It's wet and it's warm but I'm not sure how palatable it will be!'

'An expression my mum always uses too – wet and warm.' Annie sips at the scalding liquid and pulls her mouth sharply away. 'Oh, it's boiling hot!'

'Yes, be careful,' says Richard. 'Marla was telling me about a woman in America who sued McDonald's for a million dollars when she spilled a cup of really hot coffee on her legs. Can you imagine trying to get away with that here? They'd laugh you out of court!'

'Here's the Chesterfield coach, at last!' Annie replaces the lid and drops her tasteless coffee into a nearby bin. 'I'd better go and find my friend. Thanks,

Richard – have a nice weekend with your cousin.' Annie stands on tiptoe to see above the heads of the people around them.

'Yes, you too, Annie. Perhaps we can get lunch one day next—'

But Annie has spotted Betsy, and she leaves Richard in mid-sentence.

Only a handful of people get off the Chesterfield coach and Betsy is the last to dismount. She clings to the chrome rail, balancing herself against a large tote bag, as she steps gingerly down. Although it is only a matter of weeks since Annie last saw her friend, she is horrified by Betsy's appearance.

'You don't have to say anything, Annie love. I can see it on your face,' smiles white-haired Betsy, dumping her bag so she can reach around Annie in a frail attempt at a hug. 'OK, I've lost another four pounds since the wedding, but now can we steer clear of that subject for the rest of the weekend, because I've had enough of it already from me mum?'

'Oh, it's lovely to see you, Betsy!' And Annie is surprised to find a prickling of tears in her eyes.

'What do you think of the hairdo?' asks Betsy, turning slightly to show Annie the back of her head. 'Had it done at that new salon behind the market.'

'Smashing! You look good with shorter hair.' But Annie is really thinking how much smaller it makes Betsy look – how tiny and fragile she appears in this huge, clumsy place.

'I could kill for a cuppa. Is there a caff somewhere close? I need a wee as well, while we're at it.'

'Come on, there's a place I saw on my way from the tube station.'

'Hang on a sec. I've got to collect my case. Oh, and this is for you, from your dad.' Betsy hands Annie a plastic carrier bag that contains a neatly packaged newspaper parcel. Annie doesn't have to guess; she can smell the fish even before she peeps inside.

Suddenly she realizes that everything has changed. As she watches Betsy struggling with her tiny suitcase, she sees the scene as though projected on the screen of a home-movie set-up. There is no sound except the noise of the projector and the 8mm film as it rattles across the spools. The colours are not true, everything seems slightly speeded up and the ground is not quite level as the flickering light blurs the edges of reality.

This is how it really is.

A small, inconsequential moment in time being captured on film.

Everything is different now. Annie is married, living in London and working for a high-powered legal firm. This is her link with the past, this National Express coach that just a few hours earlier had stood on the friendly tarmac of Chesterfield coach station. Here is her best friend – friends since junior school – come to visit for the weekend with her best clothes and a purse stuffed with fivers. No more popping round there for a coffee and a chat. No more Friday night pizza binges with a Blockbuster rental and a bottle of Blue Nun. No more old life with everything that Annie once took for granted. Now everything is new and strange and distorted, as though she is seeing her own life through the bottom of a milk bottle.

'This is so exciting, Annie!' giggles Betsy, looking around at the cavernous building in which they stand. 'I'm actually in *London*. I can't believe it!'

Annie smiles back, but it is an automatic reflex that has nothing to do with her state of mind. Betsy would think she was mad if Annie even hinted that she would actually prefer to be back home in Chesterfield right now, dropping by the Kiwi Cafe for a milky coffee and a slice of ginger parkin. 'Come on, Bets, give me that case. You take the carrier, and let's get out of this bloody place.'

'So who was the bloke you were nattering with back there? I noticed you through the window as we drove in,' asks Betsy, hitching up the shoulder pad on her oversized jacket.

'Oh, just some bloke from Spencer's office.'

'He looked nice – friendly like.'

'Mmm, come on, let's make a dash for it,' and the two women duck their heads against the rain as they race across the road at a convenient green light.

'Crikey Moses, Annie! Look at all the taxis.'

'I hadn't really noticed,' replies Annie, holding her umbrella above Betsy's head, 'but you're right – the street is full of them. Taxis and double-decker buses. I suppose nobody wants to stay in one place for very long in this city. Come on, this is the place,' and Annie leads Betsy into an Italian coffee bar with plate-glass windows and bistro chairs.

'This is a step up from the Kiwi,' whispers Betsy, clinging to Annie's coat for support. 'Just aim me in the general direction of the loo and order me a frothy coffee.'

Annie takes a seat by the window, leaning her umbrella against the glass and removing her coat. They are playing contemporary jazz and the waitress has a ring through her nose. 'Two cappuccinos please and two pieces of that chocolate cake,' says Annie, pointing at the glass counter.

'Which one?' demands the waitress, pen poised above pad. 'We've got four chocolate cakes and they're all different.'

'The one with the nuts on the top.'

'Praline Mocha Torte,' she scribbles. 'Double espresso or single?'

'I'm sorry?'

'In your cappuccinos. Single or double shot of espresso?'

'Oh, single I think, with extra milk if possible.'

'Skimmed or normal?'

'Normal.'

'Tall, Grande or Mega-Jolt?'

'Just the small, please.'

The waitress turns away without another word as Betsy returns, casting a surreptitious eye around the cafe as she takes a seat. 'They've got johnnies in the ladies'. There's a machine next to the Tampax!'

'Did you buy any?' laughs Annie.

'Did I heck as like! What do I want with johnnies? They give me the willies! Imagine having to put one of those things on right in the middle of having it off. No wonder blokes want a girl to be on the pill these days.'

'But there's AIDS to think about as well, Bets.'

'Not in *Chesterfield*, Annie love. In Chesterfield they think that safe sex is having it off with the person you're married to.'

'There's a fella at the office who's got it.'

'What? AIDS?'

'Well, he's HIV positive. He's got the virus.'

'It's the same thing, isn't it? Is he queer, then?'

'No, he's married with a couple of kids. Caught it when he was in Tokyo or something – prostitute, I think.' Annie whispers these final words. 'He's a really nice bloke as well. Catholic. And a volunteer fireman.'

'Crikey! You see it all here, don't you? The closest I come to scandal in our office is catching Maureen Blake nicking paper for their Barry's drama club newsletters.'

'Two tall cappuccinos.' The waitress delivers their coffee.

'What was that on her hand?' whispers Betsy across the table. She is suppressing a grin and Annie finds the mood contagious.

'It's henna, you know, like the stuff you put in your hair to make it go red? They paint those patterns on themselves, like temporary tattoos; it's an *Indian* thing I think. Madonna invented it. It washes off after a couple of baths.'

'I think I've seen it in the Body Shop in Sheffield. I thought for a minute she'd got psoriasis!'

'Don't!' laughs Annie, jiggling the table so much that the froth on their coffee slops messily into their saucers.

What a relief to have a bit of a laugh. Annie suddenly realizes that she hasn't really laughed since before the wedding, and this thought worries her. Isn't she supposed to be happy? Don't newlyweds drift around in a haze of sickening euphoria, making barely concealed jokes about their excessive love life?

'So what's it like, then?' asks Betsy, picking at the edges of her chocolate cake with the tip of a pastry fork, without actually eating any of it.

'What's *what* like?'

'Married life? Living together? *Sex*? Come on, Annie, I want all the gory details.'

'It's certainly different,' admits Annie, scraping the final smear of chocolate from her plate. 'I don't think I've got used to it yet.'

'There's nothing to get used to, is there? Spencer is so gorgeous, don't you just go to bed with him as soon as you get in from work?'

'Hardly! He works so late and gets up so early. I barely see him during the week and then at weekends he's always got something or other that he has to do. I don't know, Bets, I feel a bit lonely sometimes, you know. His house is lovely, but it doesn't feel like home. Well, you'll see what I mean. Sometimes I wish we could have lived up in Chesterfield.'

'Are you barmy? I'd give my right leg to be where you are right now. Everybody at home is pig sick that you caught him.' Betsy switches plates with Annie.

'I'm not very good at the sex thing either,' says Annie, lowering her eyes.

'What do you mean? I would have thought it was pretty easy really, although I'm probably not the best authority on bedroom matters. Don't you just lie there and let *him* do all the work?'

'It's embarrassing, Bets, and he doesn't seem all that fussed about it. The few times we've tried, he's been too tired or it has hurt. It's not very comfortable, you know. I've been reading about foreplay in *Cosmopolitan*, and I don't think we're doing it right.'

'Isn't it the same as using a Tampax?' asks Betsy.

'Spencer is a bit bigger than a bloody Tampax, Bets! And he expands width-wise *before* he goes in!' They both start to laugh uncontrollably.

'What you need is a shoehorn and a handful of Nivea!' screams Betsy, leaning forward to catch her breath.

'No, what I need is a bloody car jack!' And neither of them can speak for a good five minutes, by which time their coffee is cold and they have to order more.

Eight

'Are you sure this is the right place?' asks Annie nervously.

Spencer looks at the scrap of paper in his hand. Marla had scribbled the address out for him this afternoon in the office, pleading with him to relinquish his Friday evening for the sake of business relations. 'Michaela is our biggest client, Spencer, we need to show a united front if we are to land that contract. She is planning to bring over thirty employees to the UK next year. You'll just have to bring Annie and her friend with you – make it a party!'

Michaela Fox is not Spencer's favourite client. Actually she is Marla's client, but more often than not Spencer gets roped in each time Michaela comes over from New York. She is a high-maintenance, high-profile kind of woman, the kind of gutsy American businesswoman who epitomizes female emancipation at its most militant. Her brashly visible fashion empire is up there with Tommy Hilfiger and Calvin Klein, and she is beginning to make it big in Europe.

'It's the right address,' says Spencer, peering through the taxi window.

'But there's no sign, no windows.'

'This is it, mate, if you're looking for the restaurant.' The cabbie turns in his seat and addresses them through the partition. 'Get a lot of politicians come over here.'

'OK, how much do I owe you?' As Spencer pays the cab driver, Annie and Betsy step out on to the wet pavement, practically clutching on to each other for emotional support. This is not a place for the faint-hearted. The narrow street is dark and many of the buildings appear ready for demolition. There is a betting shop nearby with metal bars on the windows, but its lights are out. Annie steps back on to a loose paving stone and immediately her pale satin shoes are drenched in muddy rainwater.

'Oh bugger!' she exclaims while Betsy clings to her arm, obviously in need of assurance that they are not going to be mugged and beaten.

'Michaela picked the place,' explains Spencer, watching the taxi now disappearing around the bend in the road as though it was his last hope. 'She always picks bizarre places whenever she comes over. Last time I was in New York, she took me to some horrible place in SoHo that had no air conditioning and no windows.'

'There isn't even a sign,' says Annie. 'How do we even know that this is the place? It doesn't look like a restaurant?'

'I suppose I'll have to ring the doorbell to find out.'

The door is painted black and studded with large nail heads arranged in diamond patterns. The only light comes from an iron lantern inside the porch, and it illuminates a framed menu that has been hand-written in black ink.

A very tall, very thin woman, wearing what can only be described as a black PVC tube, opens the door. Her hair is scraped up and twisted painfully into a tight little knot on the top of her head, and her face is ashen white with a tortuous crimson slash of a mouth. Spencer looks down at her boots: black leather platform boots which lace all the way up to her knees.

'Good evening,' greets the woman. 'Welcome to La Maison d'Esclavage. Do you have a reservation?'

'We are with Michaela Fox, table of five at nine.'

'Lovely! Ms Fox is already at her table. Please follow me.'

Spencer ushers Annie and Betsy ahead of him. They are in a long, narrow hallway that is hung with heavy metal lanterns on industrial-weight chains, each one casting the barest minimum of light against the dark metallic walls. The music is barely audible; a low-frequency disco beat that seems to come from behind the walls. At least the food smells good to them, even before they enter the main restaurant.

'This way, please,' says their hostess, walking stiffly in her ungainly footwear, and they follow through into a cavernous space that is filled with tables and thick with cigarette smoke. Shafts of coloured light slant down from the high ceiling, and candles flicker through the darkness. In the centre of the room there is a raised platform, rather like a circular stage, on which appears to be some kind of scaffolding structure criss-crossed with leather bands. As they get closer, Spencer realizes that there are people on the stage. A semi-naked woman appears to be strapped to the scaffolding; face down so that a second woman, wearing leather hot pants and six–inch heels, can thrash her exposed back and but-tocks with a cat-o'-nine-tails. She doesn't whip too hard, but just enough to make the submissive woman writhe against the metal framework.

What the hell is this place?

Spencer turns to look at Annie and Betsy. They are still clinging to each other, but now they are barely progressing, so terrified are they of the scene that is being played out before them.

They find Marla already seated at the table with Michaela Fox. The two women are smoking cigars and drinking dry Martinis.

'Welcome to hell, Spencer! Isn't this place totally cool?' Michaela screams across the table, seemingly unaware that there is absolutely no need to raise her voice to be heard. 'Read about it last month in the *Village Voice* and just had to come here to see it for myself. Total S and M! What a blast!'

Michaela stands up to offer Spencer her cheek. She stands taller than Spencer because she is wearing very high heels. Her hair is fluorescent orange and it stands out from her head like an exotic cactus flower – short and spiky with bleached white tips. Her perfume reaches him before her cheek does. It is heavy, musky, masculine.

'This is my wife Annie and her friend Betsy. Annie, I'd like to introduce you to Michaela Fox.'

Annie extends her hand and Michaela grabs it and pulls it against her chest. 'Honey, you are absolutely gorgeous! I had no idea that Spencer had married such a beauty! You have perfect bone structure, and your hair – it's just beautiful!'

'Well, thanks,' stutters Annie, valiantly trying to extricate her hand from Michaela's bosom.

'And who is this?' asks Michaela, turning her attention to Betsy who is now cowering by a wall display of medieval torture instruments. 'Come over here, sweetness. Let me get a look at you.' Betsy moves forward into the light and Michaela does nothing to suppress an audible gasp of astonishment. 'My God, you are *emaciated*! What's wrong, honey? Do you have an eating disorder or something?'

Spencer closes his eyes. *Oh Christ! This is going to be a disaster.* He sees Annie glaring at Michaela as though she has just raised her skirt and relieved herself on the table.

'Anorexia, actually,' whispers Betsy, holding her head up with a proud defiance that Spencer finds quite surprising.

'Oh honey, how long have you been suffering? You can't weigh more than seventy pounds. Come and sit over here by me. I think you and I need to have a little talk. I'm no stranger to eating disorders; in fact I just recorded a show with Roseanne about my bulimia. You'd never believe it now but I was as skinny as you were in 1995. I'd stuff my face with Häagen-Das and cookie dough, and then bring it all up ten minutes later so that I could stuff myself all over again.'

'Sit down, for God's sake!' groans Marla, knocking back her drink and stubbing out her cigar simultaneously. 'This is the freakiest place I've ever been to – our waitress is wearing an outfit from *The Wizard of Oz* but with her tits hanging out and chains clamped on her nipples. They've been dripping hot wax on that fella over there ever since we came in, and he's loving it!'

Once they are seated, Spencer takes a moment to look around. He is astonished to see that the majority of the clientele consists of very normal-looking business types. There is the odd obvious deviant here and there

– a few leather-clad Village People types with beards and cropped hair, one or two dominatrix types with ratted-out hair and pointy breasts – but on the whole the diners are the type who could be eating quite comfortably at L'Escargot or the Ivy.

'Please, sir, let me fetch you a drink.'

Spencer finds a muscular slave boy in leather studded jockstrap kneeling by the table at his feet. He is licking Spencer's shoes.

'C'mon, Spencer, give the boy a thrill. Let him fetch you a cocktail!' screams Michaela, punching Spencer quite forcefully in the arm. Marla cackles through a mouthful of cigar smoke while Annie appears to be shrinking down below the level of the table with embarrassment. Betsy, on the other hand, seems to be quite interested as she leans sideways to get a better look at the slave boy in his skimpy attire.

'I'll have a bourbon on the rocks. Annie? Betsy?'

'Oh, can I have a Malibu and pineapple?' asks Betsy, clinging to the edge of the table, staring with concentrated fascination at the slave boy's pierced nipples.

'I'll just have a Diet Coke,' says Annie, holding the lapels of her jacket tightly across her chest.

'You're not on a *diet* are you, Annie?' shouts Michaela. 'You don't need to be on a diet, honey, you look fabulous!'

'Well thanks, but I really do need to lose a couple of stone.'

'How much is that in pounds, honey?'

'Erm, twenty-eight pounds.'

'Christ! Are you kidding me? *Twenty-eight pounds?* You must be cuckoo for cocoa puffs! Forget it, honey, it's not worth shit to be thin. Look at your pal here, where did it get her? Am I right? Miserable and thin – where's the point in that, huh?'

Spencer sincerely hopes that Annie is not listening seriously to Michaela and her homespun philosophy. He wants her to fit into a size 14 before next summer.

The slave boy has now pulled down Spencer's sock and is licking at his ankle. Spencer smiles uncomfortably, pretending to be a good sport, but he is getting an erection and there is a line of heat just below his collar that is making him very nervous.

'I think he likes you, Spencer. You should take him home!' laughs Michaela.

'Perhaps he's got a sister?' laughs Spencer with an unconvincing smirk. He looks over at Annie but she is staring with wide-eyed disbelief at a pinstriped gentleman being led around the restaurant on a lead by a buxom woman.

The menu, when it comes, seems pleasantly refined and very expensive. The dishes have quirky names spiced up with appropriate innuendo: Marquis de Sardine Salad, Sir Loin's Beefcake with whipped garlic butter, that kind of thing. There is also a secondary menu which outlines 'Specialities from the Rack'. Apparently diners are invited to indulge in sadomasochistic fantasies up on the stage area, and each item is priced appropriately – from a mild bottom beating at £20 to a lesbian bondage adventure at £120.

'Isn't this just *too much*?' squeals Michaela, grabbing Annie by the arm as they are approached by a muscle man wearing a leather harness and biker boots. He hands Michaela a bottle of body oil.

'Grease my body, bitch!' he grunts.

'Oh sugar, any day!' and Michaela squirts the oil across his chest and starts rubbing his glistening pectorals with enthusiastic aplomb. The muscle man kneels before her, gripping her thighs in his meaty hands, with his head thrown back in apparent ecstasy. Spencer glances at Annie and sees her expression of disgust and horror at the scene before her. She has slipped so far down in her seat that only her head and shoulders are now visible above the table edge. He attempts to offer her a sympathetic look, shrugging his shoulders desultorily, but he can see that she is not placated by his effort to show a united front against the debauchery around them.

'Come on, honey, it's your turn,' and Michaela hands the bottle of body oil to Betsy, who is practically hanging out of her seat with excitement. Spencer imagines this is the closest she has come to a naked male body in her entire life and she is practically slavering.

Betsy is up and on the man before he can protest. Unabashed and audacious, her slippery fingers work their way across his washboard stomach. She allows her fingers to slip beneath the leather belt of his jockstrap – and Michaela is screaming enthusiasm while Marla looks on with mild amusement, yet another Martini in hand. They are drawing quite a crowd.

'Come on, Annie, it's time for you to have a go.' Michaela grabs Annie's hand, but Annie snatches it back and conceals it safely beneath the table.

'Oh, come on now, don't be a party pooper.'

'Leave me alone!' snaps Annie, turning her head away to stare at the wall.

Spencer smiles broadly at Michaela and shakes his head as if to say his wife is better left alone, but

Michaela is not the kind of woman to give in easily. She pulls Annie up from her seat and stuffs the bottle of oil in her hand, spilling a considerable amount across the front of Annie's new dress.

'Now look what you've done, you silly woman!' yells Annie, dropping the bottle and glaring at Michaela with open hostility.

'It's just a little massage oil, honey. It'll come out at the laundry. What's your problem, anyway?'

'*You* are the problem, actually. You and this bloody horrible place you've brought us to. I don't care what kind of pervy stuff you're into but I don't want anything to do with it. If my dad could see me now, he'd die.'

Marla places a steadying hand on Annie's arm. 'Annie, it's OK. Just sit back down and let's get some dinner, huh? Michaela was just having a bit of fun, so stop beating yourself up, honey.'

Annie looks at Spencer, and he nods for her to sit back down. Michaela and Betsy are meanwhile busy with the muscle man, and Spencer is, quite honestly, more interested in the oily flesh than the contretemps between Annie and Michaela. How he would love to grease up his own hands and run them across the perfect planes of that extraordinary body. The muscle man is staring right at him, and his expression is one of amused acknowledgement. Does he know what Spencer is thinking?

Spencer excuses himself and goes in search of the toilets; he just can't sit there another minute watching Michaela and Betsy running their hands over that perfect physique. It is like a kind of torment – one that twists in his gut, pumping blood into places he would rather not think about right now.

When he locates the toilets, the stalls are all occupied and he cannot bring himself to use one of the exposed urinals, knowing that he would be unable to pee due to some kind of nervous neurosis that has plagued him ever since he first realized that he possessed a fascination with other men's penises. He stands by the hand-dryer, leaning nonchalantly against the distressed black walls, with his shirt glowing white beneath the ultraviolet light. There are suspicious groans coming from the end toilet stall, and Spencer can quite clearly see two pairs of feet beneath the door. He averts his eyes and breathes slowly.

Standing at one of the urinals there is one of the leather-clad barmen; he is wearing cowboy chaps with nothing underneath, so his arse is hanging out, smooth and alabaster white against the black of the leather. He turns to look at Spencer, not smiling, just looking – as a dairy farmer might appraise a piece of cattle. He is handsome in a rough kind of way and Spencer is running out of places to avert his eyes.

One of the stalls becomes free. Spencer dashes forward and locks himself in; falling against the closed door with his eyes screwed shut. Oh God, is this some kind of test? Can a child stay away from the chocolates in a sweet factory? Can an alcoholic remain completely sober in an off-licence? This is unbearable.

And when Spencer opens his eyes he sees the penis.

Hard and arrogant.

Waiting for attention, projecting through the hole in the toilet wall.

He needs no further prompting. Spencer throws open the toilet door and practically runs through the restaurant towards the table where Marla and Michaela are snatching more drinks from a waitress dressed as a French maid. 'I'm sorry, I have to leave. I feel ill.'

'Oh no, sweetness, what's up?'

'Stomach bug or something: I've been sick and I feel terrible.' The sweat on Spencer's brow and his unearthly pallor give credence to his claims and Michaela offers him a sympathetic smile.

'I'm sorry, Annie, but I think I need to call a cab.'

Annie is up and out of her chair before he can even finish his sentence. Betsy is less enthusiastic as she wipes her greasy hands on a large white napkin.

They leave Marla and Michaela just as a flogging display begins on the central stage. The muscle man stands by the cloakroom, running the palm of his hand idly across his left nipple. Spencer practically pushes Annie out of the door and into the street.

'You poor thing, you look awful,' she says, placing her hand across his fevered brow.

But all Spencer can think about is sex: sex with another man.

What the fuck does he think he's playing at?

Spencer looks at Annie and suddenly, without any warning whatsoever, he dissolves into a racking mess of tears, clinging to his wife for support.

I can't go on like this.

And, like words scribbled in wax crayon, he just cannot seem to paint over that painful truth.

Nine

Inspector Blake sits on Marla's white sectional sofa and drinks the coffee that Julie brought in for him. Behind him, in smeared, dripping scarlet letters, someone has spray-painted three condemning words across Marla's office wall. It happened last night and the cleaners discovered it this morning when they came in to vacuum.

MOTHER FROM HELL!

'Unless there is somebody you are not telling us about, Miss Philips, we have reached a cul-de-sac. Quite honestly we are stumped. Have you absolutely no idea who could be doing this to you?'

Marla shakes her head and stares at the tip of her burning cigarette. This is all getting way out of hand, and she genuinely has no clue who is doing this to her.

'No signs of forcible entry, and the only people who came into the office last night, apart from yourself, were the cleaning people. We are coming up with nothing every time we investigate these incidents. The Internet advertisement was placed by an unidentifiable person who used an anonymous email address, and the blouse could have come from any one of hundreds of retail outlets. There is no way we can trace the purchaser.'

Marla lights up another cigarette from the butt of her last and inhales deeply. She knows that this is not something that will just go away of its own accord. This isn't a toothache or a grumbling appendix. 'I have no more idea than you do about this, Inspector, but somebody out there wants to give me the creeps, and I want to know who that person is before they do something more drastic. I'll be changing my phone number, the security code on my alarm, and my email address, but he seems to have a way of finding such things out. I don't tell a single other person what the new numbers are, and yet *he* knows. How can that be?'

'We don't even know that it is a "he", Miss Philips.'

Marla is growing increasingly tired of this whole charade. She has more important things demanding her time than worry about the actions of some fruit loop with nothing better to do than intimidate a complete stranger. It is probably some nut who got her name from the phone book and decided to stalk her for the hell of it. He probably leads a pathetic kind of life and needs the excitement.

'And you are not in any kind of relationship right now, Miss Philips? Platonic even?'

'Zilch. It's so long since I had a man, Inspector, that I've forgotten what it is I'm supposed to be missing.'

Inspector Blake rewards her with a smile. He's not half bad, if you like middle-aged guys with greying temples.

'Are *you* hitched, Inspector?'

'Divorced.'

'What happened?'

'She got fed up with my moods, my hours and my proclivity for professional wrestling.'

'You sound like a great catch!'

'I *am* a great catch. It's just that nobody is fishing!'

Annie appears at the open doorway, hesitant in a salmon-coloured two-piece.

'You can come in, Annie. Inspector Blake doesn't bite.'

Annie crosses the threshold but keeps her distance. 'I just wondered if there was anything I could do to help? Perhaps I could get cracking on that wall? Maybe try and clean some of it off?'

'Don't worry about that, Annie, we've got cleaners to do that kind of thing. Anyway, they need to take photos of it as evidence before we can start cleaning up. Inspector Blake, this is my partner's wife, Annie Noble.'

'Pleased to meet you, Annie,' smiles Inspector Blake, offering her his hand.

'Do you have any idea who might have done this, Inspector?'

'Not yet, Annie, but we're working on it.'

'Marla, you know you can come and stay with me and Spencer if you want to get away from your place for a while. It must be very worrying with all this going on. I had no idea.'

'Thanks, but I think I need to face up to this myself. I'm not going to let this bastard get the better of me.'

'Well, the offer is there if you want to take us up on it.'

'Appreciated, but right at this minute I think Inspector Blake is going to take me down to the Five Feathers for a couple of stiff drinks. What do you think, Inspector?'

He looks at his watch and raises his eyebrows. 'At ten forty-five in the morning?'

'Call it an early lunch. My nerves are shot.'

'Then the Five Feathers it is,' and Inspector Blake

finishes his coffee, stands up and escorts Marla over to the lifts.

Reflected in the surface of the shiny stainless-steel doors, she looks a total wreck. She hasn't had her hair done in almost a week, and the collar on her Versace blouse is bent upwards because she didn't hang it up properly last night. 'I look like shit.'

'You look perfectly fine.'

'Oh, you Brits would say that to a bag lady. Don't you ever feel like telling it as it is?'

'Who needs the aggro? Anything for a quiet life.' And Inspector Blake ushers Marla ahead of him into the lift.

The Five Feathers is empty. In fact, the cleaning lady is still doing her polishing in the snug, and the barman has to ask them to wait a few minutes before he can serve them. Marla and Inspector Blake take a seat in the corner by an artificial coal fireplace. The gas hasn't yet been turned on so the hearth is dead. Marla wonders why a pub smells so sour and unhealthy when it is empty. How come she never notices that when the place is filled with people?

'Have you thought about taking a little holiday?' asks the inspector, flipping a cardboard beermat on its side and tapping it gently against the surface of the table. 'It might do you good to get away from all this for a while.'

'I have an important trip to New York coming up, so I can't afford to take time off right now. Vacations are for the idle and I have never been idle, Inspector.'

'Please call me Mark. I'm not on duty now.'

'Aren't you, Inspector? I thought policemen were *always* on duty.'

94

'Well, I just knocked off for lunch, so call me Mark, please.'

'Then you have to call me Marla. It's only fair.'

'Fine.'

'Mark, can I ask you a question?'

'Fire away.'

Marla takes cigarettes from her handbag and taps a filter absently against the side of the box. 'Is it normal for a woman of my age and profession to be afraid of the dark?'

'I'm not sure I know where you're coming from, Marla. Do you mean figuratively or literally?'

'I mean the dark, at night, when the curtains are pulled and the lights are dimmed, and I lie awake in the night and I stare into the shadows and I wait for them to come for me. From the shadows.'

'And who are *they*?'

'I have no idea. That's the problem, you see: if I knew who they were I might be better equipped to deal with them, but unknown quantities are hard to combat and I worry that I will have no suitable defence.'

'Look, Marla, this has all been a terrible ordeal for you – a much heavier strain than perhaps you can imagine. Stress can be deceptive; it can manifest itself in the most peculiar ways. Some people refuse to acknowledge what they view as the weakness of surrender, they ignore the physical signs and pretend that everything in the world is rosy when really they are internalizing it all. I know this sounds like New Age psychobabble, but you know what happens when you brew home-made ginger beer.'

'*Ginger beer*? I was anticipating some kind of analogy here.'

'Well, then, let me offer you one. You see, when you make ginger beer at home, the bottles tend to explode from the unregulated pressure. My dad used to make us put the bottles out in the garage so that they wouldn't blow up inside the house.'

'Believe me, Mark, I'm not about to blow up. I've seen enough shrinks in my lifetime to turn Charles Manson sane. There's really nothing wrong with me; I'm just a bit strung-out that's all. And at night it all seems so much scarier. I guess I just need better sleeping pills from my doc.'

'I think a fortnight on a desert island might do you even more good.'

'Now, if anything is likely to send me nuts it would be that. I don't cope with solitary confinement very well – maybe that's why I get so crazy at night. You know, I have to leave the TV on all night in order to get some sleep; something about the voices makes my apartment feel that much more alive. You know, even when I was married to Lester I had problems sleeping.'

The barman calls over to tell them that they can order drinks now. As Mark fetches them from the bar, Marla lights up another cigarette. She watches him chatting with the barman and there is something about his easy style that pleases her. Would it be too much of a cliché for her to find him attractive? Isn't that what happens only in detective stories?

The last relationship that Marla had with a man was almost two years ago now. His name was Pierre and he was a concert pianist. They were totally unsuited, that much is quite clear in retrospect, but there was a strong physical attraction and Pierre was drawn to Marla's strength. He was weak, you see, talented but insecure, and ambiguous regarding his abilities. For a while Marla enjoyed his weakness; he was also several years younger than she was, so she had the upper hand. Unfortunately his musical talent, and the fact that he had been forced to forfeit his general education in deference to the piano, made Jack a dull boy. Or, in this case, Pierre – he had no sense of humour. He constantly attempted to appear erudite by misusing sophisticated words, and his grammar was atrocious. Even as an American, Marla could see that Pierre was something of an embarrassment, and that people only tolerated him because he performed at the Albert Hall.

Pierre now lives in New York. Marla still sees him occasionally, as he is married to a good friend of hers who runs a PR firm in Manhattan. Charlotte is as culturally challenged as Pierre is dense, but they seem to make a good couple. Marla has not thought much about Pierre with regard to these recent occurrences but maybe she should consider him a suspect?

'What would his motives be?' asks Mark, after she expresses these thoughts.

'I don't know. We parted on good terms and he's always very civil when we meet. I just wondered, that's all, and we haven't talked much about him. There are just so few people in my life who would be warped enough to do this kind of crap.'

'Well, we could check him out, but I doubt that a busy concert pianist living in New York would have the time or the inclination to hang around in London purely to put the wind up you. I think it is more likely that we are looking at some casual crank who has nothing better to do with their time. And, then, the recent change of tone in the messages suggests that this person knows all about your tragic past . . . your baby girl.'

'Yeah, I could just about cope with the sex stuff, but now that it's getting even more personal it brings everything back. Oh, this is all so fucking inconvenient. I've got work to do, and I don't have time for all this bull.'

'Your handbag is ringing,' observes Mark.

Marla flips open her mobile phone: 'Y'hello.'

It is Michaela Fox. She is still in town, organizing new office space on Newman Street and she wants to 'borrow' Annie for the afternoon.

'What on earth do you want with Annie?' asks Marla.

'Special assignment. I want to have some test pictures taken of her and I've got studio space free this afternoon.'

'Test pictures? Of Annie?'

'I might want her to do some modelling for me. I've designed a new range of clothing for larger women and I need some models for the catalogue. I'm not going to steal her away from you, honey, but this would be a huge favour and I'll pay for her time of course. Is that OK?'

'I guess so. Is *she* OK with this idea?'

'She thinks I'm crazy, of course, but if you say she can take the time off she'll just have to go with the flow.'

'Just don't make a habit of it, Michaela. I'm not running a modelling agency, you know.'

'Thanks, sweetheart, you're a saint.'

'Consider me canonized,' and Marla flips off her phone without even saying goodbye. Just like Americans do in the movies.

'Have you got time for a spot of lunch?' asks Mark, surveying his empty beer glass.

'Not really, but if you're offering . . .'

'Oh, I'm not offering anything. I'm just starving hungry and there's a cafe round the back of this place that does great fried egg sandwiches.'

'I can't resist a fella with sophisticated tastes.'

'Then that makes me practically irresistible.'

'I'm sure there's a clever retort built into that statement somewhere but I'm too jaded to catch it.' Marla finishes off her drink, stubs out her cigarette, and follows Police Inspector Blake out of the Five Feathers and into a mellow slice of October sunshine.

Unexpected pleasures . . . The kind that are found in last winter's coat pockets, tucked away with the lint and the flavourless peppermints, like banknotes waiting to be discovered on a rainy day. Marla feels like she just reached down and found one.

Ten

Shani's stepdaughter Aurora is celebrating her thirtieth birthday and Lester has been invited along to the brunch at Chez Maurice. He hasn't seen Aurora for a couple of years: she has been working at EuroDisney as an events coordinator since she injured her ankle and had to give up dancing at the Moulin Rouge. She is a tall, slender woman with porcelain skin and long fair hair that she keeps in a ballerina bun. She is engaged to a Frenchman called Didier, who wears his hair long and sports a peculiar little beard.

'I'd like to thank Shani for arranging this little gathering for me today,' spouts precious, lithe Aurora as she stands at the head of the table with her champagne glass raised. 'I think of her as my mother, but I know she wouldn't thank me for saying that as she prefers me to think of her as an older sister.'

Polite laughter. Shani smiles and bows her head. The waiters hand out plates of chocolate crème brûlée and dole out the coffee.

'I would also like to thank my darling Didier for being here despite the fact that he's in the middle of producing a very important documentary for Canal Plus Television.'

More raised glasses and smiles. Didier gives a modest frown and taps his spoon against the tabletop, maybe with embarrassment. Aurora runs her free hand across the side of her perfectly groomed head, and her nails are long and well manicured.

'If only my father could be here now to see his little girl grown up to be thirty. His life was taken from him at such an early age and I only wish I had been able to know him as an adult. Well, thank you, everyone. Cheers!'

'*Cheers!*'

Lester raises his glass which is prudently filled with orange juice (he has a hangover resulting from another of his wife's impromptu parties) and he toasts Shani's stepdaughter. At his side, Tina has already started poking at her chocolate brûlée, pissed out of her head on wine and champagne and grumbling under her breath for the 'little bitch' to shut her mouth and get on with it.

Lester's young wife is not what you might call a classy drunk.

Actually, she's not very classy at the best of times. Massage therapist and ex-pornstar Tina Philips, née Stardust, is about as classy as grated cheese.

'Can I get you a digestif or liqueur with your coffee, madame?'

Tina squints at the waiter with blurry eyes and wipes chocolate from around her smudged mouth.

'I'll have a double Bailey's, mate, and make it choppy – this coffee is nearly cold already.'

Aurora shoots a look down the table that could harpoon a whale, but Tina is oblivious to her scornful observation.

Shani pats the back of Lester's hand sympathetically and offers him a reassuring wink. 'Are you sure she'll be all right tonight for the documentary?'

'Oh, I'll probably leave her at home to sleep it off. She's not really bothered about seeing me on the telly. And she doesn't have a clue who Karl Steinbrenner was anyway.'

Both Shani and Lester had been approached – along with others – to offer their thoughts and memories of the infamous film director. The resulting documentary will be shown this evening after the nine o'clock news.

Tina struggles out of her seat to find the ladies' room, catching the back of her jacket on the chair so that she has to tug angrily at the fabric to release herself. The chair topples noisily on to the marble floor but Tina just leaves it there, weaving through the other tables, swearing under her breath.

'I think you need to get her home, darling. She's totally pickled,' says Shani, diplomacy preventing her from saying more. Aurora is glaring down the table, obviously furious that her younger friends have had to witness such behaviour. The said friends all look as though they have got something sharp up their arses.

'Come over to my flat at about eight tonight and we'll have some supper before the broadcast. You don't mind that I've invited Marla, do you? She's bringing a *man* with her, can you believe?'

'Well, as long as it's not that pianist prat, I don't care. It's about time she found herself a decent bloke. She's seemed so sad recently.'

'I think it's just the strain from all this *bother* she's been having with that loony who's stalking her. She pretends to be coping with it all but I know that she must be feeling the strain. Anyway, this chap she's bringing with her is actually the police inspector working on her case.'

'As a bodyguard or a boyfriend?'

'No idea, darling. She was very cagey about it over the phone. I tried desperately to get details but I couldn't weasel them out of her.'

Aurora is opening birthday presents. She shrieks with disgust at a cut-glass vase and holds it up for ridicule. 'Look what Auntie Violet sent me – isn't it hideous!'

Everyone laughs. They are probably scared stiff that when Aurora gets to *their* gifts she will react in the same way. She isn't an easy person to buy things for. Lester got her a voucher from Harvey Nichols, costing an extravagant £100 that he really didn't want to part with, but anything less would have been met with the same derision as poor Auntie Vi's Ravenhead vase.

'Oh, if I get one more perfumed candle from L'Occitaine I'm going to vomit!' Aurora's unsparing comment turns several brunch guests pale with anxiety.

'No fucking paper towels!' Tina is back from the ladies' wiping her damp hands down the front of her leather skirt. It appears that she has thrown several handfuls of water over her face for some obscure reason, so the front of her hair hangs in dripping ringlets across her shoulders.

'You're wet through, Tina!' observes Lester. 'What happened?'

'I fell in the fucking toilet, if you must know – banged my sodding head on the bowl and practically passed out.' It is definitely time to get Tina home.

He collects their coats and waves goodbye to Shani from the cloakroom door. Aurora has just unwrapped a turquoise-coloured Tiffany box with great enthusiasm only to be shot down by the apparent unsuitability of the gift inside. 'Just what I needed, another crystal paperweight shaped like a hedgehog!'

'Come on,' says Lester, taking Tina's elbow, 'let's get you home.'

'Stop pulling me around, Less. I feel . . .' But before Tina can actually express how she feels, she demonstrates her sentiments in a noisy, undignified display of projectile vomit which hits the marble floor with such violent force that Lester has to jump back to avoid being splattered.

'Fuck me, must have been something I ate!' and Tina wipes her mouth on a folded linen napkin that she grabs from a nearby table.

Shani's flat is not large. It is on the fourth floor of a Victorian building not far from Holloway Prison and she has lived here for years. Her living room looks out on to a charming but unpretentious square that has iron railings and trees. In October the square is already heavily littered with fallen leaves, and a group of industrious kids have started building a bonfire. Lester finds a convenient parking space just a few doors away from Shani's building. He has brought along some wine that he will not himself drink.

Shani buzzes him in and he begins the climb: five flights of narrow stairs, creaking and crooked, and carpeted with something ugly and worn. The light is dim; the smell is damp and overcooked, as though someone is perpetually boiling cauliflower with the windows tightly closed.

'You're horribly late, darling!' admonishes Shani, as

she appears on the landing above Lester's head. 'We're all desperate to eat and my Yorkshire puds are a disaster!'

'Yorkshire pudding? How very working class of you,' jokes Lester as he completes his final steps and bends to kiss Shani on both cheeks. She smells familiar and warm, of faded perfume and something fruity.

'It's all the rage these days, darling. Working-class English food has suddenly become de rigueur in all the top restaurants. I had Barnsley chops last week at Bibendum.'

'Does that mean jam roly-poly for pudding, then?'

'Actually, Marla brought some dessert.' Shani lowers her voice to a whisper. 'Frozen M and S cheesecake. Aurora is being very rude about it.'

'What else did you expect? There is a permanent track in Marla's kitchen running from the fridge to the microwave. The last time she attempted to actually cook something, several people were laid up for the weekend with chronic indigestion.'

Although Shani's flat is small she has decorated it with little consideration for its proportions. The entrance hall is painted dark burgundy, and the walls, which are very high, are crowded with framed pictures and gilded angels. There is an oversized crystal chandelier dimmed down to the wattage of a wavering candle, and a console table that could easily look over-the-top in Buckingham Palace. The smell of roast beef fights with a strong, heavy fragrance from scented candles.

Lester knows where to hang his coat. He hands the bottle of wine to Shani and she disappears into the tiny kitchen which has been faux-painted to look like the ceiling of the Sistine Chapel. Above the cooker there is a bas-relief of *The Rape of Dejanira* in several subtle shades of terracotta.

Shani pours a generous glass of orange juice for Lester and tops up her own glass with wine. 'Come and meet Marla's mysterious new beau. He's actually rather dishy in a fogeyish kind of way.'

The living room, which doubles as a dining room, is very cramped. Huge overstuffed sofas and chairs, numerous table lamps and bookshelves, and walls painted a deep salmon pink to offset the cheerful, chintzy curtains that swag heavily across both windows. It is like a condensed version of a Merchant Ivory film set. The Renaissance meets Baroque meets Victorian whorehouse. Oddly enough it works, and Lester has always liked this room. It is very theatrical, very Shani.

When they enter the room, Aurora is feeding Didier cooked asparagus dipped in garlic butter and Marla appears to be falling between a crack in the sofa cushions, with her companion perched high at her side. The man is somehow too large for this room and his jacket is rucked up around him as though constricting the blood flow. He is quite handsome in a grey, tweedy kind of way and Lester experiences an unexpected frisson of jealousy when he shakes Mark Blake's hand and feels his strength.

'I believe some of my colleagues have already questioned you, Lester. I hope they weren't too bothersome.'

'Not at all. Anything I can contribute to find out who's doing this to Marla . . .'

Lester kisses Marla lightly as she shifts uncomfortably to extricate herself from the clutches of the upholstery. Her cigarette is in danger of setting fire to the fringe around a brocade cushion.

'We have to eat now, darlings, otherwise all will be lost. The documentary starts in fifty minutes, so we'll have the pudding and coffee afterwards.' Shani stands by the dining table with her arms outstretched. 'Poor Didier can't believe that we're actually having roast beef for dinner. He thought I was joking. You see, the French have a giggle about the Brits and their beef.'

'*Le rosbif*, it is a little like the way you call us the frogs.' Somehow Didier manages to make his statement sound accusatory, and Aurora shrieks a silly little laugh as though to add levity to his observation.

'Sit, sit!' claps Shani, pulling out chairs and smiling broadly. When Lester sees her like this, in entertaining mode, he wonders why she never found herself a suitable husband. There has been a string of suitors but none of them ever got beyond the boyfriend stage. At fifty-six, Shani is still very beautiful.

'How is your wife, Lester?' asks Aurora with mild sarcasm. 'Is she sleeping it off?'

'Yes, I left her suffering for her sins.'

'She certainly knows how to make an exit. I was telling Marla and Mark earlier about that scene by the cloakroom.'

'I'm sure you were,' replies Lester, averting his eyes from Aurora with her brittle enthusiasm. Marla offers him a wink across the table and Lester feels immediately better. Everyone knows about Aurora's habitual nastiness.

Shani comes in from the kitchen carrying a hunk of roast beef on a silver platter. 'Darling, do you mind carving for me? I've never been the same since that episode with the electric knife at Gerald's.' She offers Lester the carving implements.

'I hope it's still pink inside, Mummy, Didier can't eat beef unless it's haemorrhaging on to the plate.' Aurora pokes at the beef with the tip of a fork and screws up her arrogant little nose.

'Aurora darling, there is only so much I can do – and I'm not blaming you, Lester, sweetheart – when the dinner was supposed to have been served forty minutes ago. And, *please*, you know how I hate it when you call me Mummy!'

'I like my meat cremated, so there's no worries on my account,' quips Marla, blowing cigarette smoke over her shoulder to avoid the buttered sprouts that have just appeared before her.

'Me too,' adds Mark, smiling at Shani in the way that one might smile at an unfortunate child.

Lester is cutting through the third slice of medium-rare beef when Marla's broken scream shatters the calm of the dinner table, as she stares down into her open handbag with blanched horror. 'Oh my God!' she moans, dropping the bag on to the floor and steadying herself against Mark's shoulder.

'What is it?' he demands, reaching down to retrieve the offending handbag.

'My purse, how did he get to my purse?' she wails.

'Somebody stole your purse?' asks Shani.

'She means her handbag,' explains Lester, still poised for action with his knife and prongs.

'Christ!' Mark hisses the expletive under his breath as he reaches into the bag and pulls out what looks like a handful of raw liver.

'Ugh! What is it?' cries Aurora, pushing her chair away from the table with hands fluttering at her neckline.

'It's a heart,' says Mark. 'Looks like a pig's heart, and some sick bastard has pinned a photo of Marla to the top of it.'

Eleven

When Annie sees the photographs she starts to cry.

'Whatever is the matter?' asks Richard as he observes her sitting at her desk wiping tears from the glossy eight-by-tens.

'These photographs that Michaela sent to me, they're smashing,' and Annie's voice breaks again.

'I don't see how they could have been anything *but*: I think you really do underestimate yourself, Annie.'

'Oh, Richard, you're always so nice, but I'm not totally thick, you know! I've been ridiculed all my life for looking the way I do, so you don't have to be kind to me. It must be trick photography: they've magicked me beautiful.'

'Annie, I am not being kind. Michaela saw something special in you the moment she met you in the restaurant, and although I know the two of you don't hit it off she *is* a professional and those photographs prove my point. What does she say in the note there?'

Annie wipes the corners of her eyes with a Kleenex and flattens out the crumpled yellow paper that is stuck to the back of one of the photographs. '*Annie, these are even better than expected. Rave reviews from the guys here in New York who are working on the catalogue. We are talking front cover material here! Forget Delta Burke and Roseanne, you are going to be a sensation!*'

'Who is Delta Burke?' asks Richard.

'Don't know. Probably another overweight American. She goes on to say that they would like me to do another session in New York this time, and they'll discuss a contract with me when they've talked to Marla. What has Marla got to do with this? She hasn't been in the office for a week and Michaela seems to think I'm going to *jump* at the chance of being a model for her clothes. I don't *want* to be a model. People will kill themselves laughing when they see me prancing around in these kind of clothes.'

Annie looks up at Richard, who is holding one of the photographs and smiling at her.

'You do look very nice in this one . . .' and he holds up the one of Annie wearing a full-length black jersey dress with a flared transparent jacket that is cinched in at the waist, giving the illusion of a much taller and slimmer woman. The hairdresser did something clever with her hair, and the make-up girl had somehow used cosmetics to give Annie a look that was even more natural than if she wasn't wearing any make-up at all.

'I have to admit that particular get-up was a knockout! But who would ever wear such a thing? It's not as though I spend my life going to balls, and I doubt that I'd feel very comfortable traipsing around Waitrose with that jacket thing floating a mile behind me.'

'I don't think that's the point, Annie. They just want to sell the clothes to women who *do* go to a lot of balls.'

'Spencer is going to die when he sees these.'

Richard falls silent. Annie suspects that most of the staff at the law office are suspicious of her odd little marriage and that people have stopped referring to it because they are embarrassed to bring the subject up.

Just the other day Richard had asked Annie if she minded Spencer being away so much and she had had to admit that life was somewhat easier with him away.

The house is easier to handle without Spencer's constant scrutiny. Bedtime is a relief as Annie can watch late-night TV with a tub of ice cream or a couple of Mars Bars and not have to worry so much about personal hygiene. (Not that she's neglectful of such things; it's just that Annie suspects Spencer is easily offended.)

He won't let her use talc because it messes up the bedroom carpet. Aerosol deodorant pollutes the atmosphere and speckles the mirrors.

And is it absolutely necessary for Annie to keep her tampons in the linen cupboard when they would be much better hidden away somewhere private? Let's not even mention the unspeakable 'first period' when Spencer was forced by his own distaste to sleep in the guest bedroom, while Annie sprinkled her knickers with baking soda (a little tip passed on by her mother years ago).

Since that strange night at the sadomasochistic restaurant when Spencer burst into tears outside in the street, Annie has sensed a distinct cooling towards her, and even Betsy had noticed it during the weekend she had been down from Chesterfield. 'It's as though he's being very careful all the time, afraid that he might break something if he steps in the wrong direction.'

He has been in New York with Marla for most of the week. There has been talk of Marla moving back to America on a permanent basis, since this thing with the stalker commenced. The police seem unable to find any clues, even though Marla has been going out with that lovely Police Inspector Blake. They are installing security cameras all over the office building as well as in

Marla's flat – she has refused to come back to London until everything is secure. Spencer reckons she's close to having a nervous breakdown, but somehow Annie cannot imagine a woman like Marla going gaga. When Annie's Auntie Sybil had *her* breakdown they had to coax her off the garage roof with the promise of a fortnight in Blackpool, and then she spent three months crying in the spare bedroom with the lights turned permanently off.

The promise of modelling stardom does nothing to assuage Annie's current feeling of oppression. Two months of marriage have left her feeling more alone and miserable than she ever felt previously as a single woman. Her friends and family are miles away, she lives in a house that feels more like a showroom, and she has a husband who has made love to her only once and that was after several large glasses of whisky and a Viagra (the container for which Annie discovered the following morning in Spencer's toiletry bag). What kind of life is this for her?

Annie looks at her desk diary and finds she has no appointments for the entire week ahead. Her in-box is empty and her out-box contains two personal letters and an application for a credit card offering a reduced interest rate. It has been fairly obvious from the start that this job was created for her merely because she is married to Spencer. When she asks for something to do they only provide her with unskilled tasks such as invoicing or time sheets. Yesterday she took a three-hour lunch break and went shopping in Oxford Street.

The days pass so slowly with Annie watching the clock – dividing up the day into palatable segments so that she can get herself through to the next snack or similar diversion. She drinks so much coffee that by mid-afternoon she is overdosed on caffeine and has to eat cake to stop herself from shaking. She has put on weight but she isn't sure how much, because Spencer's scales are metric and Annie still works in pounds.

Homesickness strikes like a blow to her heart. It happens quite often these days, and she sometimes has a little cry in the ladies' when she thinks about the simple things that she used to take for granted. At this time of the morning she would be having elevenses with the girls, sharing gossip and flipping through magazines in the staff canteen. Roxanne would be complaining about her oversexed husband and showing them all her love bites. Susan would be griping about her next-door neighbours and their surround-sound TV. And someone would have tuned in to Radio 2 so they could answer the questions on Ken Bruce's Popmaster Quiz.

Everything here in London is so impersonal. Annie has not yet taken up any offers of a drink after work from Julie or Richard, because all she wants to do is rush home to Spencer's house and hide away where it is quiet and safe. There she can turn on the telly and watch familiar programmes that offer her some sense of continuity. She can soak in the bath and listen to Barry Manilow and almost believe that she isn't bewildered and lost.

Some evenings she merely sits by the conservatory window in the dark and stares out at her reflection, lost in a world of her own. Time passes quickly like that.

Richard gets up and makes his way across to the office door. Annie no longer notices his pronounced limp, she merely accepts it as being part of Richard, like the colour of his hair or the way he hesitates before he makes a statement. 'Do you want some coffee?' he asks.

'Yes, please. And bring a packet of Jaffa Cakes with you as well.' Annie needs *something* to get her through the morning.

'He isn't home at the moment, can I take a message?' Annie has a biro at the ready.

The woman at the other end of the line hesitates before she answers, 'Oh, no, there's no message.'

'Shall I tell him who called?'

'This is Maggie, a friend from . . . university. We haven't seen him for a couple of weeks and we were just wondering if everything was all right.'

'University? Spencer has never mentioned you. Have we met?'

'Don't worry, just tell him Maggie called,' and the line goes dead.

Annie is perplexed. Who is this woman, and if Spencer has known her ever since university why hasn't he spoken about her? It's not as though this should be a guilty secret between them. Annie would be only too happy for Spencer to see his old friends, if that's what he wanted.

But Annie feels as though she knows so little about her husband. He is like a closed book. When they were previously just friends Spencer had always confided in her, telling her stories about his latest girlfriends and the work he was doing on his house. They used to sit up late and watch old films together; they have similar tastes in British films from the '60s and many a night was spent in front of the telly, by the light of Dad's aquarium, lamenting over the fate of Rita Tushingham in *A Taste of Honey* or laughing at the raucous street brawls in *Up the Junction*. Now that they are married, they never watch TV – not together, anyway. When *Room at the Top* was on last week Spencer claimed he was too tired to sit up, and left Annie alone with a large bag of Kettle Chips and a giant bottle of Tizer.

Marriage has ruined their friendship, it has ruined everything and Annie wonders now why they even bothered with it. It's not as though they enjoyed any kind of courtship. Spencer had just phoned her up, out of the blue, and asked her if she would marry him. Hardly a proposal forged from true romance. Why had she said yes so easily? Was it because Annie had loved Spencer all along but thought him beyond her reach? Or was it that she was merely afraid of being left on the shelf? A bit of both perhaps? Annie is beginning to think that she should have thought things through before she leaped off the edge of the cliff.

This Maggie woman . . . now, who is she? Spencer has never mentioned anyone of that name before. Could she be one of the women he was seeing before they got married? It would make sense that he is currently having an affair with a beautiful woman – she has already imagined that this Maggie woman is beautiful – and Annie is quite surprised to register only the smallest prick of jealousy. It is difficult to be jealous of a man who has continued to show little or no interest in sexual relations with oneself, but it does lead to a degree of self-doubt and insecurity. Annie has always been insecure – hardly a surprise, having gone through life as a fat person. Sometimes she wakes in the middle of the night with those familiar taunts ringing in her ears: on the hockey field, in the changing rooms, at the social club, and even later in life with insensitive teenagers screaming at her from the top of double-deckers as she walked home from work.

'Hey, fatso, your arse is falling out of your pants!'

Or sometimes there would just be the rude snorting noises that children make when they want to imitate a pig. Cruel, heartless children who will grow up to be respectable husbands and wives with cruel, heartless children of their own. Annie knows the type because she has seen the way her classmates have grown up. Some of the worst name-callers are now dentists and green-grocers and they nod and smile when they see Annie, forgetting the vile names that would send her crying to a locked bathroom stall. They smile and say 'Aren't kids terrible?' as though being a child is a valid excuse for unprovoked victimization.

It is not yet eight thirty but the evening already seems so late. Spencer hasn't called from New York yet, but it's only half past three in Manhattan and he's probably busy.

It has started to rain. The sound of it against the glass roof of the conservatory is unsettling so Annie decides to go to bed early with her new paperback and a box of coconut snowballs. She is just passing through the hallway when the unexpected sound of the doorbell practically sends her scurrying back into the kitchen with fright.

She peeps through the security viewer but cannot see clearly who is standing on the doorstep. This is London, so it could be *anybody*. 'Hello?' she shouts through the letterbox.

'Oh, hello. Is Spencer at home?' It is a man's voice.

Annie unlatches the door and peeps around the crack. It is Spencer's client, the airline bloke with the white smile and the perfect blonde hair. Annie opens the door fully and apologizes for her caution. 'He's in New York at the moment, won't be back for another few days. Perhaps I can pass on a message for you? He'll probably call tonight sometime.'

There is no outside porch so he is getting quite wet from the driving rain. 'Please, come inside for a minute. You're drenched through.'

'That's OK, don't worry, I can call again.'

'Come on in, *please*, just for a minute.'

'Thank you. I *am* a bit soggy. Had to park my car a couple of streets away – the parking around here is awful.'

'Oh, I know, and nobody has a garage or a nice driveway like they do up home.'

'Where do you come from? I detect a northern accent.'

'Chesterfield. I'm Annie, Spencer's wife.'

'Same town as Spencer. Pleased to meet you, Annie, I'm Nolan. Actually I've heard Spencer talk about you before. You are an old school friend, aren't you?'

'That's right. We've only been married a few weeks. And I've heard *your* name before, as well – it's unusual, more like a surname than a first name.' Annie shows Nolan through into the kitchen where she turns some of the lights back on.

'It was my mother's maiden name and she couldn't bear to part with it so they decided it would be an interesting first name for a boy. Wow, this is a fabulous kitchen!'

'Thank you. Take that jacket off for a minute, Nolan, and I'll make some tea.' Annie is quite animated now that she has company, and the prospect of a nice cup of tea and some conversation lightens her mood.

'So Spencer has mentioned me before, then?' asks Nolan, removing his dripping jacket and handing it gingerly to Annie.

'Yes, when he used to come up home on a visit, he'd tell me all about what he'd been up to, and he was always going on about Nolan this and Nolan that. Funny though, when you called round the other night he told me you were just a client.'

Nolan doesn't respond to this. Instead he just shrugs and smiles and fingers the workmanship on the built-in plate racks.

'Spencer used to have a ring like that, too,' says Annie, recognizing the unusual design, 'but he doesn't wear it any more.'

Nolan looks down at his hand and twists the gold band around his finger; he doesn't look directly at Annie when he replies. 'Yes, we both bought them at the same time actually, a couple of years ago when we were on holiday in France.'

'I wonder what he's done with his?' Annie places Nolan's wet jacket over the back of a chair and goes to fill the electric kettle. 'You two must have been very close, so how come you didn't come to the wedding?'

'Oh, I was living in Singapore since the beginning of this year, and only came back to London a few weeks ago.'

'Well, I'm going to tell Spencer off when I see him. Fancy passing you off as a client the other night when you came round! I don't know what he was thinking.'

119

'So when's he getting back then?'

'Oh, in a few days or so. He never tells me exactly what his plans are. I'm getting quite used to being here on my own.'

Nolan moves slowly around the kitchen, touching things as though familiarizing himself with every small detail. Annie watches him from the corner of her eye as she prepares the tea, and she senses some kind of uncertainty in his manner, a sort of sadness that she can't put her finger on. It seems a bit odd that Spencer hasn't mentioned this friend once since they got married. Maybe they had some kind of falling out and Nolan is here to patch things up. Annie knows how awkward things like that can be.

'So . . .' ventures Nolan, pausing at the built-in microwave, 'how come you and Spence got married after all these years. I mean, I know you've been friends forever, but I didn't know there was anything going on between the two of you.'

'I was more surprised by his proposal than anyone, to tell you the truth,' admits Annie, spooning Darjeeling into the pot like Spencer has shown her. 'It came out of the blue, but I have to admit that I was over the moon. I think I've loved him ever since we were at school. I always thought he'd marry some rich, beautiful model type, so you could have knocked me down with a feather when he phoned me to see if I'd marry him.'

'Didn't it seem a bit strange to you? I mean, to suddenly propose like that? I would have been more than a bit suspicious if it had been me.' Nolan looks at Annie intently and there is something about his expression that puts her on guard. Who is this person really? And, if Spencer has never mentioned him to her, is she safe having him in the house like this? After all, he could be almost anybody.

'No, it wasn't strange.' It was romantic,' and Annie wonders how quickly she could get to the front door if she has to.

'Funny, I never had Spence down as a romantic myself. Now *I've* always been the romantic one. I'm the one who remembers to send flowers, light candles, remember anniversaries. Spencer was always too much into his work, too much into himself to care about those kind of things. But he has his moments.'

This doesn't sound like the kind of friend who is here for a cosy chat, does it? This sounds like somebody who is bitter and brittle, somebody who runs their every word like a fingernail down a blackboard. What actually happened between Spencer and Nolan? Perhaps they fell out over another woman. Perhaps Nolan is married and Spencer fooled around with his wife. All kinds of scenarios run through Annie's head as she pours boiling water into the pot and fiddles with the milk carton.

When the phone rings it sends a jarring crack right through the glaze of their silence and Annie almost drops the sugar bowl. Nolan himself is so startled that he appears to press himself back against the oven.

It is a relief for Annie to pick up the phone. It represents a connection with the outside world and she feels foolishly nervous when she says hello.

'Darling, it's me!'

'Spencer!'

Nolan looks at Annie with the fear of a startled animal.

121

'I've got your old friend here – Nolan.' Annie is careful to smile as she says this, disguising any fear as she fiddles with the phone cord.

Spencer doesn't answer at first. There is a silence that crackles, then he asks if he can speak to Nolan. Annie hands the phone over and busies herself with stacking a plate of bourbons. But she listens carefully to the one-sided conversation. Nolan is turned away from her, talking into the wall as though he doesn't want her to hear what he is saying.

'I didn't know you were out of town and you didn't return my calls . . . No, it's raining and your wife let me into . . . No, no, oh *please*, give me *some* credit, Spence! We were just having a cup of tea, actually.'

Then there is a considerable listening pause as Nolan crouches silently over the phone. He is picking the edge off a table mat with skittish fingers, and Annie unravels her own thoughts and picks through them while she pretends to be busy with a dishcloth.

'Fair enough,' says Nolan, 'I've got to get home anyway: I never intended to stay. I'll see you next week then? At your office? OK, give me a call when you get back.'

Nolan turns to Annie with a smile. 'He wants to talk to you now, Annie,' and he hands her the receiver that is warm from his touch.

'Spencer?' Annie is looking for some kind of reassurance, but Spencer makes no reference to Nolan or his unexpected arrival on their doorstep. Instead he rambles on about clients and business meetings and gives her a list of things to do before he gets home. When Annie puts the phone down she feels dissatisfied with the entire conversation and she wonders if it is normal for newlyweds to converse that way when they haven't seen each other for over a week. Not once did he say that he loves her. Not once did he make any kind of reference to their relationship, or even that he was missing her. Nolan has his coat on, and has been waiting for her to finish on the phone before he leaves. Annie doesn't attempt to dissuade him even though the tea is now perfectly brewed.

'Hope to see you again, Annie,' says Nolan, extending his hand.

'Yes,' says Annie and she holds the front door open. It is still chucking it down out there. 'Miserable!' exclaims Nolan as he turns and runs down the pathway with his collar turned up.

'Yes, miserable,' says Annie. And she goes back indoors to scoff the entire plate of chocolate bourbons, without even stopping to consider the consequences.

Twelve

Spencer grows more confused by the hour. For a hot-shot international immigration lawyer he is almost as fucked-up as his boss, and that's saying something as Marla continues to deteriorate under the pressure of her personal torment.

Being in New York helps, but it doesn't solve anything for Spencer. He can pretend that everything is OK as long as he is working with clients, attending business meetings or eating out with casual acquaintances, but back in London nothing will have changed. Annie is still there, in his house, sucking up his life like a massive vacuum cleaner. She occupies his future with all the darkness of imminent death, and Spencer knows that it is all his fault. He has used Annie to paper roughly over the cracks in his own self-assurance, and it is now quite evident that she is not strong enough to maintain the surface tension. The cracks are beginning to tear through the surface of Annie's tenuous hold and Spencer wishes now that he had chosen someone less vulnerable as a means to keep him together.

Manhattan's Upper East Side is busy at this time, late afternoon. The sky is already turning inward as evening draws close, and the trees in Central Park are clustered together, forming a tight network of skeletal branches above a ground littered with fallen leaves.

Christmas has already arrived in the shop windows; barricades are being erected outside the largest department stores so that queues of people can stand in line to peer in at the spectacular window displays. Spencer stands opposite the Metropolitan Museum in his grey trenchcoat and looks up at the darkening sky with a sense of being swallowed whole by an invisible vortex that sucks him upwards into oblivion. Everything whirls around him – noises and people and buildings spiral and twist as though uprooted by a tornado. Spencer stands alone, firmly rooted to the pavement while the rest of the world is in chaos.

He has a couple of hours to spare before he meets Marla at Michaela's loft apartment in SoHo. The taxi ride will take about thirty minutes at this time of the day so he walks down to one of his favourite boutique stores where they have a cafe amidst the ecologically friendly assortment of expensive household goods for sale. He needs a sanctuary from the whirlwind of the streets and he knows he can find calm if he surrounds himself with understated opulence.

The cafe is on the third floor. Arched windows look down on to the bustle of Madison Avenue and he finds a seat with a view. New York seems so much more glamorous viewed through plate glass. He orders a double espresso and a slice of comfort cheesecake that comes sprinkled with finely grated chocolate, displayed on a bed of raspberry coulis. The dessert makes him think of Annie. And with Annie comes the baggage of reality.

If Spencer could turn back time, he would.

But he isn't Superman. He is floundering in the shallow waters of his own polluted tide and he has

125

dragged Annie with him – pulling her from the safe, clean life she knew previously in an attempt to save himself from the scum that had been blocking off his oxygen supply. He sits here with his double espresso and his eight-dollar cheesecake, contemplating life as a monk somewhere in the Italian mountains. But he is too superficial, too caught up in his own little world to do anything so profoundly life-changing. Even now, as he sits here dissecting this dilemma, he has half a mind on a celadon-glaze soapdish that he spotted on the way up to the cafe. It would be perfect for his downstairs toilet.

Nolan always said that Spencer was more interested in the wrapping than the contents of a package, and maybe he was right. The idea of homosexuality is still an unacceptable lifestyle for Spencer and it represents weakness and a break with conventionality; it represents something that is less than perfect. Spencer has spent his entire life trying to be perfect. At school, with friends, with family, and then in his career – he was the envy of everyone he knew. People admire him, they seek his advice, and they wear him as one might wear a talisman for good luck. His charisma is like gold dust that powders the fingers of those who touch him.

There is nothing very charismatic or golden about a man who sometimes hangs around in men's changing rooms in the hope of a casual encounter. What kind of admiration would he instil if people knew that he spent every transatlantic flight lusting after the male flight attendants? They might feel slightly nauseated at the mere thought of such things. Men loving men. Men kissing men. Men fucking men. Ugh! It is the kind of thing that gives most heterosexual males the creeps.

And yet to Spencer it is beginning to appear increasingly natural.

For the three years that Spencer was friendly with Nolan he never once wanted or needed anyone else in his life. Even without the sex he could believe that he was complete. But he was a mess at the same time. One minute loving Nolan, wanting Nolan, feeling safe and secure in his presence; the next, blaming Nolan, hurting Nolan, feeling trapped and breathless in his company. And then Spencer decided to eschew his homosexual attachment, to pursue a 'straight' lifestyle, and that was the end of that. Nolan moved away and Spencer married Annie: an imperfect solution to an imperfect problem.

He is such a mess.

And yet, looking at him as he sits here in his subtle taupes and greys, we might mistake him for a man who has no insecurities. We might put him down as a man who always gets what he wants. A man who never prevaricates when it comes to important decisions. A man who has never even thought about the sinful pleasure of rubbing up against a hairy chest when he climbs into bed at night. How can this man be homosexual? He isn't even wearing a pinkie ring.

Of course it takes one to know one, doesn't it?

Nolan always joked about his 'gaydar' – his innate ability to spot a poof from thirty yards. Oh yes, any self-respecting homosexual would be able to spot poor misguided Spencer a mile off. One look at that perfectly gelled hair, those manicured hands, that marvellous cologne that smells of old money and of leather and of bruised flowers. And his briefcase alone is enough to give the game away – buttery tan leather with the coach label still hanging prominently from the shoulder straps.

Poor old Spencer, he's a dead giveaway.

And still he kids himself that nobody knows his secret.

'It's called dandelion but it didn't look quite like this in the salon.'

Michaela Fox is mixing drinks in her exposed kitchen while Marla, Spencer and a couple of Michaela's designers lounge uncomfortably on her low-slung inflatable furniture. She is referring to the colour of her hair which she has changed from orange to bright yellow. The colour is called dandelion and that is what she looks like – a tall, lanky dandelion with red, smudgy lips.

Marla is smoking a cigar with Michaela and the other two, but Spencer has declined the offer, even though Michaela insists that they are 'perfectly safe'. Marla doesn't look at all well. She is wearing her beige St John outfit, the one with the gold stitching at the collar and cuffs, and she looks washed out. Her hair is flat on one side as though she has been sleeping somewhere, and her lipstick has worn off. She has crossed her legs and is dangling a shoe from her toes, bouncing it up and down nervously as she puffs away at her cheroot. Her handbag sits by her side, gaping open to reveal her small silver revolver and several containers of pills.

Michaela makes a huge production of blending her cocktails, throwing in handfuls of fruit and ice to create abnormally large drinks that look virulently potent.

They are listening to some kind of abstract music which reverberates from the exposed brick walls of the loft space, a cacophony of clangs and shrieks that Michaela explains are oil-drum percussion and whale song combined artlessly by some Scandinavian nutcase.

Spencer was not in the mood for an evening of Michaela Fox and her obscure idea of fun but Marla had practically begged him to join her for the evening. It is only seven thirty but already feels like the middle of the night. Spencer is hungry and the one consolation he can count on is the fact that Americans eat so much earlier than Europeans. He helps himself to a bowl of birdfeed that he assumes is a cocktail snack. It tastes like dry Quaker Oats and he finds it difficult to swallow.

'It was all *white* chocolate,' says the woman with the slicked-back hair who is talking to her male counterpart, a fairly robust-looking guy with several visible piercings and a pair of black boots that look capable of extreme violence. 'I have never liked Leonidas for that reason: the white chocolate is so sickeningly sweet.'

'Neuhaus are the best,' says the man, waving his cigar in the air with studied nonchalance. 'You can forget Godiva over here because they use a different recipe in Europe. It's the alcohol, you know. They can't use it in chocolate over here because of the Mormons or something.'

'Oh, Danny brought back the most amazing chocolates from Paris the other week,' chips in Michaela as she distributes her buckets of slush. 'They were like miniature works of art, each one hand-painted. Of course they tasted like shit but they looked sensational! Give me a pound of Hershey's any day.'

'Oh Michaela, you can't mean that!' shrieks the slicked-back woman. 'Hershey's is like eating chalk by comparison.'

'I always buy Cadbury's whenever I can find it. They sell it in my supermarket now – the one with almonds.' The man called Taylor seems to think that he is enlightening the conversation, because he smiles broadly as he imparts his words of dubious wisdom.

'Oh Taylor, you are such a chocolate snob! I've seen you eating peanut M&M's from Tilda's jar when you thought nobody was looking.'

'Oh you bitch, Tamara! That's a lie and you know it.'

And so on, and so forth.

Spencer knocks back a brain-numbing mouthful of frozen vodka, his inflatable chair squeaking uncomfortably beneath him. Michaela is sitting in what she calls her 'butterfly chair', a metal contraption of spindly metal bars and stretched orange canvas. She looks like an insect that has been caught inside the vicious petals of a carnivorous plant – a brightly coloured Venus in the sticky clutch of a flytrap.

'That wife of yours is going to be a huge success, Spencer. Those photographs were a knock-out and that's just the beginning. With the Internet catalogue and the JC Penney contract, this line of outsize fashions is going to be hot. Annie's face is going to be on billboards from New York to LA.' Michaela toasts the room with what remains of her purple concoction.

'Oh yes, Spencer,' joins in Taylor, 'she's big but she's not vulgar. I think it's got something to do with being British – her complexion is very Elizabeth Hurley.

When I saw the proofs I said to Michaela, "That girl is going to be big!"'

'Awesome bone structure,' adds Tamara, with her own bone structure prominently displayed through the painful canvas of her face.

'You guys,' cackles Marla, 'you crack me up!'

'Why is that, Marla?'

'I doubt that Annie is going to want her face plastered across every billboard in America. She only did the shoot as a favour. She's a small-town girl with small-town aspirations, Michaela. Don't you go bullying her into something that could ruin her life.'

Spencer averts his eyes with shame, wondering just how ruined Annie's life already is.

'*Ruin?*' shrieks Michaela. 'I'm offering her the world on a plate. She'll be rich and famous – even bigger than Camryn Manheim!'

'Who the hell is Camryn Manheim?' demands Marla, losing her shoe as it clatters to the concrete floor.

'Oh, that fat actress from *The Practice* who writes all those books about being glad!'

'She's very good,' says Taylor, goggle-eyed.

'Marvellous in that Todd Solondz movie!' agrees Tamara, nodding frantically.

Where the hell am I? thinks Spencer, listening to this continuous stream of crap that seems to pour relentlessly from the mouths of these crass people. He closes his eyes and attempts to think of a quiet place, but all he can come up with is his kitchen at home: spotlessly clean and gleaming with chrome, and there is Annie filling up the empty spaces in a hideous pinny and wearing her most self-deprecating smile.

Spencer hates himself. Normally so assertive and self-assured, he feels totally out of control as his life snatches him up and drags him forcefully behind, as though dangling from a precarious rope attached to the bumper of a racing car. As he bounces and skids along the ground, his feeble attempts to recapture his stability are thwarted by the strength and speed of his runaway life.

He catches Taylor staring at him – Taylor with the nose-ring and the tattoo on his forearm. Spencer immediately looks away but he can feel Taylor watching him. It's no big surprise that Michaela's assistant designer is gay. Hell, aren't all fashion designers gay? It's like being a hairdresser or a window-dresser, where homosexuality is practically a prerequisite for the job.

Taylor slouches on his chair with his legs splayed out ahead of him, weighed down by those enormous black boots. Oh yes, he's good-looking in a New York trendy kind of way but he's probably ten years younger than Spencer and not really his type. Not that Spencer has a type, but if he did have a type it wouldn't be Taylor with his pointy sideburns and tight, tight T-shirt that cuts into his gym-structured biceps. Spencer isn't interested in men. He isn't interested in men. He isn't . . .

'Let me show you the rest of Michaela's loft, Spencer. It's quite something if you've never seen it before,' smiles Taylor, looking at Spencer with undisguised amusement.

'Yeah, go check out my bathroom, darling. It cost me too much for nobody else to see it,' says Michaela, puffing on her cigar like a Wall Street banker.

Just be cool, Spencer. Play it straight. This guy has

absolutely no idea that you are anything but an honest married man.

'Isn't this bed fabulous?' asks Taylor, bouncing at the edge of the king-size mattress with his hands resting behind him. 'Michaela designed it herself.'

Spencer remains by the bedroom door, leaning nonchalantly against the frame with both hands in his pockets. When Taylor sits forward his pectorals bunch together beneath the sheer black fabric of his shirt, and Spencer averts his gaze to the unadorned warehouse windows that stretch from floor to ceiling. Outside it is night and he can see his own reflection in the glass.

'You *have* to see this bathroom,' enthuses Taylor, leaping up from the bed to lead Spencer over to another doorway. 'It is all Phillipe Starck fixtures and the tile is volcanic rock.'

Michaela's bathroom is indeed spectacular and for a moment Spencer forgets about Taylor and his pneumatic muscles as he stands in open-mouthed wonder. He is suddenly aware that Taylor is standing very close behind him. So close that he can feel the man's breath against his hair.

'You are so fucking cute,' whispers Taylor, and before Spencer has time to react Taylor's lips and tongue are gnawing gently at the tender nape of his neck. It's a feeling that is so erotically electrifying that Spencer experiences a shudder that weakens the backs of his legs. He gasps, he falls back against Taylor's chest, and then he pulls away.

Angrily he stands his ground. 'What the hell are you playing at?' he shouts, turning to Taylor with his face burning red.

'Oh come on, Spencer, cut the macho crap. You

wanted to jump my bones the minute you walked in this evening. Man, you're damn near begging for it!'

'I'm married. I'm a married man. Didn't you know that?'

'And that makes a difference *how*, exactly?' laughs Taylor with an inflection on the 'how' in that annoyingly smug American way they have. 'I've got an email address list as long as your dick of married men who like a little ass now and then. Boy, some of those guys are hot!'

'Well, I'm not one of them, OK? Now let's just pretend that this never happened and we'll say no more about it.' Spencer straightens his tie and brushes back his hair with trembling fingers.

Taylor closes the bathroom door and turns the key behind his back.

'What are you doing?' demands Spencer.

'Giving us a little privacy, handsome,' smiles Taylor as he begins to unbuckle his belt.

'You are totally out of order, mate. Now get out of my way or I'll knock that smile off your face.'

'Ooh, so butch, Spencer, so rough! C'mon, *mate*, you know this is what you want.' And Taylor has his jeans around his knees.

Taylor is not wearing any underpants.

And Spencer has to close his eyes and steady himself against the heated towel rail.

He feels sick with lust.

He has wanted to do this for so long it has almost become a myth. He wants this so much that it is almost painful. This is the first time he has ever been propositioned by anyone but Nolan. The first time he has been offered sex by another man. Well, the kind of sex that actually *means* anything to him. He can't go on like this. He can't deny himself any longer.

So, as Taylor approaches him, Spencer sinks slowly to his knees as though in supplication. It is a convenient position for both of them, and Spencer no longer has the desire or the facility to call out for help.

His mouth is otherwise occupied.

Thirteen

Let's get one thing straight, OK? Marla Philips is not a wuss. She may be many things but she is not a coward and she is not afraid of idle threats or lawsuits. People are normally afraid of *her*, goddamnit!

So why does she feel her throat constrict with fear as she walks through the lobby of her exclusive Manhattan hotel and catches a brief glimpse of a man lurking behind the indoor fountain? It is one thirty in the morning and the only other person here is the skinny guy on reception, so what is that guy doing here, hiding away where nobody can see him?

Marla stands by the lift and counts the floor numbers as they light up in turn above the doors. From twenty-four all the way down to number one, she has to wait here fiddling with the keys in her coat pocket. She would like to light up a cigarette but she has just smoked her last one in the cab. She can taste the garlic from her dinner, she can smell the sanitized hotel smell of polished marble and vacuumed carpets. The guy at reception is talking into the phone and has turned his back as he messes around with the mail in the pigeonholes. The foyer is otherwise empty: no sign of anyone loitering. The splashing fountain and the siren sounds of the city form a backdrop to the scene as she quietly waits for the lift to reach ground zero.

Marla steps into the lift. She presses the button to ascend and stands there holding her breath because the doors don't seem to be closing. Any minute now that guy is going to step in behind her, smiling sweatily and eyeing Marla with a hungry kind of anticipation.

Close! Close! Please close!

Slowly, slowly the lift doors close and Marla begins to ascend.

What a night it has been. She didn't want to go out in the first place but Michaela is so insistent sometimes. How could Spencer just disappear like that? One minute they're having drinks in Michaela's loft, and the next minute he's racing out of the place complaining of some sudden and mysterious ailment. What is it with him? He's been looking sick for weeks now and once or twice Marla has caught him daydreaming in the middle of important meetings. She thinks it must be something to do with his ridiculous marriage to Annie. What was he thinking to do such a ludicrous thing? Everyone knows that he's a fruit but he just doesn't seem to want to accept the fact. Perhaps something happened between Taylor and Spencer in the bathroom. Taylor wouldn't elaborate. He just downed a fresh Cape Cod and adjusted his belt with a scurrilous smirk.

Marla can think of much worse things than being a fruit.

Much worse.

She wishes at this very moment that Mark were here to hold her arm. She actually misses him right now, and that is an emotion that she usually wouldn't own up to. Dependency is a dirty word to people like Marla; it represents weakness and lack of self-assurance and it rubs shoulders with words like love and trust. Marla can no longer love and she cannot trust. She went through all of that years ago and now she is hardened and impervious through experience. If somebody is stalking her then they'd better watch out, because Marla has a gun in her handbag and she's not afraid to use it.

On the twentieth floor the carpets are dark blue patterned with gold diamonds bearing the initials of the hotel. The corridors are long – long and seemingly endless when you occupy the last room and you are afraid to look back because the hairs on the back of your neck are standing on end. The double-glazing keeps out the noise of the night and behind each door someone sleeps, being too late for normal television viewing. When Marla hears the bell ting and the lift doors opening behind her she hurries the last few steps to her room and fumbles with her key card.

She gets the red light.

She tries again, and again it lights up red.

Someone is approaching behind her.

Flipping the card around the other way Marla almost drops it in her haste, but this time she hears a comforting click and the light glows green. She doesn't look back, but pushes open the door, shuts it quickly and leans against it from the inside, closing her eyes, with her heart thudding in the side of her throat.

There are three locks on her hotel room door – this is New York City, after all – so Marla secures them all to barricade herself in. The bedroom curtains are still open, so there is enough light in the room for her to see without switching on the lamps as she removes her coat and tosses it over the back of a chair. She turns on the TV for company and attempts to push open wide one of the windows but they are secured in a way that nobody can jump out, so all she manages to get is a couple of inches of fresh air. The transparent curtains billow into the room as Marla stands with her cheek pressed up against the cold glass.

'. . . *In a moment we will be talking to Sherri Townsend, the Maryland mother who lived for two years in the branches of a redwood tree* . . .' The TV voices flicker in the hotel bedroom and the ceiling is lit with an unearthly, pallid light.

Marla has never felt so alone or so abandoned; it is as though self-pity has finally caught up with her after all these years and is now gripping her throat with smug little fingers.

There are cigarettes on the bedside table: a large carton of duty-free, already ripped asunder as though ravaged in desperation. She tears open a packet and rests the unlit cigarette between her lips, heading for her handbag to find her lighter. In the unlit room her face flares up as she inhales against the butane flame, sucking smoke deep into her lungs and closing her eyes for a moment. Then she sinks down on to the edge of the bed and stares at the TV screen, and in her head she attempts to recall her last conversation with Mark when they spoke on the phone just yesterday.

'I met your neighbour,' he informed her. 'She was sniffing around when we were installing the video cameras, and I thought it might be handy to have someone in the building watching out for us. She's quite a character.'

'Oh yeah, she's some broad, isn't she? I thought at first she was a hooker but I think she's just out for a good time. To coin a quaint British saying, she's rough and ready!'

'She tried to chat up one of the installation guys. He was probably young enough to be her son but she pulled out all the stops. Invited him in for a cup of tea, then walked into the kitchen wearing nothing but a red bra and pants. He couldn't get out of there fast enough, poor chap!'

'So the security system is all set?'

'Activated, and ready for you to come home.'

'I'm still nervous, Mark. There is something about this weirdo that makes me believe he's capable of anything. Are you sure I'll be safe there? And what about the office?'

'That's rigged too. There isn't anyone who can get near you now without being screened and photographed. If we're ever going to catch this guy, we need you here in London.'

So Marla is planning her return. She no longer feels comfortable in America; it just isn't her home any longer. She listens to people here talking and she wonders if they have any idea just how insular they are. Half of them have never been to the West Coast, let alone Europe, and yet they talk as though the whole world revolves around them. They watch *Masterpiece Theatre* on their big-screen TVs and assume that England is all fog and crinolines. When there is a war somewhere it takes third billing on the news after the local weather report and a story about the new pet at the White House. They have no idea – arrogant, overhyped America, inflated and glitzy with self-importance.

Marla has become anglicized. She has grown to appreciate the minutiae of British life; to embrace the quiet traditions of a country that is so much maligned and yet still revered for its paradoxical qualities of humility and social snobbery. Although the world grows smaller and American culture infiltrates everywhere with Big Macs and Mickey Mouse, there will always be those stalwart traditions of England that amuse, frustrate and delight the Americans: teabreaks and elevenses, queues and double-deckers, pub grub and shandy. Marla now misses it all and resents the fact that somebody is spoiling it for her.

She turns on a lamp and checks her watch. It is just after two, and Mark will be eating his breakfast. Marla picks up the phone and calls him, settling back against a scrunched pillow with her cigarette making smoke spirals in the air. When he answers, he sounds as though he has just woken up. 'Hello, love,' he says, 'I'm just out of the shower.'

'You shouldn't tease me with mental images, I'm four thousand miles away right now and I'm not into phone sex.'

Mark chuckles. 'When are you coming home?'

'I thought I might get the six thirty flight tomorrow evening . . . *this* evening, come to think of it.'

'You want me to pick you up at Heathrow?'

'That would be a gracious gesture but there's no need, I can get a cab.'

'It would be my pleasure. We can drive you home together and then I can show you how to work all this hi-tech equipment we've installed at your place.'

'Don't I get a twenty-four-hour bodyguard? Some guy with tight pants and a big gun in his pocket?'

'Listen, love, this is England you're talking about. The best we can offer you is a bobby with a walkie-talkie.'

Marla smiles through a cloud of smoke. 'You know,

I'm not one for corny lines but I've kinda missed you this week. Do you think I might be getting hooked?'

'It happens all the time,' jokes Mark, 'women throwing themselves at me. I suppose it's all part of the job.'

'I guess I'll just have to accept that about you. Are you *sure* you don't have another woman tucked away somewhere? There has got to be *something* wrong with you – you're worrying me.'

'Well . . . I didn't want to tell you this, but I *do* listen to Radio 4.'

'Oh my God! That's it, then. It's only a matter of time before you'll be admitting to all kinds of degenerate behaviour: *Gardeners' Question Time*, Delia Smith, fly-fishing . . .'

'Not to mention my penchant for spotted dick!'

'Now that's something that no self-respecting Yank will ever put in her mouth.' And for the first time in a while Marla is able to laugh without having to think about it first.

As she puts down the phone, the hotel bedroom suddenly takes on a slightly less sinister appearance and Marla stubs out her second cigarette and prepares herself for another sleepless night.

In the bathroom she shies away from the harsh fluorescent light, preferring to remove her make-up in semi-darkness. She wipes away the grime of New York City with a cotton wool ball and strips down to her underwear, tossing her expensive clothes on to the bathroom floor with total disregard for their pedigree.

Rake thin and stripped of her identity, Marla appears frail, vulnerable even, as she sits on the edge of her bed and stares at herself in the mirrors of the sliding closet doors. Even in this shadowy light she knows that she is looking old, but the realization does not scare her: the older she becomes the less people will expect of her. Preoccupation with vanity is something for the very young and the very shallow, and Marla no longer concerns herself with first impressions. She plays the part when she has to, she wears the clothes and wears the face that they expect of her, but underneath the superficial gloss she knows her own limitations.

She also recognizes her strengths.

Some time later, Marla wakes with a start. She didn't even realize that she had fallen asleep, but as she wakes she remembers what she was just dreaming about. It was a strange dream of wallpaper that was slowly coming unstuck, revealing walls of bare plaster. The paste that she used on it was merely flour and water, so she couldn't get the paper to stick, and the more frantically she tried to keep it all together the more the paper peeled around her.

She has only been asleep for an hour, but the door to her room is wedged open with one of her suitcases and the TV has been turned off, as well as the bedside lamp. Light splays across the carpet from the corridor and Marla is frozen with fear. She literally cannot move.

How did someone get into her room without waking her?

She listens but there is no noise except for the traffic in the street below. Then she sees the open drawers of the dresser, and her clothes strewn across the carpet as though someone has been searching for something in a frantic panic. The closet doors have been slid apart. Her handbag is within reach but she just can't make her arm move – she is paralysed.

Then a couple of hotel staff arrive: a man in some

sort of uniform and another man in a double-breasted suit.

'Is everything OK here, ma'am? We got a call from the people in 602, who said they heard strange noises.' His voice breaks her momentary seizure of fear, and Marla grabs her handbag and reaches inside for her gun.

But it isn't there.

'My gun – they've taken my gun!' she screams. It doesn't even sound like her voice.

'Who? Who's taken your gun?' asks the man in the suit.

'I don't know. Whoever broke into my goddamned room while I was asleep.'

The first man, a hotel porter by the look of it, turns on the light in the bathroom and whispers something to the second guy. They stand together with their backs to Marla, both of them staring at something she cannot see.

'What the hell is it?' Marla leaps out of bed in her bra and panties and pushes the men aside.

Scrawled across her mirror in several shades of broken-up lipstick are the simple words: BABY KILLER!

Marla grabs the lapels of the man in the suit. 'Who's doing this to me? How did they get into my room?'

'The door wasn't forced,' says the porter, looking at the undamaged locks on the inside of Marla's door, 'so it can only have been opened from the inside.'

'That's impossible!' shouts Marla.

'Not necessarily, ma'am. Someone could have been here in your room all the time and you just didn't know it.'

Marla's eyes turn to the sliding mirrored doors of the closet and there between her skirts and her jackets, there is a gap that is just large enough to conceal an intruder. A person who could listen and wait for the right moment.

A person who knows her every move.

And for the first time in her entire life Marla has the distinct feeling that she might even faint.

Fourteen

Children's television is a tricky business. Everyone is on the lookout for something to moan about, something that might be offensive or illustrating the wrong message. If Sooty and Sweep can be condemned for sniffing essential oils in a programme about aromatherapy, then how much innocence remains? These days you just can't be too careful, and on the set of *Pigbeet and Little Pud* tensions are running high.

The problem is the new director.

She has been brought in to inject a little pizzazz to the ailing show. Apparently she is the authority on children's entertainment since her latest Saturday morning show *Mega-Brunch* eclipsed the alternative magazine shows and she went forward to win a BAFTA for outstanding creative contribution.

Kate Buckley is one of those media whizz-kids, a woman with a mission. In her mid-thirties she still dresses as though she is at art college in an attempt to project the street credibility that she constantly promotes. Children to Kate Buckley are merely unformed adults and her credo is simple: catch them young and make them tough. She is not a great believer in baby talk or Beatrix Potter except in the case of the *Teletubbies*, where she is a stoic supporter of Tinky Winky and his subversive attempts to promote homosexuality to the under-fives.

Today she is wearing a Batman T-shirt that is so tight it accentuates her emaciated body to the point of repulsion. Her shoulder blades stick out like the folded wings of a bat and her breasts are squashed boyishly and bralessly against her concave chest. Her skirt is black and narrow and split at her ankles, below which she sports black granny boots with lethal heels and rolled-down football socks. As she paces up and down the studio with her clipboard she reminds Lester of Twizzle – all angular and stick-like. Her hair is dyed very black and she keeps it knotted in several African-looking bumps on her head. Stray hair straggles down her back and gets caught in the confusion of junk jewellery that hangs around her scrawny little neck. In both ears she probably has twenty silver rings, all of them seemingly jammed into one over-extended hole.

'The premise of this particular episode is simple. I don't understand why you are all so baffled by it.' Kate Buckley glares at them all through her Dame Edna glasses and her lips are a thin black line. 'We don't have to actually *mention* substance abuse but I want it to be perfectly clear that when Little Pud experiences a head-rush from the hairspray that Mrs Woggle is using we are getting a message across. Frances, we are not playing this for laughs, I want you to go into a total tailspin when you get a whiff of that stuff. The kids need to know that this is not a good thing.'

Frances, who plays Little Pud, is leaning against part of the set in her padded costume. Lester can see that she isn't happy but what can any of them do? This is a new era and things are changing in the world. Only last week another teenager ran amok through a

California school with a shotgun, and now they're learning about AIDS in junior school.

Everyone involved with the programme is already doubtful about Kate and her radical ideas. She is spending money as though it is going out of fashion, though it was only a couple of months ago that their budget was cut. The new set was designed by a band of art students and everything is made from industrial waste. It looks like the hollowed-out inside of a rubbish tip that has been spray-painted in Day-Glo colours.

There are a host of new characters on the show: animated regulars who pop in and out to offer words of wisdom or to inject a little wacky humour whenever things are getting a little too mundane with the main characters. There is a set of talking dentures called Nash in a drinking glass – Nash has a Brummie accent and moans a lot. There is a huge pink fairy called Plumeria in a beehive wig who flies around on a winch, and a rather pervy-looking gentleman called Mr Goo who has an Elvis hairdo and a bow tie that spins.

Lester is now being upstaged by a cast of thousands, and he isn't happy. They've even changed his costume to make it 'a little less cutesy', and given him a baseball cap with a propeller on the top. He is keeping quiet until all the fuss dies down and then he's going to have a quiet word with the producer of the show. He has already called his agent to see if there's any chance of a different job. He'd even consider going back to the soaps if he could find a challenging character, but these days it's all cheap Aussie stuff. The only show worth considering would be *EastEnders* and auditions for it are notoriously tough. He's not as confident about his acting abilities these days as he used to be, but he is hoping that his appearance at the Oscars next year might rekindle some enthusiasm from the industry.

Marla got back from New York last night and she is in a right old state. Lester hasn't been to see her yet, but according to Julie at the office Marla's on the verge of a nervous breakdown. It seems that Mark fella has taken her under his wing, dragging her off to his house in the country as though he owns her or something. She doesn't even know him, as they've only been going out for a few weeks. Shani aims to head out there tomorrow to see if she can do anything, but Lester doesn't want to come across as the jealous ex-husband so he's keeping out of things for a while. Instead he's sent some flowers but the gesture seems inadequate somehow.

Kate Buckley is now rounding up her dance troupe of oversized toadstools to rehearse their jazz-funk routine, so Lester takes this opportunity to sneak off to the green room for a cup of coffee and a doughnut. He feels deflated. Tina stayed out late again last night with her friends, and Lester can never get to sleep until she's come home, so it was after two before he dropped off. On days like this he could easily jack it all in, jump in the car and drive off somewhere remote where nobody can find him, with no phones, no television, no connection with the world he knows. It isn't as though he has a bad life – hell, there are people much worse off. It's just that everything gets on top of him and he feels as though he is pinned against the floor with the weight of it all. Childhood fame and fortune have curdled around the base of his adulthood and it seems that everything he achieves in life is measured by the enormity of that brief period in his life when he was golden.

He is surprised to find Shani in the green room, involved in an animated conversation with Plumeria the big pink fairy, who is taking a cigarette break with her feet up on a pouffe. Apparently they know each other from working in a repertory theatre company in Southend.

'Oh God, darling, those were the days! Fifty-seven pounds a week and a free bus pass. How did we ever survive?'

'What are you doing here?' asks Lester, bending to offer Shani his cheek.

'Came into have a chat with Dick Robinson about that charity thingy they're organizing for the BBC next month. Something to do with Terry Wogan and spina bifida.'

Lester pours himself some coffee and takes a seat. Outside, in the studio garden, they are burning piles of leaves and the late morning sky is clouded with woodsmoke and lingering mist.

'I just had to get away from Kate for a few minutes. She's driving me up the wall with her bloody enthusiasm.'

'Maureen has just been telling me about it all, darling. It sounds dreadful. Isn't there anything you can do? After all, the show was created around *your* character.'

'They only care about the ratings these days. It gets more like America every day.'

Plumeria the fairy, aka Maureen Bloodworth, stubs out her cigarette and gulps back a mouthful of coffee. 'Well, I'm not complaining. I've been out of work since my stint on *The Vicar of Dibley* and this has been a godsend. I'd better get back before Kate sends out the search party. See you later, Shani. Lovely to see you.'

Shani pinches Lester's cheek affectionately. 'You look peaky, darling, have you been overdoing it again?'

'Tina was out late again last night. That's three times this week.'

'What does she get up to? Surely she isn't still hanging around with those people who make the dirty films?'

'Oh yes, she thinks that's all very glamorous, just because there are a few shabby film producers hanging around and unlimited Asti Spumate. I'm worried about the drugs that some of those girls take. Tina swears that she's not into that scene but I know for a fact that she's smoking dope.'

'Well, as long as it's only dope that she's smoking, darling. I'd be more worried about the people she's hanging around with.'

Lester realizes that Shani does not approve of Tina; she thinks that he undersold himself, although she is too kind to actually say that. Tina refers to Shani as 'Mummy Sha Sha' because she reckons that Shani mollycoddles Lester.

'She gets on my wick!' Tina regularly complains. 'Darling this and darling that – she's a relic. What she needs is a good fuck and then perhaps she'd leave you alone.'

But Lester refuses to be baited. Shani has been a good friend to him over the years and he has a lot to thank her for. Anyway, she is the only remaining person who knew him when he was a star, so she can empathize when he gets a little bit depressed.

'I've been talking to Beatrice about soaps, as I thought I might like to get back into some proper acting instead of this lark.' Lester indicates 'this lark' with a derogatory sweep of his ridiculous Pigbeet costume.

'Darling, are you *sure*? Remember how fed up you were by the time you left *Crossroads*. You said then that you'd had it with soaps.'

'Well, now I've had it with children's entertainment. I need to get my teeth into something more challenging, otherwise I'm going to go mad.'

'You know Jane Graves is looking for boys and girls? They're casting for a new weekly drama – one of those low-budget, late-night things with raunchy storylines and full-frontal nudity. I could have a word.'

'Oh darling, that would be brilliant! I loved that thing she did with John Sessions about the magazine editors.'

'I can't promise anything, darling, but Aurora is great friends with the casting director and I had dinner with Jane and her husband a few weeks ago. Leave it with me.'

Lester is immediately brightened by this news. He knows that when Shani sets her mind to something she can be very persuasive. *Real drama!* Oh, how he would love to get back to something mentally demanding instead of dancing toadstools and talking dentures.

'So, you spoke to Marla?' he says.

'She's a *mess*! Could hardly get a coherent sentence out of her on the phone this morning. I haven't seen her like this since that whole murder fiasco in '81. This recent episode in New York has really shaken her, and when I spoke to Mark Blake he hinted that Marla is dangerously close to a breakdown. He's going to keep her at his place for a while until she calms down. I was intending to go out there tomorrow, but he said it's better if we just let her rest for a while. She's on tablets.' 'I wish I knew *who* was doing this to her,' says Lester. 'It's not as though she has any real enemies. I wonder if it might be something *professional* – something to do with a disgruntled immigrant or somebody she has inadvertently pissed off through work. I can't think of any other reason why this is happening.'

'Marla pretty well covered her tracks after all that dreadful publicity in the '80s and anyway, that's twenty years ago now. The sexual stuff doesn't make sense to me. It has absolutely nothing to do with those other accusations regarding the baby. This freak is obviously a schizo or something. At least it's great that Marla has found Mark Blake. He seems to be a really nice bloke, very down to earth, no pretensions. And what could be better than having a police inspector at your side at a time like this?'

'I suppose so. It doesn't stop me from worrying, though.'

'Oh darling, you're not jealous, are you?'

'Of course not! I stopped being jealous of Marla years ago. It's just that Blake can't be with her twenty-four hours a day. I find it unbelievable that the police still haven't come up with any clues.'

Shani grasps Lester's wrist and squeezes it in silent sympathy.

'*Lester, can we have you back on the set, please!*' It is Kate Buckley calling for him over the speaker.

'Better go.'

'I'll call you about the Jane Graves thingy. Let's do dinner at the weekend.'

153

And Lester returns to the studio, where Kate and her sycophantic sidekick are announcing more script changes – to include a sub-plot involving Pigbeet and a downpour of artificial custard.

Fifteen

There are places that exist in the darkest corners of every big city. If you knew what went on in these places you would probably shudder in horror and disbelief. There are places where humans act like animals, where decency is chewed up and spat out like bubblegum with the flavour sucked out.

When you think about the rats that inhabit the sewers; when you imagine the millions of minuscule insects that reside in your mattress; or contemplate the exchange of thriving bacteria that accompany every kiss, how does it make you feel? Does your skin crawl? Do you rub your hands across your arms and close your eyes with repulsion?

Oh yes, we do live such blind-sighted lives. In our disinfected, Glade-scented, fresh-emulsioned homes we try not to think about the things that go on in the places we cannot see. Let the spiders and the earwigs stay in the attic and the foundations while we dust and hoover our way through life, feeling virtuous and respectable and squeaky clean.

In New York City the rats regularly come out to play. The cockroaches swarm up the U-bends to hatch their eggs amidst the scouring powders and the washing liquid. And in the shadows of the murkiest streets there are places you can go if you are looking for depravation.

For three days Spencer Noble has walked these streets.

For three days and three nights he has stumbled from one hellhole to another, submerging himself in a mire of his own making. Like an alcoholic taking refuge in a swimming pool filled with gin Spencer is drowning in the depths of depravity. He has done things that he never knew were possible in respectable society – twisted, sexual things that sometimes carried him upward on an invisible tide beyond his control. His body is no longer his own, it hangs from his shoulders like a second-hand coat, and it is crushed and torn like the soul that hides within.

He sits in the corner with a Diet Sprite. Above him there is a dim red light turning everything, including Spencer, a ghastly shade of brownish green. The music is turned up loud; it is a local radio programme with continuous rap music and it never stops, it never abates, because in these places there is no night or day, just a constant twenty-four-hour darkness that has no sense of time or season.

He has been eating from vending machines and he doesn't feel too good. Chocolate bars and crisps and fizzy drinks have sickened his stomach. He has not slept for more than a few hours and he is finding it increasingly easy to nap in the most uncomfortable of places. Knees beneath his chin, head resting against a crudely fashioned partition wall, he can sleep like that for quite a while before waking with a jerk and a crick in his neck.

This is what they call a bathhouse. A misnomer for a place that has no running water.

It is where homosexual men come to have anonymous sex. Nobody talks, nobody smiles, they just hang

around the narrow corridors of black-painted brick, and
their teeth shine luminous in the ultraviolet light. There
are cubicles with flimsy locks and tiled floors that are
easy to swill down once a day. These are men from
every walk of life who come to these places because it is
their last resort, the skeleton in their closet that rattles
its bones until they can't sleep at night.

Spencer no longer holds out any hope of salvation
for himself.

For almost a year he has yearned for redemption
from his sins but now he knows that there is no place
for him in heaven, or hell, or even in that nebulous
limbo that hangs somewhere in between. His soul is lost
for ever and he is like a person who knows that death is
lurking at the bottom of the bed. Nothing matters to
him because he has given all of himself away and if he
were to look at himself in a mirror right now he would
not know the person reflected in his eyes. He has been
bitter now for so long that the taste of his own unhap-
piness has become a pill he is forced to swallow.

He still wears his Armani suit with the silk lining,
but his shirt is open to the waist and the tails hang from
beneath his jacket, crumpled as he is himself. He has
the makings of a beard and his lips feel chapped and
rough; his scalp itches and he stinks. Despite his appearance he is still a striking figure and the men who sidle
past him make no pretensions about their interest, but
Spencer is bloated and sick with overindulgence and he
has nothing more to give.

The episode with Taylor in Michaela's bathroom
had been the final straw. The floodgates had swung
open effortlessly with that simple act of acceptance and
the poisons had come pouring out. But what do you do

when you have to accept the truth? How can you go on when your failings are finally revealed? Spencer has lived his life until now as the golden child, the overachiever, the best this and the best that. His life is supposed to be as white and blameless as his monogrammed shirts, as crisp and clean as his laundered bedlinens. The stains that he has created over these last three days will never come out; they are embedded so deeply in his warp and weft that nothing can wash them clean. He did it to spite himself – and felt good. It was like pushing at a wobbly tooth with the tip of his tongue, daring it to fall out, enjoying the exquisite pain. Once he had accepted the fact that there was nothing he could do to save himself, he was almost feverish in his desire to paint himself in the darkest of colours. Flagellation could not have satisfied his hunger for blood any better and even now – with his wounds wide and gaping – he finds pleasure in pain.

He doesn't want to think about Annie.

He can cope with his family and his colleagues but he just can't consider what he has done to Annie. He has used her so selfishly and with such calculated coldness that he cannot forgive himself that one sin above all others. He should have chosen a complete stranger instead of a lifelong friend. He should have chosen a ruthless, brittle beauty who could have used him in equal quantities for her own survival. There can be no excuse for his actions, even though he almost believes that it was Jesus who spoke to him that day, urging him to get married, to turn away from sinful thoughts.

Cut the crap, Spencer! You never believed in Jesus. You never really heard his voice, it was merely your own weakness hiding behind what it believed was an impervious shield. Your prayers were shallow and your aspirations were dishonourable. When you looked at religion you saw nothing but a pious cloak to make you invincible against the imperfections of your sexuality. What a fake! What a con artist! You even fooled yourself for a while.

There are some people who cannot settle for anything less than perfection. They scrub and they scrub at invisible marks on their kitchen work surfaces; they cannot settle if a picture is crooked or a dish is left unwashed. For Spencer, surrounded as he is by the scattered pieces of his broken life, there can be no peace. There is nowhere for him to sit down since he shredded the upholstery and pulled out the stuffing. Nowhere to sleep now that the mattress is torn asunder and the pillows are nothing but feathers. His internal house is no longer in order.

There is a man who has been watching him now for quite some time. Every few minutes he walks past Spencer and allows his foot to scrape past Spencer's shoe, assuming the nonchalance of a thief about to smash through a window. He is now leaning up against a broken pinball machine, staring straight at Spencer with unabashed interest. His hand rests against his thigh while he strokes himself through the fabric of his trousers.

Revulsion is Spencer's initial reaction.

The man is in his early fifties, he is tall and fairly well built but wearing a very obvious toupee which is too luxuriously thick and perfect to be real hair. His shirt is open, all the way down, so that everyone can admire his hairy chest, and he wears too much jewellery – several heavy rings, a bracelet, and two gold chains around his neck. He could well be a '70s sex symbol, a kind of Burt Reynolds lookalike refusing to accept the fact that he is thirty years out of date. Spencer can smell the cheap cologne from here.

He begins to hate this man. He glares at him with contempt, knowing what he wants and loathing him for it. The look of lust can be vile when reflected in the eyes of someone undesirable and Spencer is repulsed.

During the course of the past three days Spencer has shared intimacy with more men than he can now recall. There were young boys, barely eighteen, fresh-faced and smooth-skinned, wearing surfing beads and smelling of fabric conditioner. There were military men, clean-shaven and crew-cut with chiselled muscle and an indifferent attitude. There were older men wearing wedding rings who loosened their ties and worried about creasing their shirts. And then, towards the end of Spencer's odyssey, he grew indifferent and almost perverse in his selection – allowing himself to be defiled by several men at the same time in rooms that contained no light at all.

Hands against his body.

The brush of a stranger's lips against his neck, his cheek, his lips.

This was Spencer's penance for being what he is. Reconciliation came in the form of disgust and so it was necessary for him to debase himself in this way.

This man deserves what he is about to get. The man with the toupee and the tight trousers.

Spencer is ready now and Marla's revolver weighs heavy in his inside pocket.

He knows that the man will follow him. No word has to be spoken here; Spencer just stands up and makes sure that the man is following as he searches for an unlocked booth in one of the darkest corners. Spencer enters the booth and waits. The man comes in after him and locks the door with a self-satisfied smile that turns Spencer's gut.

This man will not be smiling for long.

Spencer unbuckles his own trousers and allows them to fall around his ankles. He pulls down his underpants and lifts the tails of his shirt to reveal his penis – limp and unimpressed by the man and his slobbering lips.

'Suck it,' demands Spencer.

The man crouches down, being careful not to touch the sticky tiled floor, and he lifts Spencer's penis to his mouth. Spencer looks down at the crown of that toupee and he feels no hesitancy as he carefully removes the revolver from the inside of his jacket and clicks open the safety catch.

The situation could not be more perfect. The barrel of the gun is just inches away from the man's head.

The rap music blasts from a speaker, drowning out the noise of sex all around as it groans and thrusts through the rancid darkness of this hellish place.

He is doing this for imperfection. For failure and weakness.

He is doing this for the sake of insufferable torment.

Spencer raises the gun to the roof of his mouth and without hesitation he pulls the trigger.

And nothing happens.

He never imagined that her gun would not be loaded.

The man kneeling at Spencer's feet looks up to see why Spencer is not responding to his expert administrations. When he sees the gun in Spencer's mouth he falls back against the partition wall and begins to scream like a woman, both hands clamped to the sides of his mouth as though he learned technique at an amateur dramatic society.

Spencer drops the gun and yanks up his trousers, fumbling awkwardly with his belt as the screams summon attention to the booth in which they stand.

'It's OK, it's OK!' shouts Spencer as he unbolts the door and pushes his way past the small crowd gathered outside in the narrow passageway. Bright fluorescent lights flicker above, and suddenly the whole seedy scene is flooded with garish white light that probably scares the hell out of every married man who is presently living out a fantasy with someone infinitely hairier than his wife. Security men are on their way but Spencer does not pause to observe the mayhem he has caused. He slips out through the building's insignificant entrance and hurries down the alley towards the bright lights of the main street.

Sixteen

Oak Hollow is the name of the house where Spencer grew up. It is considered posh by some people in Chesterfield, but it is really a rather modest establishment compared to some of the houses Annie has seen in London. The house was built in the '30s, but the style is Tudor.

Mock Tudor.

Like the mock roast pork that Annie made in domestic science class from sausage meat and apple sauce. Like mock turtle soup in the days when such a thing was thought sophisticated. You don't see it on the menu these days: it went out of fashion with beef Wellington and steak Diane.

Oak Hollow stands back from the main road and it has little windows in the roof. A sprinkling of early snow has turned the gravel driveway partially white, as though dusted with the sugar that bakers put on the top of Victoria sponge cakes. It isn't particularly cold, though: just the elbow of winter testing the water before the plunge.

Spencer's mother Blanche is holding up well, considering the strain. She wears a very smart little two-piece from Jaeger, with epaulettes and a fur collar. Her husband Dennis wears his councilman's suit – dark navy with the trousers too long so that they bunch over his highly polished brogues. Still a handsome man, he looks less polished than his shoes today.

People love to gossip, especially when it concerns people from a different class. The Nobles are a respected family in these parts, always have been, and Spencer is their golden boy. What a shock to hear that he has gone missing in New York – such a wicked, dangerous city. It doesn't bear thinking about . . .

Well, maybe we *can* dwell on it just for a while. Let's turn our faces to the corner and help ourselves to another portion of delicious wickedness.

Frightening.

He just ran off somewhere and nobody has seen him for over a week now. The police in New York are looking for anyone who might have spotted him but so far they've come up with nothing more than a handful of unsubstantiated sightings. There were dirty little rumours that he was seen in a male strip joint, but nobody has confirmed this yet and, anyway, what would Spencer Noble be doing in a horrible place like that? What a disgusting thing to contemplate in this nice house that smells of furniture polish.

Annie can barely register the words that fall around her as she sits by the fireplace with a glass of Bristol Cream and a small plate loaded with vol-au-vents that were recently defrosted in the Nobles' microwave. People feel obliged to offer her friendly consolation. They are awkward and they mutter things under their breath, as though rehearsing the words of a play. Nobody really knows what to say to her, because nobody understands what she is feeling. Not only has her husband gone missing but also the rumours concerning Spencer's whereabouts are weighing heavily on her mind. The few statements that the New York police have, so far, merely raise the suspicion that he might have been in places that Annie can only begin to imagine. *Sex places.* Places where men go to have sex with other men. Now it all begins to make sense, and Annie can work out for herself why Spencer Noble, athlete and demigod, married fat Annie Stamper when he could have had anyone else he wanted.

'Are you all right, love?' whispers Annie's dad as he bends from behind the wing chair with sherry on his breath.

She nods, but she doesn't really know if she feels all right or not. Mr and Mrs Noble have called everyone together today because there is a possibility that Spencer might be lying murdered somewhere. He might never come back. How should she be feeling? She's not lost her appetite; in fact she's been stuffing herself continually since the day they called her to say that Spencer had gone missing. All kinds of food – she has been indiscriminate in her choice of fare. Annie eats and eats but the hunger remains. This morning she had a fry-up with baked beans and kidneys, and still had room for two pieces of her mum's chocolate layer cake and a packet of Boasters.

Annie wishes that Betsy could be here too, but Betsy's in hospital with tubes in her arm, and they can't move her until she regains a little strength. She can't keep anything down apparently, even though the psychologist reckons it's all mental. The human brain can do funny things to a person and if you don't watch out you can acquire all kinds of symptoms just because you're a bit fed up with things.

Stress!

Everybody seems to have stress these days – even those little kiddies who have to take tablets to calm them down. They say the cause is in the sweeties they eat – too much sugar and additives – but Annie herself never had a problem with hyperactivity when she was a kid, and when your mum works in the Trebor factory there's never any shortage of things to ruin your teeth with.

Poor Betsy can't even suck on a Polo without retching. Annie tried to coax her with one yesterday but as soon as she had it in her mouth she had to spit it out again, with her eyes watering as though she was going to be sick.

'I just can't,' she said as she wrapped up the mint in a Kleenex.

'I don't really understand how you can't eat if it's just your brain that's telling you not to. Can't you just stuff your face with food and tell your brain to sod off?'

'I've tried that, Annie love. I know it seems daft but I just can't keep anything down, even though I know that I'm not physically sick. The shrink has talked and talked to me about it but it doesn't seem to make any difference.'

'But you'll die if you don't eat something!'

And Betsy just smiled at Annie and squeezed her hand resting on the hospital sheet. 'I'm not going to die, you daft ha'peth. I'll be out of here by next week and we'll be down the Fiesta knocking back Bacardi and Cokes just like the old days.'

They talked about Spencer. Betsy said that she would never in a million years have guessed that he was 'that way inclined', but she feels angry that he has used Annie in such a callous way.

'He should have told you before you got married.

He should have asked you if it was all right, instead of pretending that he loved you.'

'He *does* love me,' insisted Annie, still clinging on to the crumbling edge of her rapidly sinking illusions.

'But he isn't *in* love with you, Annie. There's a big difference, you know. He loves you as a friend but that's about as far as it goes with Spencer. If he'd told you that he was . . . *that way* before he asked you to marry him, do you think you'd still have gone through with it?'

'Probably,' replied Annie. 'It's not as though anyone else was going to ask me, and we could at least have been friends, I suppose. I can take or leave the sex.'

'You say that now but how would you have felt when he wanted to go off with a fella? Remember how hard it was for Tiffany when whatshisname turned gay in *EastEnders*.'

'That was different, Betsy. That was just the telly and Tiffany's brother was already gay so she was used to that kind of thing. Anyway, she married Grant a few weeks later so it hardly mattered, did it?'

'Funny, isn't it, when you think about it?'

'What is?' asked Annie, helping herself to some of Betsy's untouched Angel Delight.

'You know . . . thinking about Spencer with another bloke. I wonder what they do? I mean I know what they *do*, but it's just not natural, is it?'

'They can do a lot more than lesbians can. I've never understood lesbians.'

'I think that's more to do with companionship than actual sex. Men are just more sexual about things, aren't they? If they don't get their end away every couple of days, they're in the toilet with the door locked for half an hour at a time.' And they had a good laugh about that. Betsy weighing five stone two pounds and Annie stuffing her face with fruit pastilles.

Spencer's younger sister Jasmine is swanning around the Nobles' house like a primadonna. She is wearing an unsuitably tight dress that constricts the way she moves across the room. She has not spoken to Annie all morning but her spiteful glances are enough to reassure Annie that Jasmine blames her for everything. She earlier heard Jasmine whispering in the kitchen, making insinuations that it was probably Annie who turned Spencer gay. 'If she tried losing a few hundred pounds he might have been able to get it up for her.'

Annie wonders if that might be true. She had made all those promises to lose some weight once they were married, and yet she had managed to put on several pounds instead. With Spencer away on business so much, she had found it difficult to fill her free time with anything but cravings for food. When she thinks about it now, Spencer must have been repulsed by her – how could he not be? He is such a fantastic-looking bloke – everybody says so – and what on earth would he see in a fat blob like Annie? Perhaps it was the thought of having sex with her that sent him over the edge. Perhaps he thought that sex with blokes wasn't really cheating on their marriage. Maybe he did it for Annie's sake, so that she wouldn't feel too rejected.

Annie might have expected to hear from Marla, seeing as how she was the last person to have seen Spencer, but she's still hiding away in the country with that police inspector, apparently not holding up too well under the strain. She did send a massive bunch of pink and yellow flowers, but Annie knew from the unflattering choice of colours that Marla had nothing to do with their selection. It was probably her secretary Julie who ordered them, on the company account.

'And how are you holding up, Annie love? Such a long time since I've seen you.'

It is Mr Sparkle the funeral director: an inappropriate guest at this particular gathering, but he is courting Jasmine so he thinks he is already one of the family. Frank Sparkle took over the family funeral business when his father passed away with fluid on the lungs three years ago. Annie went to school with Frank but, just like David Ratchet who became a GP, she only refers to him by his surname now that he's taken up the profession. He has inherited the dour, pale-faced countenance of his family: a suitable face for such a grim vocation. There is always a whiff of formaldehyde lurking behind the lapels of his dark grey suit, and he wears his hair in an old-fashioned style that requires a lot of Brylcreem to keep it in place.

'I must say that Spencer's parents are holding up remarkably well under the circumstances. I cannot begin to wonder how they must have felt when they found out about Spencer and his . . . shall we say . . . little proclivities.' Frank Sparkle rolls the words around the inside of his mouth as though they are juicy morsels of tender meat. He is salivating and his lips are wet with the flavour of turpitude. Annie is rather disturbed by this obvious display of prurient indulgence. 'Such an athlete,' simpers Frank, 'always so good on the field and yet a scholar too. Who would have believed that such a perfect specimen would seek out the company of his own sex when he had every girl in the sixth form falling at his feet?' Frank is practically rubbing his hands together.

Annie is saved from further insult by Blanche Noble, Spencer's mother. She would like Annie to join them in the dining room for a few minutes.

'Excuse me, Mr Sparkle,' says Annie, handing the funeral director her plate of food as though he is a waiter. He smiles but there is no humour behind his expression. He should have worn braces as a child, then perhaps he could have smiled with more confidence as an adult.

In the formal dining room the walls are papered with deep-red damask and the curtains are the tied-back kind that come from Laura Ashley. Mr Noble is already seated at the far end of the mahogany table with a man Annie doesn't know, but he's wearing a tie so she assumes he must be somebody important. Jasmine is here too, leaning up against the sideboard, her pinched little face contorted with displeasure upon seeing Annie.

'Take a seat, dear,' says Mrs Noble as she offers Annie one of the tall-backed flamestitch chairs.

'Annie, this is Jim Dunne. He's our family lawyer. As you know we've had some difficulty locating Spencer's papers but Jim brought everything up from London this morning, once they'd made sure that everything was in order.'

Annie smiles at Mr Dunne. He has a friendly face – a moustache always softens a man's face – and his is thick and nicely shaped.

'If Spencer is dead and he's left everything to *her*, I'm not interested in hanging around for the party,' says Jasmine, indicating Annie with a thrust of her pointy little chin.

'Jasmine, please!' admonishes Mrs Noble, placing a gentle hand over the back of Annie's.

'That's enough, Jasmine,' warns Mr Noble with a stern frown across the width of the room.

'Actually, Jasmine, if your brother were to have died, then his will is all very simple and straightforward,' says Mr Dunne, shuffling his papers and referring to one single sheet which he holds up to the light. 'Spencer has left everything to a certain William James Clarke who currently resides in north London.'

Puzzled looks all around.

'Spencer has placed most of his assets in a trust fund for Mr Clarke and the remainder of his estate is bequeathed to the boy's mother, a Mrs Margaret Clarke, until such time that he is of age to manage his own affairs.'

'I don't even know these people, Jim. Who are they?' asks Mr Noble, glancing nervously at the lawyer.

'Mrs Clarke is a friend of Spencer's from university, and young William is . . .' Jim Dunne coughs politely at this point and looks directly at each of the family as he concludes his statement, '. . . Spencer's son.'

'Oh dear Lord!' wails Mrs Noble as her hand flies instinctively to clutch at her pearls.

'You've got to be joking!' snorts haughty Jasmine, shooting forward to grab the paper from Mr Dunne's hand.

There is a distinct flurry of emotions in the room with the red wallpaper and the tied-back curtains: an eddy in the atmosphere that stirs the air and makes everyone uncomfortable.

Poor Annie, sitting silently in her tall-backed flame-stitch chair, begins to wonder if she ever really knew Spencer at all.

Seventeen

In a recent survey, 49 per cent of men interviewed said that the one part of their body they would most like to change would be the size of their penis. Baldness and love handles came in close behind.

Billy Clarke: eighteen years old, six feet two inches in his bare feet, with a full head of dark, naturally wavy hair and a washboard stomach, has what every man in that survey wishes they could possess.

He isn't quite sure where the measuring should start but holding a school ruler against his enviable penis at a conservative starting point he measures 22cm, which in dick-measuring size adds up to over eight and a half inches. And it isn't one of those skinny jobs either! When Billy drops his pants in the school locker room, penis envy practically stiffens the air with audible admiration.

He has quite a reputation in the upper sixth and it has nothing to do with his academic virtuosity. He is head boy, captain of the school gymnastic team, and pin-up idol of practically the entire female quotient of Stanhope Comprehensive. Billy Clarke has inherited all of his father's good looks, charm and charisma, with little of his innate intelligence and scholastic prowess. Maybe if Spencer Noble had spent more time with his son he might have instilled in him a little more dedication to study.

It is the last week of school before term breaks up for Christmas. They are allowed to come in without uniform on the day of their social in the assembly hall, and there is always great excitement for the younger pupils who rarely get to see their friends in normal clothing. Of course the upper sixth eschews the childish idea of an assembly hall social and have their own arrangements to join some of the less dilapidated teachers at a West End nightclub at the end of term. That is one of the privileges of having stayed on at school for the extra two years. That and having a private common room where they are allowed to smoke and play music.

Billy has a meeting today with Miss Joyce, his English teacher. It is late afternoon so they are at her little semi on the new Bovis housing estate. She's got the fire on and the curtains drawn. Somebody next door is practising a trumpet.

'You're probably unfamiliar with D.H. Lawrence, Billy, as we have not been able to cover his work in school due to the rather explicit nature of his novels. He is known for his frequently misunderstood but basically idealistic ideas about sexual relations, and for his interest in primitive religions and nature mysticism.'

Well, that mouthful is enough to turn Billy off for a start! Whoever this D.H. Lawrence bloke is, Billy knows the kind of crap he probably writes. Too many words, too much thinking about things and not enough action. How come every writer they have to do at school writes stuff like that? Stephen King sells a lot more books than they ever do, so why can't they study something like that for a change?

Miss Joyce is sitting in her wicker chair, with a cup of tea and a biscuit perched in her saucer, waiting to be

173

nibbled. Billy has already wolfed down three chocolate digestives and a couple of those pink wafer things that get stuck to the roof of your mouth. But he didn't come here for a lecture on twentieth-century English literature.

'I am sure you have heard of *Lady Chatterley's Lover*. It was banned as obscene when it was written in 1928, and was unavailable to read until that ban was lifted in the '60s.'

'Banned?' questions Billy through a mouthful of pink wafer. 'So it was porno then?'

'It had frank language, yes, and some rather detailed descriptions of lovemaking which at the time were shocking and vulgar. He used terminology that was only ever spoken in private, and probably never at all in respectable households.'

'So words like "fuck" and "cunt"?'

Miss Joyce flinches slightly at the harshness of those words; they soil the soft pretty colours of her sitting room and offend her sensibilities as a romantic.

'Yes, words like that, Billy. I know it may appear rather trivial to you now, but you have to remember that England was a very civilized place in the 1920s. Well, at least, for the *upper* classes – there will always be a working class for whom foul language is less of an issue.'

'So what's your point, miss?' Billy shifts slightly in the chair that is too small for him. His legs stick out across the nylon blend carpet, and he is still wearing his school blazer with his tie slightly loosened at the neck. Miss Joyce has placed his overcoat in her hall cupboard, on a silk-wrapped hanger that smells of pot-pourri.

'Well, I thought that could be our "theme" for today. You know how I like to attach literary connotations to our meetings, and we haven't done Lawrence yet. He is an obvious choice but not, I thought, an author with whom we should become acquainted until we knew each other better.'

Miss Joyce looks quite pretty in this light. She has short blonde hair that has streaks in it, and her earrings are small beaded things that dangle when she moves her head. All the boys at school are lusting after her since she wore a rather short tennis skirt on sports day, displaying more flesh than she probably realized when she crossed her legs up on the judges' podium.

'You would make a marvellous Mellors, Billy. He was the gamekeeper: a big, masculine, working-class man who entranced Lady Chatterley with his overt sexuality.'

'So he was a bit of a stud then, yeah?' smiles Billy, beginning to twig on.

'Oh yes, he was very attractive but in an unassumed, earthy kind of way. He didn't really know how sexually attractive he was – that was his appeal.'

'So this Mellors bloke has sex with Lady Chatterley? How *come*, if she's such a lady? I thought people from different classes didn't mix in those days?'

'Oh they didn't, Billy. That's what made the book so shocking. Lady Chatterley was married to an aristocratic gentleman, but he was crippled and so they never had sexual relations.'

'So this lady was pretty randy, then? She was probably ready for a good going over and the gamekeeper just came in handy.'

'Something like that. Anyway, I thought we could start with one of my favourite scenes where Constance – Lady Chatterley – is taking a walk through the grounds when she accidentally catches Mellors washing himself outside his little house in the woods.'

'I wondered what the bucket of soapy water was for,' smiles Billy, indicating the red washing-up bowl sitting by the fireplace, with a pink towel and a fresh bar of Imperial Leather.

'Why don't you take off your clothes and I'll go upstairs and change into something more suitable,' says Miss Joyce the English teacher, carefully placing her unfinished tea on the little wicker side table.

That's more like it! Let's get down to the nitty-gritty and forget all this literary rubbish. As much as she likes to tart up these afternoons with fancy language, all Miss Joyce really wants is a good shag.

Billy whips off his clothes and flings them over the back of the sofa. He's already got a hard-on and he plays with it as he walks slowly around the small room investigating the framed family photos and the little knick-knacks on the mantelpiece.

Miss Joyce comes downstairs with a duvet cover wrapped around her waist and a couple of chiffon scarves covering her bare boobs. 'This will have to do,' she says as she enters the room. 'It's the closest I could come to an Edwardian gown so you will have to use your imagination.'

'It's not going to stay on for long,' leers Billy, slapping the underside of his erection with an open palm.

'I'm hidden in the trees,' says Miss Joyce as she

ducks behind a rubber plant. 'You have to wash yourself and I'm watching. Very slowly, Billy, and *all over*, not just your face.'

Billy gets the gist. He crouches over the washing-up bowl and lathers up his balls with the soap. He can see her peeping out through the sparse leaves of the plant, but he pretends not to notice. The trumpet player next door has reached a discordant fever pitch with his scales.

'Show me your bottom, Billy. I want to see you washing your bottom.'

Billy obliges. The soap slips up and down between his legs and he knows how good he looks. He likes to be naked like this, showing off, letting someone appreciate all the hard work he puts in at the gym. He soaps across his chest, up between his pectorals and around his nipples.

'What's that buzzing sound?' he asks, looking over at Miss Joyce who appears to be clinging on to the rubber plant for dear life, with the duvet cover hitched up around her waist.

'Nothing,' she croaks. 'Lady Chatterley is exploring her own sexuality while she watches Mellors take his bath.'

'Well, Mellors is nice and clean now and it's about time Lady Chatterley stopped playing with herself and came over to the house in the woods for a bit of rough.'

Billy dries himself off with the towel and Miss Joyce dumps her vibrator unceremoniously behind the clothes horse and tears off her scarves to reveal her lovely little tits, all pert and firm and ready to be sucked.

'Please respect me, Mellors. I am a lady,' whispers

Miss Joyce hoarsely as Billy pushes her back over the sofa and lunges down at her nipples with his mouth salivating. She is petite and her body feels frail in his huge arms as he lifts her up and places her on the carpet so that he can get a better grip.

'And I'm a country gamekeeper and I have no manners, so stop whining and open your legs!'

Lady Chatterley is losing some of her demeanour now and the words that are coming out of her refined little mouth are hardly suitable for a woman of class and sophistication. This is what sex with an older woman is like. And this is why Billy comes here once a week. No restrictions, no stupid girlie concerns about getting pregnant or a bad reputation. He holds Miss Joyce as wide as he can get her and buries his face between her legs, burrowing deeply with the tip of his tongue so that her pelvis rises up to meet each thrust.

'So good, so good . . .' sobs Miss Joyce, clinging to the leg of the sideboard with knuckles white and eyes clenched shut.

He knows when she is close. He can almost feel the tension mounting as her breathing becomes less deep and her cries subside to a soft gasping of disbelief.

Billy knows when to pull his mouth away.

'Get the doughnut!' yells Miss Joyce, pointing frantically at the dog's rubber toy which is just within reach, by the draught excluder.

This is the only way Billy can fuck her. He's too big for her, you see, and it hurts if he thrusts too hard, so they have devised this little procedure where he bungs the rubber doughnut over his dick and he can pound away to his heart's content without making Miss Joyce sore for three days afterwards.

Unfortunately the only drawback to this novel and inspirational appliance is the built-in squeak.

'Fill me up, Billy!' yells Miss Joyce, eyes rolling back into her head as she grabs his arse and pulls at him with every thrust.

Squeak, squeak, squeak goes the rubber doughnut.

The dog begins barking at the kitchen door.

Thank God Billy had a wank in the toilets before he came over this afternoon, otherwise he'd have come by now, and Miss Joyce is still rising to the occasion beneath him.

'Just a bit further, Billy. Just a bit further . . .'

Squeak, squeak, squeak . . .

The dog is throwing herself against the kitchen door in a frantic attempt to break free and join in the fun and games.

'Oh, oh . . . this is it, this is it . . .' and Miss Joyce goes stiff all over. She stops breathing. She is completely immobile and her fists clench the pile of the carpet.

Billy can't hold it any longer. When she comes like this his cock is squeezed by a vice-like muscular grip which finishes him off immediately. His elbows are trembling as he attempts to remain aloft but the spasms are so violent that he has to collapse against Miss Joyce, who is now writhing and sobbing beneath him.

The kitchen door suddenly bursts open and Villette, Miss Joyce's overenthusiastic mongrel, launches herself on the unsuspecting couple.

'Fuck!' yells Billy, rolling across the carpet. 'She's after the fucking doughnut!'

And the dog's bite barely misses a prominent vein as she sinks her teeth into the rubber ring that sits snugly around the base of Billy's rapidly deflating penis.

Eighteen

'Come on in and have a gander at me new settee.' Treez from number 6 stands in the doorway of her flat, wearing something skimpy from Littlewood's catalogue. She holds her door open and smiles at Marla expectantly.

Poor Marla! She's only just got back from her stay in the country with Mark, and she's hardly in the mood for polite conversation with a neighbour she doesn't know. 'I'm in a bit of a hurry . . .'

'Come on in. You've got time for a quick drink.' The diamond in Treez's front tooth catches the light and sparkles between scarlet lips still sticky with licked-off lipgloss.

The flat is smaller than Marla's but it is still a bit surprising that a woman like Treez can afford such a place. None of the units was cheaper than £220,000 and she's got two bedrooms, and a balcony with double glazing.

'It came this after – two yobbos, thick as two short planks, crashing into me Chinese screen and denting the corner of the frigging wall. I demanded compensation but they just stood there with their mouths open like a pair of bleeding goldfish. I would have thought better of Selfridges but there you go.'

Marla follows Treez into her living room. Table

lamps create pools of intimate light without really illuminating the room. The wallpaper is gold foil with some kind of oriental pattern embossed on the surface. The carpet is spongy and dark red, so that the feet of the furniture sink into it like a viscid puddle of blood. Lots of tables, lots of lamps and the ceiling is covered with pleated fabric.

'Oh, my tented ceiling . . .' says Treez, noticing Marla's stare. 'It needs ripping down but it cost me an arm and a leg, and the fella who did it for me is selling kebabs in Athens now. It's a fucking dust trap and my hoover attachments won't reach, so I'm up there with a feather duster twice a week trying to dislodge the spiders.'

'It's very exotic,' says Marla, thinking of a million excuses to get out of here without offending.

'Fashioned after a Turkish tent or something similar. We copied it from a photo in *World of Interiors* magazine – one that was left behind in the doctor's surgery. What do you think of this?' Treez presents her newest piece of furniture with a theatrical flourish which threatens to dislodge one of her dangerously loose bosoms.

'Wow!' exclaims Marla, stepping back to get a better look at the monstrosity.

'Four months I've been waiting for that to come. They told me six weeks, and it's been four fucking months. If I'd have known it would take so long I'd have gone to Court's and got one delivered off the shop floor. Mind you, this is an original. You won't see many of these knocking around.'

Marla is relieved to hear that.

'Have a sit in it. Come on, it's bloody brilliant. I'm

going to be here all night with my feet up and the fire on. I'll be like Lady Muck.'

Marla takes a seat on the edge of the surprisingly soft cushions. She can't avoid being pulled back into the sofa because of the awkward slant of its body. She has to admit that it *is* comfortable, despite the fact that it is hideous. 'Quite remarkable,' she says.

'Well, I've had a pig of a day, so I'm going to watch that film with Clint Eastwood tonight and treat myself to a couple tequila slammers. Why don't you stop and we'll have a girl's night in? I can call out for a pizza.'

'Oh, no thank you,' splutters Marla, desperately attempting to extricate herself from the cushions of Treez's sofa. 'I've only just come back from a few days away and I have got a lot to catch up on.'

'Yes, I had a word with that boyfriend of yours. He's fucking gorgeous – where'd you dig him up? He showed me the video stuff they've put in your place and told me all about the trouble you've been having. I *can* sympathize, actually, because there was a time, a few years back, when I was being stalked by a chap. He apprehended me outside the chippy one night with his dick hanging out of his trousers wanting to spunk on my chips. I wouldn't have minded but he couldn't even get the fucking thing hard. He just stood there waggling it like a bait worm so I told him to sod off and then he started following me. For about a week he was always there, loitering with intent at the bus stop or outside the tube station. In the end I called the cops on him and he gave it up as a bad job.'

Marla is out of the sofa. A cuckoo clock begins its assault on the hour from somewhere behind the partition wall that is covered with framed prints of Chinese people having sex in pagodas. 'I wish whoever is hounding me would give up so easily. The police don't even have a clue who it might be, but he's growing increasingly clever. Seems to know my every move.'

'Well, I'm only across the hall if you need me, sweetheart. You can knock on my door any time of night or day. I'm usually up half the night, watching the cable. The doctor's given me tablets, but they're about as much use as a condom in a nunnery.'

'Thanks. And your sofa is really quite lovely.'

'Smashing, isn't it? I'm dead chuffed, even though it took so long to *come*.' Treez breaks out into something close to a laugh. 'And there's a mucky joke hidden in *that* statement somewhere!'

'Goodnight, Treez, and thanks again.'

Marla escapes without turning back and she hears Treez locking her apartment door from the inside. So maybe the woman's not as hard as she makes out. Marla knows from experience that sometimes the toughest people are the ones who fall hardest when the enamel starts to chip.

Darkness greets her. And a neglected smell despite the floor polish.

It's strange to be home again. Like opening the door on a person she used to be. Staying with Mark made her feel safe and protected, and it frightens her to realize that. Marla has never before had any requirement for safety or protection in her life but now she craves it.

Pathetic. Shoulders back. Don't let them get you down.

The phone is ringing. She switches on the lights as she passes through the living room, and sits on the arm of the sofa as she takes the call.

It is Mark, of course.

183

'Everything all right?' he asks.

'I guess. But I only just walked in. Was apprehended by my wanton neighbour, Treez. She had me in to take a look at her damned sofa. It is momentously heinous.'

'You need to read the instructions for that new alarm system. I left notes about it on the hall table. I didn't set the system because it might have thrown you into a panic.'

'I'm already in a panic.'

'You want me to come over? I could be there in an hour, you know.'

'Nah, I'm just being ditzy. Christ, I'd forgotten how impersonal this place is. It's more like a suite at the Holiday Inn than someone's home. I need a decorator in.'

'Don't forget those videos are recording you twenty-four hours a day. The only privacy you can get is in the bathroom, so if you decide to dance naked around the bedroom just remember those tapes might come back to haunt you one day.'

'Honey, the sight of me dancing naked at this point in my life is hardly likely to cause anything but nausea, but I'm glad you kept the john camera-free, don't like the idea of someone watching me take a dump.'

'The panic button is by the bed. Did you notice the extra security down in the lobby? We've put one of our guys down there temporarily, just to make you feel safer.'

'Yeah, Scabby George is down there showing him Polaroids of his wife's ass. He's so gross.'

'All right then, I'll say goodnight. I've got a pile of papers on my desk that I should tackle. I'll call you before I leave.'

'Sure thing.'

'And Marla?'

'Yeah?'

'You are *really* special to me. You know that, don't you?'

'Yeah, I know that.' And Marla puts down the phone and smiles to herself in the plate-glass mirrors. She had to come back to London: without Spencer the office is in disarray and her clients are leaving distraught messages. The thought of work is comforting and she is looking forward to going in tomorrow to bury herself in something other than self-doubt. Let the bastard show up tonight. Let the cameras catch him breaking and entering, so that she can have some peace. She can't seem to remember what it was like before all of this started to happen. She can't remember a time when she could wake up in the morning without wondering what new atrocity she'll find.

There are flowers in the kitchen. There are flowers in the bedroom; people have been very kind. Hetty has obviously been round the place with the vacuum, and there is milk in the fridge along with Marla's favourite bagels and a box of Godiva chocolates from somebody called Mehmet. Probably a client.

The phone rings again.

'It's me, darling. I'm outside in my car. I've got Aurora with me and a gallon of Hagen Daz. Can we come in?' It is Shani, come to make sure that Marla isn't feeling lonely. The policeman brings them up to Marla's flat. Shani throws Marla a funny look when she walks in – a wink and a smile as if to say 'He's a bit of all right'. Aurora is wearing a tall hat made from astrakhan wool and she looks like a Russian spy. No wonder the policeman came up with them.

'I hope you haven't eaten yet, darling. We stopped at Harrods food hall on the way and grabbed anything that was left.' Shani holds up the carrier bags. 'Liver pate, smoked salmon quiche, and some gorgeous olive bread.'

Aurora drops her coat over the back of a chair and throws herself into the sofa. 'I *told* her to get the grilled aubergine, but she was making a scene in the middle of the delicatessen so I left her to it.'

'Don't listen to her, darling' – kiss kiss – 'she's grumpy because Didier is in Paris without her. I told her to get the Eurostar this evening but she'd rather play the martyr and make my life miserable, so we're stuck with her, I'm afraid.'

'I'm not going to Paris on the *train*. Imagine the kind of people who use that thing. No, if he won't pay for me to fly club on BA, he can do without me.'

'Come on, Marla darling, let's leave her here to wallow in self-pity while we fix ourselves a Martini and organize this food.'

And so the evening progresses.

'I got Lester an audition for the new Jane Graves drama, you know. I think it's tomorrow actually. He's very excited.'

'They want him to show his willy, apparently,' says Aurora, finishing off the last piece of quiche.

'Lester?' laughs Marla, lighting up a cigarette. 'They want him to show his dick on national television?'

'Oh, don't listen to Aurora. She's just being catty. There *will* be some nudity, but we don't know whether it will involve Lester or not. Anyway, it'll be good exposure for him if he gets the part.'

'Or just good exposure for his *part* if he has to drop his pants!' and Marla gives a dragon's laugh, with her mouth wide open and smoke blowing out of her nose.

'Well, it's nice seeing you laugh again, darling,' says Shani, squeezing Marla's elbow. 'I'll go and get the ice cream.'

As Shani goes to the kitchen, Marla inhales deeply and observes Aurora. The carpet is now littered with open boxes and plates from their impromptu picnic. Marla feels terrific; energized, even. It might have something to do with the vodka Martinis that Shani made, or it might just be the fact that she is home without feeling afraid.

'That'll be Mark checking up on me,' she says when the phone rings.

'Hello, babe, it's me.'

'Oh, hi, Lester, we were just talking about you.'

'Who was?'

'I've got Shani and Aurora here.'

'Did she tell you about my audition tomorrow? I'm shitting bricks.'

'Aw c'mon, Less, I thought you were a pro? Where's all that confidence you used to have when I first knew you?'

'You are talking to a bloke who has spent the last five years of his life dressed as a purple pig!'

Marla removes the phone from her ear once she hears Shani scream. Aurora's head pops up from behind the sofa, and Marla drops the receiver and dashes through to the kitchen.

Shani is standing at the sink with her back pressed up against the draining board. The ice cream is already served up in three glass dishes, but she is staring at the opened box of Godiva chocolates sitting on the granite work surface.

'Are you trying to give me a heart attack?' asks Marla.

'The chocolates . . .' says Shani, pointing at the open box.

'What about the chocolates?'

'It's disgusting. Look.'

And Marla, rolling her eyes in mock annoyance, crosses the kitchen to see what Shani is talking about.

The box does not contain chocolates.

Staring up from a wad of tissue paper is the severed head of a cat.

'Jesus Christ! When is this going to stop?' screams Marla, and she knocks the box sideways with a violent swing of her fist.

'I don't understand,' says Shani. 'What is the significance?'

'It's some sick bastard's idea of a joke. He is probably jacking himself off right now, just *thinking* about this.'

'Aurora, call down to the security chap. Tell him to come up here straight away.'

'Not much point in doing that, is there?' says Marla. 'I can't get away from this. There's nowhere left for me to hide.' And Marla lurches towards Shani, clinging to her friend as though she might somehow help her remain afloat.

Nineteen

The new drama show is called *Weird Anatomy* and the character that Lester is auditioning for is a plastic surgeon called Jonathon Jons, who basically shags his way through the entire female cast over the course of the ten-week serialization. The way Jane Graves described the role to him was a kind of Frank Finlay character, as portrayed in *Bouquet of Barbed Wire* in the late '70s. Lester went out and bought the entire series on video to see what she was talking about and was surprised at just how progressive that show was, for its vintage.

He has already learned the lines – driving Tina up the wall with his meticulously repetitive execution of every word.

'Can't you go and do that in the bedroom, Less? I'm trying to watch *Emmerdale*, but I can't hear a thing with you droning on.'

It is imperative that Lester gets this part. He is desperate to break free from children's television and eager to prove himself as a serious player. They aren't paying much, but if the show is a success he will be in demand again and they might even make another series. Since she made *Team Players*, Jane Graves has been everyone's darling, so the BBC are investing a considerable amount on this new one. It is already slated for the spring season and the hype has been enormous in the trade press.

There are probably fifty actors in the waiting room. A middle-aged man wearing a stripy tank top and a nicotine patch is shuffling papers at a makeshift desk, and he doesn't look happy. When Lester approaches him to give his name, the man snatches up a box of Silk Cut and runs off to the toilet without so much as an acknowledgement.

'He's been like that all morning, love,' says a woman with a fake beauty spot. 'Up and down to the loo, and coming back reeking of smoke.'

'How long's the wait?' asks Lester.

'Well, I've been here since nine and they've been faffing around with the appointments, so now apparently I'm not scheduled to go in until two. I would have popped out for a quick sarnie if I'd only known but now I'm stuck.'

Lester takes a spare seat between two young actresses and a fella with a fake tan and a T-shirt that illustrates every ripple in his washboard stomach. The two young women are talking too loudly, as actresses tend to do, and Lester cannot help but listen to snippets of their inane conversation.

'No way, Chloe! That stuff's for your bum; I'm not putting it round *my* eyes – puffiness or no puffiness!'

'Well, it worked for me after Alan went off with that tart from Crabtree & Evelyn. I had a shoot the next morning and I looked like shit.'

'Talking about *her* . . . Courtney saw her down the doctor's clinic last week. Of course she didn't know Courtney from Adam, but they got chatting and it turns out she's got a terrible case of thrush. We had to laugh

when Courtney told me that she'd tried rubbing it with
baking soda and yoghurt – I said her vag probably blew
up like a sodding soufflé!'

The waiting room is overheated and the windows
are steamed up. Someone has attempted to inject a little
Christmas cheer into the place with strings of red and
blue tinsel and paperchains, but the decorations merely
accentuate the down-at-heel nature of the room. Bare
untreated floorboards, littered with Wrigley's wrappers
and cake crumbs; high ceiling with exposed hot water
pipes painted brown to match the polystyrene tiles. It
reminds Lester of his old junior school and the wooden
chairs they are sitting on have the same mistreated,
undersized feel.

It is a long time since he has had to audition like
this and he feels that it is beneath him. He is after all an
Oscar winner, so why should he have to sit here for
hours on end with a bunch of unknowns who don't even
recognize him?

He has dressed specially for the role of Jonathon
Jons: he has put himself in the position of a successful,
sexy plastic surgeon, so is wearing clothes that he
wouldn't normally wear. He has had his hair cut, and
Tina touched up his grey with some Clairol she had left
over from her brunette phase. He doesn't look half bad.

When he looks around the room he can spot his
contenders. There are eight men who fit the bill, and all
of them look confident and suitable – physically at least.
One of them is actually wearing a white doctor's coat
over a shirt and tie and another has a stethoscope
around his neck. Do plastic surgeons use stethoscopes?
Lester recognizes one of the actors from bit parts on the
telly but he can't actually place him; he's the kind of

man they always choose for those sophisticated coffee adverts or for when the lady loves Milk Tray.

It is easy to be daunted by such an experience, and Lester is beginning to think that this is all a terrible idea. People go in and people come out, but nobody gives any indication of what is going on behind that closed door. The washboard stomach gives him a nudge with his arm and asks him the time.

'Half past one, mate,' says Lester.

'They're taking their bloody time,' says the washboard stomach. 'I've missed two cattle calls for Michaela Fox's catwalk show, and my agent is going to be livid.'

'Which part are you up for?' asks Lester.

'Brandon Huxley.'

'Oh right, the fella who wins the custody battle. That shower scene with him and Alexa sounds pretty raunchy. Do you think they'll actually allow it when it comes to keeping the censors happy?'

'All I know is I've spent a fucking fortune on personal training this month, and this body is camera-ready.'

'I can see that,' says Lester, and he begins to wonder if he will be expected to take his shirt off for the scene with the soda siphon. Oh God, he should have done some sit-ups this morning.

'Aren't you that chap from *Crossroads*?' asks the washboard stomach.

'Yes, that's me,' Lester replies with a wan smile.

'Yes, right . . .' says the actor, his face forming an expression of recognition, 'you're the guy whose wife—'

'Yes, that's it: the guy whose wife killed her baby. You know, I'd almost forgotten, so thanks for reminding me, mate!'

'Sorry,' says the actor, 'I wasn't thinking.'

'No, I guess not,' replies Lester with a terse, humourless smile.

It is almost four before he is called into the audition room.

Jane Graves is sitting at a trestle table with three blokes, all of whom look just old enough to be out of college. There are two cameramen, a bank of halogen lights and several video screens. The windows in here have been blacked out with sheeting and there is an acrid smell of burning coffee. Jane seems friendly enough and it is encouraging for her to mention the fact that Lester comes 'highly recommended' for the part. She remembers him from *Five Farthings* and commends him on his performance and subsequent Academy Award. *Very promising.* Lester perks up a bit.

'Daisy is going to read the parts of Charles and Francesca, and you just fall in, OK? Let's have you standing over there so we can see you on the screen.'

One of the college leavers at the table makes a joke about Lester being unrecognizable without his purple pig costume. Lester pretends to laugh but he wonders if he is being ridiculed. The chap who made the joke is one of those smart-arse types with '50s black-framed glasses and a messy haircut that only looks good because he can carry it off. His name is Darryl and he has a Scottish accent.

They run through the scene a couple of times, and then Jane asks Lester to move around so that they can get some profile shots of him. She seems very nice: unassuming in a gentle, grey-flannel kind of way – not at all the high-powered executive type he had imagined. It seems to be going very well until that dickhead Darryl asks him to read from a part of the script that Lester is unfamiliar with. It involves some medical terms that Lester is unsure of, and there is a flirtatious exchange between his character and a female art student that is almost ludicrous to act out alone. Daisy reads out the responses in a flat, deadpan kind of way, and Lester stands there like a bloody lemon pretending to kiss a woman who isn't even there. It is all very humiliating and he can feel his confidence failing.

'Do you think I could run through that scene again?' he asks.

'I don't think there's any need for that, Lester,' says Jane, smiling sweetly. 'We're on a really, really tight schedule today and unfortunately we're lagging way behind. We'll be in touch with your agent by the end of next week, OK? You did really well. Give my love to Shani when you see her next, will you?'

And Lester is dismissed.

What a cock-up that was! Lester berates himself, as he pulls on his overcoat and steps out into the cold winter afternoon. It is dark and there is a smell of snow approaching, as though the very air itself is on the verge of crystallizing. They tricked him with that sodding last scene. How was he supposed to know the pronunciation of pyelonephritis? That cocky bastard Darryl looked so smug while he enunciated the term for him in broken syllables, as though Lester was some kind of illiterate moron.

Christmas trees lean up against the front of a florist's shop, bound with rope ready for delivery, and the display window is filled with poinsettias, holly and mistletoe. It is only a quarter past five now but it feels so late in the day. Lester tries to imagine what the scene would be like if it were mid-June, but it is difficult to picture the summer when Christmas is just a few days away.

The end of next week will be Christmas Eve. He wonders if they might contact his agent before then, seeing as it will be a holiday weekend. Maybe he should just forget the whole thing and resign himself to another year of that sodding purple pig suit.

He doesn't feel like going home. Tina will be there, watching the telly, and showing little interest in how his audition went. She couldn't care less about his career as long as he's bringing home money at the end of every month. Lester wonders when things changed between them. He used to enjoy spending time with her, but these days it is a bloody chore just remaining in the same room together. He has only recently realized that his wife is basically stupid. She views the world as a two-dimensional passageway that stretches before her like an endless straight road, with the occasional open doorway that she can peep into. Emotionally she is already dead. When Lester took her to see *Schindler's List*, her only comment afterwards was, 'You'd think they'd have made the whole film in colour. It's not as though Spielberg doesn't have the money!'

Lester finds a payphone and calls Marla's office. Julie tells him that Marla is at home, so he calls her penthouse. He gets the answering machine, and is just leaving a message when Marla picks up the phone. 'I was screening my calls,' she explains, and she tells Lester about the chocolate box incident.

'I'm at a loose end right now. Shall I come over?' he asks.

So he takes the bus, crowded with shoppers and

people going home from work, and he finds Marla still in her dressing gown with three TVs on the go and a soup bowl filled with cigarette stubs. She doesn't look good. Loose pages of newspaper are strewn across the floor, and Marla is crouched in the corner of her sectional sofa with a bottle of Scotch.

'I always wondered what happened to Baby Jane Hudson – now I know!' jokes Lester as he takes the Scotch from Marla and pours himself a shot to join her.

'If you'd stayed with me, honey, this is what would have greeted you every morning. Scary, huh?'

'Not as scary as you waking up next to a washed-up actor.'

'Oh, here we go . . . I thought you'd come over here to cheer *me* up. What's brought this on?'

'Oh, I had that audition today – the one that Shani fixed up for me. It was a bloody disaster; like going back twenty years. I sat there in that waiting room and I suddenly realized that everything has moved on without me. It was like catching a sudden glimpse of myself in a mirror and seeing what other people have been seeing all along.'

'Honey, none of us is twenty-one any more. Some days I stagger into the bathroom and catch sight of myself standing in the shower like some kind of drowned plant. It takes longer and longer to make myself look presentable, and if I don't take the time I'm scaring small kids on the sidewalk and freaking out my clients because they think I'm undergoing chemotherapy. You just have to keep reminding yourself that it isn't outward appearance that matters, but then you see some young kid with skin like a baby's ass and tits like missiles and you can't help but feel disillusioned. It's a cruel joke, Lester. Life is just a cruel joke.'

Marla raises her glass to Lester and they chink before drinking. Lester is beginning to feel better already. 'So where's Mark the Nark this evening?' he asks, putting his feet up on the coffee table.

'Out catching cat burglars,' snorts Marla through an exhalation of smoke. 'He reckons they've now got some kind of lead on my case, but I'm not holding my breath. My mail is being intercepted, they're recording my phone conversations, and my computer is wired up to some central intelligence so I can't even pee without somebody being alerted. We are being taped right now' – and Marla points to a video camera mounted just above the doorway – 'so be careful what you say. It might be used as evidence against you.'

'Is it hooked up to monitors or is it just taping us?' asks Lester, slightly perturbed by the idea of constant surveillance.

'Oh, don't worry, Lester. We can tape over anything incriminating before they get their hands on it.'

'I don't know how you can live like this, Marla. Why don't you just go away somewhere, until the police find this guy? You can afford to take a couple of months off. Go to Hawaii or Australia or a little Caribbean island somewhere, with a masseur and a cook.'

'And who's going to keep the business flying, huh? With Spencer gone there's only me, and my clients can't just take two months off when they've been waiting years to get permanent residency here. Some of them have been apart from their families for months on end. Lester, you know what my job's like; I just can't bail out when the going gets a little heavy.'

'You've been doing this for too long,' says Lester. 'It's time you started taking time out for yourself. I know what you're worth, and that you could retire now and enjoy yourself. I wish I was in the same position, because I'd bugger off with no hesitation if I had the chance.'

'You're all talk, Lester. I know you better than that. If you were in that career for an easy life, you'd carry on playing the pig and not get so worked up about this new part you've auditioned for. I know you better than anyone, remember, and we're as bad as each other – overachievers both of us. You may prefer to forget what our marriage was like in the early days. With me flying backwards and forwards across the Atlantic and you spending six days a week in Birmingham, there's no wonder we forgot about having a relationship. We might as well have been room-mates for all the good we were to each other.'

'You were always more ambitious than me, Marla. I'd have been happy to stay at home more, but what was the point with you in New York half the month?'

'So you'd have given up *Crossroads* to stay at home with me, would you, Lester? I don't think so, honey!'

Lester considers this question and has to admit Marla is right – neither of them had been prepared to give up their careers for the sake of a marriage. Especially after Jessica died.

'Look, I'm starving. Now *you* might want to sit here wallowing in self-pity but I fancy a nice piece of rump steak and some chips. How about you have a quick wash and brush-up, and we get a taxi down to Soho? And I know you're going to say no, so I'm telling you *now* to go and brush your hair, put some lippy on, and I'll call a black cab – no arguments!'

198

'I can't go out looking like this!' moans Marla.

'We'll go somewhere dark, so you don't put people off their food.'

'I need a shower, and my hair . . .'

'Squirt some scent in your knickers and wear a headscarf. I'm not fussy about who I eat with these days.'

And so they brave the cold December chill together. Ex-husband with ex-wife, clutching on to each other as they cross the road to climb into the waiting taxicab.

'They're forecasting snow heading down from Scotland,' informs the cabbie with a sniff, through the open partition.

'Maybe we'll have a white Christmas,' says Marla. 'You mind if I smoke, sir?'

'Usually I'd say no but seeing as how you called me sir, I'll make an exception. Just keep the windows open and don't drop your fag end on the floor, thank you very much!'

'You're an angel,' laughs Marla.

'And I'll be a bloody block of ice by the time we get to Soho!' says Lester, pleased to see that Marla is looking distinctly perky now that she's out in the world again.

Twenty

There is something romantic about a graveyard when it has been snowing.

The white silence that muffles the ancient edges of the church and the gravestones surrounds Annie like a quilt. Her boots crunch against the virgin snow as she treads very carefully so as to avoid stepping on anyone's resting place. There are holly bushes heavy with berries against the churchyard wall, and if Annie were more artistically minded she might have stopped and thought what a lovely picture that would make.

Especially on Christmas Eve.

She is supposed to be out buying satsumas and brazil nuts for the coffee table, but the shops were crowded and she needed some peace, so she came here instead. Nobody will miss the fruit and nuts. They'll be too busy picking out the green triangles from the Quality Street and scoffing the salted peanuts to be fussed about things that need peeling. Funny, this is the first time that Annie has felt anything but joy at the thought of Christmas. She could do without it this year, quite honestly. It all seems a bit fake. A bit too much bother.

Of course Mum and Dad are being especially jolly this year. They keep giving Annie things to do, things that normally they would do themselves. Occupational therapy – or so they think. The house has been a hive of activity all week with people dropping by for a lager or a 'snowball' with Mum's mince pies spread out on doilies and *Tijuana Brass* on the stereo. Usually Annie would enjoy all the extra fuss. She would be the first one to start stringing up the cards on bits of cotton and helping Dad to get the tree lights working again. But this year it all felt too much like hard work.

They've got the carol service and midnight mass tonight. It is a family ritual and is the only time any of them step inside the church unless somebody is being christened, married or buried. There will be roast beef for tea, with Yorkshires and horseradish and then Mum will watch them all anxiously as she serves the first piece of her yule log for pudding. The telly will be on all night and there'll be cocktail sausages and cheese with pearl onions on sticks to snack on. The best glasses will be out and everyone will have something to drink, even if they don't normally much care for it. The mirrored interior of the cocktail cabinet is already filled with bottles that will still be there on bonfire night, and Dad will be down at the beer-off getting Schweppes for the gin and tonics.

The new burials are down at the far end of the graveyard: mounds of freshly turned earth that are heaped with wilting flowers and tributes to the recently departed. Annie wonders if one day soon she might be standing beside another freshly hollowed grave to bury Spencer, but there is still no word as to where he might be. Dead or alive.

'We were thinking of Clumber Park for a little Christmas Day memorial get-together,' said Mrs Noble to Annie on the telephone. 'He used to love playing

201

there when he was a boy, and there's a nice quiet spot with rhododendrons where he liked to make a den.'

'That would be nice,' said Annie, but she was not interested in Clumber Park or the nice rhododendrons. Spencer isn't dead, or at least they don't know for sure if he's dead at this point. A memorial gathering seems a little morbid to Annie, and she still refuses to believe that Spencer is not going to suddenly turn up out of the blue with a perfectly good explanation for his absence. All she wanted was to get Mrs Noble off the phone, so she could go back to her room where she was finishing off a tray of Turkish Delight and filling in a quiz about compulsive shoppers.

Here's a nice gravestone. A stone angel, slightly crooked from years of bending forward to watch over the dead, with little pads of snow behind her wings and trapped in the roses around her head. The inscription reads: *In death as in life she will be with Jesus. Mary Olivia Botts. Wife of Stanley and mother of little Gladys and Rose. 1887–1925.*

She was only thirty-eight years old when she died. Annie wonders what it was that took her away from Stanley and the girls. In 1925 they didn't have chemotherapy and radiation treatment, did they? People died of TB in those days and the doctors didn't sterilize things like they do today, so people were lucky to get out of the hospitals alive.

As Annie looks at the birth date and the death date of Mary Olivia Botts she wonders what those thirty-eight years were like for her. That short dash between the dates symbolizes the entire lifetime of one person and it doesn't look like *much* for thirty-eight years of being alive. If Annie died today, that's all her life would be: a dash. She hasn't done much with her life and she'll be thirty-eight herself next year. When Mum and Dad are gone, who will be around to bother about Annie when she finally pegs it? What happens when there is nobody left to arrange a funeral? Annie has visions of mass graves like the ones they had during the plague – bodies wrapped in bandages and sprinkled with lime to help them decompose. More likely that the Co-op takes over, paying Frank Sparkle from the insurance money to provide a basic service with a pine coffin and a bunch of carnations.

It's only quarter past three but the sun is already about to disappear behind the trees. The snow is criss-crossed with very long shadows, and everything white is tinged with a pale shade of peach. A proper Christmas Eve that looks like a Christmas card. There is no snow left to fall, just a few smudgy white clouds against the cold blue, and chimney smoke from the old pit cottages drifting aimlessly upwards with nowhere to go.

And somewhere flies an aeroplane, for there is its vapour trail like a chalk mark on the sky.

For a minute Annie thinks she is going to cry.

It's something to do with the stillness of the scene before her, the rooks interjecting with their black artless crowing and the dead people buried and forgotten all around her. She wonders what is the point to everything. What if everyone has been lying, and there is no heaven? Does that mean you get cheated at the end, and find out that you should have been making the most of life as it happened instead of always hoping for something better?

What remains after life? Memories only live as long as the next generation and then you become just a name on a gravestone. When you die there is nothing left but the equivalent of that final streak across the blue, the chalky vapour trail that remains for a while after the aeroplane has flown away. How long will Spencer's vapour trail remain in the sky, and is it really worth the effort of living only to make such a temporary scratch on a sky that heals so quickly?

This is a revolutionary concept for somebody like Annie.

She wasn't brought up to think about things like death; she was supposed to be too busy with life to think about the meaning of it. She wonders if Spencer knows the answer to these questions yet. When he dropped Marla's gun on the floor of that disgusting backstreet place in New York, did he suddenly see quite clearly that he'd made a horrible mistake and that death isn't the answer? Did he think about his son, or about Annie, or about the man who was kneeling in front of him?

Spencer's son.

William James Clarke who prefers to be called Billy.

Annie has thought a lot about that boy. Does he look anything like Spencer? What is his mum like? It occurs to Annie that if she meets these people she will be able to understand better why Spencer wanted to blow his brains out. When Christmas is over she is going to go down to London and look them up. The worst that can happen is they'll turn her away.

This morning she went to visit Betsy in the hospital.

'I haven't had a period for three months now.' Betsy was sitting up in the hospital bed with a tube in her nostril and a needle in the back of her hand. The nurses had put some Christmas trimmings up, but they didn't disguise the fact that this was the National Health and funding is alarmingly low. It's a fairly new hospital and they've tried really hard with the wards, but nothing can get rid of that hospital smell and the sound of wheels and clicking heels on the linoleum outside in the corridors.

Annie took along some of her mum's lemon curd tarts but she knew that Betsy wouldn't eat them. She only eats what they feed her through that tube in her nostril, and she is still losing weight.

'No monthly cramps and no PMT,' boasted Betsy with a flippancy that Annie could not believe was sincere. 'The drugs aren't working, so they're talking about ECT.'

'What's that?' asked Annie.

'Electroconvulsive therapy. It's supposed to cure depression. Now then, love, how's your mum and dad? I bet they're in the thick of things for Christmas now. You shouldn't have come on Christmas Eve, Annie. A hospital isn't a very cheerful place when you should be having a good time.'

'I wanted to get out of the house, quite honestly,' admitted Annie, biting into a lemon curd tart, 'as all that fuss is driving me mad. They've got Auntie Sybil and Uncle Geoff round, so I made my excuses. Nobody said anything, although I could tell they were dying to put their oar in. Auntie Sybil is still on antidepressants so she thinks she's the authority on anybody who's a likely candidate for a breakdown. What about your mum and dad? Have they been over today?'

'You must be kidding! My dad won't set foot in the place. Reckons hospitals give him the heebie-jeebies, so he's probably down the Rising Sun knocking back pints with half the other blokes on the estate.'

'What about your mum and Janice?'

'Oh, our Janice is getting ready for a night out with the girls – some do at the Adam and Eve, with a male stripper and karaoke – and me mum popped her head round the door for five minutes last night, before the six o'clock news, and left me them.' Betsy indicates a small collection of presents on the chair by the door.

'So they won't let you out for Christmas, then?' asked Annie, unbuttoning her coat because the central heating was stifling.

'It's my punishment for not trying to eat anything. They told me I could go home if I put on five pounds but I can't keep anything down, so there's no chance I'm ever getting out of this hole. Did I tell you that Pauline Worth, as was, is one of the auxiliary nurses here? She remembers you from school and told me to say hello. I wouldn't have recognized her since she had her teeth seen to. She looks quite pretty now and she's got two little grandkids up in York, so she was off up there this afternoon with a boot full of toys.'

'I wish it was all over. I don't think I can stand three days of this at our house. Thing is, I don't know *what* I want. If somebody told me I could go anywhere I wanted, I wouldn't have a bloody clue. I've been thinking a lot about Spencer's son in London. I keep wondering what he's like.'

'A total stranger, I should think,' said Betsy. 'He was brought up by people you don't even know, so I wouldn't worry about him if I was you. What about that fashion woman in New York? I thought you said she wanted you to do some more modelling for her catalogue?'

'Oh, she does, but I'm not that fussed about it. She

206

sent another letter asking me to go down to Florida for a week in January to do a "shoot", as she calls it, for the summer line, but I just feel I've got to get on with something more important than having my picture taken. What happens if they *never* find Spencer? Am I supposed to carry on as though sometime he might just turn up again? Or do I act like he's dead and get on with my life? I need some kind of direction, Betsy, otherwise I'm going to end up just like all the other girls at school who didn't move away.'

'Honestly, Annie, you don't know when you've got it good. How many women would give their eye teeth to fly off to Florida for the week – all expenses paid – to start a modelling career with a big fashion designer? *There's* your bloody direction, girl, staring you in the face! You want to nab the opportunity while it's still there, otherwise you'll live to regret it. Whether Spencer comes back or not, how can you consider living with him after he's used you like this?'

'I still love him, Betsy. I know it sounds daft but I can't help myself. Anyway, the modelling stuff isn't really my cup of tea. I don't fit in with those people, and I'd rather be here with people I know.'

'Chesterfield is a dump, and you know it! There's nothing for you here. If you're lucky, they'll take you back at Buckley & Bright's and you'll be there until you retire, with nothing to show for your effort except your old-age pension and that wrist complaint that people get when they spend too long at the keyboard. When you got married to Spencer, I really thought you'd finally broken out, Annie. It was your chance to do something different with your life, and I was envious of you. Don't let me down by giving in so easily. It's easy to accept your lot in life but sometimes you've got to get off your arse if you want something to happen.'

'So why don't *you* do something about it, then?' asked Annie, for the first time allowing her frustrations regarding Betsy's health to simmer to the surface.

'It's too late for me: I'm past caring about myself. But I do care about you and I get mad when I see these opportunities being wasted. When I saw them photos they took of you, I was that proud! I've got them framed in my bedroom at home and I've told everybody that my best friend is a fashion model. If you don't get famous now, Annie, I'll have nobody to boast about, so get off to bloody Florida and get rich quick, so I can come and get brown by your pool in Los Angeles.'

'Crikey! Look at the time, Bets. I'm supposed to be home by half past. Listen, I'll pop in tomorrow afternoon and stop till after tea, OK? I'd rather be here with you than stuck in the house with Dad snoring on the sofa and Mum whittling on about the trifle not setting.'

Annie grabbed her coat and twirled her scarf around her neck several times. As she bent to kiss Betsy on the cheek, her friend took hold of her hand and kept her there just for a second or two.

'We've had some laughs, haven't we, Annie?' whispered Betsy, smiling.

'Usually at my expense!' smiled back Annie.

'When you come tomorrow, bring your photo album. We'll have a giggle at some of those old pictures.'

'All right, duck. Sorry to dash like this but me mum'll kill me if I'm late for me dinner.'

And Annie had left the hospital that morning with a weight in her chest that has been there ever since.

Like indigestion.

There is a little girl standing by the church gates as Annie leaves the graveyard. She is probably no older than eight or nine, and she is wearing a bright red padded anorak with black fur at the collar and cuffs.

'Ay up,' she says when she sees Annie.

'Hello,' smiles Annie, closing the gate firmly behind her.

'Have you seen my cat?'

'No, I haven't. What does it look like?'

'His name's Piddle and he's got a white patch under his chin. Our Jason told me he'd seen him squashed under a lorry on King Street but I went up there and didn't see owt.'

'I'm sure he's all right, love. He'll probably be back at home when you get there.'

'I've got to keep shot of the house for a bit while me mum wraps our presents. She's on nights tonight, so she won't have time later. I'm getting a Deluxe Spirograph and our Jason is getting money towards his bike.'

'Well, I don't think your mum would want you out after it gets dark, so you'd best get on home and see if your cat's there.'

'If our Piddle's dead, I might get a gerbil after Christmas. Our Jason reckons they can bite through your finger if you don't watch 'em. Ta-ra,' and the little girl skips off across the road with her arms stretched out for balance as she navigates the piles of snow at the sides of the pavement.

Annie looks over her shoulder and the sky is already turning dark at the edges. The vapour trail has gone.

And there is nothing now but the silent night.

Twenty-one

'You'll have to get a move on, Billy. Mum and Dad will be home any minute.'

By the flashing multicoloured lights of the Christmas tree, Billy Clarke has his girlfriend Jennifer by the ankles and wears a condom barely large enough to cover the top section of his penis. The latex refuses to expand any further and threatens to cut off his blood supply.

'This thing is too small,' he complains, releasing one of Jennifer's ankles as he tugs at the rubber sheath.

'As long as the end is covered, who cares?' sighs Jennifer impatiently. She keeps looking at the clock and Billy is getting pissed off. This would never happen with Miss Joyce. That's the problem with girls his own age: they are just too immature. Only last night Billy and Miss Joyce had re-enacted a festive nude version of *A Christmas Carol*, with Billy as Scrooge in a white fur jockstrap and wellington boots and Miss Joyce as the ghost of Christmas yet to come. No need for johnnies with Miss Joyce – she's on the pill.

'Well, don't blame me if I lose this bugger inside you again!' and Billy pushes Jennifer's legs back as far as they will go – she is an excellent gymnast – so that he can watch himself sliding in.

'Don't go all the way, Billy,' warns Jennifer as Billy reaches the seven-inch mark. Maybe he should suggest buying a rubber doughnut next time they pass the pet store.

The clock strikes midnight on Christmas Eve in Jennifer's parents' living room. The gas fire is on and they have been listening to the same bloody CD go round and round on the hi-fi since eight o'clock.

'You do love me, don't you, Billy?' asks contorted Jennifer as he plunges dangerously close to the eight-inch mark without further complaint from her. But Billy doesn't reply. Billy doesn't know what love is, because he hasn't met anyone to show him yet, but he knows how much the girls like to be told, so occasionally he'll grunt out the meaningless words when he wants to get his end away.

'Oh, Billy, I think I'm going to come . . .' breathes Jennifer with her eyes rolling upwards, but Billy can see right through her theatrical attempt to hurry him up. She is a crap actress, and her pathetic faking just makes him ram into her even harder. When he gets it all the way in, up to the hilt, Jennifer soon forgets her fantasy orgasm and she cries out in pain. 'You're hurting me!'

So Billy pulls out a couple of inches and gets back into his stroke. They have moved across the carpet and Jennifer is practically buried beneath the Christmas tree now. She has presents scattered around her shoulders, and a foil-wrapped chocolate bell hanging just inches above her face.

'Come on Billy, come on . . .'

But Billy is feeling nothing. It is as though his penis has suddenly become numb and no matter how hard he tries to concentrate on the sexual act he just knows that he isn't going to come. His mind is elsewhere tonight, and has been ever since that solicitor chap called round to tell them that Spencer has left Billy everything in his will.

The few times Billy met Spencer he had no idea just what the man's relationship with his mother was. He was just an old friend of hers, and Dad hated him because he knew that there was still some kind of bond between them. It is quite a shock to find out that this bond between them had resulted in the birth of Billy himself. No wonder Dad was so pissed off whenever Mum mentioned Spencer's name.

It's one thing to find out that your mum's best friend is also your dad, but another to discover that he tried to commit suicide in a gay bathhouse while some bloke was giving him a blow job.

'Did you *know* about him, Mum?' asked Billy once the solicitor had left.

Maggie nodded her head. She had been crying, and Billy had to console her even though he himself felt nothing. 'He got married just a few months ago, to try and get round it but he's been struggling with his sexuality as long as I've known him. The women used to pester him all the time. He always had a girl on the go, sometimes more than one.'

Now Billy worries if that kind of thing gets passed down from father to son. He tries to concentrate on the business at hand, but Jennifer has stopped pretending and she's looking pointedly at her wristwatch. She has love bites on her shoulder and smudged lipstick – totally unsexy. Billy usually needs to think about chainsaws and tomorrow's homework in order to delay his orgasm, but tonight he is trying desperately to *concentrate* on the fact that he's shagging Jennifer under her parents' Christmas tree.

For the first time in his short life, Billy fakes an orgasm.

It isn't difficult to do. He even goes so far as to pump the muscles in his crotch just in case Jennifer is sensitive enough to feel whether he ejaculates inside her. There really is no need for Billy to go to such elaborate lengths because as soon as he has feigned satisfaction, she is whipping up her knickers and switching on the table lamps.

'I need to get rid of this,' he says, hiding the empty condom in the palm of his hand.

'Well, just make sure it flushes away,' says Jennifer as she fluffs the cushions and fixes her hair in the mirror.

Billy has to get a taxi home because the buses have stopped running and Jennifer does not live near a convenient tube line. It is after one in the morning when he gets back to Holloway and his mother is still in the kitchen icing cakes.

'It's a birthday cake,' she explains as Billy strolls into the stripped-pine kitchen, throwing his jacket over the back of a chair and sticking his finger in the mixing bowl.

Maggie Clarke is a woman who appears permanently harassed. She has dirty blonde hair that is too thin for styling and too slippery to be tied back, so it either hangs in worried strands across her face or is pushed hastily behind her ears. She never wears make-up, and her clothes are chosen for their practicality rather than their beauty. Tonight she is wearing jeans and a baggy sweater with the sleeves pushed up to her elbows.

'It's Christmas, Mum. What are you doing up at this time of night?'

'I can't let my customers down, Billy, and Mrs Farlow called me in desperation this afternoon because she'd forgotten their Sylvia's sixteenth on Boxing Day. What could I say? She spends a fortune on cakes every year, and next March is their Beryl's second wedding, so they'll be wanting a three-tier which, as you well know, can make us enough for a mortgage payment.'

Maggie runs a small home cake-making business called Sweet Dreams. The front room has been turned into a showroom for her creative confections, so they have to use the main bedroom upstairs as their living room. People come to the house to 'ooh' and 'ah' over her award-winning cake designs, and the house embraces a permanent smell of baking even when the twin ovens are turned off.

'You're late home, love. Did you get a cab?' asks Maggie, licking the pale apricot icing from her knuckles as she refills her icing bag.

'Yeah, double price for it being after midnight *and* Christmas. Jennifer's mum and dad got in just as I was leaving.'

'Shame she'll be away for Christmas, love. It would have been nice to have her over for dinner or something. Did she like her necklace?'

'Shit!' exclaims Billy, remembering the gift, still wrapped, in his jacket pocket.

'Language!' warns Maggie. 'I suppose that means you forgot to give it to her? Too busy having sex, I suppose!'

Maggie is a liberal-minded mother. She advocates sex before marriage and buys condoms in bulk at the cash

214

and carry for Billy, to make sure that he doesn't get anyone pregnant. Unfortunately Billy is too embarrassed to tell his mother that he needs the 'magnum'-sized Durex, and so he gives the regular size away to mates at school and buys his own.

'You know I've been thinking about Spencer a lot this afternoon – all that money he's left you in his will. If he *is* dead, it will leave you a rather wealthy young man. I hope that's not going to stop you from trying hard to get your A-levels. Even if Spencer is dead, you've got another three years before you can touch that trust fund, and even then it won't be enough to afford a life of leisure. You'll still need a job, you know.'

'I know that, Mum. I'm not totally stupid!' Billy doesn't want to talk about this stuff now. The subject of Spencer makes him uncomfortable, and he particularly hopes they won't get on to the gay stuff again. He just doesn't want to deal with all that right now.

'That house in Fulham? I was thinking . . .' Maggie finishes off the final flourish of icing on her cake and goes over to the sink to wash out her equipment.

'What about the house, Mum? Jennifer reckons it must be worth at least three hundred thousand, being right on Fulham Road.'

'Well, I was thinking, if the worst comes to the worst, you should offer it to Spencer's wife. They were living there together and, because he never had a chance to change his will, she will be left with nothing.'

'But we could sell this place and move into that house ourselves,' says Billy, 'or else we could sell both places and buy one big house, if you wanted to stay in north London.'

'Oh, we don't need a bigger house, love, I'm quite

happy living here and it just seems such a shame that Spencer's wife should not only lose her new husband but be left penniless as well. Your dad would never accept money from Spencer. It would be an insult for him – you know how he feels.'

'But Dad is never here. He spends all of his time on the rigs. He doesn't even phone unless he's nagging us about something or other.'

'Your dad works hard, Billy. He might not be very demonstrative with his emotions, but all of his money goes into this house and keeping a roof over our heads.'

'So how come Spencer never offered to marry *you*, then?' asks Billy with a sullen swipe at the mixing bowl.

'I told you, love, we were young and Spencer was very messed up over his sexuality. When I got pregnant he talked about getting married, but I knew it would be a disaster. We talked about living together and bringing you up but I felt it was all just a compromise for Spencer, who had so much ambition. When you were born, it seemed easier if he just faded into the background. I met your dad and got married, and Spencer just got on with his life. When your dad found out that you were Spencer's child, he never wanted anything to do with him after that. It was better all round, I think.'

'Better for who?' asks Billy.

'Better for all of us. And in the end it worked out all right, didn't it?'

Maggie wipes her hands on a tea towel and hooks her hair back behind both ears. She looks tired. She looks delicate and ivory-coloured like the icing she uses on her wedding cakes. Billy loves his mum very much but he would never tell her that. He writes it in birthday cards and expresses it with hugs and kisses but the actual words just won't come out of his mouth properly; they get stuck somewhere between his throat and his lips.

'You could call Spencer's wife tomorrow morning. It would be a nice thing to do on Christmas Day, to just offer her your condolences.'

And Billy isn't a selfish boy. He mows lawns for local pensioners in the summer and feeds the homeless with his mother every last Sunday. Most people like him because he has an honest, open face and a gentle demeanour.

'I suppose I could call her and ask if she's heard anything new from the police in New York,' he suggests.

'That would be nice, love,' smiles worn-out Maggie with her falling-down hair and her jumper all smudged with icing sugar. 'Shall we have a nice cup of tea before bed?'

'I'll make it, Mum. Go and put your feet up for a few minutes and I'll bring it upstairs.'

'Thanks, love.'

And Billy plugs in the kettle.

If he talks to this woman who married Spencer, perhaps she will be able to tell him something about their life together. Something about Spencer that would make some sense out of the way he disappeared. Something that would make Billy feel better about the gay stuff.

The house is silent except for the gentle hissing of the kettle as it heats up the water for tea. Christmas cards straggle along the edges of the kitchen shelves and there is mistletoe above the doorway.

Funny – Billy isn't usually a sentimental person.

But tonight he remembers other Christmases when

he was a little boy, and it strikes him as a bit sad that he's grown up now and the magic has gone.

Father Christmas doesn't exist, and Billy won't be up all night listening for reindeer on the roof. All of that has vanished, along with the tooth fairy and the taste of green jelly on birthdays.

Billy fills the teapot and stirs the leaves.

It's 'up the wooden hill to Bedfordshire' now for this little boy who is only just beginning to realize that nothing lasts for ever.

Twenty-two

Marla sits on the edge of her seat with a cigarette smouldering between her fingers and a small scattering of ash at her bare feet. She has been sitting here like this for ten minutes, and she hasn't moved once.

It is only seven thirty in the morning but the day is already shattered. Broken shards of glass litter the bedroom carpet.

When Marla woke to discover this infraction of her privacy, this violation of her personal space, she was incensed with anger and disbelief. How was it possible that anyone could break through the layers of security to get into her flat and cause such havoc without her even waking up?

She ran over to the video machine and rewound the tape.

She sat down before her TV screen, with a robe pulled loosely around her, and she waited to see *how* this could have happened.

While she waited for it to rewind she watched a morning carol service. Christmas bells and angelic voices announced impending festivities, and women wearing hats listened to the sermon with solemn faces.

Marla had to fast-forward to get to the part of the tape where she finally went to bed last night. As she turned off the bedside lamps, the camera went into night mode and Marla's bedroom became visible, bathed in an unearthly ultraviolet light. She could see herself tossing and turning beneath the covers, and the anticipation of fear crept up her spine as she waited for something to happen. At some point her persecutor must appear, and Marla would finally have some concrete evidence to give to the police.

The ghostly bedroom remained still and quiet for over an hour. Marla rushed forward through some of the footage, impatient to see what would happen. She slowed the film down again when she saw herself getting out of bed to go to the bathroom. The bathroom light went on, and then it went out. Marla paused by the bathroom door, totally naked and seemingly confused. As she now watched the scene she couldn't even remember getting out of bed in the night; she must have been half asleep.

Then something happened.

Marla watches with horrified fascination. She watches with nausea rising in her throat and a terrible lurch of mortification squeezing her throat until she thinks that she can't breathe.

She watches and she can't believe what she sees.

Naked and seemingly wide awake, Marla walked over to the chest of drawers and picked up a heavy marble ornament. With a scream of rage she hurled her missile with full force at her bedroom window, shattering the glass into hundreds of pieces.

'I killed you, Jessica!' she screamed. 'My baby, I killed you, but I did not get away with it. I will never get away with it!'

Then she proceeded to wreck her own bedroom. She swiped perfume bottles from the dressing table with a wild sweep of her arm. She stood on the bed and punched the feathers out of her pillows, transforming the bedroom into a swirling chaos of destruction – with Marla as the whirling vortex around which everything seethed.

And when she was finished with her demented ranting and her violent rage, Marla simply stood down from the bed, pulled back the tangled sheets and climbed beneath them, as though nothing had happened. She just lay there with her head resting on one undamaged pillow, eyes closed and now totally oblivious to the scene of madness that surrounded her.

Jesus Christ! I'm a fucking psycho!

Marla Philips sits on the edge of her seat and grips the remote control as though her life depends on its support. She sits in her living room on Christmas Day with her robe hanging open and her face the colour of wet plaster, and she feels physically sick.

It just doesn't seem possible that she could cause so much destruction without waking herself up. If she had not just watched herself on the video, she would not believe that it was possible, even though she knows that people can do amazing things in their sleep. She is the sanest person that she knows! But this is not the first time Marla has experienced this kind of mental blackout. It used to happen quite frequently in the days before they electrocuted her brain. In the days before they found baby Jessica stone-cold dead.

Questions riddle her brain like wormholes, and she doesn't know where to begin searching for answers. Obviously a good shrink would be the wisest place to start, but this is not just a small psychological blip such as fear of aliens or obsessive dusting. This is a huge,

huge problem that obviously involves total mental black-out periods when Marla is capable of carrying out complex actions without any subsequent recollection. And now she's terrified. The thought of being locked up in that asylum again brings back the kind of fears that paralyse her.

No wonder her 'stalker' was so clever, so well informed of her every move. The alarm codes, the email messages, the 'break-ins' with no visible sign of forced entry, all of these now make sense. But could it be possible that she would go to such elaborate lengths to send herself those horrible parcels in the post? To decapitate a cat, to handle a pig's heart, to buy herself a blouse without even remembering any of it? This goes way beyond depression or a nervous breakdown.

She is crazy. A fruit loop. *Nuts.*

Mark is due at noon to take her over to Shani's flat for lunch. Oh God, *Mark!* What the hell is he going to think when he presents him with this devastating piece of evidence? All the fuss she has created over the past few months, and no wonder they couldn't find any evidence of her so-called assailant. He is going to dump her ass faster than you can say high-security mental institute! He is going to look at her as though she is already wearing a straitjacket, and he will then consider himself lucky to have got away so lightly.

But does he ever have to know?

Marla reaches for her cigarettes and lights up. The video can easily be rewound and replaced with a blank. The bedroom can be cleared up, the broken window explained away as some simple domestic accident. Nobody but Marla knows that the stalker isn't still out there waiting to be caught, and soon everyone will be relieved when he stops bothering her. They will tell her that the ordeal is over, that the person responsible for the nightmare has obviously moved on, or simply grown tired of his tricks. And Marla, of course, will be only too quick to jump on to their bandwagon of sensible reasoning. She can meanwhile sort out this problem herself, with the help of a good psychiatrist and maybe some powerful drugs. Nobody need ever know.

She has three hours to prepare herself.

She gets out the vacuum cleaner and makes a start on the feathers, but the bag soon fills up and she doesn't know how to empty it. Broken glass gets into the mechanism and the hoover gives up the ghost with a worrisome rattling sound.

There is no way Marla is capable of clearing this up on her own. She needs help. She needs Hetty. But Hetty will be spending the day with her family, and Marla can't even call an independent cleaning service because everyone is closed. Damn Christmas! She will just have to close the door on this mess until after the holidays, and deal with it later. Subsequently she is spending the next couple of days at Mark's place anyway, so at least there'll be no complications unless . . .

Shit!

What happens if she goes loony at Marks' place tonight? That would give the whole game away. She'll have to come up with some excuse to stay at home. She'll have to invent some kind of illness that keeps her in solitary confinement until she can get to see a doctor. Maybe she should go off somewhere. Somewhere very remote where nobody knows her. She could call Mark now and say that there is some kind of emergency in New York, that she has to catch the first flight tomorrow morning. They don't have Boxing Day over there, so she could visit a shrink without having to battle through the whole weekend living on her nerves.

When she calls Mark, he isn't at home and his car phone is not responding. She will now just have to get through the day as planned, but escape early this evening. If she takes a nice hot shower, she will feel much better. Her hands are shaking. She makes some coffee, but that only makes her feel worse.

The doorbell rings at eleven fifteen. Marla thinks that it must be Mark arriving early, but when she opens the door it is Treez in her fluffy mules and a red velvet miniskirt.

'Look what Ahmed got me.' Treez holds out her hand to display a vulgar chunk of jewellery weighing down her finger. 'It's an opal, and these ones are diamonds,' she says, pointing out the tiny grains around the perimeter of the main stone.

Marla has absolutely no idea who Ahmed is but she admires the ring with as much enthusiasm as she can muster, even going so far as to agree to Treez letting her 'try it on'.

'I only met him a couple of weeks ago, at Stringfellows. There was this wet T-shirt competition for charity, and he bought me and my mate a few drinks. He's from Saudi. Usual type, you know, but very much a gentleman. Mercedes, flat in Knightsbridge – you know, the whole works. Anyway, we end up at Staki's playing the tables, and before I knew where I was we were causing some serious friction between his satin sheets! Dick as thick as a bleeding beer can, and hair all over.'

Marla hands the monstrous ring to her neighbour

and Treez slips it back on to her finger, where it nestles clumsily amongst the gaudy collection she already owns.

'I've got a little pressie for you. It's not much, just a token, but it's better than a kick up the arse with a peep-toed sandal!' Treez hands Marla a small box wrapped in silver paper with a pre-made bow stuck on the top.

'Oh, darn . . . I didn't get you anything,' says Marla, feeling embarrassed by her lack of consideration. Actually, Marla never buys Christmas gifts – she has a personal shopper who buys everything for her, gets it wrapped and shipped, and charges her Amex card.

'Well, it's nothing much,' smiles Treez with a flash of her diamond tooth. 'Go on, open it . . .'

The box contains an enamelled Limoges pillbox shaped like the Statue of Liberty. It probably cost £100 or more, and Marla is taken by surprise. She had imagined a pair of crotchless knickers from Ann Summers or something smelly from Marks & Spencer's.

'Treez, this is beautiful. I don't know what to say.'

Treez puffs herself up with pleasure, but waves one hand at the gift as though it is nothing. 'Ah, it's just a bit of nonsense, but I thought it'd go nice on that shelf in your little downstairs toilet, or something. I noticed you had a few already, so I sneaked a look underneath one of them last time I went for a slash, and made a note of the name. Got it in Harrods, no less!'

'You really shouldn't have spent so much but I really do appreciate your thoughtfulness. Thank you.'

'You're welcome, love. You've been through the mill these last few months, so I thought it might cheer you up. Anyway, I've got a butterball in the oven needs basting and I know you're off out yourself, so I won't hold you up. Oh, and if you find yourself at a loose end tomorrow night, I'm having a little party – nothing fancy, just a few friends and some booze. Why don't you bring that fella of yours over, if you find the time?'

'Actually I'm going to New York tomorrow and I will probably be gone for a couple of weeks.'

'You want me to pop in and water your plants or anything?' offers Treez, fiddling with a hooped earring that is caught in the collar of her blouse.

'Thanks, but no. My maid will be coming in and she'll see to that.'

'All right, love. Just give me a knock when you get back.'

'Happy Christmas, Treez.'

'Yeah, same to you, sweetheart. Let's hope it's a better year for you next year, eh?'

'I have a feeling it will be,' and Marla closes her door.

See, this is easy. All she has to do is pretend that everything is normal, and nobody will ever suspect that she's a fruitcake.

A brisk scrub with the cellulite cream and a new dress to wear, she'll be fine.

At least she now knows what kind of monster she is up against and, with a quick dab of Colgate on her toothbrush, she prepares to do battle with herself.

Twenty-three

Boxing Day. Lester and his wife Tina have arrived at her best friend's house in Earls Court.

It is a nice house, all white, with steps up to the red front door and bay trees in little pots that have been chained to the wall. It stands on a square just behind the main drag and it is one of the few remaining houses here that has not been turned into flats.

Lester hadn't realized that pornography was so lucrative.

It is still drizzling and the late afternoon sky is closing up for the day. There are halos around the streetlights and a lethargic Sunday evening feeling hangs beneath the bushes, misty grey and glum.

Brandi opens the red door, and light surfs out on a wave of central heating from behind her. She is wearing one of those sexy Santa outfits – short red fur-edged dress cinched in at the waist with a black belt, and a hood. Her hair is ginger – very ginger, and lots of it. It looks carefree and wild but it is welded with lacquer so that it doesn't move when Brandi does.

Tina and Brandi scream at each other, hold out their arms and kiss on the doorstep. Lester hangs behind, holding the vin ordinaire in a Christmassy bag, and he anticipates the evening with a sediment of dread that is about to be agitated to the surface.

'Lester darling, come on, come on, come to Momma!' And Lester allows himself to be swept through into the hallway on a red velvet sleeve that reeks of perfume and cigarettes. Brandi leaves sticky red kisses on everyone she touches, and as she struggles to lock the door behind them Lester is unsurprised to see that she is wearing nothing but a black leather thong under that very short Santa skirt.

'Everyone's here, darling!' whispers Brandi. 'Including that filthy bastard Angelo who is pissed out of his mind already and giving Raven one upstairs in the sauna! Danny is livid, Amber is crying in the loo, and we've got the bi-boys practically sucking each other off in the kitchen. Why is it that whenever we all get together like this is turns into a fucking fiasco? Danny reckons we should just bring a cameraman over here and shoot the entire scene. He reckons we could give it a raunchy title, put it out on the video shelves, and it'd sell itself!'

All of this before they even walk through to join the party. It is the same every time, and Lester has vowed over and over again that he's had it with Tina's porno pals. After the last party, when one of the girls overdosed on crystal meth and punctured a silicone implant, Lester had promised himself that from then on Tina could attend these affairs alone. But here he is, standing on the marble threshold of disaster once again, with his wife already ignoring him for the comparative glamour of plunging necklines and fake tans.

Two rooms knocked through into one with an archway in between and wallpaper made to look like pink marble. Chandeliers in bright gold and glass reflect from a pair of matching chimney breasts which have been clad in plate mirror. The fitted carpet is plush and spongy to tread on and most of the women in the room are wearing impossibly high heels, which makes walking practically impossible for them. There are probably about twenty people in the room: all of them dressed in American-style soap-opera 'formal wear'. The men wear black tuxedos with frothy white shirts and bow ties on elastic and the women wear cleavage-hugging, backless, strappy sheaths of clingy fabric that leave little to the imagination. Hair and earrings are big, breasts are hitched up and pushed forward.

'Look who's here!' screams Brandi as she drags Tina into the centre of the room. Several high-heeled women shuffle forward with arms outstretched, advancing upon Lester's wife like Barbie dolls with a mission. More screaming, more kissing, and Lester dumps the wine on the corner of the upholstered bar and helps himself to a large whisky.

'I hear congratulations are in order, Lester.'

Brandi's husband Danny appears from behind a badly executed copy of Michelangelo's *David*. Danny is a film producer: mid-forties, hair weave, skin the colour and texture of rice pudding. The kind of man who might easily persuade you to give up your wallet on a dark night.

'Yes, they called me on Christmas Eve. It was quite a Christmas present.'

'Brandi tells me you've got the lead – some kind of middle-aged superstud?'

'Yeah, I guess I'm being typecast again. A giant purple pig one week and a middle-aged superstud the next!' Lester finds himself smiling too enthusiastically to disguise his annoyance so he takes another swig of his drink. Danny is the kind of person Lester has absolutely nothing in common with but unfortunately, because of the friendship between Brandi and Tina, they are often thrown together like this.

'So you'll be doing some nude scenes, I hear?' smirks Danny, and Lester catches the ironic catch in the question. Danny knows about Lester's less than magnanimous views on the kind of films that Danny makes.

'A couple maybe, but nothing that would get me star billing on one of *your* films.'

'Nudity is nudity, mate. You get your khaks off and show 'em your goods, and it makes no difference if it's the BBC or the Playboy Channel.'

Lester is in no mood to argue the point so he just smiles politely. Danny has a habit of hitching up his balls every few minutes, so Lester looks away for a moment and surveys the room.

'Did you see the picture?' asks Danny, finished with his pocket billiards for the time being. 'Got it as a present for Brandi. Thought it looked the business over the sofa, what do you think?'

Lester approaches the large canvas with Danny and they appraise the artwork through a mist of cigarette smoke.

It is a modern piece depicting two semi-naked women astride a motorbike while a leather-clad biker-type with an impossible physique snaps pictures of them with a hand-held camera. It is a ghastly piece of erotic crap and Lester is stumped for words, so he allows Danny to extol the dubious virtues of the piece. 'This guy is going to be really big when his exhibition opens in Tokyo. He's American but lives here in London. I met him at a press party at the Hippodrome a few weeks back, and then I went to his studio. Fucking ace stuff! I was bowled over by these life-size canvases that he's done – he's a real artist. Just look at the way he's captured the folds in this bird's skirt; you can practically see the outline of her—'

Danny is interrupted in mid-flow by a summons from Brandi at the kitchen door. Lester can see only too clearly what the artist had in mind when he airbrushed the contours of that skirt. He turns his back on the masterpiece of sexual indulgence and takes a quick look at the food to see if there is anything worth nibbling.

Cheeses and slabs of processed meat vie for space on the side table with leftover turkey breast and pickles. It is the usual Boxing Day fare and Lester has no appetite for it. He eats a couple of fudgy brownies and washes them down with his whisky – not a particularly palatable combination, but enough to stave off his hunger for anything more satisfying.

Tina has buggered off somewhere with her friends, and Lester is stranded with the other husbands and boyfriends, most of whom he has met before and disliked for one reason or another. There is a strikingly tall woman with what can only be described as a mane of dark chestnut-brown hair and a figure that appears hand-moulded to fit inside the simple black dress that she is wearing. She has removed her shoes and is leaning against the corner, feeding herself strips of honey-baked ham from a paper plate. She has her eyes closed and her head tilted back so that the ham can slip easily between her slightly greasy lips. Porn stars just have a way with food.

Lester watches her for a few minutes. She is a new face to him, and slightly older than the rest of the girls who usually hang around Brandi and Danny at these affairs. The firm, tanned breasts are there and the witchy fingernails, but there is something about this woman that puts her a notch above the others. A kind of young Sophia Loren.

Her name is Sable.

'But my real name is Doris,' continues Sable as she takes Lester's hand and grips it with a firmness that surprises him. 'My parents lived an artless life and had little imagination beyond what they read in the *Sun* or watched on telly. I was brought up in Bangor, you see, so that should explain everything.'

Sable has a voice that most people would describe as sultry. It is throaty without being hoarse, and it is smooth without seeming practised. She enunciates her words as though choosing each of them carefully from a self-selected compendium, and as she speaks she illustrates her words with a deliberate form of eye contact that mesmerizes Lester as soon as they meet.

The room is growing warmer. His face feels flushed and the whisky must have gone straight to his head because he finds himself moving closer to Sable, inhaling her perfume in the way that the advertising companies would have us imagine is quite normal. Seductive. Obsessive. Languorous. Words like that pop up like subliminal messages on the screen of Lester's sensory perceptions.

'You'll have to forgive me,' he says, swaying slightly. 'That last drink went straight to my head and I haven't eaten anything except a couple of brownies. I feel distinctly sozzled.'

'Darling,' whispers Sable, 'you are stoned. Those brownies are loaded with dope, so you're going to be high for the rest of the evening.' And the mere brush of Sable's arm against his own produces a tiny explosion of goosepimples which shoot directly into his crotch and make him hard as a rock.

The room has dimmed around him. He can just about focus on Sable now, but his peripheral vision is a blur of melting colours. His face feels expanded somehow – *swollen* for want of a better description – and flushed with desire. Lester hasn't been stoned for years and he had forgotten just how liberating the sensation can be. He knows that he is leering at Sable. He knows that he is making a complete fool of himself, but he really couldn't care less.

'This is my husband Roland.'

Lester hears her say the words but he can't really respond without falling slightly against the edge of the table to steady himself. He is aware of a tall man with one of those fashionable little beards. A tall, handsome man with a ponytail, and hands that crush Lester's own in an athletically challenging fashion. He is saying something but Lester pays little attention. He feels slightly sick and thinks that what he really needs is some fresh air. Without announcing his intentions, he pushes himself through the small crowd of people at the kitchen door and he instinctively heads for the back of the house. Thunderbolts do the same thing apparently: they come down the chimney and head for the nearest exit, burning everything in their wake.

A stinging blast of damp December air wraps itself around Lester, awakening his numbed senses. It feels good for a moment then it instantly makes him feel worse and he begins to shiver rather violently, as though the drizzle has already permeated his clothing and soaked through to his bones. He needs to sit down. There is a low wall covered with moss, so he perches himself on the edge and lowers his heavy head down between his knees. A cold, unhealthy sweat has made his face feel greasy, and he knows that there is no colour to his skin.

He is going to be sick, yet still clings to the hope that this feeling will pass. He still thinks that if he doesn't swallow the saliva rising in his mouth he will get through this, but he has reached that inevitable moment of no return. It is like being a defenceless child again, the horrifying loss of bodily control and the panicked gasping for breath, as he lurches forward and throws up on the crazy paving.

It is a noisy affair. He is on his knees, his hands flat against the wet stone. He remains like this for a few moments, contemplating the sense of relief and the messy nastiness of his situation. Light from the kitchen windows and the sound of party voices and music merge with the cold night sounds of the surrounding city. A barking dog several houses away. An ambulance racing to someone's rescue. The constant resonance of a city that never falls asleep.

He goes back into the house and finds the kitchen has emptied. He rinses his face at the sink and tries to clear his throat. Suddenly he is ravenously hungry.

'They're all downstairs,' explains a wayward-looking woman who appears too drunk or too stoned to realize that her breasts have broken completely free of her jacket lapels. She holds the edge of the countertop as though the ground beneath her feet is undulating violently. 'They're watching Danny's latest film on the big-screen telly. Are you an actor?'

'Yes, I am,' says Lester, 'but not the kind that appears in the films that Danny makes.'

'I've seen you on something,' says the unstable woman with the liberated breasts. 'I never forget a face.'

'I used to be in *Crossroads* but you're probably too young to remember that.'

'The *pig!*' shrieks the woman. 'You're the pig! My little Charlotte loves you!'

Lester nods wearily and steps around the woman. 'Yes, that's me. I'm the pig.' And he leaves her there to contemplate the fact that she has just met a celebrity who *doesn't* take off his clothes to make a living.

The basement of Brandi and Danny's house has been turned into a movie theatre. Everyone has crowded down there to watch the film, and Lester finds them all engrossed in a graphic close-up of what they call in the business a 'double penetration'. He sees Tina sitting over in the corner with a very young chap with long hair and a cleavage. They look very cosy. When she sees Lester, she waves to him excitedly and points to the screen as the camera pulls back for a broader view of the copulating threesome.

It isn't the carefully orchestrated sexual acrobatics that cause Lester to stare at the moving pictures. It isn't even the fact that they are doing it over a billiard table. It is the topless barmaid who appears to be buffing up her cocktail shaker in the background who draws Lester further into the room for a better view.

'Doesn't she look hot, Lester!' shouts Danny from his armchair in the corner. 'A natural if ever I saw one. Cracking pair of tits.'

And Lester stares at his wife on the screen with open disbelief.

Without saying a word, he turns and leaves the room.

He climbs the stairs. He leaves the house without reclaiming his coat.

He stands at the top of the stone steps and he looks out across the square of grass and trees all hemmed in behind little iron railings, and he knows that Tina will not come after him. She has never come after him, not since those first few months when they couldn't get enough of each other. Not since she stopped telling him that she loved him.

Lester closes his eyes and counts to ten. Like they used to do when they played hide and seek in the junior school playground.

Coming, ready or not!

And Lester heads for the main road, where he will hail down a cab and travel all the way home with a driver who thinks that Princess Diana and John F. Kennedy Jr. are living in sin somewhere off the coast of Mexico.

PART TWO

Twisted

Twenty-four

People sometimes do the most unexpected things.

They sit in the armchair of life for thirty years, flicking through a catalogue of possibilities, and one day, to the astonishment of everyone they know, they stop browsing and they decide to make a purchase.

Here stands Annie Noble (née Stamper) on the threshold of her home.

The house on Fulham Road was left locked and abandoned when Spencer disappeared, and Annie has not been back since. The house is bequeathed to Spencer's son Billy but now, if Spencer never turns up, Billy intends to give the house back to Annie. An unanticipated suggestion that changes the course of Annie's future, as a fallen tree might alter the flow of a stream. She has come back to the house that never felt like home, back to the city that alienated her. And next week Annie will fly to Key West to model for Michaela Fox, at £1,000 a day plus expenses.

It was Betsy who made her take the plunge.

'There is nothing for you in Chesterfield,' she had told Annie from her hospital bed. 'Everything is set up for you – a house, a job and the chance to do something really wonderful with your life. You'd be thick not to leap at the chance. Even if the modelling doesn't work out you've still got that job in Spencer's office if you want to go back.'

So Annie has done the right thing, even though she doesn't feel so sure about it.

Here she stands in her winter coat with the fur collar, and she has pushed open the door of the house to sniff at the air within. Richard Carruthers, Marla's accountant, is with her. He drove up to Chesterfield to fetch her, and they had Sunday dinner with her mum and dad before they left. It is dark now, being January, and the house casts its shadows over the polished floors that Spencer was so fond of.

Richard goes into the house ahead of Annie. He walks with the confidence of a man who has lived all of his life with a disability and Annie no longer notices the awkward gait of this man who has been so kind to her since Spencer died. It is just Richard, after all.

Richard and his limp.

While Annie is fat.

These things go without saying.

'It's parky in here,' observes Richard as he heads for the fuse box under the stairs.

Annie remains on the doorstep with the strangest feeling in the pit of her stomach. It is a feeling that hasn't really touched her since she found out that Spencer had gone missing; a feeling that still lives in this house. Grief and mourning hang from the walls like invisible drapery, shifting slightly as though someone has just passed through.

'It's spooky without the lights,' says Annie as she peers up the dark staircase to the landing where the moon shines through the skylight. Richard is still in the cupboard under the stairs and Annie waits until the lights come on before she finally enters the house and closes the door behind her.

She feels as though they are trespassing. They don't belong here; they clutter the clean surfaces and disrupt the serene, harmonious colours that Spencer preferred. Nine shades of white on the ground floor alone. Annie knows this because she has seen the meticulous notes that Spencer keeps in his filing cabinet. The house still smells of eucalyptus oil and new carpet, even though it has been fully decorated for over two years. It is a house that speaks in quiet voices.

'We'll have to pop out to Sainsbury's to fill up the fridge for you, and I'd better get the heating going. It's like a museum in here – not a thing out of place.'

'I'd forgotten how much I dislike this house. All these things that Spencer collected. He told me that every object has a spirit, but I just get the impression that every strange object is watching me. These paintings and the African things in the living room – everything seems to watch me. I would like to get rid of most of it, if it was up to me.' And just as Annie says this, the central heating clicks on and makes her jump. She laughs nervously and Richard touches her arm.

'It'll be fine,' he says, and Annie wonders if he is right. Will things ever be fine again?

'It doesn't feel fine at all, Richard,' she says. 'It all feels very wrong. I'm not happy, and moving back to London strikes me as bloody stupid when I hated it here so much in the first place. I don't like this house, and being in it just makes me think about Spencer. Going to Florida on Thursday should be a treat, but instead it just feels as though I'm running away from everything. I don't feel as though I belong anywhere: not here, not at home, not anywhere. *Where* am I going?' And with this depressing statement she bursts into tears.

Richard pulls Annie into the hollow of his shoulder and his hand makes circles on the back of her coat as he attempts to calm her down. He makes encouraging noises, whispering words as though soothing a child, and his lips are almost touching the crown of Annie's chestnut-brown head. Annie barely registers any of this as she sobs into the tweed of his jacket. She feels very lonely and abandoned, and the cold sterile kitchen does nothing to help her regain a sense of identity.

'Let's go out and get some dinner,' she says, wiping her face on the palm of her hand. 'I don't want to eat here, and it'll take a while for the place to heat up. There's a restaurant up the street where Spencer and I *didn't* used to eat, so that seems like a safe bet.'

'Come on, then,' smiles Richard. He stands in the middle of the room with his arms still slightly open, as though they have not yet recovered from holding Annie. He himself does not look at home in this granite and stainless-steel environment. He needs a country kitchen with weathered pine and a Belfast sink. He needs a mug of tea and a shaggy dog and a wife who throws bread-crumbs out to the birds. But Annie barely registers any of this as she wipes her face clean of tears and prepares to lose herself in a huge plate of food.

The restaurant is one of those American affairs, all movie posters and television screens showing baseball games. Annie and Richard are the only people there, so they get to choose a booth by the window, beneath a flashing traffic light and several artificial ferns. Maybe there was a good reason Spencer and Annie never ate here before. It is hardly the kind of place that Spencer would have frequented. Across the road they can see the artfully lit interior of the seafood restaurant where Spencer Annie on numerous occasions. It is busy with people wearing black and beige. It has white walls and white tablecloths, and they don't have a salad bar there, or Phil Collins on the stereo.

That is Spencer's life, over *there* behind the frosted-glass panels and the plate-glass doors.

This is Annie's life, over *here* with the fake Tiffany lampshades and the ketchup bottles.

'Hiya!' chirrups the waitress with the black nail varnish. 'Can I get you something to drink from the bar? Our special tonight is strawberry margarita.'

Annie orders a Pepsi and Richard asks about the beer.

'Michelob, Budweiser, Samuel Adams, Double Diamond, Fuller's Old Winter, Red Dog, Heineken, McEwan's, Samuel Smith, Anstel Light, St Pauli Girl, Coors . . .' The waitress looks over her shoulder towards the bar and takes another deep breath. '. . . Beck's, Whitbread Pale Ale, Sierra Nevada, Young's Ram Rod, Ruddle's County, Boddington's, Bass, Newcastle Brown, Carling Black Label, Steinlager, Harp, and there's also Guinness on tap but it's playing up and the head's a bit frothy tonight.'

'So no Belgian beers, then?' asks Richard, and it takes a second or two before the waitress sees the joke.

'You've got a right one here!' she laughs, punching Annie in the arm. 'No Belgian beers,' she mutters to herself as she goes to fetch their drinks.

'It's quiet, isn't it?' Annie looks around at the empty restaurant and wonders why it feels so much like a Sunday night. Sunday nights are depressing: they are for watching the telly, but not for staying up too late, because once the news comes on it's time for an early night. They are for soaking in the bath with lily-of-the-valley bath cubes and listening to next door rattling through the embers with the poker. Sunday nights are school nights, with a clean shirt on a hanger over the door frame and a satchel filled with homework not yet finished. So depressing were Sunday nights to Annie that the feeling has stayed with her all these years, and the only time she can shrug off the gloom of the weekend's ending is when she is on holiday. On holiday the days all get muddled up, and it's hard to tell if it's Sunday or Wednesday. Everyone keeps saying how it feels like a Thursday when it's only Tuesday, and every day becomes a weekend when there's no Monday to dread.

'I wish there was something I could do to cheer you up, Annie,' says Richard. 'You seem so sad and there's nothing I can do. I feel rather useless.'

'Richard, you have done more for me today than anyone else has done in weeks. I couldn't have done this without you. I couldn't have waved goodbye to Mum and Dad without bawling all the way to London, if you hadn't kept me talking. I don't think I could have moved back into Spencer's house without you being there with me.'

'You know I'd be happy to sleep in the guest room tonight if it would make you feel more comfortable.'

'Thanks, Richard, I appreciate the offer but I have got to get used to living there on my own, so I should start as I mean to go on. Now, let's order some food before I start gnawing through the table, I'm in the mood for onion rings and a bacon cheeseburger – bugger the consequences!'

Despite the greasy food and the pleasant company, the evening doesn't manage to lift itself above the tide line of Annie's mood. The chocolate chip brownie with banana ice cream doesn't help much either so she finishes off Richard's half-eaten cheesecake with a gulp of Irish coffee. She barely tastes the food, and she isn't really hungry, but the act of eating gives her something to do and it's better than dwelling on other things.

'I'm not being very good company, am I?' she asks, wiping her mouth on a paper napkin.

'Actually this makes a pleasant change for me on a Sunday evening. There are always so many things that need doing at my house, and I never seem to finish any of them. When I'm at home I'm usually just pottering around and achieving very little. I've been in the house for six years now and I still haven't finished stripping the paint off the door frames. So much for good intentions. At least Spencer's house is finished – ready to live in.'

'Finished, yes, but I'm not sure I'm ready to live in it,' smiles Annie. 'Spencer is so proud of that house, but it just isn't me. I can't stand all those mucky colours he has used upstairs – his "taupes" and his "birchwoods". I have always liked cheerful colours myself. I saw a nice lavender and pale green duvet cover in John Lewis the other day, but Spencer would never dream of using such cheerful colours.'

'Well, I would be more than happy to help you paint the bedroom if . . . well, if it turns out that the house becomes yours,' offers Richard. 'I'm always happier helping other people with their DIY projects than I am with doing my own.'

Annie stifles a yawn; she feels exhausted. It has been a long day and the food has made her sleepy.

'Come on, Annie, let's skip the supermarket and get you home to bed.'

And the house is just a short walk away.

Centrally heated and artistically lit.

'Richard, I don't know how to thank you.'

They stand in the shadows of Spencer's hall, against a limited edition print that is expensively framed in black burl walnut. The house is very quiet: just the distant hum of the refrigerator in the kitchen and the traffic in the street outside.

'It was my pleasure,' says Richard, and his hands are pushed deep inside the pockets of his padded jacket. The recessed lights turn his glasses opaque and Annie cannot see his eyes. She feels numb and frozen.

When Richard kisses her it comes as something of a surprise.

He keeps his hands in his pockets and his lips are soft against her own. When he pulls away Annie raises her fingers to her mouth.

'I'm sorry . . .' Richard mumbles and steps away.

For a moment Annie sees herself in Richard's shoes. She sees the vulnerability, the uncertainty and the good intentions, as though she is looking into a mirror. She wants to say something that will break the silence, something that will bring them back into the present time. They stand inside the arch of light, with the beige walls all around them and the polished floorboards beneath their feet, barely breathing.

'I'm not sure how sensible this suggestion will sound, but I *would* like you to stay here with me tonight,' whispers Annie with a voice that comes up from somewhere so deep inside that she barely registers its existence until it is floating between them.

'All right . . .' says Richard, shrugging his padded shoulders but still maintaining his distance. 'I've never been one for sensible suggestions myself.'

'Not in the guest room,' Annie says. 'I mean . . . I don't want you to sleep in the guest bedroom, I want you to sleep with me. Does that sound awful?'

'I understand, and no, it doesn't sound awful at all. In fact it sounds rather wonderful,' and Richard smiles with an expression so heartbreakingly honest that it splinters the surface of Annie's resolve.

'I have only just realized that I don't want to be alone tonight,' she says. 'And I don't want that to sound so . . . casual.'

Richard, as though released from a spell, moves forward and places his hands on Annie's shoulders. 'You're going to be just fine, Annie. These things take time. And from my own selfish point of view, I have to say that your invitation is something I have hoped for.'

He kisses her again, this time with less hesitancy. His fingers run through her hair and they both fall back against the wall, knocking the framed print slightly askew on the flat beige surface.

And if Annie keeps her eyes closed, she can almost imagine that Spencer is still here.

Back in his house.

Back with his wife.

Where he belongs.

Twenty-five

Always a variation on a familiar theme.

Marla's dreams are beginning to haunt her by day and she lies awake in the early hours of the morning, attempting to decipher their portentous symbolism.

She is staying at a small hotel on the Upper East Side where nobody knows her. From the window of her small sitting room she can just see Central Park, wedged prosaically between two tall buildings of drab grey stone whose windows and their inhabitants have become familiar to Marla since she arrived here on Boxing Day.

It has been snowing again: heavy New York snow that stops the traffic and clogs up the news reports with repetitious warnings and mindless speculation. At this time in the morning it is still night and the sky won't begin to lighten for at least another two hours. The hotel is quiet – just for these couple of hours when everyone is asleep. Like a sick woman, Marla is propped up in the very centre of her huge, huge bed, with a packet of cigarettes and a plastic lighter that she rolls between the palms of her hands as she sucks on her first intake of nicotine for the day.

The dream is getting clearer every night. It is a frustrating dream that thuds in Marla's head like a sinus pain, like a memory that just won't come to the surface. She will discuss it with Dr Ramirez again on Thursday, and he will offer no explanations. He will merely sit in his chair with his legs crossed and he will look directly at Marla as though she herself should provide the answer. He prompts her with teasing questions, attempting in his cleverness to disguise the fact that he *knows* why Marla is so bewildered. If Marla thought that her current fears were based purely on a long-buried guilt trip over Jessica, she wouldn't be paying Dr Ramirez $120 an hour, now would she?

Long-buried. An unfortunate turn of phrase. A Freudian slip?

She is convinced that there is more to it than that.

Every night since she started visiting Dr Ramirez she has had the same dream. Never *exactly* the same, always a variation but with the same overwhelming sense of fear. The fear of discovery and the fear of punishment? Punishment for the heinous crime she has committed? Marla could never survive in a prison. She would rather receive the death penalty than be incarcerated for the rest of her life. She wonders who it is in the grave that she sees in these dreams. She hears her victim calling to her through the woods – a death rattle filled with the frightful tones of retribution.

Last night the dream was again slightly different. It was one of those horrible nightmares when lights wouldn't come on, and when they did they only flickered in the darkness as though drained of power. Long corridors with sharp corners, each turn looming with all the premonitory dread of an approaching ghoul. There was a baby crying somewhere but Marla could not move quickly enough to find it, and the cries became further and further away. She knew that the baby was Jessica, but where was she? Each door that Marla opened revealed just another empty room: bare, dusty floor-boards and peeling wallpaper, and always a single, bare light bulb that refused to illuminate more than a quivering halo of empty space.

Outside the house are the woods – the woods where she would find the grave. And Marla knows that it won't be long before they come to get her.

Then she had woken with a start.

Just like the other nights. And the lingering sense of guilt and fear stays with her even when she turns on the light and forces herself to stay awake until dawn. She has a photograph of baby Jessica, less than one month old, and she keeps it in her bedside drawer between the pages of a Bible. When Marla looks at that photograph she tries to remember what it had felt like to be a mother but, as hard as she tries, she can only remember what it felt like to be accused of murder.

The murder of her own baby.

What can be more upsetting than that?

The guilt alone is enough to last her a lifetime and even though they say that she is coping very well these days, she is beginning to think that maybe the experts were too optimistic with her prognosis. Guilt is like an oily knot in a piece of cheap timber, and it is only a matter of time before that ugly stain begins to show through the paint again, oozing and resinous and unfailingly persistent.

Marla attempted to leave the scandal behind when she divorced Lester. She needed to move on with her life and to find safe harbour from the cruel and thoughtless taunts of people she didn't even know. People who had nothing better to do than throw sticks and stones. Funny really, she had always clung possessively to her

maiden name when she was married, but in order to
purchase a certain amount of anonymity she took Lester's name when they got divorced. She left Lester but
she took his name. Like a memento.

And people soon forgot about her. There was something new in the papers, something else for people to
get riled up about. Marla had escaped, but she would
never be unscathed.

She calls the office in London. Things are going to
pieces over there without her and several clients are
threatening to find more reliable lawyers. A friend of
Marla's has been helping out, but he doesn't have the
experience or the knowledge of her clients to perform
more than the most rudimentary of services. She should
be over there herself – she needs a new partner, her staff
are floundering without her direction. But if she goes
back now she will have to face up to Mark, and so far
he suspects nothing of her schizophrenic attack at
Christmas. She needs more time, more therapy, more
isolation.

There have been no disruptions since she came to
New York, no nocturnal wanderings as far as she can
tell. She is taking tranquillizers which seem to be helping. She tries to keep up with her workload via fax and
the Internet, but she can't concentrate on anything for
very long before her mind wanders back to that freshly
dug grave and the ghostly sound of the wind in the
trees.

There will be a short respite from all of this for the
next couple of days. Marla is flying down to Key West
to catch up with Michaela Fox so that they can hammer
out some of the kinks in their immigration strategy, for
Michaela's London office. They could have met up in

Manhattan but Michaela had suggested Key West as a chance for Marla to unwind. They are working on a summer catalogue down there. She will have a guaranteed stress-free environment.

Marla smokes another cigarette and decides to take a shower. They'll start serving breakfast at six, and then she can watch the *Today* show and drag herself back into the reality of a world that apparently continues unhindered by Marla's current non-participation.

To make a jarring transition from one climate to another can be quite disorientating to a woman who is currently on the verge of an identity crisis. Marla arrives in Miami – following a three-hour delay on the frozen tarmac of JFK Airport – to cloudless skies, palm trees and the mercury just prodding 80 degrees. She has to wait an hour or so for her connecting flight to Key West, so she sips freshly squeezed Florida orange juice – with just a little vodka – at an open-air bar where the waiters wear short-sleeved shirts and khaki shorts.

The puddle-jumper gets her into Key West at half past five, and Marla is just a little bit tanked. The medication she is currently taking does not mix well with alcohol, so she is feeling strangely euphoric and the taxi ride to the guest house is a blur of colour and warmth. The windows are open and she can smell a tropical ripeness that obliterates the concrete and ice of New York City.

The guest house is blindingly white, even though the sun has dropped low on the horizon. A Victorian-looking house with an assortment of verandas, balconies and louvred shutters, it is surrounded by lush vegetation and lusciously saturated colours. No wonder Hemingway settled here in the '30s. On the main front porch there is a swinging bench from which a middle-aged gentleman dangles a sandal from his big toe. He is sipping iced tea and fanning himself languidly with a straw hat. He raises the hat to salute Marla as she approaches the house, and she waves back, although she has no idea who he might be.

'Charles Farlow, proprietor and house-mother. Welcome to Shangri-La.'

He stands in the coolness of the hallway beneath a slowly turning ceiling fan, and a small transparent lizard scuttles across the floor to hide in the shadow at the bottom of the staircase.

'They're all down by the ocean,' he explains, 'still taking pictures and probably taking full advantage of this marvellous sunset. They really couldn't have picked a better week to come down – it has been extraordinarily beautiful for the time of year.'

Michaela and her entourage have taken over the guest house for ten days, filling the rooms with models, photographers and stylists from New York. Charles offers Marla an informative tour of the house and then shows her up to the third floor, where she will have the 'last remaining room'. He apologizes for the size of the attic bedroom and for the fact that it does not have its own bathroom, but Marla is too tired and too befuddled to register much of what he is telling her. She only sees the single brass bed with its patchwork quilt. She feels the trapped evening warmth that radiates from behind the closed teakwood shutters, and she breathes the pleasantly dusty scent of a house that has spent its life baking in the sun.

'No air conditioning, just the fans,' says Charles, indicating the switch by the door, 'but at this time of the year there's no humidity, so you should be comfortable. We leave the pool open twenty-four hours a day and bathing suits are optional if you like to bare it all. Breakfast is served outside by the pool at seven thirty and it is buffet-style, so you can wander down whenever you feel up to it. We'll be serving cocktails when everyone gets back, which should be – ' Charles checks his watch – 'in about half an hour, so I'll leave you to unpack and see you downstairs at six-thirty.'

Marla flops down on to the brass bed, and the mattress yields unhealthily beneath her. She could do with a good sleep. A clock strikes six somewhere in the house, and there must be parrots outside because Marla can hear them chattering mindlessly from beyond the closed shutters. She is now glad that she came. This was a good suggestion and she will thank Michaela for bringing her here. She folds the pillow beneath her head and closes her eyes. Like a lullaby the house surrounds her and she can feel herself falling down amidst the gentle folds of the dusty evening warmth.

When she wakes the room is completely dark. There are voices in the hall outside and laughter drifts up from the back of the house where, presumably, everyone has gathered for drinks by the pool. She only slept for forty minutes or so but she immediately feels refreshed. No dreams that she can recall, and she has a sudden desire for a sharp gin and tonic with plenty of ice and lemon. She switches on the bedside lamp, brushes the creases from her already dishevelled linen suit and goes in search of company.

On the second-floor landing she encounters a very

muscular young man wearing nothing but a pair of square-cut swimming trunks and a baseball cap. His nipple is pierced and he has a decorative black band tattooed around the top of one bulging biceps. When he sees Marla on the stairs he smiles brightly and rattles a glass filled with ice at her.

'Cocktails by the pool, sweetheart! It's getting a tad cool out there, so I was just fetching a shirt.'

'I think we've met before, haven't we?' croaks Marla. 'I'd never forget a body like that.'

He laughs self-deprecatingly and looks down at his expensively moulded chest. 'Yes, we have – at Michaela's loft last fall.' He offers Marla his handshake. 'Taylor Hess, pleased to meet you again, Marla. I was really sorry to hear about your partner. I just couldn't believe it when I heard that he'd tried to kill himself like that. I suffered terrible guilt for days afterwards. Maybe if I hadn't seduced him in Michaela's bathroom that evening, he wouldn't have run off like that and tried to blow his brains out.'

'I guess he would have flipped sooner or later, and I'm sure that if it hadn't been you, Taylor, it would have been some other guy. Now, show me where the party is: I need cigarettes and I need alcohol before I turn back into a respectable human being.'

'Follow me, sweetheart – although I have to warn you that these models are not of the Kate Moss variety. We're talking serious body fat here. You should see the way they inhale their drink. It takes an entire bottle of Absolut before they're even feeling it!'

'They sound like my kind of people,' laughs Marla and she follows Taylor's tight little butt down to the back of the house.

There is a cool breeze blowing through the ground floor of the guest house and the temperature has dropped considerably in the last hour or so. Marla follows Taylor through the conservatory where the caged parrots continue to chatter amidst a jungle of potted palms and luscious ferns. Two overweight women wearing brightly coloured sarongs occupy wicker chairs that appear rather too fragile for adequate support. The women smile at Taylor and he cracks a joke about that being their fourth Martini in fifteen minutes.

Outside, where the tropical evening is lit with coloured lights and hurricane lamps, Marla finds Michaela holding court by the poolside. Her hair has changed colour once again and she is sporting a sleek look with a collection of plastic clips that look as though they were purchased for a dime a piece at the drugstore.

'At last!' she cries when she sees Marla. 'I thought you were going to stay up in your room all evening. I was just about to send you a fuzzy navel. Charles makes the most *fun* cocktails, sweetheart!'

Kiss, kiss. This is Michaela and her group of sycophants.

Marcie and June, Forrest and Blair, Thom the Sexiest Photographer on the East Coast, and of course you already know our darling Annie.

Marla accepts a seat by Thom and Marcie.

'It's lovely to see you, Marla,' says Annie. 'I'm still feeling a bit overwhelmed by all of this and it's nice to see a familiar face. I feel like I'm in a film. I don't think it's quite sunk in yet.'

'You'll soon get used to it, honey,' says Michaela, slurping back the last of her drink. 'A few more exotic photo shoots and you'll be complaining about the size of your room and demanding a 50 per cent increase in your fees.'

Marla has heard that Annie and Richard have been seeing quite a lot of each other since Annie moved back into Spencer's house. It has become something of a scandal at the office; particularly as Spencer is still missing and could turn up at any moment. Marla was oblivious to the fact that Annie and Richard even much knew each other, beyond the inevitable contact of working in the same office together. Richard is one of those people whom Marla never imagines having a private life. He is her accountant, and to Marla he just represents gross annual income and tax returns. And what happens if Spencer isn't dead?

But who is Marla to begrudge Annie a little happiness? After all, even if Spencer does come back, he'll probably want to get a divorce so that he can get on with his life. He can't deny his sexuality any longer, now that it's been spread over almost every tabloid in Britain. Perhaps Annie deserves a chance of real love with a man who has no ulterior motive.

'Make sure you get yourself a good agent, Annie, because I know Michaela – she'll have you working for peanuts.'

'Hush that big mouth of yours, Marla! You're off duty now and I don't want you spreading dissension amongst my highly paid and gorgeously pampered employees. Anyway, for your information, Annie has just signed a contract with the Swank agency in Manhattan. I introduced her to Val Rosen yesterday afternoon – they are mad about her already. Our little orphan Annie is going to make a big splash on the West Coast, where outsize fashion has become de rigueur.'

257

'Congratulations, Annie. I know that Spencer will be very proud of you.'

Marla isn't sure if she should have said that, because her comment causes an awkward stillness in the general conversation. Fortunately Annie rises to the occasion and does not take umbrage.

'I don't know if he'd be chuffed to know that I'm going to be famous for being *fat!*' she says.

'We don't use that word around here, sweetheart!' admonished Michaela. 'Can you imagine the outrage if we launched our new catalogue for plus-sized garments as "clothes for fat people"!'

Charles appears by Marla's side and offers her a selection of tantalizingly named cocktails.

'Whatever has the largest alcohol content,' quips Marla, accepting a pink cigarette with a gold tip from Marcie with the painfully flat chest.

'Well, I have good news for you too, Marla,' announces Michaela, reaching forward to squeeze Marla's knee. 'Mark has called three times today trying to get hold of you. He said you can call him whatever time you get here – it's important.'

Marla feels sick. *Oh God! He's found out that he's been dating a psycho.*

'Did he say what it was about?' she asks with as much nonchalance as she can muster.

'They've caught the freak who's been stalking you! He's been arrested and they're holding him for questioning. Isn't that fabulous?'

'One very potent Long Island iced tea with plenty of ice,' says Charles, handing the glass to Marla.

'You'd better mix me another,' says Marla, 'I'm going to chug this one back in thirty seconds.'

And she feels as though her nightmare is coming true.

They've found the grave and it won't be long before they find the murderer.

Twenty-six

They have just released *Five Farthings* on DVD. The director's cut – in honour of the late Karl Steinbrenner.

One of Lester's musical numbers has been reinstated from the original cut, and he has been watching it over and over again as though mesmerized. It is like finding a small piece of his past that he had forgotten about. Like the page from a diary or a roll of undeveloped photographs buried in one of those time capsules that were so popular with schools back in the '60s.

He barely remembers shooting the number but the song comes back to him even now, thirty odd years later. It is an ensemble scene that involves a lot of extras but Lester is the central character. The song is called 'Never Say Never', and Lester can see why it was cut from the original: it is much weaker than the other songs and it doesn't really relate to the main storyline. He sings it with Shani at one point, the two of them sitting at the back of a horse-drawn cart surrounded by baskets of vegetables. The sight of them both on the screen, so young and yet so instantly recognizable, strains at Lester's throat and he feels a sense of loss so profound that he could easily cry.

But he doesn't.

The award-winning musical that captured our hearts.

That's what it says on the front cover. And there,

too, is Lester, perched on a carousel horse, waving his cloth cap in the air along with the rest of the cast.

Tomorrow he will tape the last of his *Pigbeet* shows in studio 6. He was rather upset that they let him out of his contract so easily; his agent had prepared for a legal battle but there was no contest, and Lester is now free of all obligation. He has heard on the grapevine that Kate Buckley is bringing in teen idol Sean Flynne from *Kidsville Junction* as a replacement. Just another kick up the arse for Lester, who is already feeling much older than his forty-seven years.

'Don't worry darling, this is just the break you needed. Your career is bound to get a kick-start from this new thing you're doing with Jane Graves, and you've been moaning for months now about the purple pig. This is your chance. You've got the Oscars in March, and then *Weird Anatomy* will be coming out in October. Nothing to worry about, darling. We'll get you a few adverts, too, and you'll be fine.'

This was his agent's attempt at encouragement but Lester is unconvinced, and the more he thinks about his new role the less confident he becomes. Everyone else in the cast has serious drama experience and the preliminary read-through was awful, with Lester tripping over his lines as though his tongue was numbed with novocaine. He heard someone snigger when he mispronounced 'awry', and the blood rushed to his face as though he were back at school reading Shakespeare out loud to the class.

Rehearsals don't start in earnest until the beginning of February, and they will begin filming a few weeks later. Lester has eight weeks to improve himself both mentally and physically for this challenge. He has been teamed up with a personal trainer who is going to torture him every morning in the gym in order to give him the kind of body that his character is supposed to have. Apparently it worked for John Cleese when he made *A Fish Called Wanda*.

Tina is in the bedroom, rummaging through the wardrobes for the last of her things. She is moving out and going to live with a girl called Fern in Brixton. Fern's boyfriend is helping Tina to fill her cardboard boxes, and Lester is having no part of it. He has barely spoken to Tina since Boxing Day, when he walked out of the party at Brandi's house and came home alone. Tina didn't even have the decency to call him that night. She didn't come home for three days and when she did she announced her decision to 'move on' with her life.

Moving on for Tina means a renewed career in porn movies. She is young enough and stupid enough to believe that there is glamour in removing her clothes and getting shagged in front of the camera several times a day. Funny, really – sex with Tina has never been that exciting; it was always far better with Marla. Tina is the type who could easily be filing her nails or singing along to a CD while Lester did all the hard work. Granted she has a nice body and her tits are big, but Lester hopes that she is going to put a bit more effort into her performances for the camera, otherwise she'll be out on her heels in no time.

These days, when Lester thinks about his marriage to Marla he can no longer see why they didn't give it a better chance. Admittedly they were ridiculously young: he was barely twenty and Marla was only a couple of years older. Both of them were much too immature and ambitious to realize what marriage meant; they just thought it would be fun and it expedited Marla's immigration process so they just did it. The few photographs that Lester still has of the wedding make him cringe with embarrassment, but they illustrate just how lightly the two of them took the oath of marriage. It was 1976, it was an East London registry office, and Lester's trousers were so wide at the bottom that it is hard to tell who's wearing the dress.

Maybe it isn't a good idea to look back to a time when one was young and reasonably successful. Lester was making a decent wage on *Crossroads* and Marla was holding her own as a junior at the law firm, and they were renting a furnished flat just off the King's Road that had Habitat floor cushions and track lighting. It was all very modern, very progressive and they thought they were 'it'.

There is a nostalgic sadness that sticks in Lester's throat when he remembers those early years with Marla. It all seems so distant now that it could have happened to different people; it could have been a film he saw or a story he read. Life was very colourful then: the '70s were brash and vulgar but nobody took things as seriously as they do now. It was before the Thatcherite excess of the '80s, and before the bleak, pared-down beige of the '90s. When Marla and Lester spent time together in London there always seemed to be a party, and they used to mix with the celebrities of the day. What happened to everyone? Where are they now? When Rula Lenska had her party to celebrate the success of her TV serial *Rock Follies*, Lester recalls quite clearly the excitement of drinking champagne in the jacuzzi with Julie Covington, Polly James and Tim Curry.

Where are his celebrity friends now? These days the only person who returns his calls is Shani. Once Lester and Marla had hit the headlines with the whole dreadful baby incident, the fair-weather friends soon disappeared, closing the shutters on friendships that were based purely on social connection. Nobody could afford to fraternize with baby-killers. By the time Marla was acquitted of the crime, it was too late to sop up the stigma that had spilled over their life, staining it with an indelible sense of disrepute.

So that was the beginning of the end for Lester and Marla. The halcyon days were bruised like rotting fruit and with the death of their baby came the death of their marriage.

'I'm taking this.' Tina's head appears around the living room door. She holds up the electric neck massager that somebody gave them as a wedding present. Next week would have been their first anniversary.

Maybe the giver of the gift had known it would turn out like this. Maybe it wasn't intended for Tina at all, but she can have it. She can take whatever she wants, just as long as she clears out every last vestige of her presence in Lester's life. He wants no reminders of his foolish mistake. He wants to rub her out, like a pencil smudge at the edge of a crisp clean line.

'You'll need to get yourself a new iron and ironing board 'cause I'm taking ours, seeing as how it was mine in the first place.'

'Oh, just take what you want, Tina: I honestly couldn't care less.' Lester doesn't look at his wife as he speaks; he keeps his eyes glued to the television screen as he continues to watch the lost scene from *Five Farthings* over and over again.

'You're not still watching *that*, are you?' Tina's ongoing rhetoric grinds against Lester's nerves and chips away at his patience. He ignores her.

Fern's boyfriend – a hulking black man in ripped jeans and a leather waistcoat – comes through the room carrying a large cardboard box piled high with shoes. 'All right, mate,' he mutters as he disappears into the kitchen.

He says the same thing every time he passes through. There are landmines in this flat, and so far they have been lucky, but Fern's boyfriend knows that it is just a matter of time before somebody loses a limb.

The living room is awkward with vacant spaces. There are dents in the pile of the carpet where things once stood. There are nails now evident in the wall and dusty circles on the tables. Lester no longer has a microwave, a vacuum cleaner, a full-length mirror or a guest bed. He has too much space to hang his clothes in, and too little cutlery to host a dinner party.

If he were to delve much deeper than the surface tension of his mood right now he would find a jumble sale of conflicting emotions. He likes to think that he is in control of his anger, resentment and fear, but they are merely bubbling away beneath a stretched-thin layer of superficiality. He doesn't want to be the bitter husband, the pugnacious antagonist who fires his insults as a way of releasing his frustrations. He wants to be fair, to understand why Tina is doing this. There seems little point in attempting to patch things up between them when it is so obvious that she is doing what she really wanted all along. He doubts that she ever loved him, even way back when they first met and she used to wear his underpants as a way of being closer to him when he was away. Theirs had never been a romantic coupling, and Tina's idea of affection was a calculated business that usually involved an ulterior motive. She has never done anything for nothing.

So why does Lester feel so lonely right now? Why does he look at the gaps in his living room and wish that Tina would come back and fill them all up again? Maybe it's just that something is better than nothing and, although Tina has never been the ideal wife, she did at least break the silence.

'I think that's it then,' says Tina, standing by the kitchen door with her plastic bin bags filled with the last of their married life. 'I've left Fern's number on the kitchen table and the keys on the peg in the hall. You can forward any post that comes for me. Can you write me a cheque for the money you owe me?'

'I'll send it to you,' replies Lester.

'Well, I kind of need it now . . .'

'Well, I kind of don't want to give it to you now, OK?'

'It's *my* money, Less. You have no right to—'

'Don't tell me what my rights are, Tina. I think you waived all involvement in my rights when you walked out on me. Now, I've given you everything that you want without creating a fuss so why don't you just toddle off and make your porno films and let me get on with my own life.'

Tina drops the bin bags on to the floor and stands her ground. She already looks like a porn star, with her big hair and her tight satin blouse straining the buttons.

She could be beautiful, but instead she has chosen to be a tart.

'Fuck you, Less!' she spits. 'I used that money to buy Christmas presents for *your* fucking friends, people I don't know and don't give a toss about. That five hundred quid is mine, and I'm not leaving here until I get it.'

'You'd better go and make up a bed for yourself in the spare room then, darling, because I am not writing that cheque for you until I do an inventory of everything that you've taken from here that belongs to me.'

Lester is as surprised by this statement as Tina, but now that he has voiced himself so succinctly he can see the sense in it. She is digging her own grave, and would have done much better just by leaving quietly.

'You can't do that!' she screams. 'I'll get a solicitor on your back and I'll clean you out. I'll claim half your earnings for the next ten years, and make you sell this place. I know what my rights are, Lester.'

'Maybe I'll claim half *your* earnings, sweetheart. After all, this is the age of equal rights and you'll be earning much more than me once that pussy of yours gets to work. Yes, I think that sounds like a great idea – thanks for making me think of it.'

'You bastard! You're not going to get away with this. I'm going to get you for every penny you've got. I'm going to ruin you. I know enough about you to spread your pathetic face across the front of every paper in England. Hell, I could even get paid for it!'

'Go and do your worst, Tina. It can't be any more demoralizing than the last year I've had. Marriage to you has been about as fulfilling as a premature ejaculation.'

'And you'd know all about that, wouldn't you?' snaps back Tina, teetering on her five-inch spike heels.

'Darling, you should be lucky that I came at all when I was having sex with you – there were times when I would have had more fun fucking the pillow.'

Tina's laugh is a shrill, cracked sound that lacks any humour, and she tosses back her lacquered curls with an attempt at theatrical contempt. She is going to be such a great porn actress!

'Lester, let's not get into that right now, OK? Because once I start listing your sexual inadequacies I might be here until next Christmas. Let's just say that you should invest in a good sex manual or get yourself a blow-up doll to play with, because all the time you were searching for my G-spot, I was thinking about my next threesome with Brandi and Danny.'

'You disgust me!' snarls Lester. 'Just get out! *Get out!*'

And it pleasures him to see the way Tina stumbles back, reeling from his sudden outburst.

'Everything all right in here?' It is Fern's big black boyfriend, stepping in from the kitchen to check on the situation.

'Everything is fine, mate,' smiles Lester. 'Tina was just leaving, weren't you, darling?'

'Just you wait, Lester, I'm going to show you—'

'Darling, you've already shown me everything that you are incapable of, now why don't you just buzz off like a good little slut and go show the world instead? I'm sure that your physical attributes are far more photogenic than your mental inadequacies. After all, in your new business a capacious cunt sells so much better than an O-level in domestic science. Correct me if I'm wrong, darling, but isn't that about the extent of your academic qualifications?'

'Steady on, mate,' says Fern's big black boyfriend.

'Go and fuck yourself!' shrills Tina – as a child might retaliate by sticking out its tongue. 'It might just be the first good orgasm I've had, since I met you!'

With that, Tina grabs her bin bags and leaves the flat with Fern's boyfriend following obediently behind her. As she slams the door, a picture falls from the living room wall and glass shatters on to the corner of the table.

All enveloping silence.

On the TV screen the sound is muted, but *Five Farthings* continues to play.

Lester feels deflated now. There was no joy in arguing with Tina; there was no sense of achievement from having allowed his anger to break through like that. He has just done what he said he wouldn't do – he has acted like the bitter, pugnacious jilted partner, and turned himself into a cliché.

He *needs* to talk to someone, so he calls Shani. With Marla in America, there is no one else he can confide in and Shani can always be counted on for emotional support.

'Oh, darling, I was just going to call you. Isn't it dreadful?'

'Isn't what dreadful?' asks Lester.

'The car wreck, darling – it was just on the news. Jane Graves and her husband were killed this morning when a juggernaut threw them over an embankment off the M25.'

'Oh no!' is all Lester can say when he hears the terrible news.

He wants to feel sorry for the loss of an acquaintance, for the death of a young and talented director who had been kind enough to offer him a starring role in her new TV drama.

But Lester only feels sorry for *himself*.

He is doomed.

And he sits in the wreckage of his life, and watches a last piece of its ceiling as it finally crashes down into the rubble.

Twenty-seven

'You know they use Calvin Klein's Obsession to mate ocelots?' says one of the make-up boys, as he finishes off Annie's translucent face powder. 'It must have some kind of pheromones in it, so I've been using it to see if it works on guys.'

The second make-up boy is working on Candy, another model, and he replies to his colleague via the mirror as though neither Annie nor Candy are even there.

'What's an ocelot? Some kind of bird?'

'No, it's a leopard I think.'

'So does it work? On guys, I mean?'

'Well, I get a lot of compliments from *women* but I can't say that I've noticed much of an increase in my sex life.'

'Well, just don't go to the zoo, honey, otherwise you'll have them big ole leopards sticking their dicks through the bars of their cage!'

The make-up boys laugh uproariously, and Annie exchanges subtle eye contact with Candy, who is on her third doughnut since she sat down.

'Watch it with that powdered sugar, honey,' warns her make-up boy. 'You're ruining my lips!'

Candy is several pounds heavier than Annie, and she has been modelling outsize clothing for years. She

271

wanted to be an air hostess but no airline would take her because of her weight – the aisles in a 747 are not wide enough, and they were worried that she might block an important exit during an emergency. She has been very nice to Annie since she arrived in Key West: a kind of mother figure even though she is only four years older.

'I've been doing this stuff for years now and I've seen it all. Michaela is one of the best, she knows how to treat her staff, but I've worked for some doozies in my time. You are a real knockout, Annie, and you are going to be big, I can see that even now.' Candy had said this to Annie last night after dinner. Right after she announced that this would be her own last photo shoot.

'I'm getting my stomach stapled in Phoenix next week,' she explained. 'I've tried everything else and none of it works, so I'm planning on a size fourteen by the fourth of July.'

'Isn't that dangerous?' Annie had asked.

'No more dangerous than crossing the road, honey. Anyway, I'm getting a special deal from the doctor who fouled up my sister's breast augmentation. Poor thing needs to have steel girders sewn into her brassiere to keep them monsters pointing north since the surgery!'

'But you are beautiful,' said Annie. 'Can't you just lose a few pounds by dieting if you're so worried about your health?'

'Annie, honey, I've tried every diet there is – from high-protein to low-fat, from grapefruit and egg to cabbage soup – and all that happens is I get cranky and hungry and my face breaks out. I even had my jaw wired for thirty days, but it didn't stop me from throwing everything in the blender and sucking it up through a goddamned straw!'

In the space of five days, Annie's life could not have altered more dramatically if she had just woken up on the moon.

She spends all day being photographed in gorgeous clothes, with her hair and make-up done by people who have worked on Julia Roberts and Sigourney Weaver. She sleeps in a king-sized bed, with her own bathroom and cable television, eats cantaloupe melon and onion bagels for breakfast under the palm trees, and gets paid a thousand quid a day for doing this. Betsy was right when she said that there is a world beyond Chesterfield. There is an entire universe, and Annie is just beginning to enjoy it.

'You're done, sweetheart,' says her make-up boy with a final dab at her nose with an oversized brush, 'and you look fabulous. Doesn't she, Troy?'

Troy agrees.

Candy winks, and searches through the Dunkin' Donuts to find the last Boston Creme. Annie removes the tissues from around the neck of her blouse and goes to the gazebo, where they are shooting the daywear collection beneath a canopy of ferns.

This is their last day on location. Annie will fly back to London tomorrow evening from Miami. It has been quite a week, and one that she will not forget in a hurry. Just the experience of summer weather in the middle of January is novelty enough for a girl who has spent her entire life living in a country where the weather is often discussed but seldom exalted.

Tomorrow night she will be back with Richard.

Sharing a bedroom with Richard has been another revealing experience for Annie. On the few nights that she spent with Spencer, there had always been the underlying tensions of sexual inadequacy, the rigid embarrassment of unspoken fears. With Richard it has been different – much different. For such a quiet unassuming man he is not bashful when it comes to intimacy, and Annie has been surprised by his boldness. He has no qualms about standing naked in the bathroom doorway, drying himself off after a shower while telling her an anecdote about his childhood. He takes off his clothes there in full view of the bedroom, unlike Annie who prefers to disrobe in private, covering her body, before emerging like a virgin bride into the darkened room.

Richard turns on the light when they have sex.

'I want to see who I'm making love to,' he tells her, running a moist tongue across the sensitive part right below her ear.

And Annie is exposed and naked, and her eyes are closed while Richard moves down the bed and makes coloured sparks explode behind her eyelids as he does things to her private parts that make the soles of her feet tingle. If Annie were a little less inhibited she would like to groan and wriggle with ecstasy but instead she keeps very still, holding her breath – almost afraid that if she moves, he might stop.

She wonders where he learned these things. Quiet Richard with his moist lips, his soft tongue, and a seemingly inexhaustible capacity to keep his neck rigid while he reaches down like that to feed in her unmentionable places. She can't wait to get back to London!

Once they tried watching some porno videos together but Annie found them repulsive and ugly. Cheap girls with bouncing bosoms and shaved whatsits and the men treating them so roughly, calling them horrid names and spunking on their faces. Richard seemed to like it and got quite excited but Annie asked him to turn it off while she went to the kitchen to help herself to the last of the chocolate fudge cake that had been calling to her from the fridge.

But the truth of the matter is, Annie never experienced an orgasm. She's tired of being led up the garden path only to find the door to her dream house is barred and bolted. It's a kind of torture – like seeing an advert for ice-cold Pepsi in the middle of a parched, endless desert. And, to give him his due, Richard has tried to make it up to her in other ways, but once the moment has passed she just doesn't seem able to recapture it. No matter how frantically he works his talented tongue.

The cuddling is nice though.

They sleep naked, with Spencer's monochromatic duvet pulled over their bodies. Richard comes up behind her and presses himself in to conform to the shape of her legs and her back. One arm comes over her so that his hand can rest between her breasts. It is a safe feeling. A warm feeling. Like falling asleep on the sofa with the fire hissing and the clock ticking on a quiet weekday afternoon.

Falling asleep in Richard's arms is one of the things that Annie has missed the most since she came to Key West. She misses the fact that they can talk in the dark about things that in the daylight would be intrusive and personal. Annie asked Richard about his leg and he explained to her that he had something called Perthe's disease as a child and it affected his hip joint due to inadequate blood supply.

'I was five when I started having the pains,' he said, 'and my mother passed them off as "growing pains" for several months, until I was crying out in agony every night and could barely walk across the room. There are drugs to treat it now, but back then they didn't even know what it was. The doctors recommended that I spend as much time in bed as possible, restricting my activities to the minimum. They wanted me to stay in bed for years, they wanted me to go into a wheelchair, but my mother refused to give in – she didn't want a cripple as her son. And so she ignored the medical advice and she made me go to school like everyone else, even though on some days I could barely make it down the garden path to the car.'

'Oh, Richard, that must have been horrible,' whispered Annie with her back still turned to him and his fist buried in her cleavage. 'How long did it go on for?'

'Oh, about ten years. The pain subsided as I got older, but I was still getting twinges when I went to grammar school at eleven. Of course, by then, my hip had not developed properly and so I was left with my lopsided gait.'

And Annie had turned to him then, seeing his eyes glitter in the dark, and she had kissed him. She kissed him . . . and for a moment she almost forgot about Spencer. She almost believed that it was Richard she was kissing, until she opened her eyes again and knew that this was only sympathy she was feeling. Sympathy so profound that it had momentarily blinded her to the fact that it wasn't *love*.

'You are a very special person, Annie,' whispered Richard on that fourth night at Spencer's house.

'So are you,' she replied. And they fell asleep like that, with their noses almost touching on the pillow.

And so they are now 'an item', as Betsy put it when Annie told her that Richard has slept with her every night since she moved back into Spencer's house. Annie isn't quite sure what that means as far as an emotional investment, but it feels very nice to have a boyfriend who dotes on her instead of one who makes her feel perpetually insufficient. Dating Spencer had been like trailing behind a comet, herself overshadowed and overlooked in the fire of his brilliance. When Annie is with Richard she feels confident and pretty, because she knows that is what he is seeing when he looks at her. His eyes are on her constantly. He sings her praises to everyone they meet and keeps his hand at the small of her back when they are out together.

If Spencer was a black panther, then Richard is a damp-eyed spaniel.

'That colour really suits you, Annie,' says Saya, the black lesbian stylist, as Annie steps up to the gazebo where the photographers are waiting for her. Saya doesn't look like a lesbian, but then what kind of reference does Annie have for comparison? In Chesterfield there aren't any black people, let alone lesbians, and if there were they would probably move to London with all the gay men and the drug addicts. Betsy would die if she knew the kind of people Annie is knocking around with these days.

She has three changes of clothing and they break for a late lunch at two. Michaela has already gone back to New York, so the atmosphere is slightly more relaxed at the lunch table. Taylor has been left in charge, but he's been out all night with a bloke he met at Sloppy Joe's so they haven't seen hide nor hair of him all morning.

The recent warm weather has broken and there is an empty, last-day feel about the luncheon party that reminds Annie of her Sunday night depressions. A cool breeze has blown clouds in from the north, and she is glad of her cardigan. Tomorrow she will be back in London. The thought of morning frosts and perpetual drizzle does nothing to lift this current mood of despondency that has settled around her shoulders like a damp towel. She could easily stay here, in Key West, for ever. She could sell Spencer's house in Fulham and buy a little cottage with palm trees and a veranda, and paint it soft pink with shutters of buttery yellow. It wouldn't have to be anything fancy; just one bedroom and a living room with bare plank floors and white walls. She could live there alone, making friends with her neighbours and buying fresh mangoes at the street market, dressed in a large straw hat and sandals.

Do real people actually do things like that? Is it possible to run away from responsibility completely and find peace in a place where there are no connections with the past? Annie doubts that things are ever that easy. She had a school friend who got divorced and ran off to Edinburgh – just because it was a place she had always admired in the Green Line Coach Tours catalogue. She only stayed up there for a fortnight before she got fed up with the cold and the incomprehensible accent.

'It wasn't what I expected,' she confessed. 'The sun didn't come out once, and my landlady was charging me fifty pence every time I had a bath, even though the water wasn't even hot.'

Annie moves on from her lobster salad to the pineapple slices with a desultory fork, not really hungry for anything right now. There is a purple orchid in the middle of her salad, grown and picked merely for the purpose of temporary decoration. It seems such a waste when this exotic flower will end up in the pig bin with all the other scraps at the end of the meal. Annie reflects that she too is enjoying her last day of temporary decoration, and tomorrow she will be thrown back into the pig bin just like the purple orchid in her salad.

She has never harboured thoughts like these before. Annie has always been an optimistic person, the kind of person who smiles in the face of adversity. Is it possible that she is changing? Can just one week of sunshine and glamour rust the seams of her cast-iron irrepressibility? A tin of John West sockeye salmon just isn't the same once you've tasted the real thing.

When she sees Taylor approach, she knows that he is the bearer of bad tidings. He is walking too fast and his face is set in a grim line of determination, as he hurries towards her across the grass.

'What's up?' she asks him, even before he has stopped to catch his breath.

'There's been a fire, honey,' he gasps, 'at your house.'

'Oh no! Are Mum and Dad all right?' shrieks Annie, pushing back her chair, prepared to charter a plane to fly her home immediately.

'No, not your parent's house – *your* house in London,' says Taylor, holding Annie's forearm to keep her from running across the park.

'Oh, *Spencer's* house,' she says, suddenly deflating from her panic with a huge sense of relief. 'What happened?'

'Didn't get the details, but a guy called Richard phoned to say that there is a lot of damage to the back of the house.' Taylor pauses at this point as though unsure how to proceed. 'They don't know how it happened yet, but they think it might have been an electrical fault.'

'Just when everything seemed to be going all right for a while, and now it looks as though I'm homeless again!'

Annie stares at her salad. She pokes at it with the prongs of her fork. 'Can I borrow your mobile?' she asks.

Taylor hands her his phone and walks away to chat with one of the photographers.

Annie calls Richard. He is still at the office and he answers on the first ring.

'I've been trying to get hold of you all morning,' he says. 'I suppose you've heard what happened?'

'How bad is it?' she asks. 'Can I still live there?'

'Not really, it's pretty bad. The parts that weren't damaged by the fire are ruined from the smoke. It's going to take quite some time to get it all repaired.'

'Would it be all right for me to stay with you for a bit, until I get back on my feet?' asks Annie. 'I don't really want to go straight back to Mum and Dad's again.'

Richard hesitates, but Annie can hear him breathing.

'Richard? Are you still there?'

'Yes, I'm here. It's just that . . . well, my place is very small, Annie, and I only have a single bed. Why don't I have a word with Marla and see if you can use her guest bedroom for a while? I'm sure she wouldn't mind.'

'Oh no, I hardly know her, Richard. I'll go to a bed and breakfast.'

'Marla is hardly ever at her place, Annie; it would practically be your own. She'll be in the office tomorrow morning, I'll ask her then.'

'Well . . . if you think it would be all right. I don't want to get in the way or anything.'

'You won't be in the way, and I'll be there to look after you. Well, that's if you still want me now that you're an international model . . .'

'Don't be silly, Richard. I've really missed you and it would be more comfortable for me staying at Marla's if you were there with me.'

'Consider me your official chaperon,' he laughs.

And Annie, with the phone tucked between her ear and her shoulder, mashes down the orchid in the middle of her salad – and attempts to make light of this new set of circumstances.

At times like these she really misses Spencer.

Where is he? And if he is still alive why hasn't he been in touch?

'See you tomorrow, darling,' says Richard. And Annie hears something in Richard's tone that makes her slightly nervous.

She hears love.

Annie knows that she will never feel the same way about Richard, because she used up all her love when she married Spencer.

You see, she has made up her mind. If Spencer ever comes back she is going to stay with him, even if that means she must carry on a life with a man who cannot love her in the way a man should love his wife.

For Annie there is only one man, and Richard, like a small silver trowel loaded with moist plaster, is merely filling the jagged cracks that appeared in her heart when she discovered that Spencer had never really loved her at all.

Twenty-eight

Marla sits in her office late at night, smoking one cigarette after another by the ghastly green light of her computer screen. Like an underworld goblin she stares blankly at the piles of unattended files and papers on her desk – representing weeks of accumulated case files and of post to be opened. But she just cannot concentrate on work. The phone rings and she ignores it. Her answering machine is full and cannot take any more messages. She has over 200 email messages to open but instead she watches the ever-decreasing circles of her screen saver.

She has to turn herself in. She *can't* go on like this. The police are holding a young guy under arrest, charged with all kinds of misdemeanours against her when she knows that he is innocent. If she doesn't confess to Mark about her psychological breakdown, this guy might be put away for something that he didn't do.

The obvious thing is to own up. She should call Mark right now and tell him that she is to blame for everything.

So why doesn't she call him?

'I thought I'd find you here.'

Marla almost sucks her cigarette down her throat with fright.

'Christ! Lester! Don't ever creep up on me like that! You nearly gave me a fucking heart attack!' She is coughing now; reaching for a glass of water that was perched on top of some legal documents.

'Sorry,' says Lester, coming into Marla's office. 'I let myself in – I still have a key, you know, and I could see the light on from the street.'

'Don't normal people phone before they call round on a social visit?'

'I *have* been calling – since six this evening, but I keep getting your damned message machine. What's going on, Marla? You've been home from Florida for three days and I haven't heard a peep from you. I left seven messages at your flat and you haven't returned one of them.'

Lester removes his coat and clears a space on the leather sofa to sit down. Marla lights up another cigarette and spins around in her chair so that her back is facing the computer screen. She indicates the stacks of paperwork on her desk with the match as she waves out its flame and inhales.

'As you can see, my darling, I have got a lot of catching up to do and Richard persuaded me to let Annie move into my spare room. There was a fire at her house so she needed somewhere to stay for a while. It's been a busy few days.'

'You look like shit.'

'Thanks for the compliment.'

'You look as though you've slept in that blouse. Have you even changed your clothes since you came back from America?'

'Oh, stop mothering me, Lester. I'm two years older than you, and if anyone is going to get maternal it'll be me. I can look after myself – I have been doing it for quite some time now.'

Lester sighs. He is sitting in the dark shadows so he reaches across and turns on a lamp.

'You don't look so hot yourself, Lester,' smiles Marla. 'I don't think I've seen you with that much of a beard in all the time I've known you.'

'Why do you think I've been calling you?'

'What? You can't shave or something? You haven't needed me to help you in the bathroom since we got divorced. Doesn't Tina buy your razor blades for you?' Marla sucks on her cigarette and then squints at Lester through the smoke as she exhales.

'She's left me.'

Marla stops swinging in her chair.

'She's gone to live with one of her sleazy friends in Brixton and she's going back to the porno business. I walked out on her at a party on Boxing Day night, and she moved out the last of her stuff a couple of days ago.'

'Whoa! Did you have any idea that this was coming?'

'Oh, you know Tina. She's been knocking around with those tarts as long as I've known her and I always suspected that she envied them in some ways. It turns out that she's been having sex with half of them for as long as we've been married.'

'Oh God, honey, you should get tested for HIV. You don't *know* what kind of crap those sleazebags are into.'

'I've already thought about that, so I went to get a blood test yesterday. I have to wait a week to get the results.' Lester says all of this with a kind of resigned lethargy, as though he has already come to terms with everything that he is telling her. For him, it is old news.

'You know what I'm going to say, don't you?' asks Marla, leaning forward across her desk to study him more closely.

'I never should have married her in the first place . . . I know.'

'Everyone thought the same thing, honey. She was a tramp and you deserve better than that. None of us could see it lasting as long as it did – that scag was destined for the gutter.'

'And there's more,' says Lester, running a weary hand across his unshaven chin, 'I'm out of work. I got myself out of the *Pigbeet* contract, and then Jane Graves got killed in a car accident and the BBC have canned the series. I don't even have any adverts lined up.'

'Christ, Lester, what have you been doing since I left town? Did you get the clean end of the wishbone at Christmas or something?'

'I just don't know what to do, Marla, I feel so fucking hopeless. I can't keep my marriage together and my career has totally collapsed. I'm too old for this kind of shit. I should be established by now. I should be sitting back and thinking about my pension fund, with a dog at my feet and a pipe in my hand. I should be playing *Hamlet* or writing my memoirs, but instead I'll be signing on for unemployment and watching *Cagney and Lacey* repeats in the afternoon.'

'Oh, come on, Lester, it's not like you to give in to despondency so easily. Everyone has their problems, you know. You're not the only one who feels that their life is collapsing around their ears. Look at me!'

Lester looks at Marla. She stubs out her cigarette and gets up to open the liquor cabinet. 'Time for some medicine,' she says, pouring out two very large glasses of Scotch. She hands one to Lester.

Lester takes a drink from his glass. '*You've* got your act together, Marla. How can you possibly compare your life with mine?'

Marla raises her glass and takes a long drink before answering Lester's question. 'Oh yes, Lester, my life is so peachy keen, isn't it? So why am I still here at eleven thirty on a Friday night, chain-smoking myself to death when I should be at home with my fabulous fella having sex on a sheepskin rug by candlelight? Answer that one for me, Lester, because I sure as hell don't have the answer.'

'Because you're driven, Marla, and you always have been, and when there's work to be done you simply won't rest. Anyway, you should be happy – they've caught the bloke who's been pestering you, haven't they? Who is he? Do you know him?'

Marla shakes her head. She doesn't want to talk about the poor innocent guy they have locked up. 'I don't know who he is and I'm not even sure he's the right guy; he just happened to be in the wrong place at the right time and the police put two and two together and came up with five. He has no apparent motive but he *was* in New York at the time of my hotel room break-in, and he *has* been in trouble before – he was harassing a school teacher for giving him low grades or something. He's only in his mid twenties, computer programmer apparently.'

'You don't sound convinced that they've got the right bloke.'

'I just think they're jumping to a lot of conclusions.

I've been thinking about calling the investigation off. I haven't had any more trouble since the cat-in-the-chocolates business, and I kinda feel that things have cooled off since I went to New York.'

'But what about the fella they've arrested?'

'He hasn't been charged with anything yet, and I guess if I decided not to press charges they'll have to let him go. It's not as though this is a murder case or anything.'

Lester looks astounded; he obviously thinks she is going mad.

He could be right.

'But breaking and entering, defacing personal property, stalking, threatening messages – you have no idea what this chap is capable of. I don't think it's very wise to let him off the hook so easily, Marla. You're just feeling secure at the moment because nothing has happened for a few weeks, but perhaps that is just because your madman is currently behind bars.'

Marla pours herself another drink and lights up a cigarette. She fills Lester's glass too, then walks around the office saying nothing. She wonders if she can trust Lester with her secret. If she doesn't tell someone soon, she is going to collapse under the burden. He knows her better than anyone and perhaps it would help to finally admit to her problems.

'Look, Lester . . .' she begins, turning her back on him and squinting between the slats of her window blinds down at the street below. 'I'm going to tell you something, but I want you to swear that whatever decision I come to you must abide by it. I don't want any lectures on morality or legality. I just need you to listen and to keep an open mind OK?'

'Oh God! What are you going to tell me?' laughs Lester. 'You've not been abducted by aliens while you've been away, have you? Or maybe you've been embezzling money from the business?'

'Get real, Lester!' snaps Marla, impatient now to have his understanding and support. 'This is serious.'

'OK, OK, spill the beans, darling, but don't expect me to keep quiet if you've turned lesbian or suddenly become intimate with Jesus.'

'There is no stalker, Lester.'

'What?'

'There is no stalker. There never has been anyone doing all those things to me. That's why I know they've got an innocent guy under arrest right now.'

'What are you talking about? We've seen the evidence, and you can't just pass it off as a figment of your imagination.'

Marla blows smoke straight up into the air and looks directly at Lester in order to get her message across. 'Nobody did those things, Lester. I did them all myself. I've been having my blackouts again, the same ones I used to have before . . . well, before Jessica died. I can't remember what I've done – usually at night when I'm sleeping but also during the day. I saw myself recorded on videotape on Christmas Day: I was like a crazy person, screaming obscenities to myself and basically causing a lot of damage to my bedroom. That's why I dashed off to New York: I needed to get away before Mark found out, and I knew that I badly needed professional help. I've been through all of this before, Lester, and it scares the shit out of me. I feel totally out of control and I don't know what I might be capable of if I'm left alone during one of my crazy spells.'

Lester has not stopped smiling. 'This is a joke right? You're taking the piss . . .'

'No, Lester, this isn't a joke. Do you think I'm totally sick to joke about something like this? I have a problem and I don't know where it's coming from. All I know is that I can't let them arrest a guy who is definitely innocent just because I'm scared to admit that it was me all along. If anyone finds out about this, I'll be ruined. My business will fold and I'll have nothing left. Nobody wants a lawyer who is nuts, and all that crap about Jessica will be back on the front page of every rag in town. I can't go through all of that again, Lester; it will kill me.'

Lester has now stopped smiling. He shifts uncomfortably in his seat and stares at her as though she has just announced that she has thirty days to live.

'Suddenly, Lester, your own problems don't seem half so bad by comparison, do they?'

'But what about the other stuff?' he asks. 'The heart in your handbag, and the blouse in the post . . . and what about the cat's head in the chocolate box? Are you telling me that you did all of those things while you were somehow . . . sleepwalking?' He doesn't sound convinced, and Marla cannot blame him. She barely believes it herself. This is just like it was when Jessica went missing: the same sense of dread, the same feelings of disbelief and fear.

'I know it sounds off the wall, and believe me I wish I could blame somebody else, but I've seen that tape and it all makes sense when I look back. There was never any physical evidence of another person being involved, and it has been baffling the cops ever since about how this guy got into my apartment, my office and hotel room without ever breaking through the locks or being witnessed.'

'What did your therapist say?'

'Nothing conclusive, but I've been having these dreams, real vivid dreams that have something to do with Jessica and . . . the circumstances surrounding her death. You know I'm still punishing myself for that – I think I always will. I'm scared, Lester. If the truth be known, I'm *terrified*. In these dreams there is always a grave in the woods, and I think I might have murdered somebody and blocked it out of my mind. Maybe I did murder somebody during one of these blackouts I've been having. I don't know, but the dreams are really *vivid*. If I can kill my own daughter without even knowing it, isn't it possible that I could have killed someone else?'

'Come on, Marla, you didn't *kill* Jessica, and dreams mean nothing – they probably just represent something else, some kind of symbolism, perhaps. This is just a kickback to the past. Stress-related, perhaps. You went through a lot back then, and I was surprised at the time how tough you were under so much strain. What does the shrink say?'

'Same as you, but I can't shake the feeling that I have done something bad and just can't remember what it is. It's so damned frustrating – like having a word on the tip of your tongue but not being able to spit it out.'

'Have there been any more blackouts since the one at Christmas?'

'Not that I know of.'

'So what are you going to do?'

'I don't know, Lester! If I knew the answer to that I'd be able to fix the problem, wouldn't I?' None of this is helping matters, and Lester is merely confirming everything that she has already ascertained. They are going round in circles. 'I'm going to drop all charges so that they'll let that guy go free, and then I'm going to find out just what it is that I did to make me act this way.'

'And where are you going to start?' asks Lester.

'I have no idea, but all I know is that these blackouts were the cause of our daughter's death and I am not going to let them take over the rest of my life. I have to get help, and I have to do it fast, but I'm scared, Lester, really scared. Will you help me?'

Marla reaches out to grasp Lester's hand.

It is a gesture that obviously surprises him but he clings to her fingers and nods his head. 'Yes, Marla, I'll help you in any way I can.'

And it all feels horribly familiar. *Déjà vu* at it's most disturbing.

Twenty-nine

Billy chose the venue.

He has never been to Planet Hollywood before and Annie said that he could choose any restaurant in London, so he chose this one. He is wearing his new Nikes, the ones with the neon speed stripes and the gel insoles, also the Diesel jeans he got for Christmas.

'Can't you wear something a bit more dressy?' Maggie had suggested as he came down the stairs. 'I don't want Annie thinking that you're a slob.' His mother was icing a christening cake, and she had yellow food colouring down the side of her cheek. 'Well, at least you've washed your hair,' she smiled, pausing to admire her son as he stood in the kitchen doorway.

'She's *fat*, isn't she?' asked Billy.

'What does that have to do with anything, love?'

'Well, I want to recognize her when I see her.'

'Darling, she will recognize *you* immediately – you're the spitting image of your father. And it's not very nice to refer to someone as fat, now is it? She's a fashion model, darling. She's very pretty. I only met her the once, at the solicitor's office when we went over the legal papers for the house, but she seemed very nice.'

'So she's fat, then?'

'On the heavy side, yes.'

So here he is, gulping back his second beer at the

bar, alongside a chap who's been going on about his tight foreskin to somebody on the other end of his mobile phone for the last twenty minutes.

The restaurant is brilliant.

The walls are covered with framed rock and roll memorabilia and it's mind-blowing to think that at any minute Sylvester Stallone or Bruce Willis could come walking in. Billy wonders if they have a special table where they always sit. He can't see anybody famous now, but he's keeping his eyes peeled just in case. He brought a disposable camera but he's not sure how cool it would be to ask Stallone for a photo in the middle of eating his bacon cheeseburger.

There is a girl with schoolgirl bunches and a scoop-neck top at the other end of the bar, and she's been giving Billy the eye since he got here. She's drinking something from a large glass, and every time she sucks on her straw her eyes wander over to Billy. He knows what she's thinking. He sees that same look every day.

'Billy?'

He turns around on his stool, to face Annie.

Blimey! She looks like a film star!

A huge, glamorous, beautiful film star.

'I thought it was Spencer sitting there for a minute. You could be him, you know, when he was still at school. The spitting image.'

'That's what Mum says. Nice to meet you, Annie.' And they shake hands.

'You'll have to forgive . . .' starts Annie but she can't talk, she has started to cry, and she can't find a tissue in her handbag.

'What's up?' asks Billy, looking around to see if anyone's watching.

'I'm sorry, love. It's just a bit of a shock to see you. I can't believe how much you look like Spencer. I wasn't prepared for the similarity, that's all.'

Billy hands her a paper napkin from the bar.

'What's all this then, darling?' says the cheeky, chirpy barman with the waistcoat. 'We can't have tears in here. What's this young chap been saying to upset you?'

'Oh, don't mind me,' laughs Annie through her tears. 'It's just a bit of a reunion, that's all.' She turns back to Billy. 'Have I smudged my make-up? I've come straight here from a test shoot – the agency that I've signed up with needed some photos to send around. I'm not usually tarted up like this.'

'You look *great*,' says Billy.

'Well, it's not really *me* – they like to plaster on the foundation, and this lipstick is a bit bright for me. I'm a No.7 girl, usually – a dab of blusher and some eyeliner has always done the trick. But I have to admit that I love my nails.' Annie holds up her hands, fanning out her fingers for Billy to admire. 'I've never had a manicure before. This is called a French polish. See the white lines at the ends? That's *painted* on – it's not real! Isn't it clever?'

Billy couldn't care less about blusher or manicures, but he is polite enough to show interest while Annie rattles on about her manicurist – some poof who looks just like Pierce Brosnan, apparently.

They share a booth right under Madonna's bra.

'It's very noisy in here, isn't it?' shouts Annie. 'You'd think they'd turn the music down just a bit. I can hardly hear myself think!'

'I love this one. It's the Manic Street Preachers. The

video is brilliant!' Billy is trying to impress her. He knows that she has no idea who the Manic Street Preachers are. She probably stopped listening to the charts about the same time as his mother did. Oh yeah, she probably hums along to the occasional Top 20 hit, but it's a safe bet that she probably still listens to Duran Duran and Spandau Ballet on vinyl.

'I don't know anything about pop music,' yells Annie. 'I've always liked something I can sing along to, even when I was a teenager. I remember being teased because I liked Boney M and the Bee Gees when everybody else was listening to Queen and the Electric Light Orchestra. Spencer . . . your dad . . . was always more into music, when we were at school. He used to go to concerts in Birmingham and London on the train with his mates, and I always thought how awful it sounded – all those crowds of screaming people pushing to get to the front of the stage. I don't think they ever really heard much of the music, but it didn't stop him from going again and again.'

'It still sounds a bit funny you calling him my dad,' says Billy. 'I keep thinking about my *real* dad, well, my adopted dad, I suppose – and he's totally different from Spencer, if what I've heard from Mum is true.'

'What's your *real* dad like, then?'

'Well, he's probably never been to a pop concert in his life, but he's been to a lot of Manchester United matches. He works on the oil rigs so we don't see much of him, and when he's home he just sleeps all the time or watches the telly. He's always been a bit like a lodger, I suppose, but when he's home he treats me and Mum really well, and we go abroad once a year to Spain or the Canaries.'

'Sounds like *my* dad,' says Annie, 'although my
mum and dad have never been abroad – they're suspicious of the food and Dad reckons there's nothing
wrong with a fortnight in Rhyll, if the weather doesn't
play up. We went to the same guest house there every
year, and all I can remember of those holidays is sitting
in the back of the car with Mum divvying out the tea
from the flask, and Dad chuntering on about the rain.
We weren't allowed to go back to the guest house until
half past five because that's when the landlady would be
finished cleaning the rooms, so we spent a lot of time
sitting in car parks or wandering around amusement
arcades with a handful of pennies.'

'So how come you were friends with Spencer, if he
was so posh?'

The waiter brings them menus and takes their order
for drinks. Billy has another beer and Annie asks for a
glass of white wine which, she explains, is something
she acquired a taste for in Key West.

'It's true, Spencer and me came from opposite sides
of town, but we went to the same school, so the only
time we ever really thought about the difference was
when we went to each other's houses. I think he liked
my sense of humour, and perhaps he felt a bit sorry for
me because I was overweight and unpopular. You'd
think that he'd have been really stuck-up and horrible
to me, but he was so popular that he never had to prove
himself to the other kids. Whatever Spencer did or said
was always what everyone else wanted to copy. When I
went out with him, I always thought that a little bit of
that would rub off on me, but as soon as I was out on
my own I was just boring old Annie again.'

Billy likes her accent. He likes the way she rolls her

eyes when she talks, and the way she smiles. He can understand why his dad liked her, why they were friends. She doesn't look as old as his mum, because she doesn't have any wrinkles on her face. She's *sexy*. That's something that Billy had not expected to find, and he wonders how much it has to do with that black dress with the plunging neckline. He's never seen such a big pair of tits in his life, and they're freckled from the sun. He wonders what it would feel like to push his face between them, to breathe in their scent, to suffocate in her cleavage.

'I'm sorry to hear about the fire at your house,' he says, averting his eyes from Annie's chest.

'Yes, it has all been a bit of an ordeal really. The place is a complete mess. Anyway, this was supposed to be a thank-you dinner for your kind gesture about the will and everything – it was really generous of you, Billy. Not many young lads would do something that nice for somebody they don't even know.'

'It was Mum's idea,' he admits. 'She's the one with the social conscience.'

'She seems really nice – very quiet.'

'She reads a lot. I think she would have liked to have done something more with her life than baking cakes, but Dad never liked the idea of her going out to work, and anyway, she had me to look after. You know she has a law degree? She could have been a barrister.'

'That's a shame,' says Annie, sipping her wine. 'I always wanted to be a hairdresser but I ended up being just a secretary – there was more money in shorthand typing than perming people's hair.'

'So how did you become a model?' Billy can't believe that Annie was ever 'just a secretary'; when he thinks about secretaries he thinks of scratchy tweed skirts and glasses on gold chains. Annie would be too big, too overwhelming, to sit meekly behind a desk. It would be like one of those stupid elephants that they train to stand on a tiny painted drum at the Christmas circus.

'It's only just happened. Michaela Fox is one of Spencer's clients, and I met her at dinner one night. She was starting a line of clothes for bigger women and thought that I'd make a good model. Can't say I was fussed about the idea at first – I thought she was having me on – but now that I'm doing it, it's a good laugh!'

'Wow! Michaela Fox! My girlfriend wears a lot of her stuff – it's really cool. What's she like?'

'She's from New York, so she's very loud. She's very thin with short, bright hair that changes colour every time I see her, and she's got sticky-out front teeth so she looks a bit like Janet Street-Porter.'

Billy isn't sure he knows who Janet Street-Porter is, but he keeps quiet. She's probably somebody famous who he ought to know, so it's better not to make an idiot out of himself.

'I'll tell you what, Billy, next time she comes to London I'll introduce you to her. She's a really nice lady once you get over the shock of meeting her.'

'Wow! Do you mean it? Could I bring my girlfriend as well? She'd be *pissing* herself!'

Annie laughs – that really nice laugh that sounds so genuine. Billy can't help but laugh along with her. This has got to be the coolest day of his entire life: having dinner in Planet Hollywood with a model who is going to introduce him to Michaela Fox, and probably loads of other famous people too.

'This is so brilliant! I can't believe it!' yells Billy across the table.

'It is, isn't it?' agrees Annie. 'You've cheered me up no end.'

And to mark the occasion Billy asks the waiter to take their photo with his disposable camera.

'That's lovely!' says the waiter as he gets them to move closer together so that he can fit them into the viewfinder. 'Mother and son.'

And the camera catches the laughter on their faces as they share their private joke in the flare of the flash-bulb.

Thirty

Lester has a red label stuck to his forehead. It says 'NEW IMPROVED DESIGN'.

He has forgotten that Shani stuck it there this morning after she peeled it off the side of her new aluminium stepladder. She is decorating her guest bedroom and Lester, being currently unemployed, had offered to help her.

'And you have to promise that you won't breathe a word of this to anyone,' he said as they covered the skirting boards with masking tape. 'She told me this in the strictest confidence.'

'Poor Marla!' gasped Shani in the kind of theatrical way that only she can carry off. 'I always wondered if that thing would come back to haunt her, but I'm really surprised that she's been keeping it a secret from the police – Marla of all people! Do you think Mark'll dump her when he finds out? Surely he already knows about the baby? It was all over the papers at the time.'

'I don't think she has any intention of him finding out about these latest blackouts,' said Lester. 'She's hoping that, once they let that suspect go, she will be able to convince Mark that it's all over. She wants to find out what it is that's been disturbing her, what those dreams mean. Personally I just think she's been working too hard and it's all stress-related.'

'Well, darling, we all get stressed out, but we don't go around putting pigs' hearts in our handbags, do we? She obviously needs professional help.'

'She's going to see a hypnotherapist next week.'

'Well, if he's anything like the one that I went to when I wanted to quit smoking, she might as well save her money. Four sessions at a hundred quid a time, and all he did was play tapes of birdsong and waterfalls, while I lay there watching the clock so that I could get outside and light up a fag.'

'This one is renowned, apparently. He's American, of course, and he's very popular with the Hollywood set. There was a write-up about him in some medical journal. Marla seems to think that he's her only hope.'

'Well, that's smashing, darling, but I just hope she gets some *real* help as well. A friend of mine was having acupuncture for back pains, then it turns out that she had cancer. By the time she was diagnosed, it had spread too far to do anything about it. If she'd gone to a real doctor in the first place, they might have been able to do something.'

So now Lester is standing in the office of his agent, and she has just pointed out the label on his forehead. He has been wearing it all the way on the tube from Shani's place.

'Good joke! I like a bloke who can laugh at himself in times of crisis,' grins Beattie Churchill with an expression that would terrify a rabid dog.

'You've redecorated the office,' says Lester, sheepishly removing the label from his forehead and searching around for a paper bin.

'It *has* been a long time since you last came in, Lester. We had this done eighteen months ago. It's our

'70s motif which, quite frankly, was a bit worrying at the time, because we all lived through it the first time and none of us ever thought we'd be able to stomach it again. But there you go – fashion dictates once again! Some of the younger staff think it's hip, but quite honestly I feel as though we've moved into George Best's bachelor pad circa 1973.'

'So?' says Lester from the centre of Beattie's office.

'So, darling?' sighs Beattie shuffling papers on her glass-topped desk as a way of avoiding his eyes.

'Have you got anything for me yet?'

'Take a pew, darling,' says Beattie, indicating an egg-shaped plastic chair opposite her desk, 'and let's have a look at what we've got.'

Beattie has been Lester's agent since he first got the contract with *Crossroads* in 1975. She handles a lot of big names in showbusiness, and because of that Lester quite often feels neglected. He is put on hold whenever he phones these days, and every year at the Christmas party he is seated further and further away from the top table where Beattie and Co. entertain their constellation of stars with sycophantic aplomb. Last year he was forced to sit with the Crankies and an Indian chap who was booted off *Coronation Street* for being a drunk.

'Have you seen what they've done to poor old Pigbeet since you left?' says Beattie as she rifles through a filing cabinet. 'That Sean chap just doesn't seem right for the part – he's too young and chirpy. It's all becoming so Americanized.'

'That's what kids want these days, Bea. They want all that fast-paced computer-generated stuff. I can't even watch *Blue Peter* these days without feeling totally out of touch with children's entertainment. Whatever happened to the days of *Michael Bentine's Potty Time*? I definitely need to get back into something adult, something that I can relate to on a personal level.'

'Well, there's not much out there right now, darling, unless you fancy doing some rep over the summer? It doesn't pay much, but it might be a way of getting back into the public eye.'

'I've never done theatre,' says Lester, 'I don't think I could handle it. I'm used to working in front of a camera. If you cock up on stage there's no second take, no chance to put it right before the audience sees it.'

Lester sees Beattie sneak a look at her outsized watch as she buzzes through to her secretary. 'Janet, will you tell Rupert that I'll be with him in five. Give him some Perrier and that new copy of *Hello!* until I'm done here, OK?'

'I'm sorry to just barge in like this, Bea, but you weren't returning my calls and I was beginning to get an inferiority complex. I know you've got much bigger fish to fry these days, but there was a time when you used to call *me*.'

'Look, I'm sorry, Lester, but there really isn't anything out there for you at the moment. Now I've promised I'll get you some adverts to tide you over, and you've got that thingy at the Oscars coming up, so I'll put out some feelers in LA. That's all I can do for you right now. You'll have to sit tight – something is bound to come up. And meanwhile you could always take a temporary job to earn a bit of extra cash.'

Lester stands up and places the palms of both hands on the highly polished edge of Beattie's desk. He leans forward to bring his face within a few uncomfortable inches of her own, and he delivers his words in precise, hushed tones.

'I am not going to start waiting on tables, after almost thirty years of being in showbusiness. If you can't find me a modest but respectable job, then I will find myself another agent who can. I do not appreciate the fact that I have to practically force myself in here to see you for just five minutes, and I'm fed up with being treated as though I'm some kind of second-rate citizen. You were all over me when I was making money, but as soon as I hit a slump you've got better things to do.'

Beattie returns Lester's glare with a steady, impassive expression. Behind her large black-rimmed glasses, her eyes employ the colour and obduracy of a battleship. Without saying a word to Lester, she leans over to her intercom and buzzes her secretary once again. 'Janet, would you bring Lester Phillip's contract through for me.'

Lester steps away from the desk, and his hands fall to his sides. Beattie must be calling his bluff; she must be teaching him a lesson for stepping over the line. But there is no mirth in her tone when she tells Lester that it is probably for the best if they cancel their contract – leaving him free to approach other agents and get the work that he so obviously thinks he deserves.

'You can't just dump me like this,' says Lester. 'I've been loyal to you for twenty-five years.'

'Then it is time for a change, Lester. You said so yourself. And I have no intention of representing someone who is under the impression that I am somehow swindling them. Your complete lack of faith in me is demoralizing and, quite frankly, upsetting. This is a tough business and I only hope that once you are out there on your own that you will begin to realize just how difficult my role is.'

Janet comes in with a manila folder which presumably contains Lester's contract.

'Null and void,' says Beattie, as she signs the papers with a flourish.

'Stick it up your arse!' says Lester, and he knocks the pen out of Beattie's hand and strides out of the office with as much dignity as he can muster.

Outside in the street it is cold. There have been gale warnings, and the temperature is falling rapidly now that evening has arrived. Lester pulls the collar of his coat up around his ears and lowers his head against the wind as he crosses the busy road to stand at the bus station. There is a long, straggling queue of people. They look up the road with a kind of hopeless expectancy, all of them knowing that the first bus to arrive will have been held up in a jam somewhere, and will already be too full to accept any more passengers. They know that they won't be home for ages and although the work day is finished, it will be at least an hour before they can take off their shoes and turn on the telly.

The cold chill of a January evening represents more than just physical frigidity. It is a subjective misery that seems to settle in the folds of the flapping awnings above the newsagent's shop. It is the bleakness of hardened furrows where corn once grew, the desolation of a strip of Christmas tinsel still trapped against the ceiling beneath a square of Sellotape. There are very few people who would cite January as their favourite month of the year: surely it is the most joyless of all the months? A time for planning summer holidays. A time for extra blankets and Cadbury's Drinking Chocolate. If every occasion in life had its appropriate season, then January would have to be the best time to plan a funeral. Lester shuffles his feet on the pavement. His nose is running and his vision is slightly blurred by the wind as it gusts around the corner with gleeful impertinence. He is feeling almost as wretched as the weather, and has little desire to return home where the magnolia walls mock him with their austerity. There is still no sign of a bus, and the traffic moves just a few inches at a time. He can't afford the extravagance of hailing a taxi, and there is a bomb scare on the District Line so the tube will be a disaster. Bond Street is only about a mile away from here. Maybe Marla is still in her office and they could get some dinner together?

This thought cheers him up: it brings a little colour to his cheeks and offers him a glimpse of hope. A brisk walk down Oxford Street will do him good, and even if Marla is too busy to have dinner with him, she always has time for a drink and a chat. That will be enough to bolster his resistance to this current emotional malady.

The Christmas lights are still there, but they won't be turning them on now that Christmas is over. Up high, oversized snowflakes and reindeer sway violently in the wind, and a plastic carrier bag swirls high above the streetlights, filled with air like a miniature balloon. As Lester hurries through the crowd he feels totally isolated, even though seen from the air he would look merely a part of this vast human stream – innocuous in his preoccupation for self-preservation. For every person in this street there is a different life, but Lester walks in a straight line and his mind thinks only of himself.

There is a light on in Marla's third-floor office.

Lester has his key. He lets himself in and takes the stairs instead of the lift. The warmth of being indoors is prickly against his skin, and it smells dusty in here, like the smell in the bottom of an airing cupboard where the lagging has split apart.

Marla's secretary is still in reception. She is sorting through some papers, and looks up when Lester appears.

'Oh, hello, Mr Philips, is she expecting you?' asks Julie, casting a cursory eye across the day planner spread out on the desk before her.

'No, I just dropped by on the off chance, to see if she is free for a spot of dinner,' says Lester, unbuttoning his coat. 'Can I go through?'

'She's got Inspector Blake in there with her at the moment, and said that she didn't want to be disturbed. Why don't you have a seat anyway, and I'll let her know that you're here. There's some coffee in the pot but it probably tastes disgusting – it's been there since half past eight this morning.'

'Thanks, Julie.' Lester removes his coat, unwinds his scarf and plants himself down by the coffee table scattered with copies of *Time* magazine and various ashtrays. A courier comes in with packages to be signed for. A vacuum cleaner starts up somewhere along the corridor, and nobody answers a phone that rings and rings.

Richard comes through the double doors, dragging on his coat, and his briefcase is bulging unsteadily under one arm as he struggles to coordinate his actions. He stops when he sees Lester sitting there. 'Hello, Lester, I haven't seen you for ages. Did you have a nice Christmas and all that?'

'I can't say that it was the best I've ever had, Richard, but at least it's over. How about you?'

'Fantastic!' smiles Richard, beaming from ear to ear.

'Well, something has certainly lit you up – or some-one. Can I hazard a guess that she's of the female persuasion?'

'Did you ever meet Annie?' asks Richard.

'A couple of times, and I believe she's moved in with Marla for a while, hasn't she?'

'Just for a couple of weeks while they clean up her house.' Richard attempts to keep his briefcase in place on a chair while he continues to struggle with the sleeve of his coat, but it falls with a thud to the carpet and spills its contents across the floor. Papers and files slide everywhere.

'Damn and blast!' Richard is on his knees gathering things up with a kind of frantic desperation.

'Here, let me help,' says Lester, leaning forward, but Richard holds up his hand and practically barks at Lester to stay where he is.

'I've got it, I've got it,' he repeats, stuffing everything back into his briefcase with little regard for order or neatness. 'I'm already late,' he explains as he fastens the last of his buttons and heads for the door. 'See you later.' Then he is gone.

Lester wishes that he could be somebody like Rich-ard; somebody who has no real ambition and is content to plod along in the same boring little job for the rest of his life. If Lester had been an accountant he might have found peace, he might have found contentment. There is comfort in quiet routine for people like Richard; they would only find disquiet in a profession as unstable as acting. But there are also people – people like Lester –

who would wither and die if they were forced to stay in one place for longer than a few months. And Lester knows that for every door that closes there is another just on the verge of shooting open. It is all a matter of patience.

Inspector Mark Blake breaks through Lester's silent reverie as he pushes his way between the swinging doors. He crosses the reception area, and leaves without acknowledging Lester's presence. In his wake there is a tight wire of tension that seems to zing like a recently plucked guitar string. Like a dog sniffing the air, Lester is aware of undercurrents. He gathers up his coat and heads through the swing doors towards Marla's office.

Julie and a couple of other office juniors are putting on their coats outside the staff room.

'Goodnight, Mr Philips,' says Julie. 'Her door's closed, but she said you could go in once Inspector Blake left.'

Lester taps lightly on the door before entering.

Marla's office is dimly lit and thick with cigarette smoke. She stands by the window with a large Scotch in one hand and a cigarette in the other – a familiar pose for a woman like Marla. She is wearing her deep pink skirt and her jacket with the black collar and cuffs, and her hair has been done up so that she looks more professional than Lester has seen her looking in weeks.

'How come you Brits find it so damned hard to say fuck off?'

Marla doesn't turn to look at Lester as she asks this question. She puffs on her cigarette and continues to look down into Bond Street through the horizontal lines in her aluminium blinds.

'Perhaps we're just too polite,' replies Lester. 'Is

there any of that stuff left for me, or have you finished the bottle already?'

'Help yourself,' says Marla, waving an indolent hand towards the bottle on the corner of her desk.

'So what was wrong with Mark? He left like a bat out of hell.'

'Verbally constipated, that's what was wrong with Inspector Blake. He couldn't even rise to the occasion and tell me to fuck off, even though that's what he so desperately wanted to say. Instead he tried to spare my feelings, and in doing so he lost all my respect. He's a wimp, just like every other guy I've known.'

'Thanks,' mutters Lester as he helps himself to a drink.

'Oh, you know what I mean,' says Marla, and she holds out her glass for a refill.

'Was I a wimp too then?'

'Oh, honey, you wimped out on me years ago. Left me to go in search of yourself, and look where *that* got you. Twenty years later and we're both as pathetic as each other. We should have stayed together and perhaps things would have worked out for the best.'

'Here's to us,' says Lester, raising his glass to Marla's. 'Two of a kind.'

'Yeah, you've got that right.'

'So you told him, then? That you're dropping the case.'

'And the rest.'

'You mean . . .'

'Yep! Told him he's been dating a fruitcake who chopped off the head of a pussycat and sent it to herself in a box of chocolates. For some strange reason he wasn't too keen on arranging another date with me.'

311

'Christ, Marla! I thought you weren't going to tell him? I thought we'd agreed?'

'Had to come clean, Lester. There's no point in basing a relationship on lies. He would have found out sooner or later anyway, and then I'd have been in even deeper shit.'

Marla takes a seat at her desk and stubs out her cigarette in an overflowing ashtray.

'What did he say?' asks Lester. 'He must have been floored.'

'Yes, to put it mildly, sweetheart. He looked at me as though I'd just peed in my slingbacks. He couldn't even look at me after that. I tried to explain that I'm getting help and all that jazz but he wasn't listening. I could see that he had stopped listening to me, and that all he was hearing was the desperate ramblings of a madwoman. So in the end I just stopped talking, and that was when he wanted to tell me to fuck off. I could see it on his face. It was that black look, that tight-lipped anger that comes when you just discover that you've been duped. I've seen it before on the faces of my clients – the ones who don't get their immigration status, or the ones who get deported. They want to stick up their fingers and scream obscenities, but they're still afraid that they might lose their final vestige of pride. Or maybe they still think that there's a chance that the decision will be reversed or revoked. In Mark's case he just couldn't get the words out, because he is a coward.' Marla slams the palm of her free hand against the edge of her desk. 'Damn!'

Julie knocks at the office door and steps inside without waiting for a response. 'You left this in reception, Mr Philips. It was under your chair.'

Julie hands Lester an envelope.

'It's not mine,' he explains. 'It must be Richard's – his briefcase fell open and everything went on the floor.' He checks the address. 'Does he live in Ealing? There's no name, just an address.'

'Yes, leave it here on my desk. I'll give it to him in the morning,' says Marla. 'Did Bahrain call, Julie?'

'Yes, they've sent the documents over by FedEx. Should be here tomorrow morning.'

'Great.'

'Goodnight, then.'

'Goodnight, Julie.'

'So? You want me to take you out to dinner then, Lester? I presume that's why you're here.'

Lester laughs. 'Am I that transparent?' he asks.

'Honey, if you were a shower curtain I'd now be staring at your bony white ass.'

'Why don't you kiss it!'

'Been there, done that – wasn't up to much.'

And Lester, with a playful snarl, gives Marla the finger.

'Now, that's what I *call* a man,' laughs Marla. And she links her arm through Lester's as he reaches for his coat. 'Who needs a police inspector when I can have an unemployed actor?'

'An unemployed actor who no longer has an agent,' replies Lester as they leave the office.

'Oh Christ! What have you done now?'

'I guess somebody finally told *me* to fuck off.'

'Beattie?'

'Yes, the bitch has fired me.'

'Sounds like this story is worth a corner table at L'Escargot,' and Marla turns to smile at Lester. 'You know, just when I think my life can't get any worse, you come along and tell me about yours. You *do* cheer me up, Lester darling.'

'Ditto,' laughs Lester.

And they dodge the cleaning lady outside in the corridor as she vacuums the carpet with steady, monotonous diligence.

Thirty-one

Annie has been at the house all day. She needs to get three comparative estimates from all of the contractors who will be working on the redecoration of her house and she is already finding that very few people are as reliable as their adverts profess. Two electricians turned up more than an hour late; one painter brought his two infant daughters with him; another reeked of alcohol and couldn't stand up straight; and four men didn't even bother to turn up.

If the house seemed depressing before, it is even worse now.

The back of the building, on the ground floor, had suffered the most damage. The fire had started in the kitchen and quickly spread through the conservatory and up into the master bedroom and adjoining bathroom. Most windows are now boarded up, and the conservatory is sealed off completely with hardboard panels, because the glass roof had caved in completely. The one window that remains intact has been left open all day, and Annie must have used at least two cans of Country Berry air-freshener, but the acrid stink of smoke pervades the house like a virus. Her dad was going to come down from Chesterfield to help her but Annie had reassured her parents that everything was under control.

If Annie disliked this house before the fire, she likes it even less now that it is so dark and dismal. The fire has reduced her marriage to nothing more than a charred ruin, and there is something poignant in the fact that the only thing that remained for her of Spencer is now demolished. Richard has convinced Annie to stick with the house, to see through the repairs and redecoration even though that is the last thing that she wants right now. Spencer had added Annie's name to the deeds when they got married so she has no legal problems with claiming it as her own if Spencer really has disappeared for good. Richard has organized a lawyer who asked Billy to sign a document that says he will relinquish any rights to the house, should Spencer's will come into effect.

It all feels rather too final to Annie, who secretly hopes that Spencer will pole up any day now with a feasible excuse for his absence. But she has to be sensible, and if she's going to live here alone she will need to feel more comfortable with her surroundings. She must choose new colours, new furnishings, and she must start thinking of herself for once, because she cannot live here with Spencer's ghost hanging around like a monochromatic shroud.

Yesterday she spent the entire day in the West End, looking at fabrics and furniture. Once she got started, it was almost fun and the only thing that was missing was Betsy – Annie has never been out on a major shopping spree without her best friend before, and she missed the companionship, the support and the coffee breaks. There is something rather anticlimactic about shopping alone. Annie did call Betsy before she went out, though. Her friend is back at home but she is still not gaining any weight. The electroconvulsive therapy doesn't seem to have worked.

Betsy gave Annie a list of places to look for colour schemes and accessories. 'I've got nothing better to do with my time than read endless home magazines, so I've got lots of ideas,' she said.

Annie spent two hours in Next, choosing wallpaper, curtains, duvet cover and sheets, lamps and even pictures for her lemon and apricot master bedroom. In the kitchen she is painting over the distressed concrete walls in a lovely shade of lavender. Somebody from Dorset is coming in to paint all the white cabinets in a shade called Butternut, a kind of creamy coffee colour that ties in with the colours of the floral Austrian blinds that John Lewis are making for her.

She had lunch in John Lewis – spinach quiche, macaroni salad and a carbonated apple drink – and then it was on to Marks & Spencer's for the wallpaper border Betsy had told her about, for the bathroom – blue and white seashells with matching embroidered towels and a tissue box cover. By the end of the day Annie was drunk with consumerism.

She was spent with spending. There was no point in totting up exactly how much money she had burned through in one day because the insurance was going to cover everything, and Spencer himself had much more expensive taste than Annie does.

She met up with Richard in a pub at six o'clock for a gin and tonic, and he remarked on just how elated she looked.

'I'm up on a billboard in Leicester Square,' bubbled Annie, practically swallowing her slice of lemon in a thirsty gulp of gin, 'right up there where everybody can see me. Nobody told me that the advert was coming out yet. It was a right shock, I can tell you!'

'How does it feel to be famous?' smiled Richard.

'I'll tell you when I've got used to it,' joked Annie. And for the very first time since she came to London, she caught a glimmer of hope as it fizzed to the surface of her excitement. Maybe she could learn to like it here.

Perhaps it *is* possible to bring the country girl to the big city.

A man from Sotheby's has come to the house to assess Spencer's artwork and furniture. It is mostly modern or tribal art but the man with the bow tie and cufflinks still seems impressed, and is making all kinds of notes in his jotter. Annie wants to get rid of it all. She doesn't like the dark, menacing wooden sculptures and the paintings that look like crayon scribble. There are genuine shrunken heads in a perspex box on the landing wall, and they watch her every night when she climbs the stairs. Some of the black and white photographs are all right, but Annie wants something with a little more colour, and for the cost of one single painting, she can buy prints for the entire house from John Lewis. Spencer is going to go mad if he does come back, but then it'll be his own fault for buggering off like that without telling her.

The man from Sotheby's seems very impressed. He knows a firm who will repair the smoke damage on the pieces most affected by the fire, but he is pleased to report that no serious damage has been caused.

'This Paul Wunderlich, although a fairly recent work, should fetch about thirteen thousand,' he says, stroking his chin as he stares at the one painting that

Annie absolutely loathes. It is a painting of a man with a head shaped rather like a distorted vegetable, and Annie can't believe that anyone would fork out good money for something so ugly.

'And these Patrick Procktors will probably go for about seven thousand apiece. Your husband has a wonderful collection of twentieth-century art, Mrs Noble – some of these pieces are investments that you may wish to hold on to.'

'But I don't *like* any of them,' says Annie, staring at a huge black canvas smudged with grey and green ovals and squares, 'they're depressing. And if my husband ever reappears he can start collecting all over again. They mean nothing to me, and I prefer something with a bit more colour.'

The man from Sotheby's smiles as he continues to make notes with his gold fountain pen, he refrains from comment, but Annie can guess that he's labelling her a philistine. And maybe she is. She comes from the kind of background where 'art' is for museums and 'pictures' are for homes. Pictures of flowers and trees and sometimes buildings, but pictures that *look* like something, to show that the artist could at least draw a decent representation of his subject. Some of Spencer's paintings have nothing much to do with their titles, and Annie just cannot see how anyone could daub crimson paint across an orange canvas and call it 'Woman with Child'. The only original oil painting that Annie ever saw that she liked was by an artist called Thomas Kinkaid, but it was for £5,000 in a shop on Bond Street. £5,000 for a picture of a thatched cottage, with the sun setting behind the trees – how ridiculous!

The phone interrupts Annie's critique of the art world. She excuses herself from the man from Sotheby's and takes the call in the kitchen.

'You're on the telly!' screams Betsy. 'Right now, on Gloria Hunniford, Channel 5!'

'What do you mean, I'm on the telly? Quieten down a bit. I can't hear you properly.'

'She's interviewing Michaela Fox. I didn't even know it was on, I was just flicking through the channels and then I saw Michaela large as life on the screen. She's talking about her new collections, and they've already shown loads of photos of you wearing her clothes. They even mentioned your name. Oh God, Annie, this is like a bloody dream come true. I can't believe it. Go and turn your telly on now.'

'I'll call you back!' laughs Annie and she rushes up to the bedroom where there is a small portable TV hidden inside a Moroccan chest. By the time she finds Channel 5 Gloria and Michaela are having a laugh about hemlines, and they're just moving on to talk about the popularity of Michaela's brand label with fashion-conscious teenagers in Britain.

'It's all connected to black culture in America,' says Michaela, grinning her toothy grin while Gloria fiddles with a clipboard and a halter-neck top that presumably she was holding up for the camera a few minutes ago. 'The black kids have been setting fashion and music trends for years now, but they never got the credit for it before. In New York, as a designer, I keep my eyes on the streets to see what's buzzing, what's happening. I get such a kick when I see young black kids now wearing my clothes. I see the MF label in huge bold letters across their sweats, across their jeans, and I think, wow! It's come full circle.'

Gloria is nodding. She is pretending to be interested when really all she wants to do is complete her list of formulated questions before time runs out.

'And yet, Michaela, you also manage to produce these upmarket, very sophisticated evening lines for women who still like to look glamorous. My daughter Karen had one of your dresses on the other week, and she looked stunning.'

'Gee, thanks!' gushes Michaela, leaning forward to fondle Gloria's knee.

'And I'm afraid that's all we've got time for today. Thank you for joining us, Michaela, and good luck with the new plus-size collection. I'm certain it's going to be very successful.'

'Thanks, Gloria, it's been a pleasure.'

'And please join me here again tomorrow, when I will be talking to June Whitfield about her long and very varied career in television. Until then, goodbye.'

And there, on the TV screen, as they roll the final credits, is a full-colour photograph of Annie standing against a palm tree, wearing a navy-blue satin trouser suit with a fuchsia crossover blouse and matching sandals.

Oh . . . my . . . God!

Annie has to clench her thighs together to stop herself from peeing on the carpet. This is just too much for her to handle. It's like winning the lottery and not being able to comprehend the vastness of the fortune.

The phone starts to ring. This time it's Annie's mum calling from a payphone.

'Oh love, I was just walking past Rumbelows in the high street, and there you were on every telly screen. I ran in to see what they were saying about you, and I was that proud I couldn't contain myself. I told everybody in the shop that you were my daughter. They must have thought I was potty! Oh duck, you must be over the moon. Your dad's going to be chuffed when I tell him; he's already blowing your trumpet all over the market. You know they've put one of them posters up near the Pomegranate Theatre? Dottie Hindle saw it from the top of a bus yesterday, and thought she must have got a tile loose. She really thought she was seeing things! Everybody's talking about it, love. You're a real star up here in Chesterfield . . . Oh, that's the end of my money, so I'll talk to you later, love—'

The man from Sotheby's is now standing in the kitchen doorway. It appears he has finished with his inventory and is ready to leave. Something seems to be bothering him. He hesitates by the front door as Annie goes to see him out.

'Is there something else, Mr Blatchford?' asks Annie.

'Oh, this may seem a trifle impertinent of me, and I hesitate to broach the subject with your husband missing, it's just that . . .'

'Yes?'

'I wondered if perhaps you would like to have dinner with me one evening? Nothing heavy – just a bite to eat somewhere quiet?'

Annie is quite taken aback. This was the last thing she expected to hear from a neat little man like Mr Blatchford.

'Oh,' she says, feeling the colour rise to her cheeks, 'that's really nice of you but I'm . . . well, I'm already seeing someone at the moment. Sorry.' She wonders how that sounds. Husband missing, possibly dead, and she's already seeing somebody else. What a cold-hearted slut!

'I apologise,' says Mr Blatchford, blushing slightly with embarrassment. 'I should not have been so familiar.'

And Annie, for the first time in her entire life, begins to understand what it feels like to be popular.

Dinner at Mezzo is a noisy affair. Michaela always chooses these kinds of restaurants – the kind where food is secondary to the people who are eating it.

This evening they are six. Michaela, Annie, Billy, Lucas Halliwell – yes! *The* Lucas Halliwell – a PR person called Andy, and the assistant editor from *Vogue*. They created quite an atmosphere when they walked through the 700-seat restaurant, and Annie could barely keep her eyes off the floor she felt so embarrassed. Several people have already been up to their table for autographs – from Lucas Halliwell of course! – and the waiters are being particularly attentive.

Annie had no idea that Lucas Halliwell was going to join them for dinner, so this is an amazing coup for young Billy, who can't keep his eyes off the pop star long enough to look at the menu. Further excitement was generated when both Michaela and Lucas agreed that Billy is model material.

'Even better looking than your dad, and just the right age!' enthused Michaela when Annie introduced the fashion designer to Billy. Michaela took Billy's chin in the palm of her hand and swivelled his face from left to right as she scrutinized his features through squinted eyes. 'Very Milan,' she said, 'and the perfect height too.'

When Lucas Halliwell had joined them for drinks at the Hempel, Billy practically dropped his champagne with excitement.

'He's coming to dinner with *us*?' he hissed to Annie, as all around them they solicited discreet stares and whispers. Annie was just as shocked and impressed as Billy. What will Betsy say when she hears about this?

'I've seen the photographs, Annie. They're fantastic. Very nice to meet you,' said Lucas as he shook Annie's trembling hand. 'And who is this?'

Annie introduced Billy.

Billy looking gorgeous without even having to try. Billy wearing a pair of loose-fitting Michaela Fox jeans with a silver key chain that hangs to his knee – purchased especially for the occasion, even though his mother had begged him to wear something less casual.

At the dinner table they have to talk very loudly to be heard above the din of the restaurant. Annie is wearing one of the outfits that Michaela gave her in Key West, even though it is theoretically a summer costume. She took time to apply her make-up just as they showed her, and her hair is simple to blow-dry, now that it's been cut properly. Everyone agrees that Annie looks like a million dollars. Just a few months ago her wardrobe was all from Evan's and the outsize department at the Co-op, but now she is wearing dresses that cost more than her parents make in a month. The Chesterfield girl is now a cover girl.

'Where's Richard this evening?' asks Michaela, flagging down a waiter for another Martini.

'He's at his computer class. Marla is getting an

updated accountancy system installed next week, so he's having to learn the ropes.'

'He's way too quiet, sweetheart. You need to bring him out of himself. Don't look so worried, honey, I'm sure he'll perk up once he gets to know us all better. He just needs to get out more, especially if he's going to be dating one of my top models! I have to say, though, he's a bit of a dark horse.'

'What do you mean?' asks Annie.

'Well, for a start I never knew he was engaged to be married a few years ago. One of Marla's secretaries, apparently, a girl called Sally. She was killed in a car accident or something: I don't know the details but it was all very tragic.'

Annie has stopped playing with her drink. She stares at Michaela without blinking. 'Marla told you this?'

'Oh my God, sweetheart, you didn't know!'

Annie shakes her head.

'Well, it's not that important, is it? She's *dead*, she can't be much of a threat if she's six feet under, can she?' and Michaela laughs with an embarrassed shrug. 'Now, who's ready for another round of cocktails?'

Annie is more than a little surprised to find out that Richard was engaged. He has never once mentioned this to her. Did he somehow think it might put her off to know that he had been so close to marriage? It is unsettling to think that he couldn't share such a big part of his life with her, when Annie has told him *everything* about her relationship with Spencer.

Dinner is an extensive affair. They are still sitting at the table after midnight, and Annie can barely keep her eyes open. They have been joined by two models from the Swank agency, who know everyone at the table except for Billy. They assumed that he was just another model until he explained the situation.

'God, darling!' exclaims the emaciated blonde with the limpid eyes. 'I thought you were one of Michaela's.'

'Isn't he divine?' laughs Michaela. 'I've already told him that he just has to sign on the dotted line and he'll be on the front cover of some gorgeous magazine by the end of the year.'

'I don't think I'm cut out to be a model,' smiles Billy, obviously flattered by the attention. 'Mum wants me to go to university.'

'An education!' exclaims Michaela in mock horror. 'Darling, with a face like yours who needs tedious old qualifications?'

'I appreciate the offer, Michaela, but modelling just isn't my bag.'

'Oh well, you can always give Auntie M. a call when the university thing gets old. Look at Annie here – she was a reluctant candidate too and now she's going great guns!'

'I think Billy's right, Michaela,' says Annie. 'At his age it's more important to get an education and – not to belittle the profession at all – I do think that modelling is the kind of job that only lasts so long.'

The models from Swank exchange catty looks but say nothing. They probably don't have two A-levels to rub together between the two of them.

'I think we'd better change the subject before this conversation turns sour,' laughs Lucas Halliwell. 'Although I do have to say that I think the old cliché about models being thick is a bit passé these days.'

The models smile but refrain from comment.

Michaela directs Annie's attention to one side while

the discussion regarding models and their relative IQ continues at the table, and she speaks in an uncharacteristically quiet tone. 'How's Marla doing these days?' she asks.

'Quite honestly, I don't see a lot of her; she works so late, and I'm out of the flat before she gets up in the morning. She seems OK, I suppose, considering the way things have been lately.'

'Do you know anything about these rumours that are going around?'

'What rumours?'

Michaela checks to make sure that she is not overheard and she moves closer to Annie, placing her hand on the back of her chair so that she can turn sideways. 'I wondered if it's true that Marla had a child that died. A baby?'

'It's the first I've heard about it,' admits Annie, 'but then I really don't know her very well, and Spencer never told me anything about there being a baby.'

'Well, I've heard that she had a baby with Lester years ago, and that she had some kind of schizo attack and killed it. Apparently she—'

But Michaela is cut off mid-sentence by the arrival of her pork tenderloin and they do not get another chance to resume the speculative gossip.

Annie wonders if it can be true. And if it is true, how did Marla get away with it?

The party finally disbands at one thirty, and Lucas Halliwell offers to give Billy a lift home to Holloway in his limousine. How could Billy possibly refuse such an offer? Annie is going back to Marla's flat at Canary Wharf, so Michaela's PR person has offered to drop her off on his way to Rotherhithe.

As they wait outside the restaurant for their cars to arrive, Billy corners Annie. 'This has been the best night of my entire life and it's all because of you.' He squeezes the top of Annie's arm through her jacket and kisses her full on the lips.

And for just a moment, as they stand together like this, Annie can almost imagine that Spencer is back. A new improved Spencer. A Spencer who is capable of loving her as more than just a convenient sidekick.

What a ridiculous thought. Annie must be drunk.

This is a boy we are talking about. He's only eighteen years old – young enough to be Annie's son. So why does she tremble when he looks at her that way? And why, for the first time in months, does she experience the same reckless feeling that she felt when Spencer asked her to be his wife?

Seemingly impossible things do come true.

Get a grip, Annie. A few glasses of wine, dinner with Lucas Halliwell, and you're losing all sense of reality.

'Are you ready, Annie?' shouts the PR person from the window of his car.

'I'm ready!' she replies.

And that is just how she feels right now. Ready for anything – whatever the outcome.

Thirty-two

When Marla sees the words SEX STARVED BITCH scrawled across her bedroom door, she has to steel herself against the wall, with bile rising in the back of her throat.

She calls to Lester, who is in the living room fixing a drink.

'I can't do this, Lester,' Marla whispers. 'I can't go through much more of this.' She covers her face with her hands and feels the sting of tears. Humiliation and nausea make her feel faint.

Lester comes bounding up the stairs and Marla points to the bedroom door.

'You can't have done this, Marla. You've been at the office all day and with me all evening,' says Lester, pulling her into his chest and stroking the back of her head as she begins to sob.

'I'm cracking up, Lester. I'm really cracking up.'

'Don't be silly, love, you couldn't have done this. It has to be someone else.'

Marla pulls herself away from Lester's arms and places her hands against his chest so that she can look up at him.

'It was me – I'm sure of it. I came home at lunchtime to get some files that I forgot. I wasn't here long and I certainly don't remember doing this, but it had to be me. I'm scared to look inside. Will you look?'

Lester pushes open the bedroom door.

Marla is dismayed when she hears him sigh, 'Bloody hell.'

'What have I done? Let me see . . .' Marla pushes past Lester and halts at the threshold of the bedroom.

The bedside lamps are switched on. Across the neatly folded bedspread there is one of Marla's new dresses – a black jersey ankle-length affair with black beads sewn around the neckline.

Resting inside the beaded neckline sits the butchered head of a pig, and wedged inside its mouth there is a monstrous rubber phallus. Across the mirror behind the bed, in black magic marker, spiteful letters spell out the words ROTTING FLESH, OPEN WOUNDS, SLUTTY BITCH, DIE, DIE, DIE.

'Where is Annie?' asks Lester, checking his watch.

Marla doesn't answer. She is staring at the pinkish-purple flesh of the pig's head in total horror. This is getting worse by the minute. This is the work of a dangerous maniac.

'Call my doctor, Lester. I can't go on like this. I need serious help. I need to be locked up.' As Marla says these words, she can feel the blood rushing from her head, and she gets a tingling sensation at the backs of her knees. 'I think I'm going to faint . . .' She sinks down against the carpet, pressing her forehead against the base of the bed.

'Let me get you some water,' says Lester, rushing through to the bathroom. 'We're not going to lock you up in some asylum, Marla. If this was *really* something that you did, we just need to make sure you're under constant surveillance while you get the help you need.'

'Why am I doing this?' croaks Marla. 'What's wrong with me?'

'Here, sip this . . .' Lester hands her a glass of water and crouches beside the bed. 'Now then, where is Annie?'

'She's gone out with Michaela for dinner somewhere, I think. She'll be home any minute. Oh Christ, Lester, how are we going to explain this to her? I'm going to have to tell her, otherwise she'll freak out when she sees this.'

'OK, let's be a little more rational about this, Marla. Why don't you go through to your study and lie down on the sofa for a bit. Let me sort out this mess before Annie gets home.'

'But how, Lester?'

'I'm going to clean up the bed, chuck out this monstrosity, and wash the mirrors.'

'You're going to stay here with me tonight, aren't you? You won't let me out of your sight, Lester.'

'Yes, I'm going to stay. Now go and lie down, because Annie could be home any minute.'

'Thanks, Lester,' says Marla and she hauls herself up from the carpet. 'I'll take a couple of pills; they'll probably knock me out for the night.'

But Marla knows that she will not sleep. No medication is going to offer her the solace of a restful night, and she isn't going to sleep naturally again until she is cured. When she attempts to explain the emotional exhaustion that she feels to anyone else, she just cannot find the words to describe it. Frustration and anger seem to be the two most prevalent reactions to this waking nightmare, and the only situation that Marla can compare it to would be the imprisonment of an innocent person. That is how it feels to Marla – like she is trapped behind bars, shouting out the truth, but nobody is listening. She feels framed and, without any evidence to prove herself innocent, she must believe that she is guilty of the crime. It is all happening again. The police will come and take her away. They will tell her that she has killed her baby daughter, and she will scream at them to believe her denial. But the evidence will be damning.

In this bedroom, Marla can now witness the fruits of her madness. Although the window has been repaired from the last incident, she still has no curtains and Hetty has pinned up blankets to offer her some privacy and to keep the room relatively dark when the sun comes up. Hetty has been a great help these last few weeks; she seems to understand what Marla is going through because Hetty's own sister was a paranoid schizophrenic. They thought her sister was getting better, until the summer of 1999 when she witnessed a total eclipse of the sun whilst on holiday in Cornwall. She thought it was the end of the world and she threw herself off a cliff in Polperro, dragging her youngest child with her.

'I know all about the goings on of the human mind, Mrs Philips,' said faithful Hetty, polishing up a new copy of *Vanity Fair* with a squirt of Mr Sheen. 'The manifestations can be something chronic if you don't watch it.'

Hetty is the kind of faithful servant who never questions the activities of the people she considers her 'betters'. She was brought up on a Bermondsey council estate, sharing a room with two brothers and a Border collie called Shep. Her father was a steelworker who lived up north most of the year, and her mother – as far as Marla can tell by reading between the rather wavering lines – was a part-time prostitute who took in laundry at weekends.

'Life's not that easy for some folk, Mrs Philips,' said Hetty as she sorted through a laundry basket filled with whites, 'but these days is easy compared with how it was then. I've now got satellite telly, a fridge-freezer, and a sing-song down at the Weary Ploughman every Saturday night.'

How Marla wishes that she could say the same sort of thing about her own life. There was a time when she thought that she too had it all. She used to wake up in the mornings and her first thought would concern her work. Her itinerary would unravel itself before her eyes as she pulled back the curtains to face the grey light of dawn. She would revel in the prospect of tackling a difficult legal problem, of helping another person cross the international borders to find the refuge they sought in England. She would work late, dine out with colleagues or clients, fly around the world with a cell phone, a laptop computer and a change of underwear. These days she can barely make it to the wardrobe to choose a suitable outfit.

She turns on the TV for company and helps herself to a large whisky from the bottle that remains by the bed from last night. The room is a mess, with clothes strewn across the furniture. There is a bra on the bedside table, and the remains of another microwaved meal on a scabby plate by the bathroom door. Hetty didn't come in today – she doesn't come in every day now that she's past retirement age – and Marla clearly doesn't know how to look after herself any more. She also knows that the bathroom will be littered with damp towels. She knows that the shower door will be hanging open, that the tap will be dripping, that there will be powder spilled across the marble vanity top. There are no tidy places left for Marla to go. She has only chaos in which to dwell, and at this precise moment she feels like screwing herself up in a little ball on the bed, where nobody will see her. A little ball so insignificant that it cannot be found amidst the folds of the continental quilt.

In Marla's adjoining home office there are patio doors that lead on to a narrow terrace where, on nice summer evenings, she can sit and contemplate the complex pattern of the city across the Thames. She pushes open the doors and gasps as a sharp blast of frosty night air cuts through the airless vacuum of the room. The night has a sharp smell: it is slightly metallic, like the smell of coins in a sweaty palm. The flat, unemotional hum of London lies like an impassive beast somewhere beyond the shrill whistle of the wind as it tears around the concrete and buffets the long-dead geraniums in the window boxes. Marla takes a deep breath and steps out on to the terrace.

This is definitely a summer place.

Two iron chairs sit back to back in the corner, draped with some black plastic to protect them from the seasons. They form a misshapen hump and the plastic rustles as the wind swipes against it with sharp little slaps. Breath comes out of Marla's lungs in huge clouds of vapour, only to be whipped away into the night before she can even register the fact that they exist.

There are no ships on the river. The NatWest

building blinks with a red eye above the lower structures over which it presides. Clouds of steam rise up behind it, as though the earth is about to erupt – as though giant fissures are opening up in the tarmac upon which the city is built, to release the surging gases from the planet's core. And the river is dark: it has no reflection tonight, it has no light. The water rushes quietly by, a strong, menacing presence that makes Marla shiver even more than the bitter north wind that stings her cheek with blatant reproof.

She could quite easily climb the railings. They are only waist-high and there is a narrow ledge on the outside where she could stand long enough to say her final farewell. It would be a quiet way to go. It would be a neat way to go, like a sharp cut through a piece of paper with a large pair of dressmaker's scissors. *Snip, snip!* A nice clean line that cuts her free of all obligations to this sorry little life. No more endless searching, no more desperate longing to understand, and if that is all there is to life, then why bother continuing with it anyway? If all she has is this insignificant lifeline of seventy-odd years in which to prove herself, then why not fuck the lot of them and see what's waiting for her on the other side?

It's tempting.

It's very tempting.

Marla approaches the ice-cold railings, against which her hands burn. The wind makes her eyes teary, her hair whips back from her face, and she looks down at the silent river to see if she can decipher any kind of sign from the next world that might make her less afraid. That water is black, and it is deep. She wonders if Jessica is down there, just under the surface of the water, with outstretched arms, waiting for her mother to come home. If Marla threw herself into the river she would be sucked under a freezing vortex, and it would pull her down until her lungs were filled with nothing but water. She might hear hymns being sung, like the ones that people profess to have heard as they are brought back from the dead. She might see that faraway light, the one with God in its centre, the one with dead relatives beckoning, dressed in white robes.

Go towards the light. At that point there would be no other direction in which to head. Her decisions would be made, and she would just give herself up to the flow of the river and the call of those voices. How comforting that would be.

'What on earth are you doing out here? It's bloody freezing!' Lester appears behind Marla just as her hand reaches out to grab the drainpipe. She is so startled by his voice, so shattered by the interjection, that she utters a shrill little scream and falls against the railings as though suddenly kicked in the small of her back.

'You're not even wearing a jacket. Come back inside! I've finished in the bedroom, and Annie hasn't come home yet. Let's go down to the kitchen and get something warm to drink, eh?' Lester places a reassuring arm around Marla's thin, vulnerable shoulder and she caves in against him. His hand rubs against her skin, to cause some friction of heat. His breath is warm against her cheek as he talks.

'It goes round and round in my head and I can't make it stop,' she sobs. 'I haven't got the strength left to fight it, Lester, I thought I was strong but I'm not.'

'You *are* strong, love, you've always been a fighter, you're not going to give up now, are you?'

'I should be in an institution. You need to get me locked up otherwise I might hurt somebody. Please, Lester, promise me that tomorrow you'll find me somewhere to go, because if you don't, I'm flying straight back to New York and I'm booking myself into a clinic.'

'All right, all right . . .' whispers Lester, stroking Marla's hair. 'Come on, love,' he says. And he takes her by the arm and slowly, responsibly, leads her towards the light.

Thirty-three

It has been raining for three days.

Everything appears blurred at the edges, as though gradually dissolving into a coarsely textured canvas, and St Valentine's Day rattles against the windows with relentless despair.

February the 14th was always a poignant time for Annie when she was growing up. At school she stood by and watched as the popular girls flaunted their Valentine's cards. Huge padded cards that came in cardboard boxes with hearts and flowers and mice wearing lacy bonnets.

> *From Your Boyfriend*
> *To The One I Love*
> *Will You Be Mine?*

Annie was seventeen before she received a Valentine's card of her own. It came from one of the married men in her office building who sometimes sat next to her on the bus in the mornings. His name was Stan and he had hair on the backs of his knuckles. The card was supposed to be from a mysterious admirer, signed only with a question mark, but Annie could tell, by the way Stan questioned her the next morning on the number 7, that it was no mystery.

Every year after that, Annie had received a card faithfully from Spencer. Not romantic cards that spoke of love and devotion, they were more like 'friendship' cards, as though Spencer merely wanted to reassure her that she wasn't forgotten. Of course last year he sent her the real thing along with a massive bunch of flowers that came already arranged in a glass vase from Sheffield. When they arrived at her office, she was the envy of all her workmates. A dozen long-stemmed roses: the colour of very dark blood, or red velvet. Compared to the puny scarlet things that Isabel from accounting received, Annie's roses were of a much superior pedigree, and everyone agreed that Spencer Noble had incredible taste.

Annie had bought some cufflinks for Spencer. He was one of those people who seemed to already have everything, and she always suffered hours of indecision when buying him gifts of any kind. Even at Easter, she had to specially order him a dark chocolate egg from Betty's in Harrogate, having made the mistake the year before of getting him milk chocolate, iced with his name at Thornton's Cabin. (He didn't say anything but she could tell by the look on his face that this really wasn't his style.)

She had bought the cufflinks in York. Dad took her up there one Saturday because the only jewellers in Chesterfield were of the H. Samuel kind, and Annie knew that Spencer would never wear a pair of rolled-gold, diamond-etched cufflinks that came in a plastic, flock-lined box.

She found a small antique shop in The Shambles that sold silver tea sets and crystal decanters. They had a small glass display case filled with antique jewellery and, as luck would have it, there was one perfect pair of cufflinks. The man who owned the shop was very nice. He let her hold the cufflinks while he explained how old they were. Solid 9-carat yellow gold that was patinated with age to a soft, mellow sheen. Each cufflink was twisted in such a way that it resembled a small knot of rope and they were stamped with the Cartier insignia.

The price was exorbitant – but Annie had expected that. She used her credit card for the very first time. She had opened an account specifically for that purpose, so that she could pay it off in monthly instalments. If her dad had known how much she was spending he'd have had a fit, but Annie fibbed and told him they were £40 from Samuel's. Even then, he balked at the price and suggested that maybe a bottle of rum would have sufficed.

Spencer was thrilled with the gift. He loved beautiful things and although Annie knew that he already had a drawer filled with cufflinks, she derived great satisfaction every time she saw him wearing hers. It was a mark of approval, and Annie was proud of herself for having the intuition necessary to procure such a suitable present.

This year the long-stemmed roses came from Richard. Almost as handsome as those from Spencer, but not quite as dramatic. There was a card as well. It was a Hallmark job, very pretty, with cherubs and trails of ivy, but it wasn't from Spencer, and Annie was saddened by her ungrateful attitude as she read the romantic verse inside. There was once a time when she could only have dreamed of receiving such a card, but Spencer has spoiled her. Like they say in the Galaxy advert: why have cotton when you can have silk?

Annie is back at Spencer's house. She still can't call

it home, even though it all now belongs to her. Sotheby's have taken the artwork for auction and the decorator has stripped the walls, ready to be painted and wallpapered. The floors are covered with plastic sheeting and the windows in the kitchen have been replaced. Annie rubbed Windoline on the front windows to keep prying eyes from looking in, so the house now looks unoccupied from the street. She moved out of Marla's flat because Marla seemed very unhappy with having her around, even though she never said as much. Marla had offered up her own bedroom to Annie while she goes away to a health farm in the Cotswolds, but Annie didn't like the idea of living there without Marla – it was too much of an imposition on someone she still barely knows.

So now Annie is living in the small study upstairs. Spencer had put a single bed up there, piling it with Thai silk cushions and calling it a daybed. She has set the portable TV on a stack of legal books, and it's very cosy at night with the blinds closed and the desk lamp creating a shallow pool of light against the bookshelves. It's also a bit scary at night when the empty rooms around her are so quiet and dark, but she locks the door and won't even nip out to use the loo until daylight arrives. She leaves the TV on, with the sound muted, while she sleeps.

This morning, even with the lights on, it is depressingly grey, with the rain battering on the outside of the hardboard sidings where the conservatory used to be. Annie has made some tea, and she is watching the news as she eats her way through a box of untoasted cinnamon Pop Tarts. She is due for a photo shoot this afternoon at Kew Gardens, for Michaela, and tonight she is having dinner with Richard at an Italian place somewhere in east London.

A busy day.

It is unusual for the doorbell to ring so early in the morning, unless the postman has brought something that won't go through the letterbox, but the postman has already been today so it can't be him.

It is another florist: a different girl from the one who brought Richard's roses at the crack of dawn this morning. This must be a very busy day for them, so they have to start early.

It is a basket of pink carnations from Interflora.

Annie takes the flowers through into the kitchen, and removes the little card that has been spiked into place on a plastic holder.

HAPPY VALENTINE'S DAY, ANNIE. WITH LOTS OF LOVE, BILLY. And there are three kisses in red biro.

Annie quite suddenly feels short of breath. She has to sit down on a counter stool, and her fingers play lightly at her throat. She feels very close to tears. Annie is beside herself with joy, and she doesn't stop to wonder why she feels so elated by this simple gesture when Richard's romantic tribute had left her so unimpressed earlier. These carnations, so simple, so unaffected, seem to embody the feelings that Annie has for Billy. He has an enthusiasm for life that reminds Annie of Spencer when he was first at university. It is a fresh-faced, unlined vivacity that Annie never possessed but that she so admires in other people. Everything that Spencer once inspired in her, she now sees in his son Billy. It is like being offered a second chance to put things right and, despite the age difference between them, Annie can quite easily relate to the eighteen-year-old, as though she has never grown up herself.

Annie phones Billy's house, and Maggie answers. As they make polite conversation Annie senses instinctively not to mention the flowers to Billy's mother. Maggie reveals that she is uncertain about Billy's involvement with Michaela Fox and the fact that she might be 'tempting' Billy with thoughts of glamour. She is concerned about her son's future and wants him to go to university in the autumn, but she is sensible enough not to stand in Billy's way if he chooses another path.

'I'll just get him for you, Annie. I think he's still in bed.'

Annie smells the carnations but they don't have any perfume. She can hear Maggie calling upstairs to Billy's room. She can hear classical music on the radio in the background.

Billy picks up the extension. 'Hello?' He sounds groggy, and Annie imagines him rubbing the sleep from his eyes.

'Billy, it's Annie. I just wanted to thank you for the flowers. It was a lovely surprise.'

'Oh yeah, sorry, Annie, I'm still half asleep. I forgot what day it is. Happy Valentine's Day.'

'You too, Billy. I expect you'll be doing something with Jennifer today?' The mere mention of Billy's girl-friend brings an edge to Annie's voice.

'Yeah, there's a school disco tonight – everybody's going. I doubt that it'll be much cop. It's more for the girls, really.'

'No school this morning, then?'

'Not until one. Free periods this morning.'

'I've got your dad's picture here, the one you chose before they took everything off to the auction house. Why don't we have dinner this week and you can pick it up?'

'How about tomorrow? I'm not doing anything then,' suggests Billy.

'Tomorrow would be great. Why don't you come over to the house and we'll go to one of the local restaurants.'

'How about some of them chips of yours? I was telling Mum about them, but she said she's not getting a deep-fat fryer.'

'Chips it is,' says Annie, 'and I reckon there's still some of Mum's mushy peas in the freezer to go with Dad's cod. It'll be a Stamper family joint effort.'

Annie puts down the phone and runs her fingertips over the pink carnations.

The rain continues to bounce from the guttering, splashing down against the window sills and tapping insistently against the roof.

It is going to be a good day.

Richard meets Annie at the restaurant of his choice. It is a small, intimate establishment called the Little Prince and it is folded quietly away in an unpretentious part of Shoreditch. It has a used record shop above called Slipped Discs.

'You look beautiful,' says Richard, standing up as Annie approaches his table. She still doesn't know how to accept a compliment and so she giggles and accepts the seat that he has pulled out for her. Only one other table is occupied. The restaurant is dark and lit only by candles which stretch the shadows. The music is low.

'It's still pouring down outside,' says Annie unnecessarily, because she has never known how to launch herself into a conversation.

'Some wine?' asks Richard, holding up the bottle he has already started on.

'Lovely,' she says.

Ever since Annie received the carnations from Billy today, she has been thinking feverishly. Her head has been jumbled with thoughts about Spencer and Billy and Richard. Without a definite conclusion to Spencer's disappearance, she finds it almost impossible to settle down to any one thing. It is rather like sitting up late, waiting for someone to come home, while reading the same page of your book over and over again because you can't stop looking at the clock. Annie is tired of sitting up, she is tired of reading the same page over and over again without comprehending the words, and she now wants to progress. This is one of the reasons she has allowed herself to take control of Spencer's house. By selling his artwork and by repainting his walls, she is staking her claim. She is establishing herself as a person in her own right.

Every time she talks to Billy she allows herself to think that she is talking to Spencer. They have the same voice, and over the telephone she can forget for a while that he is only eighteen years old. Every time Annie meets with Billy, she is astounded by the familiarity of his face and his gestures. It is uncanny how he resembles his father, and it unsettles her with a kind of trembling disquiet. Being with Billy is like crying over the photograph of a person she once knew.

And then there is Richard.

How does Annie feel about this man who gives her so much and yet keeps his personal life so private? She feels . . . untouched. It is as though she places the palm of her hand up against Richard's but finds there is a sheet of glass between them. When they kiss it leaves no impression, and the sex has started to feel forced somehow. It is as though Richard must prove himself to Annie while she stares at the bedroom ceiling and wonders how long it will be before he realizes that she isn't going to climax. Afterwards, in the period that lovers call the afterglow, Annie longs to jump up and take a nice long bath. She wishes that she had the bed to herself, and the mere smell of Richard on her fingers brings with it an unsettling feeling of mild disgust. Disgust that she has allowed herself to fall from grace so easily.

How then can she tell Richard all about this? After she has allowed him to believe that she feels as strongly as he does? She may even have led him on in an unconscious way. She has never told him that she loves him, but there were moments of great tenderness, especially at the beginning of their relationship. He represented someone kind and sweet who liked her for being who she is instead of what she might become. Unlike Spencer, Richard allowed Annie to feel attractive and sexy; he told her constantly what a wonderful person she is, and made her feel special. Why then can't she love him? Why does she still love a man who showed her little physical tenderness and yet feel indifferent towards a man who appears to provide everything that she should need? It doesn't make sense.

'Richard?'

'Yes?'

'How come you never told me that you were engaged?'

For a moment Richard is caught off guard. His hand falters as it reaches again for the bottle of wine, and Annie notices the creases between his eyebrows as he considers her question.

'I wondered how long it would be before someone told you,' he says. 'I suppose I just didn't want to drag all of that up so early in our relationship. I didn't want you to see me as some kind of pathetic charity case for you to feel sorry for. It's happened before with women I have dated. Once they find out about Sally and the accident, I can see that glassy-eyed sympathy that blinds them to accepting me as a person who has reconciled himself to the tragedy. I'm over it, Annie, and I want to be liked for the person that I am *now*. Can you understand that?'

'Yes, I can understand your reasons for not telling me, Richard, but don't you think that under the circumstances – with Spencer missing and my own personal mess – that it might have offered me some kind of support to know that you have come through a similar situation? Don't you think that perhaps you see *me* as some kind of charity case? That certainly crossed *my* mind in the beginning.'

'You have never been a charity case, Annie,' says Richard. He reaches out for her hand across the table. 'The very first time I saw you I thought you were a beautiful woman, and I just couldn't understand what you were doing with a pompous egotist like Spencer. I'm sorry to say that about him, but you have to admit that he was only in love with himself. I couldn't bear to

347

see how upset you became every time he went away on yet another business trip. It was obvious he never loved you.'

'Actually, Richard, you've got it all wrong. It might have looked odd from the outside but I know that Spencer loves me. He might not be capable of falling *in* love with me, but we have known each other since we were at school and it hurts me to hear you say that there was no love between us.'

Richard clasps Annie's hand and there is candlelight in his eyes. Annie's instinct is to pull her hand away, but it would seem childish at this point.

'When you love someone, Annie, when you feel the way that you feel about Spencer, it is very difficult to tell yourself that they don't feel the same way about you. Believe me, I've been through it myself, and unrequited love is something that can ruin your life if you don't prevent it. You now have to come to terms with the fact that Spencer may never return. And if he does come back, do you think that he's going to fall right back into your marriage as though nothing ever happened? If he loves you so much, how come he's been missing for three months now and not even bothered to give you a call?'

'We have no idea what's happened to Spencer,' says Annie. 'He might be dead for all we know.'

'And you might never find out, Annie. You might have to live the rest of your life without that answer. So you have to move on. You have to realize that, whatever happens, Spencer is never going to love you in the way that you need to be loved.'

Annie doesn't want to hear this. Least of all from

Richard. She resents this intrusion and the fact that he presumes to know what is best for her. She removes her hand from his grasp and flips open the menu so that she can divert her anger.

'Now I've upset you,' he says.

'I'm fine,' sniffs Annie.

'You have to move on, you have to come to terms with the truth—'

'The truth? Richard, how come you know so much about the truth when you hardly even know me? I know you're trying to be kind, but I really don't like you talking about Spencer as though he is the scum of the earth. Now can we drop the subject and get something to eat, please?'

'Of course,' says Richard and he motions to the waitress. 'Could we order, please?'

Annie takes a cursory glance down the list of main courses and chooses the most expensive thing on the menu.

So what if she's never tasted venison in prune gravy before? It costs £28 and Richard is paying, bugger him! The least she can get out of this lousy evening is a good plate of grub!

'And bring us more wine,' she tells the waitress. 'I feel like getting pissed.'

Richard coughs uncomfortably.

It is time for Annie to assert herself. To stop letting people use her as a convenient doormat. She is old enough and intelligent enough – not to mention beautiful and soon to be wealthy enough – to get through life on her own if she has to. She's read about independent women in her monthly magazines, she's seen them on

American soap operas. It's time to get tough, and the first casualty on her list is going to be Richard.

Annie Noble has reached the end of her tether and there's only one thing for it – she'll have to bite through the rope and set herself free.

Thirty-four

Are some people really born lucky and others not?

Looking at Lester's life right now, one might be excused for believing that the silver spoon of fortune never touched his newborn lips. But it wasn't always this way; he's had his fair share of luck – a lot more than some people could ever dream of. He's just going through a rough patch right now, and things are bound to get better.

Life's funny like that, isn't it? One minute you're about to declare bankruptcy and the next there's a letter in the post with a tax refund, or an uplifting letter from the building society giving you another month to pay your overdue mortgage.

If Lester had not been such a successful child actor, he might be better equipped to deal with the current situation. They say that what you never have you never miss, so does that mean it is better *never* to have had, just so that you can't miss it later? It's like those people who wish they had never fallen in love because the pain of losing that person is too overwhelming for them to bear, but life would be a sad and rather pathetic business if we had to play safe all the time. If we avoided things like success and love just so that one day we wouldn't regret having lost them.

Lester has stopped watching his newly purchased

DVD of *Five Farthings*. It upsets him too much. There was just so much hope back then – and so much time. At such a young age it seemed that the stretch of life was almost infinite, like looking through the wrong end of a telescope and reducing the horizon to a pinprick of light. There was a time when a year was such a long time that he had to break it up into convenient, bite-size chunks in order to acknowledge the mere passing of time. Clocks ticked slower, daylight lasted longer, and the weekend seemed never to arrive. These days a year hurtles by so quickly that there is barely time to get used to writing a new year date on a cheque.

Since Marla admitted herself to the special hospital in Avon, Lester has been left with a nauseous feeling of rejection and loneliness. He has always counted on Marla to be the beanpole in life, to stand tall and solid, offering support to the struggling plants at her feet. Right from the beginning she was the sensible one, the one with all the common sense. Now that she has fallen to pieces, Lester begins to realize that nothing can be relied upon and everything has a breaking point.

When he left her at the hospital last week, he couldn't even turn back to look at her. She was standing in the glass doorway with reflections of the well trimmed shrubbery obliterating everything but her hand as it waved to him. He couldn't look back; he just sat in the taxi and fixed his gaze on the tatty little advert that was stuck to the back of the driver's seat. The past has come back to torment him, like a fly that buzzes around a darkened room but hides whenever the light is switched on.

They maintain that she is free to leave whenever she wants to, but stressed that a twenty-eight-day minimum stay is usually standard in cases of extreme mental disturbance. Of course they have to evaluate just how bad Marla actually is, but private hospitals don't cut corners when it comes to your health. They can afford to be thorough at £700 a day.

When Marla called him last night she sounded pretty good, even though they are restricting the amount of cigarettes she can smoke and there is no alcohol allowed.

'I feel like Leona Helmsley,' joked Marla, 'shut up in a prison with wall-to-wall carpeting and twenty-four-hour room service.'

Lester and Shani had lunch together today and they both feel relieved that Marla is receiving the treatment that she obviously needs. Shani is as surprised as Lester at Marla's breakdown.

'I honestly thought that she was over all that,' said Shani over a plate of mussels at Belgo. 'I always thought *I* was the one teetering on the edge of insanity, not Marla. Even when she was going through hell with the baby and everything, I admired her courage.'

'Maybe the stress of all that finally caught up with her,' suggested Lester, 'but she always seemed to be in control of her life, so I imagined that she was well adjusted to her hectic lifestyle.'

'Darling, even the most powerful people get bogged down by it all eventually. Look at poor Princess Diana. Who would have guessed that while we were watching her in a documentary about landmines that she was throwing herself down the stairs at Kensington Palace? We all like to put on a brave face, but I can tell you, darling, sometimes it takes more than a lick of face paint to fool the audience.'

And then they saw Marla's neighbour, Treez.

'What is *she* doing here?' hissed Shani, leaning forward over the mussels. 'I would have thought she'd be more at home with a quiche and some pasta salad at Garfunkel's.'

'Don't act like such a snob, Shani. It's not like you to judge somebody so harshly. Marla is quite fond of Treez, actually – did you know that she gave Marla a Limoges ornament at Christmas? Anyway, this is hardly haute cuisine, my love – chips and mayonnaise, beer and mussels, we could have got the same thing for half the price down the East End.'

'Yes, but people don't really come here for the food, darling. It's the atmosphere and the waiters in those robes that makes it special.'

'Now I can see why Aurora turned out the way she did,' laughed Lester.

'Oh my God! Look who she's with!'

Lester turned around in his seat and watched Richard Carruthers cross the restaurant to take a seat opposite Treez.

'That's Marla's accountant, isn't it?' asked Shani. 'What on earth is he doing out with *her*? I thought he was seeing Annie – or at least that's what Marla told me.'

'Well, obviously it isn't an exclusive arrangement,' said Lester, unaffected by the personal scandals of people he barely knows. 'I haven't set eyes on Annie since she moved out of Marla's place a couple of weeks ago.'

'He also took Marla out a couple of times, you know,' whispered Shani, once again leaning forward with a conspiratorial hand to her mouth.

'Who? Richard?'

Shani nodded. 'Yes, *years* ago, when he first started working at the office. I think it was just before Marla met Pierre, or maybe it was during their first break-up, I can't remember now, but anyway, Marla and Richard went out on a couple of dates together but it didn't turn into anything. Marla said he was boring as hell and couldn't keep it up in bed.'

'They *slept* together?' Lester found that information rather surprising, and the image of Marla with Richard *was* a trifle incongruous. Like trying to imagine a poodle mounting an Alsatian.

'Only the once. You know what Marla's like, darling – she doesn't mince her words, and Richard was definitely not man enough for her.'

'I suppose I should take that as a compliment, then.'

'Lester, darling, you know Marla loves you to death. It was just unfortunate that you both met when you were so young. Pierre was a total waste of space and since then there's only really been Mark, and that's died a sudden death, hasn't it?'

And Lester has been thinking about that ever since.

He had a dream last night. It was one of those surprising dreams when the brain decides to unlock a little drawer that you thought was empty, and out pops a memory that is so vivid you could almost believe it is true. People Lester had forgotten about years ago suddenly rematerialized and held conversations with him, as though the last twenty years never happened at all. They were still living in their flat, Marla and Lester, with the same furniture and everything in its familiar place. The only thing that was different was the bathroom. It wasn't where it was supposed to be. There was no door for it. Lester knew that something was wrong, but he couldn't quite put his finger on it until he woke up this morning. There was no bathroom, and Marla wasn't the young woman that he had been married to. Instead she looked like she does now, but she was wearing a dressing gown and oversized slippers – something that Marla would never dream of wearing, then or now.

It is the first dream that Lester has ever had of Marla for as long as he can remember, and he woke with something similar to regret in the very pit of his stomach. There is something else as well, something that perhaps has been there all the time, like a photograph turned face-down.

He still loves her.

This comes as quite a revelation to Lester after all this time, and yet even with this silent admission comes the ready acceptance of something he has known all along. His marriage to Tina – after a long period of unsuitable relationships – had obviously been just another desperate attempt to bring some stability into his life at a time when his career was falling stagnant. In the beginning she had seemed to Lester like an antidote to the undulating waves of depression he was then experiencing. Tina was young, she was funny, and she was the total opposite to Marla. Lester wanted a stab at being the *man* in a relationship for once. Every woman he had dated since Marla had mirrored the same character type: independent, bossy, opinionated women who were more mature and more established than Lester himself. He felt safe beneath their maternal wing, he didn't have to think for himself, he could just straggle behind in their jetstream, safe in the knowledge that they would turn back for him should he lose his way.

It isn't that Lester is a particularly weak individual; he has his strengths like everyone else. No, Lester just lacks the confidence that he used to have when he was sixteen. It has been knocked out of him over the years, and these days he can't even look at himself in the mirror without a total lack of conviction. Marla and Shani are the only women who have remained constant in his life, but Shani is like an older sister to him – he couldn't even contemplate any kind of sexual relationship with her at this point. Even at his lowest ebb, Marla has been there with an encouraging word or with dinner at an expensive restaurant.

But how does Marla feel about *him*?

Her most recent fling, with the police inspector, knocked Lester for six. It finally seemed that she had met her match: a man who was both intelligent and authoritative. Lester has to admit that he was jealous when he first saw the two of them together. And that jealousy bled like ink into blotting paper when Mark began to take such obvious care of Marla during those first upsetting weeks of her harassments.

It has been dark in Lester's living room for over an hour now, and yet he seems unaware of the change. He sits in a narrow wedge of light that steals in from the kitchen, where the hob light is constantly switched on due to a faulty connection. He has been sitting here since he came in at three thirty this afternoon, and a mug of instant coffee remains untouched on the table beside him.

It is the telephone that finally rouses him from this apathetic position, and its shrill jangling makes him jump up from the sofa as though an electrical current just passed through the room.

The phone is out in the hall. It is Marla's secretary Julie calling from her office.

'Mr Philips? I'm sorry to bother you but I wasn't sure who I should call.' Julie sounds uncharacteristically wary, hesitant almost.

'That's perfectly all right, Julie. What can I do for you?'

'Well, I've been going through Marla's post. Her desk is a mess and things keep piling up in here every day, what with Federal Express and the couriers arriving every few hours. Anyway, I opened an envelope addressed to Richard Carruthers by mistake – it must have somehow got muddled up in Marla's post, and I didn't check the address on the front. Anyway, I opened his envelope and found this . . . stuff. Porno stuff. A catalogue.' Julie pauses, obviously embarrassed by this admission.

'So shouldn't you just put it back in the envelope and leave it on Richard's desk?' asks Lester, wondering what on earth this has to do with him.

'Well, it's just that this isn't the normal kind of porno stuff. It's perverted.'

'I don't think this is any of our business, Julie. What Richard gets up to in his own time has nothing to do with any of us, has it? Unless . . . Oh God, don't tell me my wife is in that catalogue.' The sudden thought hits Lester like a fist in the small of his back.

'Your wife?' Julie sounds confused.

'We split up, Julie, not long ago. She's working for a company now that makes porno films.'

'Oh, I'm sorry.' Julie continues to flounder. 'Well, no, this hasn't got anything to do with your wife, Mr Philips.'

'So what is it, then? Child pornography? Sex with animals?'

'Well, it's kind of sick stuff. There are some photos from films with people being tied up and whipped and others with car accident victims – pictures of men with women who have been involved in a car crash, you know, *doing it* with them.'

'OK. Well, yes, that does sound a bit sick, but I still don't see what this has to do with us, Julie.'

'There's one film in the catalogue about a woman lawyer and a man who is stalking her. It's called 'Litigious Bitch', and some of the descriptions sound exactly like the things that have been happening to Marla recently. There's a bit about a dead cat in a box of chocolates and even a pig's heart in a handbag. There's no way this is just a coincidence, is there?'

'The bastard,' whispers Lester.

'Mr Philips? Are you still there?'

'Yes, I'm here, Julie. Look, tell me what Richard's address is. I think I should go over and tackle him about this.'

'Don't you think I should call the police? This is brilliant evidence and they could reopen the case.'

'Well, let me make sure we're on the right track first, Julie. I don't want to get Richard involved with the police if this has nothing to do with him.' Lester is not going to tell Julie all about Marla and her blackouts, and he doesn't want to get the police involved again if everything leads back to nothing more than a strange coincidence.

He takes the man's address from Julie, and assures her that she can contact the police tomorrow if it turns out that Richard is definitely a suspect. The first thing he wants to do is check Marla's video collection. If for some bizarre reason she has a copy of this sick pornographic tape, it might be that she has been subconsciously reliving it during her blackout periods. That seems highly unlikely, as Marla has never indicated the slightest kind of fascination for sexual degradation, but Lester has to rule out all possibilities before he approaches Richard on the subject.

Lester calls a cab. At this time of day the traffic in London is heavy, and it takes him over an hour to get from Kensington to Docklands. There is a light rain misting the windows of the cab and the radio is tuned to a sports channel. As they drive, Lester's mind works overtime, and the one hope that lights his path is one of freeing Marla from her purgatory. If he can prove that she was being persecuted by Richard, then it will help her to understand *why* she has been sleepwalking. Hell, with the kinds of horrible things she has had to put up with over the past few months, Lester wouldn't blame anyone for going a little crazy. She only has actual evidence of one sleepwalking episode, and that could have been triggered in response to everything else she has experienced – the constant pressure of being stalked by a maniac who appeared to know her every move.

The sight of an ambulance and police cars outside Marla's building bring panic to Lester's throat. But there are sixty flats in the building, so there could be any number of emergencies arising for other residents. Yet why does Lester instinctively know that this has something to do with Marla?

He pays the taxi driver and hurries over to the doors of the lobby.

'Are you a resident here, sir?' asks a young police-man as Lester attempts to enter the building.

'Yes, I am,' lies Lester, fingering his set of keys to Marla's flat as proof of his identity.

'Which floor are you on, sir?'

'Sixth.'

'We've got a situation up there right now, sir. I may have to ask an officer to escort you up to your flat. Which number are you?'

'6C,' says Lester, watching the lift doors open to reveal two ambulance men with a stretcher on wheels. On the stretcher there is a body. A body wrapped in a zip-up bag.

'What happened?' asks Lester. 'Did somebody die?'

'We don't know the exact circumstances yet, sir,' says the policeman. 'Officer Dunfree here will take you up to your flat.' Another young policeman appears, holding his hat in his hand.

In the lift Lester questions Officer Dunfree.

'Looks like murder,' the policeman admits, 'the lady who lived opposite you.'

'Treez?'

'She called for help, but by the time the ambulance got here it was too late. Multiple stab wounds, appar-ently. She bled to death.'

'Do they have the person who did it to her?'

'Not yet, sir. We're working on it.'

And Lester keeps his thoughts to himself. He could easily have tipped off the policeman about his recent suspicions regarding Richard, but he doesn't want to incriminate the man until he has had a chance to find out more for himself.

Does the mere fact that he saw Richard having

lunch with Treez yesterday condemn Richard as her murderer?

So, running the risk of causing obstruction of the law, Lester says nothing as he steps out of the lift with the young police officer. The door to Treez's flat stands open, and on the marble tiles of her hallway there is a trail of blood that ends, like an exclamation mark, with a bloodied handprint on the wall.

Lester lets himself into Marla's flat, closing the door on the horrific scene outside. He stands for a moment in the darkness of the hallway and runs a nervous hand over his face. He then turns on the light.

He sees blood smeared across the light switch: blood that is still sticky and congealing.

Lester walks cautiously through the living room, turning on lights as he goes. The landing light is on, casting shadows down the staircase.

'Hello?' he shouts, but there is no response. It remains dead quiet.

Upstairs there is more blood on the banister rail, and fingerprints on the edge of Marla's bedroom door. Lester reaches out to push open the door, just as the phone starts to ring. He pulls back his hand as though it has just been burned. He listens to Marla's answer-phone message, as it requests any caller to speak after they hear the beep.

'Hello, Mrs Philips, this is Dr Greene from the Greystone Foundation. Could you please call us immediately? I cannot stress strongly enough why it is imperative that you come back to the hospital to complete your analysis. We can send a car round to pick you up. Please consider your own health and safety. We hope to hear from you very soon.'

Lester pushes through into the bedroom to grab the telephone but Dr Greene has already rung off.

'Shit!' screams Lester, punching the pillow on Marla's bed. Why did she go and do a stupid thing like that? She has obviously walked out of the hospital without telling anyone.

There is more blood on the corner of the bedside cabinet.

And on the mirror, above the bed, just like before, is the writing on the wall.

Lipstick sentiments in hot pink anger. 'YOU'RE NEXT!' the words proclaim.

A profound sickness that Lester had almost forgotten floods back as he reads those words, remembering the day they found baby Jessica.

Oh God, Marla, what have you done?

Thirty-five

Annie is burning her clothes.

That might seem a drastic way to reduce her wardrobe but she needs immediate gratification and there are no charity shops in this part of the Fulham Road.

Charity begins at home. What does that saying mean exactly?

As Annie stokes her bonfire with man-made fabrics, she ponders this thought: is it really possible to be *charitable* in your own home? Annie's perception of charity is something that extends beyond the family unit, beyond the people with whom you have a personal connection. Surely charity is supposed to be a selfless act of kindness or generosity that has nothing to do with personal gain or favour? How can that be possible inside your own house?

She watches her old life go up in flames, and adds another squirt of lighter fluid to expedite the process. Polyester burns very quickly: it shrivels and melts and makes blue flames in the heart of the bonfire. Annie wants to make a fresh start, and these clothes have no place any longer in the wardrobe of the woman she wants to become. No more jolly patterns designed to disguise the girth of each dropped waistline. No more shapeless sacks in vertical stripes or elasticated flares. Annie is going for quiet sophistication now. She will buy

364

one new outfit every month, and she's sticking to muted tones of taupe, brown and black. Spencer would be very proud of her right now.

She probably should have done this during the day, when the flames of her renewal would be less evident to the neighbours, but it gets dark so early at this time of the year and she couldn't bear to wait until tomorrow. So, Annie stands like a phoenix in the light of her flames, and she watches, feeling the warmth of her past as it goes up in smoke to drift off over the rooftops. A charitable contribution to the destruction of the ozone layer.

After the bonfire has died down to a few glowing embers Annie douses it with a bucket of water and goes back indoors. She herself smells of smoke, and this smell is at home in this charred, burnt-out shell of a kitchen. Fire is a great cleanser, and Annie is beginning to look upon the destruction of Spencer's home as a sign that he isn't coming back. A sign that she needs to rejuvenate this house and make it a place where she can live by herself contentedly.

She is going to Los Angeles at the end of next week to do some work for the agency. They are putting her up at a lovely hotel where she will have her own suite. She has invited Billy to join her over there, and even bought his plane tickets, but Billy's parents are not too happy about this suggestion as it will mean him missing several days at school. Maggie had therefore called Annie and suggested, in a friendly kind of way, that it might be better to wait until the school holidays before Annie made this kind of gesture. She also managed to make several insinuations regarding Annie's motives for befriending Billy. She didn't come right out with it, but

Maggie has made it clear that she does not approve of her teenage son sharing a hotel suite with the thirty-eight year-old-wife of his estranged father – sofabed or no sofabed!

But Billy has a mind of his own, and although Annie certainly wants to cause no friction with Maggie or her husband, she cannot disappoint him now that she has already made the offer. So a compromise has been reached: Billy will fly to LA on Thursday morning and he will return to London on Sunday evening, making sure that he is back at school by lunchtime on Monday for his first lesson. He is a little miffed at this because the Oscar ceremonies take place on that Monday evening, and he had wanted to go star-spotting outside the new auditorium. But Maggie had insisted that academic qualifications are more important than a quick glimpse of Sandra Bullock in a backless dress.

Annie has been having dirty dreams about Billy. Oh yes, she is ashamed to admit it, but she wakes up in the middle of the night and she can still feel the red-hot imprint of his lips against her throat as though he was actually there beside her. In these dreams Billy whispers that he loves her, as his tongue trails down the side of her neck. He then makes love to her, and sometimes he turns into Spencer, so that it is difficult for Annie to know which one of them is taking her. Does it really matter? Billy or Spencer, she loves them both, and they have become interchangeable in her nocturnal fantasies.

Since Valentine's Day, Annie has not spoken to Richard, and he has stopped leaving her messages. He obviously wasn't as besotted with her as he made out, and Annie has to admit that she doesn't miss him at all. Sleeping with him had been a mistake; she can admit that now, but at the time she had felt vulnerable and insecure. Coming back to London and living in this house alone would have been too much for her and Richard was the only person available to give her what she needed then. Annie had *used* him. She had used him as a convenient segue into her new life. She used him as a substitute for Spencer.

There is no need for Annie to go back to her old job at Marla's office since she is now making enough money with the modelling, and then there will also be a large sum coming in from the sale of Spencer's artwork. The insurance company will pay for the redecoration of the house, so Annie doesn't have to worry about finances right now. It was nice of Marla to offer to have her back, though.

Annie still misses home. She misses the warmth and comfort of being with a family and friends who love her for what she is rather than for what she is becoming. Betsy still calls her most days, but doesn't seem to be improving at all. Her depression is getting worse and she's down to weighing four stone. The doctors are talking about some kind of radical surgery, where they remove part of the brain. Betsy is scared, and says that it is the same operation that killed Lena Zavaroni. Annie would like to get her into a private clinic that deals specifically with eating disorders – one of the models once told her about a doctor somewhere in the Lake District. But it isn't cheap and Betsy probably wouldn't accept Annie's charity.

Charity begins at home.

Maybe that's what the saying means, after all.

Annie sits down for a moment. She sits on a stool by the central island of the kitchen and she looks around at the mess created by the fire and the decorators. They are skimming the walls and ceiling with a new layer of plaster, and plastic sheeting drapes the fitted furniture as though each piece has died and is awaiting the final journey to the morgue.

The day's post sits on the plastic sheeting, untouched since this morning. Mainly circulars and coupons for pizza, there is only one respectable-looking envelope in the entire pile. It has an airmail stamp and a California postmark. When Annie recognizes the handwriting, she is overwhelmed with a sudden sickness that makes her hands tremble.

It is a letter from Spencer.

The taxi driver has a bit of a problem finding Richard's house. Lester has the address but cannot help the driver with directions.

'It's outside my usual district see, guv'nor.'

They wind around on a seemingly endless lane where the houses are set back from the road, surrounded by trees and difficult to identify in the dark. There are no street lamps, and a drizzling rain makes visibility even more impossible.

'Blimey, mate, this is like looking for a bleedin' needle in a haystack. I can't see the numbers on these places.'

'Slow down at this next one and I'll get out and see if I can find a house number, so that at least we'll know we're on the right track.'

Lester jumps out of the taxi and approaches a darkened driveway with large wooden gates. The number on the gatepost is 207.

'We've got twenty more to go,' he says to the driver as he climbs back into the back seat.

They count the houses that they pass until they reach 247. They can't see the house itself, but there is a metal lamppost with a number fixed to it. The gate to the driveway is open.

'I'll hop out here, actually. No need to pull into the drive. And I think it'll be best if you wait for me here, if you don't mind.'

'Can't do that, mate. I'm off duty now. You'll have to call somebody else. Sorry and all that, but I've been up since five this morning and I need some kip.'

Lester isn't too thrilled at the prospect of being abandoned in the middle of nowhere but he has no choice. He pays the driver and watches the taxi pull sharply away in the same direction from which they have just come. Everything falls silent as soon as the rear lights disappear around the bend, and all Lester can hear is the barking of a dog somewhere in the far distance.

He walks through the gate of 247 and follows the asphalt driveway. Its surface is uneven where weeds have pushed through the surface. Fallen twigs and small branches litter the drive, and on either side the grass grows tall and straggly, as though untended for years. The house is quite close but, because it is dark and there are no lights on, Lester comes upon it almost without warning.

Trees hang low above the building, wooden shutters are closed across the downstairs windows, and it appears that the curtains are drawn shut in the bedrooms too. It doesn't look like the kind of house where strangers are welcome. It crouches there, under the trees, and it watches Lester as he pushes his way through the unkempt shrubbery to have a peep round the back.

The tall grass is soaking wet and his jeans get drenched. At the back of the house there is a small clearing with some old garden furniture stacked up against the wall. It is hard to make out anything else, and there are no lights round this side either. He knocks on the back door, but the thudding of it falls like hollow stones and there is still nothing but silence. He attempts to peer through the glass but it is so dirty that it is impossible to see anything of any significance. He knocks again, just for the hell of it, but still there is nothing.

He then tries the door handle. It is locked. He rattles a window but years of paint have glued the sash firmly into its frame. He goes back to the front of the house and tries the door there, but it too is locked.

What is he going to do now? He's come all this way out, and now he's stuck without a taxi and still none the wiser as to Richard's involvement with Treez's murder. If he could just find enough evidence to convict Richard, then he can rest assured that today's incident had nothing to do with Marla's disappearance from the institute. As much as Lester wants to believe that Marla is innocent of the ghastly crime, he still can't rule out the possibility of her having experienced another blackout.

He tries running the edge of his credit card between the door and the casement but that seems only to work in films and the lock doesn't budge. He attempts to slide his hand through the letterbox, but there is no way he can reach anything through such a narrow slot.

He will have to break in.

★

It is a long letter, written on heavy, unlined paper. Annie knows that if Spencer was in any kind of danger or distress he would not have taken the time to choose such beautiful paper. She takes a deep breath and begins to read.

Dear Annie,

This is a difficult letter to write and I'm not exactly sure how I should begin. I realize that the mere arrival of this letter will have caused you great consternation, but I feel that I have already left it way too long to offer you some explanation for disappearing in the way I did. It has been a strange and disorientating few months, and only now do I feel able to face up to my responsibilities.

By now you must already know that I am gay. It is something that I have always known about myself but was unable to accept. To me, homosexuality represented failure, and I have never before failed at anything in my life. I thought it was possible to bury my sexuality, to pretend that it wasn't there. Like someone with an incurable disease, I fooled myself that it would get better on its own, that one day I would wake up and the tumour would have melted away of its own accord. Of course this was naive of me, but that's how I felt.

The only person who knew about my feelings was my old university friend Maggie. She guessed it not long after we met and then, for the only time in my life, I didn't deny it. Maggie is a true liberal and was very supportive, although she never understood why I couldn't just come out and accept myself for what I am. She made me call Gay

Switchboard, she took me to a gay pub, but in both instances I just wasn't ready to stand up and say that I had failed. You see, that's what it seemed like to me: total failure as a man.

Agreeing to have a baby with Maggie seemed like a good idea at the time. It was a way of affirming my manhood, and when she became pregnant I even imagined that I could be a father and a husband and that these things would cure my 'illness'. Maggie wouldn't have any of it, she told me I was delusional, and she was right. Anyway, she preferred the idea of bringing up Billy on her own, even though I was desperate to be a part of the process. When she got married I was conveniently ushered out of the picture and made to feel like a nuisance. So I stopped visiting Billy, and allowed Maggie to have the family life that she had always wanted.

My friendship with you has always been very special, but there were just some things that I felt you wouldn't understand. You are an honest, decent person, Annie, and I didn't think you could cope with the idea of me being gay. You seemed to think that everything I did was wonderful, so how could I spoil that image? I could see that you were in love with me and I did nothing to dissuade you, in fact I sometimes encouraged it. (Forgive me, it was vanity and ego that pushed me to be such a total bastard.)

My friend Nolan, the air steward who came to the house just after we were married, is gay and we were friends for a long time. I think I might have been in love with him, and I know that he was certainly in love with me. I never admitted my

*feelings towards him, even though he could tell that
I was on the brink of a breakdown at that time.
Once or twice we came very close to having sex but
I always backed out at the last minute, blaming my
indiscretion on drink and throwing myself into a
guilt trip. I always took out my frustrations on
Nolan, but can see now that it was myself I hated,
not him.*

*When things became almost too much to bear,
I told Nolan that we couldn't be friends any longer.
We had a big row and he went off to work abroad.
That was when I thought that I could redeem myself
by getting married. That was when I started
thinking about my relationship with you – how easy
and undemanding it would be to have you as my
wife. As much as it hurts to say this, Annie, I was
not in love with you. I just wanted people to see me
as a normal guy and I thought that we, as friends,
could make as good a job of it as anyone else. I
know now that I was terribly wrong to put you
through that, but I was sick in the head and
thought only of myself and my manic desire to
succeed.*

*Obviously it was never going to work. You were
unhappy while I was falling apart. I had made a
huge mistake and couldn't see any way of getting
out of it. It was claustrophobic. It was a bloody
mess. And then, at Michaela's loft in New York,
I had sex with one of her employees in the
bathroom. And it felt so right and I wanted it so
much that I totally freaked out and ran off like a
child, unable to face up to the cold truth of the
matter. I felt so dirty. I felt as though I had let*

everyone down, including myself. So I spent three horrible days wandering around the sleaziest places in the city – having sex with strangers, degrading myself as a way of punishment. I wanted to prove to myself that I was as bad as I thought I was. It reached the point where I practically lost control of my own actions.

I had Marla's gun. I stole it from her handbag as I left Michaela's loft that night. My intention was to kill myself, but I was thwarted by the fact that the gun was not loaded. It was one of those simple twists of fate that saved me, and it gave me reason to believe that maybe I was not supposed to die. As you know I'm not a religious person, but after that episode with the gun I began to think that perhaps I could salvage something from all the mistakes I had made. It was comforting to imagine that I was no longer in control of my destiny, that there was some higher power to guide me to salvation.

I didn't want anyone to find me. I wanted to be anonymous. I had a small amount of cash on me, and knew that I couldn't use my credit cards or passport if I wanted to disappear, so I went to Taylor – Michaela's assistant, the one I had sex with in the bathroom. He fancied me and probably felt sorry for me as well, so he helped me to rent a car which I used to drive across the country. I transferred funds from my Swiss account into Taylor's and he gave me his card to use whenever I needed the money. He was very trusting, very kind. I know you've met him, because he told me so when he got back from Key West. He felt bad deceiving you in that way but I had begged him not to say anything to you. It is comforting to know that you have found your feet, and that makes me feel a little less guilty.

Anyway, I travelled slowly, and I stopped whenever I grew tired or found somewhere interesting. It was a very therapeutic time for me, spending all that time alone. Some nights I would just sit there, in a cheap motel room with the late-night TV filling the room with shadows, and I would cry and cry – not really knowing what it was that I wanted. It was a sort of loneliness that filled me up. It frustrated me and there were times when I could have bashed my brains out just trying to cope with my feelings of desolation. What a mess! One night, in Phoenix, I got pissed out of my head and ended up walking down the middle of a six-lane highway at two in the morning. I got picked up by the police and spent the night sobering up in the courthouse jail. I thought they'd identify me, but they just let me go with a warning.

So I ended up in California. All roads seemed to head to Los Angeles, and it seemed like as good a place as any to lose myself. I booked into a Howard Johnson under my assumed name, and spent a few weeks familiarizing myself with the neighbourhood. It didn't take me long to find a gay bar. It took me even less time to meet a man. The first night I went out, I met a Puerto Rican immigration lawyer (yes!) called Basilio. He is a few years younger than I am but very mature in his attitude to life and his sexuality. After just three days I moved in with him, and this is where I have been ever since.

If it wasn't for the mess I left behind in England this would be the happiest time of my life. I have never felt so complete, so sure of myself as I do right now. Basilio is fantastic and he wants me to join his partnership. If anyone can sort out my immigration papers it should be us! And here in West Hollywood you can be yourself and nobody bats an eyelid. Men walk down the street holding hands, and just about every business here is gay-owned and run. Yes, it's a ghetto, but it makes me feel 'normal' for the first time ever. I want to stay here and make it my home.

    I know you probably hate me, and I don't blame you for feeling like that after the way I've treated you. I want you to know that I acted out of confusion and fear, and it had nothing to do with malice or any kind of personal vendetta against you. You were always a dear, dear friend to me, Annie, and I love you for that.

    I have already written to my lawyers in London. The house and everything in it is yours. I have instructed them to pay off the mortgage so that you'll have a clean slate to start off with. I have also set up an Abbey National account for you and transferred £200,000 from Switzerland. The lawyers will get in touch with details of all this, but I wanted to write to you first. If you ever need any financial help, or any kind of help at all, you can always get in touch with me. I feel I owe you at least that much for everything I have put you through.

    If you cannot forgive me, Annie, I hope that you will at least remember me as a half-decent

*person who never meant to do you any harm. I
would like to think that we can still be friends, but
that will be up to you. You are welcome here
whenever you like.*

*I saw you on a Michaela Fox advert on a giant
billboard off the Sunset Strip yesterday. I am so
proud of you, Annie. You're going to be a huge
success, and that is something that you have
achieved alone. You should be congratulating
yourself.*

Hope you can accept my love,
Spencer

And his name dissolves on the page as Annie's tears
smudge the ink of his final farewell.

Thirty-six

Lester is now inside Richard's house.

He has to remind himself why he is doing this as he crunches over broken glass in the musty darkness of the rear hallway. He needs to convince himself that it was Richard – and not Marla – who murdered Treez this afternoon. He needs to be *sure*.

He is afraid to turn on the lights for fear of being discovered, but it is very dark here at the back of the house and Lester can barely see his hand in front of his face. The passageway is narrow and the floor appears to be littered with something that crunches slightly underfoot as he shuffles blindly forward. Wood chippings? Dry leaves?

It smells like a house that is rarely exposed to fresh air. Damp and fusty like the smell of peeling wallpaper and crawling insects. Lester places his hand against the frame of a door and feels the blistered paintwork beneath his fingers. It flakes against his fingernails. He cannot see into the room, but the door is open and he can hear the steady drip-drip-drip of a tap against porcelain. He is not going to achieve anything if he can't see what he is doing.

As he feels his way around a corner, there is the slightest glimmer of light at the far end of the passageway and he is able to aim himself towards it, one careful step at a time. His eyes are gradually adjusting to the darkness and he can see now that he has reached the main entrance hall at the front of the house. The downstairs windows are covered with shutters, but a small amount of light filters down from the landing window at the top of the staircase. Lester takes hold of the banister rail and climbs up to the first floor, where there is more light.

Up here the air is slightly warmer than below, but the smell of neglect is more prevalent. It is the kind of smell that lurks at the bottom of a laundry basket – slightly moist, and capable of generating its own heat. There are three doors leading off, two of them standing wide open to the landing where Lester now stands. He enters the first door and finds a small bathroom with one of those cumbersome free-standing bathtubs jutting out into the centre of the room. A curtain is pulled roughly halfway around the bath, hanging from an oval of chrome railing suspended above, and Lester can see that the curtain is torn in places where the rings have pulled through the plastic.

He next tries the second door and finds the master bedroom. He *assumes* that it is the master bedroom because it is large, and because there are clothes strewn across the unmade bed and over a threadbare carpet that covers most of the linoleum floor. Lester takes a chance by switching on a bedside lamp. It casts light downward on to the crumpled pillows, and illuminates the contents of the open bedside drawer.

Matches from a West End restaurant.

A nasal spray for summer allergies.

Coins, loose buttons, and a spool of fuse wire.

Johnson's Baby Oil in a smeared, greasy bottle, still

open and oozing into the grain of the wooden drawer lining.

The bedroom curtains are drawn across the windows and Lester sees his own reflection in the dressing table mirror, as though he is looking at someone else in this grainy half-light. *He* is the intruder now. He has broken into Richard's house and he is breaking the law. What would Marla say if she could see him now?

It is dark in the room where Marla awakes.

Totally disorientated and confused, she attempts to focus her eyes on something familiar, but all she can make out is the faintest outline of a window.

When she attempts to sit up she becomes aware of the straps that restrain her to the bed. Her wrists are fastened to a metal headboard. Her ankles are strapped so that her legs are spread apart, toes pointing to the two bottom corners of the bed. She is pinned to the mattress like a specimen in a biology lab, waiting to be dissected.

Not only does she have no idea where she is, but she cannot recall how she got here. The last thing she can remember is sitting in her room at the clinic. They brought her lunch on a tray and she was listening to a radio show – she remembers that quite clearly. After that, nothing.

Is this perhaps some kind of therapy that the doctors are experimenting with? Maybe she is in solitary confinement, restrained and alone in a darkened room as a way of assessing the extent of her mental illness. Who knows what kind of Draconian measures these shrinks will resort to in order to better their reputation in the expanding field of mental health. Marla might even find herself the subject of an intense psychological study in next month's medical journal.

But this doesn't *feel* like a room in a clinic. Its smell is wrong and the faint light that comes from the windows suggests more of a domestic arrangement. She can just make out the pattern of the curtains. Marla can hear movement in another part of the building – footsteps on stairs and the creak of floorboards as someone moves around. She would call out for assistance but her mouth is taped with something wide and adhesive, which pulls at her skin if she moves her mouth. Something similar to claustrophobia clutches at her throat as she attempts to struggle free from her bondage. Immobile and trapped, she gets the feeling that there is insufficient air for her to breathe, so she strains her neck forward as far as she can.

She is naked!

Marla has only just realized that she is naked and exposed to the cool dampness of this room. This cannot be any kind of medical experiment. Could it be that one of the doctors is taking advantage of her vulnerable position? Was she drugged and abducted and dragged off to a secret place where her body will be violated by an unscrupulous madman? Stranger things have happened to people, and Marla reads about them all the time in the newspapers. Mental asylums have long been associated with this kind of professional corruption.

If this was a Stephen King novel, she might begin to hallucinate, or hear the wet, hungry growl of a guard dog about to gnaw through her ankle bone. Marla attempts to focus her attention on her shackles; she wants to understand the workings of her restraints so that she can figure out a way of escape. But she is no Houdini. These straps and chains are the work of a seasoned jailer, and there is no way in hell that she is going to wriggle her way out.

It doesn't take Lester long to find the videos in Richard's bedroom. They are scattered across the chest of drawers beside the portable TV. There are several titles that sound innocuous enough – Lester has been no stranger to pornography since Tina introduced him to her friends in the industry. A couple of the videos appear to be amateur films and have hand written labels marked *Undercover II* and *Terminal Torment*. The film that had caught Julie's attention – *Litigious Bitch* – is here amongst Richard's collection.

Lester reads the back of its cover:

Alexa Dutson (played by Coral Canyon of *High-Class Whore*) is a smart, intelligent, successful lawyer in Los Angeles. She takes no bull in the courtroom and she's a ball-breaking bitch in bed. Alexa works hard by day and even harder by night, but the guys in her life can't keep up with her insatiable appetite for sex. Beneath that pinstriped suit, while she busts the asses of hardened criminals, she's wet with lust – and that lust makes her totally ruthless in the sack. When Alexa first starts to receive mysterious messages on her computer, she passes this off as the work of a crank. Then she receives gifts in the mail – gifts that come from a warped and demented stranger who seems out to destroy Alexa. It doesn't take long for Alexa to realize that she is in danger, and gradually, with a mounting sense of explosive tension, we witness the satisfying sexual breakdown of Alexa Dutson – Litigious Bitch!'

So this is what turns Richard on?

There is no way that this is mere coincidence, and Lester is certain that the video tape will prove Richard is the one who has been tormenting Marla for all these months – almost sending her over the edge. Perhaps Richard was already having a relationship with Marla's neighbour, Treez. Perhaps he was preparing to scare *her* in the same way that he had scared Marla, getting his kicks from the observation of women in distress.

As Lester stands in the deep shadows of Richard's landing he pauses for a moment. Was that a creaky floorboard in the hallway down below? Lester stands very still. He can almost hear his own heart beating, and has to hold his breath as he listens to the silent house. Then there comes an unmistakable thud. It sounds like something hitting the wall beside him and Lester drops the videotape in fright. It clatters to the floor, shattering the silence with unnerving alacrity, and the sound seems to prompt a second thud from behind the closed door at the far end of the landing.

Despite a nerve-tingling apprehension, and with a courage that Lester was unaware he possessed, he crosses the passage and presses his hand to the closed door, leaning forward to listen. He should have some kind of weapon. He may need to defend himself. But there is nothing nearby that can help him so he steels himself and turns the handle of the bedroom door.

The room itself is in total darkness, but something is moving in there. Something is shifting and grunting and rattling as though caged and furious and ready to strike. Lester feels along the wall for a light switch, but when he finds it he is almost too afraid to use it. Another creak on the stairs behind him forces the issue, and he switches on the light. It isn't bright: it must be a very low-wattage bulb in that shabby fabric shade that hangs from the ceiling. Dark red shadows spill down the walls like blood, illuminating an alarming scrawl of virulent graffiti on the floral wallpaper.

Marla is strapped to the iron bed!

Her wrists and ankles are bound and her mouth is covered with a broad strip of silver carpet tape. She is almost totally naked, but her breasts have been bound in a tight lacy bra and she is wearing fishnet stocking held up with suspenders. When Marla sees Lester standing there, she closes her eyes and starts to cry. Her body sags limply, and in this state she looks totally degraded and fragile – it is a scene that brings horror and anger to Lester's throat.

'Oh Christ, Marla! What has he done to you?'

Lester pulls the tape from Marla's mouth as gently as he can. She looks at him with an expression of humiliation and fear: a combination of emotions that Lester has never seen on her face before.

'Where am I?' she asks. 'I don't know where I am.'

'You are at Richard's house. Richard Carruthers?'

'*Richard?* What am I doing at Richard's house? The last thing I remember is being in my room at the clinic. How did I get here, and who tied me up like this?'

'It was Richard, darling, he did this to you. I came here to find some evidence that he has been stalking you, and I've found it. It was Richard all the time. He managed to work you up into such a state that you started having nightmares and sleepwalking again. It must have stirred up all those old forgotten feelings about Jessica. He's a fucking psycho, Marla, and he's been copying the storyline from a porn video about a female lawyer who is terrorized by a pervert. He gets his kicks from scaring the shit out of women and watching their reactions. Come on, darling, we've got to get you out of here. Let's see if I can get you loose.'

As Lester reaches forward to the straps that hold Marla's wrist to the bedpost, her eyes widen and she gasps. Lester spins around to see what has frightened her, and finds Richard standing in the doorway. He has a gun in his hand and appears to be trembling. 'This is getting out of hand, totally out of hand . . .' he mutters, staring at Lester. 'It was never supposed to go this far.'

'How far was it supposed to go then, Richard?' asks Lester, his hand still resting on the cast-iron bedpost. 'How far did you *need* it to go for your twisted little games? I'd say that actual murder is taking things much *too* far, wouldn't you?'

'I would never have killed her,' says Richard, 'I just wanted to frighten her, but she threatened to go to the police. She said that she guessed that I'd been sending things to Marla. We'd watched some of my videos, you see, for a bit of fun, and I left them at her flat. She watched *Litigious Bitch* and put two and two together. She confronted me with her accusations and threats. What else could I do? I had to kill her.' Richard moves slowly around to the end of the bed, keeping the gun firmly aimed at Lester's head.

'But why Marla?' asks Lester. 'Why pick on her? She's never done you any harm.'

'She's *hard*. It had to be somebody I could break, not just any old girlie-girl who would faint at the first sight of blood. I wanted a challenge, and Marla is the hardest woman I know. She's *perfect*. And then, this evening, after I stabbed Treez, I panicked. I went to Marla's flat to think things out. I still have the keys, you see – the keys I had cut from Annie's set. And there, in the bedroom, I found Marla, lying across the bed in a kind of trance. She wouldn't speak, she wouldn't look at me, but it was an opportunity too good to miss. She was the perfect candidate to take the blame for Treez – crazy in the head and suffering from violent mental blackouts.'

'How did you know about those?' croaks Marla, still fastened tight to the bed in her fragments of cheap, polyester lingerie.

'It was common knowledge,' laughs Richard. 'Do you think people in our office don't talk? Do you think I haven't heard the things they say about *me* when they think I can't hear? Nothing is sacred, Marla, and especially when it's the boss who's cracking up.'

'So why didn't you just leave me there, then? In my flat so the police could find me?'

'I thought about that. I thought about smearing you with the blood, about getting your fingerprints on the knife, but then I thought it would be better if you just vanished rather than risk the chance of future hiccups. Anyway, I wasn't finished with you, so I thought, why not kill two birds with one stone? – if you'll pardon my pun – so I brought you home with me. No complaints, no struggle, you just allowed me to lead you away, your eyes as dead as a doornail.'

'How come the police never stopped you?' asks Lester.

'There was nobody there, and, anyway, we left by the fire exit. That's where I'd parked my car – at the back of the building in the guest parking lot.'

'And then, like any normal person, you stripped her naked, dressed her up in these demeaning clothes and tied her to a bed. Well, that seems very sane, Richard. What were you planning to do to her next?'

Richard appears defeated, even though he still holds the gun – even though he has every opportunity to defend himself. He even seems close to tears.

'I don't *know*. It all just got out of hand and I wasn't thinking straight. I thought that I might do like they did in the film. I wanted her to stay here in the dark; I wanted her to be scared, to beg me for forgiveness. I wanted to torture her, very slowly, so that she knew exactly what was happening to her. So that she would look at me and respect me for all the power I held over her.'

'Why do you hate me so much, Richard?' Marla manages to speak through her tears. She twists her head to look at him, but he cannot bear to meet her gaze. 'Is it because of my baby? You found out about the death of my baby and decided to persecute me?'

'It isn't you. It was never you, Marla. And I didn't even know about your baby until you started having those seizures, scribbling your guilt on walls, punishing yourself. It was quite handy, actually, when you started joining in with the games. You were a brilliant red herring.'

'So what did Treez have to do with all this, Richard?' asks Lester, straightening up very slowly as though afraid that any sudden movement might set Richard off again.

'Oh, we just went out on a couple of dates, that's all. I met her while I was seeing Annie, when Annie was staying at Marla's place. And so, when Annie dumped me, I went out with Treez – it was just sex. She was a slag. Too easy, if you know what I mean.'

Lester realizes he needs to stall Richard for as long as he can. He needs to keep him talking. But how long before Richard gets wise to his tactics and shoots the both of them?

Without any precognition of his intentions, Lester finds himself lunging at Richard in what feels like slow motion. Richard has barely a chance to realize what is happening before Lester has knocked the gun out of his hand. The gun fires a shot. The bullet hits the ceiling. And Lester pushes Richard against the wall.

In an uncharacteristic frenzy of emotion Lester lays into Richard with what can only be described as unbridled fury. He holds Richard's shoulder with one hand as he smashes his fist against Richard's face, over and over again. Lester feels his own knuckles begin to split and bleed against the sharp bones of Richard's nose and cheekbones. He hears the startled grunt as his hands encircle Richard's throat and wring out the man's air supply. He presses hard against the flesh, his thumbs sink deep, and he watches Richard choking, choking, choking.

'Lester!' shouts Marla. 'Stop! You'll kill him!'

But Lester has no intention of stopping. He forces Richard to the ground and he smashes the back of his skull against the hard floorboards with a relentless, single-minded passion. Richard does not fight back. His head flips back and forth as though his neck is broken, and his face has become purple and swollen. Blood flies from his mouth each time Lester yanks his head down against the floorboards, and he no longer makes any noise.

And when Lester is spent, when he allows Richard's body to fall immobile from his bloodied grasp, he drops his face against the sticky fabric of Richard's sweater and he sobs.

He can't seem to catch his breath. The tears clog his throat and his chest is heaving with emotion.

'Lester, honey. Please, can you get me untied?'

He had almost forgotten that Marla is in the same room.

'I think I've killed him. He's not breathing.' Lester looks down at Richard in the glowering light from the torn silk lampshade above. There is a creeping puddle of blood forming at the side of the man's head and it appears black in the sombre shadows of this dilapidated room. 'What'll happen if he's dead, Marla? Will that be murder? Can they get me for murder, or was it self-defence?'

'Lester, honey, it's going to be just fine. But, please, get me out of these straps.'

With a sting like the taste of bile, Lester swallows back the sudden memories of the day they found baby Jessica. Of the policeman who held that tiny body in his hands, and presented her as though he had found a dead animal. The deathly pallor of her skin horrific to acknowledge, but both Lester and Marla just stood there as they stared at their daughter. They stared and they said nothing, but Lester can remember this exact same feeling of disbelief and panic. It is like screaming inside. It is like too much knowledge in too small a space.

Lester unfastens the straps that hold Marla to the iron bedposts, and she rubs at her skin as successively each wrist and ankle is released. She is crying now and it seems that she is never going to stop. Lester hands her a blanket to cover herself, then sits on the edge of the bed to take her in his arms. They sit like this, rocking slowly, both of them, now weeping.

'I'm sorry, Lester,' whispers Marla into his shoulder.

'Sorry for what?' he asks, pulling himself away from her grasp to look into her face.

'For what I put you through when Jessica died. For pushing you away when I should have been clinging on to you for dear life.'

'You weren't yourself back then,' says Lester, brushing a tear from the side of her nose.

'I don't think I've been myself ever since. I've buried myself in my work and fooled myself into thinking that I've gotten over it all – that I am cured. But obviously I was wrong. These last few months have proved that I was incredibly wrong.'

'You can't blame yourself for any of this, Marla. Richard brought this on himself, and if he hadn't wound you up into such a state with his perverted hounding, you would probably never have suffered this relapse. Everything is going to be all right now, I'm sure of it.'

And beneath the circle of drab crimson light they cling to each other and they wait to be rescued.

Thirty-seven

'Is it just me, or does this place stink of Dettol?'

Annie stands at the back of the little crematorium, with Marla and Lester, and she sniffs the air. 'I think it's supposed to smell like this,' she says, 'like in hospitals.'

'Don't ever let them bring me to a crummy place like this when I kick the bucket,' whispers Marla. 'I want something glamorous, with a white casket and Broadway show tunes.'

'You want to be cremated?' asks Lester, messing with his black tie.

'Hell yes! The last thing I need is to come around in some black hole with my nose pressed up against the silk lining! Back home they vacuum seal you, sucking all the air out of the casket with a hoover attachment to preserve the body in a permanent state of non-decay.'

'Why do they do that?' asks Annie.

'Hell if I know, honey! Who cares what you look like once the embalmer's laid his hands on you.'

'There aren't many people here,' observes Lester. 'I always imagined that Treez was the kind of person who had lots of friends.'

'Not the kind who come to funerals,' smiles Marla sadly.

They seat themselves in the back row of chairs.

Annie checks her watch and wonders how long this is going to take. She has a flight to catch at lunchtime, and Billy will be waiting for her at Heathrow. He was so excited on the phone this morning, and his mood was contagious. Annie feels deliriously happy but she is keeping her emotions under her hat, because it doesn't do to look overstimulated at a funeral. There is a woman over there who looks decidedly incongruous, and Annie wonders if anyone else has noticed that she is eating a Whopper and fries from the inside of a black satin handbag.

'The pastor looks half-cut,' says Marla, curling her insinuations behind an upheld glove.

Annie follows Marla's line of vision and sees the vicar wandering around amidst a collection of artificial ferns, apparently searching for something on the stage area. There is a huge gold-painted cross hanging from the ceiling above his head, and it is swaying in a slight breeze from the open doors. The piped music is the kind that department stores have in their lifts at Christmas – angels and harps and surging brass instruments.

Annie wonders if Treez would have appreciated any of this. Did she leave a will? She was still young, so probably unprepared for sudden death. Not many people under the age of sixty think about dying these days – it's not like the old days when people popped their clogs from all manner of minor ailments. These days they can keep you alive with one lung and a plastic heart.

Annie didn't really know Treez very well. They had chatted a few times in the hall outside Marla's flat, and Treez had shown Annie her collection of fake Fabergé eggs. She kept them in a glass display cabinet: the eggs were the size of chicken eggs but they were propped up on little gilded stands, with their shells encrusted with plastic jewels and gold rickrack braiding. 'Sixty quid a piece down Brick Lane market,' said Treez proudly. 'Made by a woman in a wheelchair who used to be high up in costume design.'

Treez wasn't the kind of person you would expect to get murdered. But, then, Richard never struck Annie as the murdering type either. She was dumbfounded when she heard the news. The police had come to talk to her; they wanted to know everything she could remember about Richard. Did he ever hurt her? Scare her? Talk about sexual fantasies, etc.? But Annie couldn't think of anything like that. Richard had always been a perfect gentleman, and the idea of him slitting poor Treez's throat and tying Marla naked to a bed seems almost ludicrous. 'Are you sure you've got the right person?' Annie had asked them. But it seems that the evidence did all point in Richard's direction and, once he has recovered from the bashing that Lester gave him, there will be a full investigation. At the moment Richard is lying in intensive care with a steel plate in his head.

The police have now reopened the case of Richard's dead fiancée, Sally. Apparently there were mysterious incidents leading to her death, and now it looks as though Richard might have killed her too.

At least Marla looks cheerful. She's back with Lester and he's moved in with her. It makes Annie think about herself and Spencer, how they were friends for all those years, and then suddenly they were married. Of course it's a bit different for Marla and Lester: they've already been married and divorced, but they stayed friends for all the years since then. Annie supposes that Lester must be something of a hero to Marla now. He certainly looks chuffed with himself. They were on *Kilroy* the other day, talking about stalkers, and apparently somebody has offered Lester a part in a television play. What with that and going to the Oscars next week, no wonder he's looking so pleased with himself.

Annie sucks on an extra-strong mint and ponders the mysteries of life. Funerals are like that, aren't they? They make you wonder what it's all about. When she was very young, she never used to think about death, but these days she finds herself thinking about heart disease and cancer and wondering what she will die of in the end. This probably has something to do with spending so much time with Billy. He is still young enough to imagine himself immortal. He doesn't worry about calories or fat intake; he crosses the road without looking, and probably rides rollercoasters with his hands up in the air. Invincibility is a luxury that only the very young or the very foolish can afford.

Since Annie received that letter from Spencer, she has been up and down like a yo-yo in her emotions. At first she was just sad – crying all the time and feeling sorry for herself. Then she was angry with him for mucking her about like that, for using her just because she was so easy to manipulate. But Annie has loved Spencer for so long now that she just can't turn against him. He is ingrained in her life, as though somebody has pushed him into the whorls and cavities of her fingerprints. Spencer is the pestle that has ground Annie down in the mortar, turning her to a fine white powder that could be blown away with a single breath. It sounds pathetic – even Annie can see that – but you can't stop loving somebody just because they don't love you.

'I'm dying for a smoke,' whispers Marla, nudging Annie with her elbow. 'I wonder how much longer it's going to be before they get started?'

Just as she says that, the music quietens down and the vicar climbs up to his makeshift pulpit, and coughs loudly to gain everyone's attention. He is Scottish and he has a very broad accent that is practically indecipherable. It appears that he is delivering a kind of bland, generic eulogy that is unspecific and tedious. It makes light of loss and loneliness, passing them off as a kind of post-weekend blues. Don't worry, says the vicar, you'll soon get over it, and before you know where you are you'll be having a laugh with your friends down the pub. It's like having your appendix out: a couple of weeks being careful, with your feet up on a pouffe, and you'll be back at the Top Rank doing the Macarena.

Are people really so dispensable?

Annie is certain that when her parents die she will never get over the space that they leave behind. She might learn to get used to it, but she will never truly get over it. Just look at Marla: all these years after she lost her baby daughter and she's still blaming herself for what happened. Mind you, it's not surprising, considering the terrible circumstances. Annie was quite horrified when she found out what had happened.

The whole story came out in the papers again after this recent episode with Richard and Treez. There were news reports about it, and a whole hour on *Panorama* devoted to dragging up the past. It was fascinating in a

morbid kind of way, especially with Lester being somewhat famous and Marla being a wealthy lawyer. The
News of the World had a field day with it.

You see, in a literal way, Marla *did* kill her baby;
there is no denying the fact that she was ultimately
responsible for baby Jessica's death, even though she
wasn't herself at the time. It was a kind of seizure, they
said, a blackout like the kind that epileptics have when
they are exposed to rapidly flashing lights. Marla is
susceptible to them, apparently, and she used to get
them quite often before she had the same kind of electric
shock treatment that the doctors recently tried on Betsy.

The baby was less than one month old when she
went missing. Neither Marla nor Lester could find her
anywhere, even though she had been in her cot just an
hour before. They searched frantically but finally had to
call the police. Marla was hysterical, and they had to
sedate her while they searched through the house with a
fine toothcomb, pulling up sofa cushions – even going
so far as to check the attic and the airing cupboard.

It was a lady policewoman who found the baby.
Goodness only knows what made her look in the chest
freezer, but when she did she found Jessica there, still
wrapped in her little white cotton blanket. She was
dead, of course. Yes, it's true! This isn't an urban myth
invented to scare teenagers around the campfire – this
actually happened. Marla put her baby in the deep-
freeze during one of her blackouts, and froze her to
death.

How could Marla survive after that? How could
anyone forgive themselves for doing such a horrible
thing, even though it was during one of her blackouts?
In clips from an old television interview with Terry

Wogan, they showed Marla saying that one of the worst things about it was the fact that people made jokes. They thought it was funny. There is something shockingly comical about things like that, and it happened at a time when dead baby jokes were all the rage.

No wonder Marla suffered a nervous breakdown. What with Richard stalking her as well, it's hardly surprising that she went bonkers and started smashing her windows in the middle of the night. Looking at her now, sitting here in that lovely black tailored two-piece, you'd never believe that just a couple of weeks ago she was tied up to a bed with a gun pointed at her head.

Annie looks at her watch. She is going to have to leave otherwise she'll miss her flight to LA. They haven't even moved the coffin yet.

She makes her excuses and edges her way past Marla and Lester. 'I'll see you both next week,' she whispers, 'at the Oscars.'

Doesn't that sound thrilling? Annie Noble, née Stamper, arranging to meet friends at the annual Academy Awards in Los Angeles.

Whatever next?

They have adjoining rooms, Annie and Billy.

They are staying in what Val Rosen described as an 'urban resort', which means that their hotel is ultra-modern and ultra-chic, with all 238 guest rooms designed by a French designer who Annie has never heard of. She can't see what all the fuss is about, quite honestly – white walls, white curtains, and nothing in the minibar except bottles of Italian water. Floor-to-ceiling glass walls offer a spectacular view across the sprawling city which, at this time of the day, is looking decidedly worn out.

Val Rosen is the chief executive officer of Swank modelling agency here in LA. It represents some of the biggest names in the fashion industry, and Annie is barely aware of how amazing it is to be part of such a prestigious entourage. Val has arranged a contract for Annie with a retail chain called Lane Bryant, and they plan to feature Annie in their advertising and promotional campaign for this coming autumn.

It's all very exciting.

'This place is the business,' says Billy as he peers into the bathroom and plays with the lights. 'The bath is big enough for a football team, and this shower turns into a steam room. And we've got a kitchen and a living room – it's like having our own flat.'

'I'm not so sure about that chair with the eye on the back, and I'm not sure they had to write SLEEP on the wall over the bed in such large letters, but I do love king-sized beds,' says Annie, sitting on the edge of the white linen bedspread in her jersey wool trouser suit. 'I think this one is about the size of my entire bedroom back in Chesterfield.'

'Shame they're not waterbeds though,' says Billy. 'I would love to try one of those things out, but I'd probably get seasick.'

'Oh, Billy, isn't this brilliant? I can't believe that we're here – it's like a dream come true. If only Betsy could see me now, she'd wet her pants.'

'You'll have to bring her on one of your trips, when she's better.'

'Yes,' smiles Annie, but she is beginning to wonder

if Betsy will ever get better. She is to undergo brain surgery in just a few days, hoping to put an end to her chronic depression. It is as though Betsy has given up on life, and only yesterday on the phone she told Annie that she no longer experiences feelings or emotions about anything. She can't even follow the storylines on her favourite soaps.

'Let me take a picture, hang on . . .' and Billy goes back into his own room to fetch his camera. 'It's got an automatic flash, so we can have our picture taken together. I'll prop it up on the edge of this table.'

He sets up the camera and dashes around to jump on the bed beside Annie, flinging his arms around her neck from behind.

The camera flashes.

Annie laughs but Billy doesn't move away. His hands are conspicuously close to her breasts and she feels a flush of embarrassment colouring her cheeks. Billy kisses her ear. 'You don't mind do you?' he asks.

'Why should I mind?' she replies, but she feels very uncomfortable right now.

He kisses her again and his hand drops lower against her breast. Annie can feel her heartbeat in every breath she takes, and she has to close her eyes for a moment to steady herself. When Billy finally places the palm of his hand over her entire breast she twists around to look at him.

'We'd better not, Billy,' she says. 'It's not right.'

'What isn't?' he asks. 'I'm old enough to do it, you know. It's not as though you could be done for seducing a minor or anything. You know Jennifer and me have been at it since we were in the upper fifth. My mum knows all about it.'

'I was thinking about Spencer. He's your dad, Billy, and you're twenty years younger than me.'

'I bet you wouldn't say that if I was fifty-eight. I bet you wouldn't think it was strange if I was twenty years older than *you*.'

'I just don't think it's a good idea, love. It could spoil everything, you know, and you are so young . . . What about Jennifer, anyway? I doubt that she'd be thrilled to find out that you had sex with somebody else.'

'I've finished with her – last Saturday. Anyway, I've had sex with other people since I've been going out with Jennifer, and one of them is almost as old as you.'

'Crikey, Billy, you're only eighteen! I didn't have sex at all until I married Spencer.'

'Why not?'

'Because nobody ever asked me.'

Billy moves around to sit beside Annie and he takes her hand between his own. 'I find that a bit hard to believe. I've fancied you ever since that first day at the Hard Rock Cafe. I thought you looked like Dawn French.'

'Is that a compliment?' laughs Annie.

'She's really pretty. Well, I think so. Anyway, you're a model, and you wouldn't be here in this posh hotel room if they didn't think you were pretty.'

'It's a shame your dad never saw it. He's the only one I ever wanted, you know. I loved him a lot. Still do, even after what he's put me through.'

'Spencer was a selfish bastard, and he was gay. You were fighting a losing battle right from the start. Anyway, he *must* love you, otherwise why would he give you the house and all that money?'

'Guilt perhaps?'

'I'm not my dad, you know. I fancy you like mad and I really, really want to make love to you. Do you fancy me?' Billy looks at her with complete seriousness.

'Billy, who wouldn't fancy you? You're perfect! You could have anybody you want so why would you bother with a big old lump like me? I'd be embarrassed to take my clothes off in front of you for a start.'

'So I'll take them off for you, then,' jokes Billy.

Annie is trembling inside. This is what she has wanted to hear for such a long time. This is what she has been dreaming about since she first met him – her dreams convoluted but heavily sexual, with Billy and Spencer merging as one. They could be the same person. But she's scared stiff. She's worried that Billy will have it off with her and then, once he's had his way, he'll lose interest, and she'll feel worse than she did before. Rejected again.

'Look, Billy, I'm completely shattered after the flight. It's the middle of the night in London and my head's spinning with all this. Why don't we get some sleep, then go out for a late dinner? We can get spruced up and go up to that rooftop skybar if you like. We might even see some stars.'

'Can I sleep in your bed with you?' He holds up his hands as though this is proof that he holds no weapons. 'No sex, just a cuddle.'

'I don't think—' starts Annie, but Billy closes her mouth with his fingers.

'It's what *I* want,' he says. 'This is *my* holiday, and I'm used to getting my own way, so shut up and get into bed.'

What can she say to that? 'Only if I'm wearing my nightie, then,' she says.

'In that case I'm keeping my pants on. I'm not showing you mine until you show me yours.'

And Annie has to laugh.

He's a cheeky beggar, but he's so blooming gorgeous that she's giving in. If this is really what he wants, then she's not going to deprive herself of the experience. This is her new life – *Annie Supermodel* – and, as Michaela might say, in her new life she's not going to take any crap.

'Oh, fuck the lot of them! *I'm* the one in the hotel suite on Sunset Boulevard,' laughs Annie, and Billy laughs as well.

It's time to think about herself for a change.

Thirty-eight

In another part of town, several blocks from where Annie and Billy are staying, they are already drinking vodka Martinis at the Biltmore Hotel.

Lester and Marla arrived yesterday, and they are down in the sports bar for happy hour. Shani and her stepdaughter Aurora have just arrived; they came in on the same flight as Annie but she was in first class, much to Aurora's disgust.

'I suppose it's the only way they can fit fat people on to the plane,' she now sneers. 'The seats are wider in first class, and they get more food.'

'Aurora, you really are becoming more and more unpleasant with age,' smiles Marla, barely concealing the truth behind a skim of jest.

'Well, it's true! I find it hard to believe that they're paying so much money to put her in a magazine when there are thousands of thin girls just queuing up to become models. My friend Patsy could be a runway model, but she's been turned down by all the agencies for being too emaciated. What a joke! And it was demoralizing having to sit way at the back of the plane, crammed between those awful DisneyWorld families, while *she* sat up there beyond the curtain being served smoked salmon and champagne.'

'Perhaps when you get a little job, darling, you might

be able to afford first class yourself, but unless Didier becomes a millionaire and supports you in the style to which you have always wanted to become accustomed, you will have to settle for economy class.' Shani toasts Aurora with her Martini glass and knocks back her drink in one surprising gulp.

Lester listens but he does not digest the conversation. He is too busy admiring his surroundings and wondering if he might spot somebody famous. But the Biltmore, although once magnificently popular with the film crowd, is no longer the haunt of A-list celebrities. They now flock to the Chateau Marmont or the Mondrian and apparently the Academy did not merit Lester having sufficient 'cool' to offer him a room in either of these superchic hotspots.

What did he expect? Star treatment after a twenty-year hiatus from the industry? He's lucky even to get his expenses paid for. They did at least have the grace to send a car to pick them up from the airport, but he did take note of the small stack of envelopes and cartons in the front seat that had to be delivered by the driver en route to their hotel.

It is wonderful having Marla and Shani here with him for this momentous event. He isn't sure why Aurora tagged along, but he figures that it must be the allure of dining with the stars that persuaded the arrogant little brat to freeload once again. Sadly he only gets one guest seat at the actual ceremony, so Shani and Aurora will have to watch it all on TV. They can join in at some of the less prestigious parties afterwards, but a lot of the organized party-givers were very picky about who they put on their guest list. And quite right too! Who wants any old riff-raff gatecrashing these exclusive events?

Lester wonders for a moment what it would have been like if Tina had accompanied him instead of Marla. He cringes at the thought of his wife amidst such esteemed company, and he is so glad now that they are separated. She would have become very drunk early in the evening and she would have made a fool of herself with every famous person she encountered. Tina was never very good PR for Lester, whereas Marla is the perfect companion. Looking as she does right now, there would be very few people who could not be impressed by such a formidable figure.

It is amazing how she has sprung back after that terrible ordeal at Richard's house. Lester had been sure that Marla would end up in the clinic again, but it was as though a huge weight had suddenly been lifted from her shoulders. Of course, she is still suffering from her own personal doubts and fears from the past.

But Lester is attempting to put all of this behind him. If Marla can cope with that ordeal, then so can he. The one wonderful thing that has come out of it all is the fact that he and Marla are back together again. This is a second chance that he never believed would be possible. They are even *talking* about Jessica now; they can discuss the past without sounding bitter or judgemental. They have grown up.

'Mother! How many of those things are you going to knock back? You'll be legless by the time we go out to dinner.' Aurora stares at Shani with unabashed criticism.

'I'm not your mother — how many times do I have to tell you? I refuse to be held responsible!' And Shani glares at Aurora with a steely, ironic smile.

'She's smashed!' announces haughty Aurora, with a

twist of her mean little mouth. 'I knew she'd show me up as soon as we got away from London. It's always the same.'

'So why did you come then?' asks Shani.

Aurora refuses to answer; instead she turns her attention to a large-screen TV screen behind the bar and feigns sudden interest in a commercial for Summer's Eve vaginal douche. The sound is muted, so she probably has no idea what she is watching.

Lester wishes that the girl hadn't come. Shani is always so much more relaxed when Aurora isn't around but, through some strange loyalty to Aurora's late father, Shani seems unable to refuse Aurora anything. Lester also suspects that Shani is slightly put out by the fact that he himself is back with Marla. She hasn't said anything of course, but there has been a barely perceptible strand of falseness running through her enthusiasm for this reunion of souls. You see, not only has Shani lost her role as mother figure to Lester, but she has also lost her closest single female friend. It's a double betrayal to a woman who is too long in the tooth for such inconveniences.

Shani is a good woman. Lester loves her, and in his present euphoric state he hopes desperately that she will meet a man who can satisfy her as much as Marla satisfies him. And he doesn't just mean the sex. Oh yes, the sex is fantastic, it always was, but no, he's talking about something more spiritual – a profound sense of well-being. This is what it must feel like when people try Prozac for the first time after years of undiagnosed depression. He never knew how unhappy he was until he found happiness.

Marla watches Lester as one might watch an interesting and brightly coloured bird. He has changed since the episode with Richard. He is like a reflection of himself: like the *old* Lester that she used to know before everything went wrong. Reflections can be revealing and Lester is now a reflection of his former self, but magnified, clarified and ultimately stronger.

Of course there will always be that stinging association with Jessica, and the memories of that terrible year following her death. Marla has learned not to dwell on that time but, now that she is spending her days with Lester, it is as though their daughter is always somewhere close by, like a little ghost that floats somewhere just above their heads. They don't like to talk about it much. Anyway, Marla talked most of it out of her system at the time. The psychiatrists and doctors were amazingly sympathetic, but that year that Marla spent in confinement, as ordered by the judicial courts, she was literally *shocked* into submission. Before each jolt of electricity, as she bit down on to the rubber tongue restraint, Marla would accept the numbing pain as a punishment. Her cure was her punishment, and because of that she never complained. There was even a certain amount of guilty pleasure in that electrified convulsion, as though it was purging her soul.

Here they are, then, ex-husband and wife, sitting at the same cocktail table with the same friend they had way back when. How much has changed since then? How have they grown since the last time they shared a life together? When Marla recalls the person that she was before Jessica was born, she feels as though she is looking at a flower that has been pressed between the pages of a book. The scent has gone, the colours have faded – and yet to hold the delicate stem between careful fingers is to recapture an essence of something lingering, not quite evaporated.

Lester practically leaps out of his chair, grabbing Marla's free hand in his own. 'Oh my God!' he hisses, eyes focused on the entrance to the sports bar.

Marla feels panic twist in her gut and she dare not turn around. What kind of horrible surprise is about to befall her now? Have the police come to take her away?

'What is it, darling?' asks Shani, craning her neck to see what this commotion is all about.

'Over there,' says Lester with a hushed, reverent tone. 'I think I just saw Vanessa Redgrave!'

And so Lester is finally here.

Here in Hollywood on the eve of the Oscars.

There is a feeling like Christmas Eve in the air above Hollywood tonight: a kind of reserved hysteria that froths and fizzes somewhere under the calm before the storm. They are setting up the satellite dishes and the cameras in the streets. They are laying out the red carpet.

'Let's order some champagne and drink it in the tub. I feel like being decadent,' says Marla after they leave the others to their gossip in the bar.

They go up to their room, hand in hand, and Lester calls for room service.

Marla removes her stockings and drapes them carelessly over the back of a chair. She has a cigarette hanging from her lips, and she needs to squint to avoid the rising smoke as she bends to massage her toes.

Lester pushes open the sliding doors that lead to the balcony. It is a cool evening, with a breeze that smells freshly washed. Down below, the lights of the city are spread out like the random scattering of a broken necklace, and the sky is a pale, ghostly colour that shimmers at the far edges. Police sirens wail with the lonely cry of wounded animals.

It is one of those moments for Lester.

One of those small moments when his senses are more acutely alert, and emotions run close to the surface. He breathes in the air and closes his eyes for a brief moment, tasting the bittersweet melancholy that aches sometimes on nights like this.

It is the feeling he gets on a warm summer's evening when standing outside a house that is filled with music and laughter, when the crickets are making their noise in the grasses.

It is the feeling he gets when snow starts to fall late at night, and the coals are burning low in the hearth.

With a sudden, astonishing clarity, it brings back the darkness of the woods that were close to his childhood home, as he rode on the back of his cousin's motorbike. It was midsummer, and the midges were hovering in great clouds beneath the trees, as they bumped and jostled over the rough pathway that led through the woods to Lester's house. He had to cling to his cousin's waist in order to remain on the bike, and his eyes watered from the wind that whipped past them as they emerged into the lane that wound through the cornfields.

It was the night they were due to leave on holiday. The feeling of festive anticipation was so tangible that Lester remembers thinking that it was the direct cause of the hesitant summer lightning that flickered like a dying bulb in the sky beyond the trees.

Some feelings stay with you like that for the whole of your life.

How can you ever try to describe them to anyone else without trivializing them with the sheer bluntness of words?

Is it really possible to describe the taste of a freshly picked raspberry or the sound of the rain as it drips through the leaves of a tree?

Here he stands. Old enough to know better, and yet still hopeful for the years that present themselves before him tonight.

The fame doesn't really matter to him any more. He has wasted too much time in reaching out to grasp the one thing that continuously eluded him throughout his adult life. He made himself believe, like so many of us, that there had to be more to life than the taste of a raspberry or the sound of the rain. But he was wrong.

It is these tiny moments that prove to us that we are alive. And anyone who lacks the emotional appreciation of such fragmented sensations also lacks the ability to understand why we bother to entertain this harsh, cruel world that, paradoxically, means so much to us.

'It's cold out here,' says Marla, standing by the balcony doors in her underskirt. 'You looked sad just then, standing there like that. Are you sad, Lester?'

'No, darling, I'm not sad.' He turns to face her – and in this light she could be the woman he married twenty years ago. 'I'm incredibly happy but I think I only just realized it.'

Thirty-nine

'He's very good-looking,' says Annie, perched at the edge of a huge, oversized suede sofa. 'He looks like Ricky Martin.'

Spencer is standing by the stone fireplace, looking as though he belongs there. His trousers and shirt are almost the same colour as the sandstone, and he has a healthy tan.

The house is Spanish in style. There are twisted columns in the entrance hall, and a balcony that overlooks the main living room from upstairs. Bougainvillea hangs over the windows that face the courtyard, and Annie can hear the sound of a fountain somewhere close by. The French doors are wedged open, and it is hard to believe that she is in the middle of LA.

'Yes, he is good-looking, isn't he?' replies Spencer, almost bashful in his adoration.

'I expect you turn a lot of heads when you go out together.'

'This is Hollywood, Annie. *Everyone* turns heads in this town.'

'You should take him back with you to Chesterfield. You'd have the lasses running after you like film stars. It was bad enough when you were at school, but look at you now. You look different.'

'I'm relaxed for the first time in my life, Annie. I

never realized just how much hard work it takes to hide inside yourself like that. I wanted so badly to be accepted.'

'What did your mum and dad say when you told them? They must have been gobsmacked just finding out that you're still alive.'

'At first they were over the moon, of course, but when I told them about Basilio they soon changed their tune – you know how conservative my parents are. I think they felt threatened by the thought of gossip at the women's guild and the town hall. They asked me not to go home. They would rather pretend that I'm dead than admit that their son is gay.'

'Spencer, that's awful. I'm sure they'll come round in the end. It was just a bit of a shock for them, that's all.'

'What about you, Annie? Have you come round?'

Annie smiles. She holds no grudge. 'Oh, Spencer, I'm just glad that you're happy. Things have happened so quickly for me, with the modelling and everything, and none of it would have happened if I hadn't married you in the first place.'

Spencer takes a seat, leaning back and crossing his legs in an easy manner. He appears to have made this place his home.

'Thanks for bringing Billy with you,' he says. 'I haven't seen him for such a long time, and it's amazing how much he's grown up. Maggie was always a bit afraid of letting him see me, especially after her husband came down on me so hard. I suppose it was better that way, but I would have enjoyed playing some small role in Billy's life. He looks a lot like me, doesn't he?'

'Yes, he does, especially when he smiles. He even

has some of your mannerisms, which strikes me as odd seeing as how he's never spent any time with you.'

'He seems to be very fond of you, Annie. Funny how the two of you have become so close.'

Annie can't tell Spencer just *how* close she and Billy have become since they arrived in LA. She can't even acknowledge it herself: it is too fresh, too new, and it is in danger of dissolving right before her eyes if she thinks about it too closely. If she thinks about it too much, she gets a feeling like bicarbonate of soda in the pit of her stomach and she has to take deep breaths in order to regain her composure. After all, he is only eighteen years old. She must remind herself of that fact over and over again, until it buzzes around her brain like an angry wasp. Nobody would sanction their relationship. They will say that she is a cradle-snatcher, that it won't last. Worst of all, they will say that it is not possible for them to be in love.

'*I love you, Annie.*'

That is what Billy whispered to her last night after they made love in the shower. '*I love you and I want to spend the rest of my life with you.*'

Nobody has ever said that to her before, and the words had made her cry. They stood together like that, holding each other under the sharp stinging needles of water, and she had felt as though he might suddenly fly from her grasp like a piece of slippery soap. His body, sleek with moisture, was like a solid piece of marble beneath her fingers – totally unbelievable in its perfection. Beside him she feels like a shapeless lump of flesh, and yet he keeps telling her that she is beautiful, and he touches her in places that make her shiver with anticipation.

413

He also has a dick the size of a donkey!

Crikey! She has an orgasm every time he does it to her. She feels like she could have an orgasm just *thinking* about doing it with him. Even now she's getting a bit 'wriggly' in her seat, so she has to focus her attention back on Spencer. Does Spencer feel the same way about Basilio as she feels about Billy?

'He reminds me so much of you when you were at school, Spencer. Sometimes I forget that he is a different person and I call him by the wrong name. In a lot of ways he has helped me get over you, especially when I thought you might be dead.'

'I'm sorry I didn't get in touch with you sooner, Annie. I just didn't know what I was doing with my life, and I couldn't stand the thought of having anything to do with my old life back in England. I figured you'd all get along without me, and then Taylor told me about your modelling career opening up, so I felt a bit better once I knew you could look after yourself.'

'So you're going to set up an associated office here in LA with Marla?'

'Yes, isn't that great? She has been really generous, considering everything I've put her through. I thought she'd hate my guts.'

'Marla's been too busy with her own problems to think about hating you, Spencer. She's had a really rough time with this murder thing, and Richard. It's funny, when I first met her she scared me stiff, but now that I know her better she's really a very nice lady. Very kind.'

'Yes, she is,' agrees Spencer, running his hand across the arm of his chair with a contemplative sweep.

Billy and Basilio approach from the foyer. Their

voices echo around the cavernous space as they finish
their tour of the house and return to the living room.

'This place is brilliant!' says Billy, coming to sit
down beside Annie. She notices how the expression on
Spencer's face changes quite dramatically as soon as
Billy enters the picture. Can it be possible that Spencer
is actually flirting with Billy? His own son?

'Yes, Basilio has a great eye when it comes to art
and architecture. Did he tell you that this place used to
belong to Karl Steinbrenner, the famous film director?'

'Never heard of him,' says Billy, 'but the tower is
really cool. I'd have a little flat up there, if this was my
place – just cover the floor with big cushions and have
one of those Bang & Olufsen music systems with surround sound.'

'So you like LA then?' asks Spencer.

'It's OK,' concedes Billy, 'but I prefer London. You
can't go anywhere here without a car, and the people
are really weird.'

'Weird? In what way?'

'Oh, I don't know. Just different, I suppose. They
stare a lot more than they do back home. It makes me
nervous.'

'They're just jealous probably,' says Basilio. 'They
want to know who you are, and they want to get into
your pants! You're a very good-looking guy, Billy, but
then I'm sure you know all about that. With a father
like Spencer how could you not be gorgeous?' And
Basilio sits on the arm of Spencer's chair and places a
hand on his shoulder.

'Well, they can look all they like,' says Billy, 'but the
only person who is getting into my pants is Annie.'

For a moment Annie wonders if she actually heard

him say that. There is an audible gasp of silence that follows his statement, and she can see both Spencer and Basilio struggling to understand what he means. Then Billy puts his arm around Annie's shoulder and kisses her cheek, leaving absolutely no question as to the meaning of his previous declaration of exclusivity.

Annie can feel her face flooding with embarrassment. She would like to push Billy's arm away, but she is too mortified to move. Spencer is staring at her with a look both horrified and furious, while Basilio is still wearing a quizzical smirk that hasn't worn off yet.

'Spencer . . .' begins Annie, but he allows her no time for explanations. He is standing now, hands firmly on his hips, and he glares at the two of them with such rancour that Annie is afraid she might wither up and die before his eyes.

'You mean to tell me that you're letting him fuck you, Annie? Is that what he's saying?'

Basilio stands too and attempts to calm Spencer down by grabbing his shoulder. Spencer shrugs him away angrily and continues to stare at Annie with eyes as frigid and hard as a hoar frost.

'Spencer, I know it sounds awful, and I know he's your son and very young but—'

'Annie, you don't have to explain anything,' intercepts Billy. 'It's not as though he's really my dad, you know. He doesn't have any say in what I do with my life, one way or the other.' He looks at Annie with such compassion that she can feel the onset of tears burning the back of her eyes. Billy takes her hand and squeezes it tight. 'I think we should go,' he says.

'This is outrageous!' yells Spencer. 'I cannot believe

what I'm hearing. If Maggie knew what you two were up to she would never have let you come here together like this. It's sick! It makes me feel physically sick!' And Spencer is forced to turn away, grasping the mantel for support, as though he really might vomit at any moment.

'What's so sick about it?' shouts Billy. 'Is it sick to fall in love with someone? Does it upset you because of the age difference, or because I'm your son and she's your wife? What is it, Spencer? Is it any more sick than you marrying her just to prove to yourself that you're not queer? And what about that guy in New York? The one who sucked you off while you played with the idea of shooting your brains out – is it any sicker than that? I think you've got a very twisted idea of what is and isn't sick in this world.'

'You don't know anything about what I've been through, Billy,' says Spencer, quieter now. 'I've admitted that I was wrong and I've tried to put things right. If I had known what was going on between the two of you, I would never have been so generous.'

'And if you'd never left her in the first place, I might never have met her, so I suppose I've got something to thank you for. Annie is the best thing that has ever happened to me . . .'

'For Christ's sake, Billy, you've hardly started to live. You're only eighteen—'

'She's the best thing that has ever happened to me, and I love her, and she loves me. You can't stop that. I don't care what my mother says, I don't care what anybody says – we are going to be together, and if people don't like it they can fuck off.'

'Billy, love, let's go,' whispers Annie.

'Oh God,' moans Spencer, 'this is doing my head in.'

'I'm sorry about this, Basilio,' says Annie, standing up. 'It really was nice meeting you.'

Basilio makes an awkward shrug, and looks at Spencer who is now standing with his back to them all. 'I'll show you out.'

As they stand on the front porch waiting for Annie's car, Basilio says that Spencer will come around, that he's just very sensitive at the moment and had so looked forward to seeing them both. It was a shock to his system, and once he has had time to digest it he will be fine. He's very broad-minded.

'I don't care how broad-minded he is,' says Billy. 'I don't see any point in bothering with a man who can shit on everyone and then get all high-and-mighty when people don't behave how he wants them to behave. He could have ruined Annie's life, but she's made it without him, and now *I'm* going to look after her. I can be the Spencer that she always wanted but never got – the Spencer who will love her and protect her and be with her for ever.'

These are the words that Annie has always wanted to hear and yet, now that she is hearing them for the first time, they somehow leave her disappointed. As lovely as it sounds coming from Billy's heart like this, she finds herself questioning the necessity for all-encompassing love in her life. She's done all right on her own for thirty-eight years, hasn't she? Yes, she made some stupid mistakes and some gross misjudgements of character, but look at her now! She's a *model* earning £2,000 a day in Los Angeles, wearing a Michaela Fox original, and waiting for her driver to bring the car around to take her back to her £500-a-night hotel! Where is the jeering hockey team now? Where are those spiteful pretty girls who tripped her up on the lacrosse field, and called her Fatso in the showers afterwards?

Well, Annie may be fat. She still weighs fourteen stone. But she is *here*, and they are somewhere back in Chesterfield with their housing estate semis, and their handsome husbands gone to seed with boredom.

'I have to talk to Spencer for a minute, Billy. I'll be right back.'

'Shall I come with you?'

'No,' Annie touches his arm and kisses his cheek, 'I need to have a minute or two alone with him.'

She finds Spencer slumped by the fireplace hugging a pillow with one hand covering his eyes. 'Spence?'

He looks up.

'I just wanted to tell you something before I go.'

The room is just like a picture from a magazine. They look at each other across this great expanse of unpolished marble and opulent upholstery fabric, and they could be cardboard figures. Is it possible that these are the same two people who tore out the pictures of hotel resorts from Spencer's mother's holiday brochures and stuck them into a notebook, categorizing them with star ratings for glamour and desirability?

'This thing with Billy and me, it's not going to last. It can't last. He's just a boy and I'm old enough to be his mother. I'm not totally thick, you know! It's just that when you disappeared like you did and I first saw Billy, I thought perhaps it was some kind of reincarnation and that he was like a kind of consolation prize for having lost you.'

Annie moves around the gigantic sofa and sits on a gilded chair opposite Spencer. She has learned how to cross her legs demurely at the ankle, and she arranges her flowing skirt across her ample lap. She wears rings now, and one of them has a real diamond.

'Billy is at that age when everything makes a big impression. He is bowled over by Michaela Fox and the people who hang around her. We had dinner with Lucas Halliwell the other week and even I was bowled over by that! He sees me as the key to all of that, and he is mistaking those feelings of excitement and freedom as love. I remember feeling exactly the same way when you first asked me to go with you to the Christmas social. I was on cloud nine that night, even though I knew that the other girls were laughing at my frock and calling me a charity case because Fiona Blewitt had dumped you at the last minute. That's what best friends are for and we were always best friends, weren't we, Spencer? It didn't matter that I was fat or that you were the most popular boy at school, we could still have a laugh when we were on our own, and none of that other stuff seemed to matter. When you asked me to marry you, I already knew that you didn't love me. How could you? It was ridiculous that somebody like you could feel anything for somebody like me, and yet I allowed myself to go through with the whole silly escapade. I was fooling *myself*, Spencer. It wasn't all your fault you know.'

'I'm sorry, Annie . . .' Spencer leans forward as if to reach for her hand but the gap between them is too wide.

'You don't have to apologize. You've already done everything you can to make up for it, and I really meant it when I said that it doesn't matter. I will always love you, Spencer, even if you never love me. When I thought you might be dead, I imagined meeting up with you again in heaven someday, and I knew that when that day came I would still love you.'

Annie laughs. It is a quiet, self-deprecating little laugh. 'I'm such a prat!' she says. 'You'd think by now I'd have learnt my lesson but I'm still the same old spaz under all this expensive make-up.'

'I shouldn't have said those things about you and Billy,' says Spencer. 'It's none of my business now what you do with your life. I think I was more jealous than anything.'

'Jealous of *me*? Now there's a first!' laughs Annie.

'You're going to be a huge success, aren't you? This modelling thing is going to be the making of you. I can see it happening already.'

'I don't know what's going to happen to me, Spencer, but I do know *one* thing for sure . . .'

'What's that?' he asks.

'You and me are definitely going to that stupid twenty-first school reunion next year, and we're going to show the lot of them that fat girls and poofs can make it on their own!'

'I love you, Annie.'

'Ditto, Mr Noble. Now, come on out and say goodbye to that gorgeous son of yours. He's going to break almost as many hearts as his dad.'

They walk through the house arm in arm, and as they reach the porch where Basilio and Billy are waiting they break into smiles.

Annie waves from the back seat of the Cadillac, and Billy reaches for her hand. The wide streets of LA are lined with palm trees, and the sky is so blue that the car windows have to be tinted to cut down on the glare. They glide effortlessly back to their hotel, where the doorman comes out to open the car door for Annie.

'Good afternoon, madam,' says the impossibly handsome boy in the white uniform.

This is the life. This is the fairytale land that most people only ever dream about.

The concierge has an envelope for Annie.

She stands by the lifts to read the message, and a waiter passes by with a silver tray of filled champagne glasses held adroitly above his head.

Betsy died at nine o'clock this morning.

It was pneumonia that finally snagged her life and dragged it away like a loose thread on the sleeve of a cardigan.

'Is everything all right?' asks Billy.

But Annie doesn't hear his simple question; she is remembering something that Betsy had said to her when she visited the hospital at Christmas. *'I'm not going to die, you daft ha'peth. I'll be out of here by next week and we'll be down the Fiesta knocking back Bacardi and Cokes just like the old days.'*

But the old days no longer exist. They are glued somewhere at the back of a photo album, along with postcards from people she no longer remembers and newspaper clippings of the royal wedding.

'Excuse me, I hate to bother you, but my daughter was wondering if she could have your autograph. She recognized you from the Michaela Fox advertisements.' A blonde lady in a tight black dress is holding out a bar menu for Annie to sign.

'What is your daughter's name?' asks Annie, accepting the menu and a gold pen.

'Skylar,' says the woman, and Annie looks up to see a teenage girl with braces on her teeth, grinning awkwardly from under a denim hat with a huge sunflower perched on the front.

'You mean like the bird?' asks Annie but the woman doesn't understand Annie's accent, and she just grins and says, 'Uh-huh.'

When the woman returns to her daughter with the signed menu, Annie can hear their voices as she steps into the lift with Billy.

'Goddammit, Mother!' shouts the young girl. 'Can't you get *anything* right? She's written Skylark!'

And the elevator doors close silently on the hotel lobby, encompassing Annie and Billy in a hushed circle of their own.

'Is everything all right, Annie?' asks Billy, catching hold of her hand and pulling her towards him. 'Is it bad news? In the note?'

There's your bloody direction girl – staring you in the face! You want to nab the opportunity while it's still there, otherwise you'll live to regret it.

Annie looks at Billy and marvels once more at how much he looks like Spencer. The similarity brings tears to her eyes. The past is now the present. And it is time to forge ahead with the future.

'I'm not going to hang around for the parties tonight,' says Annie. 'Michaela can do without me. I think I'll change my flight and go back home with you instead. And when we get back to London, I need to have a talk with your mum. It's about time we sorted out where we stand if you are going to be my full-time toyboy.'

Billy places his hand behind her head and bends to kiss her.

Their reflections meld as one in the sheet metal of the lift doors.

And, like looking into the distorted surface of a carnival mirror, Annie begins to see her future from a brand new perspective.